Alice & Luigi

ALSO BY GRAEME LAY

NOVELS AND SHORT STORY COLLECTIONS
The Mentor
The Fools on the Hill
Temptation Island
Dear Mr Cairney
Motu Tapu: Stories of the South Pacific
The Town on the Edge of the World

YOUNG ADULT NOVELS
The Wave Rider
Leaving One Foot Island
Return to One Foot Island
The Pearl of One Foot Island

CHILDREN
Are We There Yet? A Kiwi Kid's Holiday Exploring Guide
Nanny Potaka's Birthday Treat

TRAVEL
Passages: Journeys in Polynesia
Pacific New Zealand
The Cook Islands (with Ewan Smith)
New Zealand – A Visual Celebration (with Gareth Eyres)
Samoa (with Evotia Tamua)
Feasts & Festivals (with Glenn Jowitt)
The Globetrotter Guide to New Zealand
The Best of Auckland
The Miss Tutti Frutti Contest – Travel Tales of the South Pacific
New Zealand – the Magnificent Journey (with Gareth Eyres)

EDITOR
Metro Fiction
100 New Zealand Short Short Stories
Another 100 Short Short Stories
The Third Century
Boys' Own Stories
50 Short Short Stories by Young New Zealanders
An Affair of the Heart: A Celebration of Frank Sargeson's Centenary
(with Stephen Stratford)
Golden Weather: North Shore writers Past & Present
(with Jack Ross)
Home: New Short Short Stories by New Zealand Writers
(with Stephen Stratford)

Alice & Luigi

– A NOVEL –

BY GRAEME LAY

David Ling Publishing Limited
PO Box 34601, Birkenhead
Auckland 10, New Zealand
www.davidling.co.nz

ISBN 13: 978-1-877378-07-2
ISBN 10: 1-877378-07-0

First Published 2006

The author and the publishers gratefully acknowledge the support of
Creative New Zealand.

Typeset by ExPress Communications Limited
Printed in Hong Kong

In tribute to my paternal great-grandparents

Alice & Luigi Berretti

AUTHOR'S NOTE

Although *Luigi & Alice* is a work of fiction, several of the events, settings and characters in the novel have been drawn from late nineteenth century and early twentieth century New Zealand history. The ill-fated Italian settlement at Jackson Bay, in south Westland, the fishing village at Makara, the poliomyletis epidemic of the 1890s and the various developments along the Kapiti coast in the last years of the nineteenth and first decade of the twentieth century all actually occurred. The episode involving Richard John Seddon's visit to Paraparaumu is also based on fact. Other characters drawn from real life include Tom and Harry Newman of Nelson, 'King' Macfarlane, the Resident Agent for the Jackson Bay settlement, 'French Louis' of Makara, the Beauchamp family of Karori and Frances Hodgkins and her companion, Dorothy Richmond. The rest is fiction.

PROLOGUE

William and Abigail sat in silence at the dining table. The funeral was over at last; all the others had left. Abigail held her wine glass tightly by the stem, taking tiny sips. Staring through the window, William watched a 737 on its final descent into Wellington Airport. The plane appeared to be drifting, almost floating, above the waters of the harbour. Eyes still on the drifting plane, he broke the thick silence between brother and sister.

'Dad was going to research his mother's family background. Try to find out about his grandfather. The Italian one.'

Abigail looked at him sharply. 'I didn't know that.'

'I didn't either. He'd only just started.' William reached into the inside pocket of his suit, and took out a letter. 'I found this on his desk. It's to his cousin, Gina Knowles.'

'I didn't know she was still alive. She wasn't at the funeral, was she?'

'No. She's nearly ninety now, I worked out. But apparently she knew a bit about Dad's family history. On his mother's side. He was going to talk to her about their grandfather.' He paused. 'Our great-grandfather.'

William unfolded the letter and read it to her.

Although Abigail kept her eyes closed, tears streamed from under the lids. Eyes still closed, she murmured, 'That's so sad. He sounds so determined. Like he always was.'

'Yes. He loved a challenging project. Especially after Mum died.'

'What're you going to do with the letter?'

'Keep it.' He stared out at the harbour again. 'And his appointment with Gina.'

'Why?'

'Dad started the job. I'm going to finish it for him.'

ONE

The room was in darkness, apart from the glowing embers in the grate. They shed just enough light to illuminate the framed photograph of their mother, in her best black dress, hanging above the sideboard. Luigi stared at it for a few seconds. How beautiful she had been, how she had loved them all. Then he turned away, moved stealthily across the tiny kitchen and pulled aside the curtain which hung across the alcove beside the fireplace, the place where he had always slept. A soft, steady breathing was coming from the curtained alcove on the other side of the fireplace. Violetta. From the tenement's one bedroom came the sound of his father's snoring.

Groping under the bed, Luigi found the box containing his passport. He took the document out and slipped it inside his shirt. Was there anything else he'd need? He remembered his silver Roman coin, the one he had dug up in their vegetable plot. If ever he needed a talisman, it was now. Finding the leather pouch and his coin collection, he located the silver one, slipped it into his fob pocket next to his watch, put the pouch back, turned to leave.

'Luigi! What are you doing?'

Violetta, in her nightdress, her long auburn hair hanging loose.

'Leaving.'

'What do you mean?'

'Leaving Pesaro.'

'To go where?'

'Far from here.'

Violetta's eyes were wide with fright at his air of desperation, his unruly appearance, the vomit stains on his shirt. With a terrible little cry, as if she had touched a burning pot, she ran to him. Holding her tightly against him, Luigi felt her laboured breathing through his jacket.

'Violetta, Violetta. I can't explain. But ...' He released her, caught his breath, found his voice. 'Something dreadful has happened. And all I can tell you is ...' Gripping her shoulders, he stared into the shadowy planes of her face. '... I am not to blame.' She stared back. Letting his hands fall to his sides, he said again, '*I am not to blame*. Do you understand?' Clamping her mouth tightly, shaking her head, she said in a desperate whisper,

'No, no, I *do not* understand. What has happened, Luigi, *what has happened?*'

Drawing her close to him again, Luigi whispered in her ear. 'We mustn't wake Papa.' Pressing his lips to the crown of her head, he whispered again. 'It is not possible for me to say.' He ran his hand over her hair, down the back of her head. 'Oh 'Letta, little 'Letta. When I am safe, I will write, I promise you.' Releasing her, moving towards the door, he heard his father's rattling cough, coming from the bedroom. Luigi turned back. 'I must go now. Take care, 'Letta. And remember, *I am not to blame.'*

Seconds later he was running again, in the direction of the town's railway station.

It wasn't until the train began to clank and rattle its way out of the station that he furtively counted the money, huddling against the corner of the hard wooden seat. In his haste to pay for his ticket, he had merely peeled a 1000-lire note from the roll. Now, turning his back on the wizened woman in the black head scarf sitting next to him, he flicked over the notes and counted to himself. Ninety-nine 1000-lire notes. *Ninety-nine thousand lire!* Yet as he gripped the roll, the sourness rose again in his throat and the trembling which had afflicted him for the last few hours became more pronounced, until he thought he must look like Signor Giannoni, the palsied, dribbling old man who lived next door to their tenement.

Tucking the roll of notes into the side pocket of his jacket, Luigi tried to recall the map he had often studied in the Pesaro railway station, of the railway lines of the Piedmont, the network that had spread so quickly over the last ten years, so that it now linked all the towns of northern Italy. Pesaro to Bologna, Bologna to Milano, Milano to Genoa, Genoa, to...The map had gone no further, but Luigi knew that beyond the last Italian town was the border, and beyond that border lay the city from where his escape would be made complete. Marseilles.

The crone beside him had fallen asleep, her head tipped back, her mouth with its sucked-in gums wide open. Getting whiffs of her repulsively stale breath, he moved away from her as far as he could, backing further into the seat corner, but sneaking a look into the basket at her feet. His stomach grumbled at the sight of the panini in her basket. But food would have to wait, at least until he reached Bologna.

Hearing the train's whistle blast twice, Luigi stared out the window. Black smoke streamed past, then cleared, revealing a man, his horse and a cart heaped with maize, waiting on a road crossing for the train to pass. As it did so the horse reared, turning away in fright. The shafts of the cart shot upwards, sending some of the maize flying backwards onto the road and almost unhorsing the man. Seconds later, they had disappeared. The morning mist that had hung over the plain had melted, replaced with a soft brown haze, the figures toiling in the fields were the size of flies. He was leaving it all, perhaps forever. He put his temple to the carriage's grimy window. The hand in his trouser pocket found the Roman coin, and he began to finger it like worry beads. He heard the insistent clickety-clack of the train wheels, over and over, over and over, bearing him away, away, away. Then, sitting up, he took from his jacket the letter he had received last month, and read it for the umpteenth time.

Okuru, Westland, 23 March 1878.

To my friend Luigi,

I am very sorry to have taken so long to write to you, my apologies for this. It is now over two years since I left, and to wait so long before writing is not good. But so much has happened to me since I left, I hardly know where to begin. I won't bore you with the voyage, it was almost three months of rough sea and bad food. The only unmarried women aboard, nuns going to Melbourne, and many crying children and seasick adults. Meals of porridge, rice, ship's biscuit, salted mutton, pickled cabbage and carrots. As well as Italians, there were some Danish and Bohemians. Not very good company as they spoke no Italian and did not appreciate our singing, especially the squareheads. They were as bad as Austrians! Without humour, either.

We arrived at the port of Wellington, the capital of Nuova Zelanda, late in October 1875. From there we were taken by train to where the line ended, a railway camp at the foot of mountains called the Rimmertuckers.

A miserable place it turned out to be, for a fisherman, out of sight of the sea. Rain on many days, snow on some. And the work laying railway lines was very hard. Dirty and rough. Not well paid, either. You remember that the advertisement in Pesaro had promised ten shillings a week for work in Nuova Zelanda? Well, we got only six. All us Italians were unhappy about this deception, and one day we put down our shovels and travelled back to Wellington to make a protest to the railway manager there. But he refused to pay us what we had been promised. So when we read an advertisement in the Wellington newspaper, wanting immigrants for a special new settlement, in the other, larger island of Nuova Zelanda, with grants of land if we would grow crops there, several of us agreed to go. And that is where I am now, since one and a half years, at Okuru, in the southern province that is called Westland. I live near the mouth of a river, also called Okuru, beside a fine, wide bay that is called Jackson Bay. Okuru is a Mowri name, and there are Mowri people here too.

What a beautiful country this Nuova Zelanda is, Luigi! Enough fertile land for every settler, for the growing of crops and fruit. Also, clean rivers, great forests and beaches. There was gold too, taken from the rivers and beaches some years ago. There are fine timber trees everywhere, ideal for building. I have seven milk cows which graze the land around my house, a house I built with my own hands. Imagine that, Luigi, seven cows, around the house I made myself! I make my own butter and cheese too, and I have ten bee hives. The land of milk and honey, infatti! Before long I will be making my own wine, from the vines I planted a year ago. There will be silk from the silk worms which will feed off the leaves of the mulberry trees I am going to grow. Now all I need is a wife to warm my bed, and she might not be long in coming to me. There is a young woman who I think is interested. But she speaks no Italian, so I have been learning the local language in order to court her.

That is all my news from the other end of the world. How are you? Still playing your accordion at Emilio's? How is your little sister? And your papa, I hope he is well.

Please send them my best wishes.
And it would be good to hear from you, Luigi.

Your friend,
Leopoldo.

He had watched Violetta as she read the letter after he had, her small hands clutching it, eyebrows knitted with concentration. Like Luigi, she had left their church school at the age of ten, her labour needed at home, just as his was needed on the family's fishing boat. But their mother had taught them both to read and write Italian, and a little German too. And later the family priest, Father Benassi, had carried on their mother's work. Luigi could see that the letter excited his sister, noticed too the way her face fell as she came to the end, to the mention of Leopoldo's young woman. Although she had been only twelve when Leopoldo had left, Luigi knew how Violetta felt about his friend. Confirming this thought, when she looked up her expression was crushed.

'He will not come back,' she said sadly. 'Now that he has all that.'

Luigi looked away. Out in the estuary a fishing skiff, its sail reefed, was beating into the westerly wind, fighting the muddy currents of the Foglia River as it made its way back to the quay. Silvio's boat. He had stayed out later than the others, hoping for a bigger catch. God knew, with eight children to feed, he needed a decent haul. Luigi held out his hand for the letter, took it back, read it again.

Leopoldo's letter disturbed him. His friend had made the great break, turned his back on his homeland, travelled about as far from Italy as it was possible to go. *Alla fine del mondo.* To the end of the Earth. And Leopoldo was thriving, as Luigi knew he would. If only he had done the same, two years ago. Taken the coach with Leopoldo, across the mountains to Livorno, on the Ligurian Coast, and joined the emigrant party. They had both seen the advertisement in *L'Eco di Pesaro*, their town's newspaper. Migrants Wanted for Nuova Zelanda. Fares Paid, Work and Land Waiting, Good Wages. Luigi had even gone to the municipal office with Leopoldo and obtained a passport when his friend did. But after he had told his father of their plan, Ernesto Galoni had erupted with anger.

'Why do you make this crazy plan, boy? *Why?*'

'I have to leave the Marche. There is nothing here for me.'

'*Nothing?* This is your home, where your family has lived for generations.'

'Yes, and every generation is poorer than the last.'

'We have the boat, we have the garden. We don't starve.'

'There is no proper work here, no prospects. In the new lands …'

'*The new lands.*' His father's voice took on a sneering tone as he mimicked his son's words. 'Where there is no culture, no history. Here, in Pesaro, the birth-place of Rossini, is where you belong.' He began to thump out his pipe bowl fiercely against the fireplace. 'Forget this migration foolishness. I tell you, the ones who've gone will be back, and full of regrets.'

That night was the closest Luigi had ever come to striking his father, the clearest he had ever seen his narrowness. It was not that Ernesto Galoni was ignorant. He could read and write, he loved the opera, he identified with the Garibaldini, had followed avidly the newspaper reports of the progress of the patriot and his red-shirts, had recited accounts of the great leader's battles to Luigi when he was a boy. And he was a fervid supporter of Italy's unification, the Risorgimento.

Yet it was this very nationalistic pride which made his father suspicious – afraid even – of the outside world, a fear which took the form of a determination to ensure that his two surviving children – three others had died in their infancy – were not exposed to the world that lay beyond the Alps. At the age of forty-two Ernesto Galoni had been to San Marino once, to Urbino once, and that was it. The rest of the world he was content to visit through the pages of *L'Eco di Pesaro*. Furthermore, he seemed more than happy to deny his only surviving son the right to see it.

Violetta laid a hand on his forearm, gently.

'What's wrong, Luigi?'

'Nothing.'

'It's the letter, isn't it?'

He shook his head. Staring out over the estuary, he said, 'Seven cows. Who needs seven cows?'

He walked along the Quai de Joliette. The harbour was filled with ships, steamships mainly, their great cranes swinging to and fro, nets dangling from them, stevedores shouting from the decks of the ships to the men on the wharves. Others humped sacks on their backs from stacks on the wharves and up ramps to the ships' decks. Arab men in long white cloaks and head-dresses sat about talking in small groups. Tall, fine-boned Africans squatted as they played cards in the shade of the plane trees that lined the quay. There were many stalls along the wharf, selling foods that Luigi had never seen before: spiced fish balls, little cubes of lamb on sticks, peppers stuffed with minced pork. The braziers gave off gusts of smoke and tempting smells.

His ship, *Pleione,* seemed as big as a cathedral. Dark smoke was pouring from her twin orange and black stacks, but her sails were still tightly furled, gathered like huge curtains against her cross-masts. Staring at the ship, Luigi was struck by the wonder of it. To put an enormous steam engine inside something the size of this ship, and use the engine's power to turn propellers! It seemed hard to believe. A train driven by steam was one thing, but a ship? And one that could cross the world? Unbelievable. Further along the wharf he saw a seemingly endless procession of bent, leather-jerkined figures staggering up a gangplank near the stern of the ship, bearing sacks of coal on their backs to feed *Pleione*'s boilers.

Just after noon, with the Mediterranean sun burning down fiercely on the steel decks, one of the officers blew a whistle and the passengers – the families first –were beckoned aboard the ship that was to be their home for the next two months. Luigi was directed by a surly deckhand to the for'ard area of the ship, to a hatch, from where a steep companionway led to the lower deck.

As he went down the companionway, Luigi felt as if he was descending to the underworld. And at the bottom, the feeling grew stronger. For'ard steerage for single men consisted of twenty bunks, each only a couple of feet wide, arranged in two curving rows which followed the shape of the ship's bow. On each of the bunks lay a palliasse and two folded blankets. The air in the cabin was thick and hot. Already several other men – most of them about his own age – were stowing their bags under the bunks, assuming ownership of their cramped space. They were dressed as he was, in caps and rough working clothes. All avoided each other's eyes, evidently reluctant, through shyness or suspicion, to make direct contact.

Noticing that the bunks already claimed were being taken furthest from the bow, Luigi moved to the starboard side and put his pack on a bunk second from the end. Next to this one a man of about twenty, with curly brown hair and a wispy beard, sat on his bunk, smoking a pipe. Luigi held out his hand and gave his name. The other man took it and said,

'Johann.'

'Osterreich?' asked Luigi.

'Nein, Bohemian,' he replied.

'I am Italian,' explained Luigi, in German. 'My name is Luigi. I am travelling to New Zealand.'

The other man's expression brightened. Still in German he said, 'I am going there too. Do you speak English?'

'A little. But I think we will need to speak English in New Zealand, so why don't we practise it now?'

'A good idea.' The Bohemian gave a polite little cough, then said carefully, 'Why are you travelling to New Zealand, Louis?'

'Luigi. I am travelling to New Zealand to visit my friend, Leopoldo.' Already he had practised the partial lie. 'And you?'

'New opportunities.' He pointed to the wooden contraption on his bunk. 'My easel. I am a painter.'

'Ah. What do you paint?'

'Portraits, mainly.'

Luigi opened his pack and took out his accordion. 'My only art is this. But it satisfies me to play.'

Boots, then a pair of legs, dressed in heavy, navy blue, came down the companionway. It was the deckhand who had shown Luigi to his sleeping area. Florid-faced, with bloodshot eyes, he looked as if he had had a torrid few days ashore. Looking around the steerage area irritably, he barked in French, 'We cast off within the hour. Be on deck if you want to wave goodbye to anyone.' He staggered off towards mid-ships, where the married couples' quarters were located.

Not understanding, Luigi looked at Johann. 'What does he say?'

The other man translated, then the pair of them scaled the companionway and walked the length of the ship to the fo'c'sle, to watch the process of departure. There were few people on the wharf to wave the ship off, probably, Luigi thought, because many of the departing families had come from parts far and away. *Pleione's* mooring lines were cast off and she was eased away from the wharf by a tugboat with a single belching stack. In a matter of minutes, the tugboat towed the ship away from the wharf and around until its bow pointed at the harbour entrance. The tug's whistle tooted, twice, and the towing lines were thrown from *Pleione's* bow.

As Luigi heard the engines' throbbing intensify and felt the deck plates tremble beneath the soles of his boots, his eyes began to moisten. He turned to the east, towards where Italy lay. Would he ever see his homeland again? As the ship slid past the lighthouse and its siren sounded three times, he watched Europe shrink into the distance. He wiped the moisture from his eyes. It had to be this way. Because of what had happened the other night, it had to be. He could never have stayed in Pesaro.

After nightfall he went up to the foredeck and stared up at the shimmering, star-filled sky. He wondered, would there be the same stars in the southern land, or did they have their own constellations there?

THE PHOTOGRAPH

'That's him,' Gina said, handing William a photograph in an oval, black-lacquered frame.

'Where did you get it?' he asked.

'From my mother. She was given it by her mother. Sometime in the 1940s, I think.'

William studied the photograph.

A young man, late twenties, thirty perhaps. A head and shoulders shot, unsmiling, his face turned slightly to the left. Formally dressed in suit and tie, the tie with a large knot. A sensitive face, well-shaped, the nose perfectly straight. But there was a suggestion of melancholia there, too, especially around the eyes.

'Handsome, wasn't he?' There was a girlish note in the old lady's voice.

'Yes, he was.'

It was true. Even in miniature the man's even features and serious countenance made him attractive. His expression exuded a blend of determination and dignity.

'He had red hair, did you know that?'

'No.'

'Flaming red, apparently. He passed it on to a few others, naturally. Your great-aunty Alicia was one.'

William studied the black and white image again, attempting to give it colour. 'Do you know where this was taken?' he asked.

'No. Not Italy, though, judging by his age. My grandmother told my mother that he was in his early twenties when he came to New Zealand. Sometime in the 1870s.'

'Did she say *why* he came?'

'No. He never told anyone, apparently.' Reaching for William's cup, she asked, 'More tea?'

'Not for me, thanks.'

Turning the photograph over, he saw that it was backed with a piece of cardboard, yellowed with age. 'I'd like to get it copied. Can I borrow it?'

Gina shuffled uncomfortably on her chair. 'Well, it's the only one of him I've got.'

'I understand. But I'll only need it for a day or two.' He pressed on. 'I'll have a copy made for you, too.' He gave her a reassuring smile. 'Don't worry, it'll be perfectly safe.'

Her eyes moved to the little portrait. 'All right then.'

Back at home in Wadestown, with the aid of a wallpaper stripping knife, William carefully prised the cardboard backing from the photo. Dry with age, it came away easily. The back of the photo was mottled, like liver spots. Looking more closely, he saw that at the bottom of the backing were two words in faded gold lettering. *Scotts Photography.* He wrote the name down in his notebook. Then, turning the photograph over, he again studied the solemn face. The image of this long-dead person already had him in thrall. Luigi Galoni. Why had this great-grandfather of his come to this country? And when? And how?

TWO

My Dear Violetta,

We are at last in southern seas. The voyage seems endless, but this is to be expected. A few days ago I began fishing. One of the crew gave me a line and some hooks, and I fashioned a lure from a small spoon and a peacock's feather which I had bought in the market at Colombo. Imagine my delight when a fish took the lure and leaped from the water! I pulled it aboard, flapping madly. It was a handsome creature – with silver flanks and a dark blue back – which the crew tell me is called a bonito. I gutted it, cut it up and one of the cooks agreed to fry it for me in exchange for half its flesh. It was delicious, darkish in colour, full of fresh flavour and such a welcome change from salt beef and pickled cabbage. The weather is growing noticeably colder now, especially in the early morning and evening. In this hemisphere it is winter still, so we can expect the cold to increase. How strange to imagine, winter in August, when the Marche and Piedmont are baking like biscuits!

Three times a week my friend Johann and I and the others have our English lessons, and we speak English to each other all the time, to prepare us for our new lives. Our tutor, an Englishwoman, is pleased, because when she asks us questions in English, we can now reply with ease. 'Good morning Luigi, how are you feeling today? I am feeling quite well, thank you Miss Pemberthy. Are you feeling well too? Not sea-sick, I hope.' 'Good morning, Luigi. How did you sleep last night?' 'I was awake for some hours, Miss Pemberthy, because of the thunder. Did you hear the thunder too, Miss Pemberthy?' 'Indeed I did hear it, Luigi, because the thunder was extremely loud last night.' And so it goes, and so my English progresses, I hope.

I will end now, Violetta, and post this to you from Wellington. By now perhaps you have guessed why I had to flee Pesaro. If you speak of me to Papa, say nothing of this business to him. Perhaps he has already disowned me. But believe me when I say yet again, my dear sister, although I had to leave Pesaro, the fault was not mine. Never forget that. Never.

I hope you are well.

Your loving brother,

Luigi.

'Land-ho! On the starboard side!'

The cry came from the top of *Pleione*'s main mast. But it was some time before they saw the land itself. At first they could see only the clouds above it, extending from one side of the horizon to the other – a long, flat-topped wall of greyness. Other passengers gathered on the deck were exclaiming at the strange, almost unnatural sight. Luigi stared at Johann's almanac, open at the small map of New Zealand. 'That must be … South Island.'

'Yes.' A tremor of excitement passed through Luigi. Leopoldo's island.

Still studying the map, Johann glanced up at the cloud bank, then down again. 'Cape Farewell,' he announced. 'We must be sailing towards Cape Farewell.'

Staring eagerly towards the cloud bank, Luigi said, 'But for us it is Cape Hello.'

They both laughed, then watched in fascination as *Pleione* moved closer to the land. Slowly the features of the coastline became clearer: a rampart of dark blue mountains, topped with cloud, a gap, then more mountains which tapered into the sea like the tail of a dragon.

Two hours later they passed around Farewell Spit. Here the sea was turbulent, the sky darkened to a graphite shade and *Pleione* heeled heavily to starboard. In the heaving, wind-blasted seas, she pitched her way through Cook Strait, driving into a freezing southerly, sails furled and plates groaning, decks lashed with hail like frozen buckshot, her stack smoke whipped away by the gale,

Then, out of the mist, the land appeared again, a long wall of rocky cliffs. Sea-sickness forced Johann below, but Luigi stayed above decks, watching excitedly as *Pleione* altered course and came beam-on to the southerly, which drove her steadily through what seemed a perilously narrow harbour entrance, with rocky shores close by on both sides.

Hills, everywhere hills. Bare, dark green hills, enclosing the harbour, stepping away into the distance in all directions. Highest to the north-west, they appeared to be layered there, each layer higher than the one below it, so that the tops of the furthermost range were real mountains, dusted with snow. The sky was pale grey and even within the harbour the cold wind was chopping the water, but as Luigi and Johann stood near *Pleione*'s stern, belongings at their feet, both were so captivated by the lake-like harbour and its surrounding hills that they paid little heed to the cold. Ahead, drawing closer as the tug drew the ship nearer to the waterfront, were the wharves of Wellington.

The waterfront was a tangle of vessels of all sizes and types: passenger steamers, unrigged brigantines, coal-carrying barques, excursion boats, trading scows, barges and tug-boats. Steam cranes like giant praying mantises were lined up on the wharf. The features of the town were becoming clearer too. Now Luigi and Johann could see lines of tall, slim wooden houses perched on the slopes above the town, and all around the edge of the harbour more buildings, like embroidery stitched around the hem of a dark skirt.

Luigi was entranced by the city's setting. There was a dark, brooding beauty about the place, he thought. Such a harbour, such a perfect place for a port. If only Leopoldo had settled here! But still, he – Luigi – had arrived, he had reached *Alla fine del mondo*!

The waterfront was clamorous. Drays loaded with bales of wool, carts piled high with coal and cords of wood, hansom cabs and carriages crowded the wharf, behind which was a row of large warehouses and a square brick customs house. Further along, to their right, were shipwrights' and boat-builders' yards, and to the left was a block of taller wooden buildings, evidently the city's central business district.

Clutching their belongings, Johann and Luigi descended the gang-plank, at the bottom of which was a small shelter serving as a reception area. As he waited in line to be checked, Luigi's anxieties returned. Then he told himself, *No-one, no-one here can possibly know me, or know what I did.* He was heartened too by the fact that there appeared to be no law enforcement officers on the wharf, only a bald, bearded man in a suit and tie behind a desk. On the desk in front of him was a pestle-shaped stamp. Johann's papers were scrutinised, then he was waved on to the wharf. Luigi stood before the man, who nodded curtly at him.

'Afternoon.'

'Good afternoon, sir.'

'Passport?'

Luigi passed the document over. The man studied it. Without looking up, frowning hard, he said, 'Where're you from?'

'Pesaro.'

'That's in Italy?'

'Yes.'

'You were born in Italy.'

'Yes.'

The man looked up.

'But you've got red hair.'

For a moment Luigi didn't reply. He felt too insulted. Then, choosing his words carefully, he replied, 'What does that matter?'

The man laughed, in an unpleasant way. 'I never saw an Italian with red hair.'

Realising he must not antagonise this official, Luigi took a deep breath, then said in as reasonable a tone as he could summons, 'In northern Italy there are many people with hair like mine. Pesaro is in northern Italy.'

Staring at Luigi for a few moments, evidently aware that he had been made to appear unknowing, the man's expression darkened. Instead of stamping the paper, he pushed it to one side of the desk, then said brusquely, 'Remain on board, I'll deal with you later.'

A hot flush began to spread through Luigi's chest. *They knew, the authorities knew, somehow, about him.* Behind them, other passengers were beginning to shove. One called out, 'Get a move on, will yuh?' Luigi, doing his best not to look flustered, said to the official, 'How long will I have to wait?'

The man tossed his head impatiently in the direction of the ship. 'As long as I take, my man.' His voice took on an irritated tone. 'Now get back up there.'

Face burning with embarrassment, Luigi walked back up onto the deck, the other waiting passengers looking at him with curiosity. Having attention drawn to himself was the last thing he wanted. He needed to get to Leopoldo's farm as soon as possible. There he could melt into the land. Now though, Leopoldo seemed as far away as ever.

At last all the others had been processed and the official beckoned him back down the gang-plank. By the time Luigi reached him, the man was scrutinising his passport again. When he looked up, he had the same cold expression on his face. Sucking at his gums disagreeably as he studied the document, he asked:

'How old are you now?'

'Twenty-two years of age.'

'And you left Marseilles when?'

'July 23.'

'And you left Italy when?'

'July 20.'

'Why did you come here?'

'To start a new life.'

'Were you assisted?'

'What does that mean?'

'Did the New Zealand government pay for your passage?'

'No.'

Annoyance at the official's thinly disguised contempt began to simmer inside Luigi. Thinking, *I must not lose my temper with this man*, he forced himself to remain unruffled. 'I paid for my passage myself,' he declared.

'You are single?'

'Single?'

'Not married.'

'Yes.'

'What is your job?'

'Do you mean, what work do I do?'

'Yes.'

Luigi thought quickly. Considering that 'Fisherman' may not quite do, he declared, 'I am a musician.'

The man raised his eyebrows. 'Really?' His tone was sceptical. 'And what instrument do you play?'

Luigi bent down, opened his pack, took out the accordion. 'This one,' he said. He pumped the instrument briskly a few times, then ran his fingers up and down the keys, producing a melodious scale. The man looked taken aback. He blinked, hard. Encouraged, Luigi played the opening notes of an Italian folk tune, then, on an upbeat note, stopped abruptly. Cocking his head, he said, 'You see? I am an accordionist.'

In a markedly more respectful tone, the official said, 'And where do you play?'

'Anywhere I am welcome.'

Looking down, the man drummed the fingers of his left hand on the desk. Then, giving a little grunt, he took Luigi's passport, picked up the iron stamp and brought it down hard on the page. Handing it back, he said, 'We've had trouble with some Italians in this country.' His expression relaxed. 'But since you paid your own way, you can enter.' Then he began to laugh. 'This country could do with more music, Luigi Galoni.'

'Johann, goodbye. We will meet again, I hope.'

'I hope so too, Luigi. When I am settled, I will write to you in Westland, care of your friend.'

'Please do. And good luck for your painting.'

'Thank you. Good luck to you too, with your music. And everything else.'

For a few moments they stared at each other, aware that the friendship they had forged in the last weeks, even if not renewed, would never be forgotten. Together they had crossed the globe, together they had reached the new world. Luigi threw his arms around the other man and hugged him. 'Aufwiedersehen, Johann.'

'Arriverderci, Luigi.'

Luigi watched him walk away. When he was fifty yards further along the waterfront, Johann paused, turned, waved once, then vanished into the crowds on Customhouse Quay.

The steamer from Wellington to Nelson took only seven hours. There, over-nighting in the small but busy town, Luigi enquired at the railway station as to the best way to travel to Okuru, in Westland. He was told that he could take the train only as far as Foxhill. From the railhead there he could use the new coach service to the town of Westport.

The train line ran through a pretty, wooded valley to Foxhill. There, outside the station, the coach was waiting, a gleaming, four-spring model drawn by two chestnut horses, with a third horse tethered to the rear. Luigi paid a shilling for his fare out of the money he had changed in the Bank of New Zealand in Wellington, his bag was placed with the other luggage in the rear of the coach, and he was directed up onto the seat at the front of the coach, alongside the driver and another man. Both were tall, rangy men with drooping moustaches, the driver a few years older than the man next to him. The driver wore a bowler hat, the younger man a cloth cap.

GRAEME LAY

As Luigi settled himself, the man in the cap held out his hand.

'Gidday there, I'm Tom Newman.' As Luigi shook his hand, the man gestured towards the driver. 'And this is my brother, Harry.' Luigi leaned across Tom and shook his older brother's hand. Tom grinned. 'His real name's Henry, but everyone calls him Harry. Harry, Tom, now all we need's a Dick. You're not a Dick by any chance?'

'No, I am a Luigi. Luigi Galoni. I am from Italy.'

Tom closed one eye and squinted at him. 'Italy, eh? Long way to come for a coach ride.'

'Yes.'

Harry gave his whip a crack, the horses started, broke into a trot and the coach moved forward along the rough, narrow road. From his elevated position at the front of the coach, Luigi stared around in wonder at the landscape that was unfolding. On either side of the barely formed road, round-topped mountains reared, their flanks clothed in dense evergreen forest. *Verde, verde.* This land seemed entirely green, he thought, just as Italy seemed entirely brown. Such grandeur, everywhere such green grandeur. But he wondered, too, where were the villages? Where were the houses? Where were the people? Since they had left Foxhill they had not glimpsed another human soul, nor a single man-made building. At home, even in the furthest reaches of the Apennines there were villages, and churches and farmhouses and vineyards. Here there seemed to be nothing but landscape and more landscape.

They entered a valley beside a river which twisted and turned and tumbled alongside them. Shadowing the river, the road took them deeper and deeper into the darkly beautiful but unpopulated land. The coach made slow progress, lurching and slithering through the many muddy stretches. The river bed was strewn with boulders which broke its flow into white water, and when the flow paused it gave way to pools of a brownish shade.

'Tannin from the trees makes the water brown,' Harry Newman explained to Luigi. The trees had straight trunks and grew thickly on both sides of the river.

'What are those trees called?' Luigi asked.

'Beech.'

'Beach?'

'Yeah. South Island beech.'

'The trees are called beach?'

24

'Yeah. They grow all over, round here.'

Luigi nodded, absorbing the information, but thinking yet again how confusing the English language could be, giving the same name to a tree and the seaside.

They stayed overnight first in the tiny settlement of Hampden, and the next at the even tinier one of Inangahua. As they moved deeper and deeper into the gorge, the rocky road following the river's serpentine course, Luigi began to feel overwhelmed by mountains and he ached to see the sea again. The gorge seemed endless, its dripping, fern-covered sides now precipitous, the swollen brown waters of the Buller river gushing angrily beside them. At one point the cliff face hung right over the road. Here Tom slowed the horses to a cautious plod, and the three men at the front of the coach had to bend their heads to avoid the dripping rock. 'Hawks Crag,' Tom announced to Luigi, turning his head away as the water ran down his brow. 'Fit for bloody hawks all right.'

For hour after hour the Newman brothers drove their team onwards, Harry clutching the reins, Tom with a cigarette stuck permanently to his lower lip. Luigi found himself admiring the brothers' determination. Half-way through the gorge, when a rockfall blocked the coach's way, Tom took shovels from a rack at the back of the coach and, working in tandem, the two brothers cleared the pile in less than an hour. Then they were off again on their tortuous journey, following the seemingly endless river. Luigi slumped forward, his hand held to his forehead, wondering, *How much further, how much further until we reach the coast?*

Another bend, then the river's course straightened and so did the road. Gradually the gorge widened to a forested plain. The road left the river, passing instead through a dense stand of bush. Now, instead of stones, the road consisted almost entirely of mud. The horses struggled to keep their footing as the coach slithered this way and that, threatening to jackknife until Harry slowed it to a walking pace. Shivering in the late afternoon cold, all Luigi could see on either side of the muddy track were beech trees and a miniature forest of ferns that sprouted from beneath the trees. But the rain had stopped, the sky had cleared to a cloudless blue and when he sat up and inhaled deeply through his nostrils, Luigi caught an unmistakable briny scent, the smell he knew and loved. *The sea!*

He sat on the wall beside Westport's Esplanade, the contents of his pack spread out to dry alongside him, counting what was left of the money.

Behind him the muddy waters of the Buller River coursed swiftly towards the river's mouth, the high tide sloshing at its edges. Across from the Esplanade a railway line ran down to the wharf area. There was a row of coal-filled wagons on the wharf and a paddle-steamer, *The Tasmanian Maid*, was berthed, its mooring ropes taut, straining against the currents. On the other side of the railway line were several hotels, a row of shops and the muddy streets of the town. Looking back inland, in the far distance Luigi could see the setting sun gilding the snow on the line of jagged mountains, and the forest that covered their lower slopes. The forest reached right to the edge of the town, and in this intense light the crowns of the beech trees were as green and bunched as broccoli. Although the sun was low and the air cold, Luigi felt satisfaction at having reached this remote coast and knowing that he was now well on the way to where Leopoldo was. Johann had torn the Westland page out of his almanac and presented it to Luigi. The map showed him that he still had a long way to go to reach Okuru, in the far south of this province. In the morning, he would set off again. But first there were certain matters to attend to.

He began to repack his belongings. Counting the unfamiliar currency carefully, he saw that it totalled six pounds. He had crossed the world, and still had six pounds left. But he needed more equipment: a waterproof cape of his own – the Newman brothers had warned him that this was a weather coast – new socks and underwear, and…he picked at the loose, leaking sole of his left boot…a new pair of boots.

He picked up his pack, crossed the Esplanade and strolled back along the main street to the Alpine Hotel, where he had taken a room. Passing the town's other hotels, he saw that their gas lights were already burning, and that there were horses tethered to their hitching rails. From the hotel doorways came the sounds of jocularity, women's high-pitched laughter and the tinny notes of a honky-tonk piano. But too tired for music, Luigi climbed the hotel stairs to his room. There he dreamed that he was aboard a paddle steamer, captained by Tom Newman, cruising the waters of the Foglia estuary.

John Harris Bootmaker was a small premises towards the Britannia Square end of Westport's Palmerston Street. Pushing open its door the next morning, Luigi caused a bell above it to tinkle madly. Blinking in the semi-light, he smelt the rich aroma of cured leather and boot polish. A chair and a sloping foot-rest were in one corner of the wooden-floored shop, and on the wall behind the chair was a long mirror. A wooden counter ran the length of the room, and behind it, taking up the entire wall, were cubicles filled with boots and shoes, some new, some labelled for repair. Near the end of the counter a slim man of about thirty-five wearing a leather apron was trimming the sole of a boot, stuck upside-down before him on an iron last. Setting down the trimming knife, the man nodded curtly at Luigi, who told him he needed a new pair of boots.

'Work or leisure?' asked the man. He was fair-haired, with wide sideburns and grey, sunken eyes. Lines ran down both sides of his narrow face, and he was thin-lipped. Not a friendly face, Luigi concluded. Still, all he needed from him was boots.

'Mostly for work.'

'Size?'

'I am not sure.'

Leaning over the counter and staring at Luigi's feet, the boot-maker said, 'Whip one of those off and give it me.' He turned the boot over, frowned at its detached sole, then took a new pair of boots from a cubicle. 'Try these. They should fit you well enough.'

As Luigi sat on the chair, put one foot on the sloping foot-rest and pulled on the right boot, the proprietor stood beside him watchfully. Luigi tugged the laces tight, stood up and pushed his foot down against the floorboards.

'How is it?' demanded the bootmaker.

'It is good.' He pressed his foot down again. 'Yes, I think the size is correct.'

The man looked at him guardedly. 'Where're you from?'

'Italy.'

'Ah, Eye-tye eh?' He gave a little grunt of displeasure.

'What is the problem with that?'

Looking away, the bootmaker sniffed. 'Had some other Italians through here a while back. Buggers didn't fit in.'

Luigi could do nothing but shrug. He began to pull on the other boot. What was it about these people? Why did they lump him in with other Italians he had never heard of?

At that moment the shop door burst open and the bell tinkled. A girl of about twelve, in a dark blue velvet dress, matching cardigan and with long, wavy brown hair went up to the man and put her arms around him.

'Hello Papa.'

Looking bashful, he held her at arm's length. 'Why aren't you at school, Alice?'

'I have a chill. Mother said I needn't go.' To emphasise the point she drew a white handkerchief from the pocket of her dress, held it to her nose and blew. Then, putting the handkerchief away, she turned and looked directly at the young man her father had been attending to.

The girl's grey eyes looked into Luigi's so piercingly that he found himself glancing away. When in a second or two he regained his composure and looked back, she was smiling, faintly, but maintaining her unwavering stare. Her face was oval, her skin as pale and smooth as a white rose petal. Below her full mouth, in the centre of her chin, was a small crease. Waves of brown hair, tied in a white ribbon across the top of her head, tumbled to her shoulders. She was petite, but her miniature body revealed the unmistakable shape of a girl on the cusp of womanhood.

Still staring at him, she said disarmingly, 'What is your name?'

'Luigi Galoni.'

Then, his face flushing, he sat down on the chair and began to lace up his new boot. The thought that he was capable of being aroused by this girl disturbed him. In the steadfast gaze of her grey eyes he recognised the intuition and allure of a grown woman.

Hoping his unease was not noticeable, he turned back to her surly father. 'How much does it cost for the boots?' he said.

Compared with the Buller Gorge, going south, directly down the coast, was easy. The gravel road was wide and well-used, and Luigi saw many other coaches, but it soon became clear that he was moving in the opposite direction to that of most other travellers. Overwhelmingly, these northward travelling people were men, crammed onto the outsides of the coaches, or on horseback. Some were also walking, heads down as if in defeat, plodding north with great packs on their backs, their bodies dangling pots and pans, like tinkers. 'It's the gold,' one coach driver explained, 'now that most of the colour's gone, there's nothing to stay for on the Coast. Mainly just the Chows left working the fields now.'

'Chows?'

'Yeah, the Chinks.'

Considering who this could mean, Luigi guessed. 'The Chinese?' He had seen some of them in the streets of Westport, small hunched men with black caps and pig-tails.

'Yeah, the slope-eyes. Little yellow bastards are everywhere, still.'

But although most of the readily found gold was gone, there was coal mining now, the man told him. The Denniston incline, an engineering marvel, had just been completed. It was bringing the black stuff down from the mine on a plateau over four thousand feet above Westport, from where it was shipped to other parts of the country. That was where the wagons he had seen by the waterfront in Westport must have come from, Luigi realised. The coachman flicked his reins irritably.

'But who wants to work in a hole without sunlight, hacking coal all day?' Some were willing to, he told Luigi, but most former gold miners were moving on, to an area up north called the Coromandel, another place where the colour had been discovered. And so the roads and the ports of Westland were clogged with men getting out, desperate to find their elusive fortunes elsewhere. Luigi wondered why they didn't do what Leopoldo had, buy land and start a farm, but he did not mention this to the coachman.

The road followed the coast closely. It was mostly elevated, and the views diverted him. The plain was only a few miles wide, separated from the alps by stands of dense forest. The mountains were enormous, snow-capped and continuous. He had never seen a landscape so wild, so grand, so raw. And the sea …

Below to his right, its dark blue waters were being whipped into white caps and driven hard ashore by a stiff westerly wind. Veils of spray hung over the waves and shore as the sea reared, surged and crashed onto the grey sand. The waves entranced him. At home the sea was almost always still. Even when storms came they usually were from the north, so that they flattened the sea or pushed it back. But here the waves seemed unending, things of beauty as well as power. As the coach travelled south for hour after hour, he watched the waves rise, curl, crash and surge against the shore, marvelling at their shape and force. His head turned constantly, from the waters to the right to the mountains to the left, from the roiling sea to the sweep of beech forest. Beach to the right, beech to the left, he thought, amusing himself with this play on the words. The trees covered the plain entirely, as well as the foothills and wall of the alps right to the snowline, covering the face of the mountains like the yashmaks he had seen masking the faces of the Arab women in Aden. There must be possibilities in this untouched land, he kept thinking.

Untouched? Not really, for he began to see the legacy the quest for gold had left. Pale green, swift-flowing rivers poured down from the mountains, and on every river bed and every terrace there were heaps of tailings. On some river banks he saw men scrambling and scratching – like the poor scavengers he remembered from the rubbish dump behind Pesaro – reworking the tailings for overlooked traces of gold. Many of these people were indeed Chinese, wearing dark blue cotton suits and round caps. As the coach rumbled over the coast's narrow wooden bridges and Luigi stared down at the miners, they sometimes looked up momentarily. But whenever he waved a greeting they just looked away, going back to the scavenging with their shovels, pans and cradles. In some places too there was abandoned dredging machinery, the rusting frames of plant and engines, half covered by shingle. It looked to Luigi as if some sort of war had taken place on the riverbeds, a war against the land that had left it littered with the broken remains of the arms men had used in their battles, one that had ended in defeat, creating the crowds of refugees who were leaving the coast.

'Did many men make their fortunes?' he asked the coachman.

The driver, an affable fellow called Albert, shook his head. 'Not many. There were hundreds of claims, and maybe one strike in a hundred.' He laughed, scornfully. 'There're always the stories, though, about a huge strike and massive payouts. But if you really struck it rich, would you let everyone know about it? Not in this lawless place.' He laughed again. 'Gold's like women; its beauty makes men lie. You should never believe what men boast about women, I reckon, and it's the same with the colour. Not many round here struck it rich. People who've made most money are the storekeepers and shipowners, going by the prices they charged the poor bastards who swarmed here.' He seemed to be talking to himself now. 'Maybe I ought t'sell me coach and move up to the Coromandel, open a general store there.'

They reached Kumara Junction in the late afternoon, then swung inland on the road to Kumara itself. Albert had recommended the hotel there to Luigi. The coach would be over-nighting there too. The sun was setting, making the snow on the mountain tops glow, as they pulled in at the front of the Queens Hotel. Tipping back his broad-brimmed hat, Albert let go the reins. 'You've arrived at a good time, I reckon, Luigi,' he said. 'There's a rally here tonight. A political rally.'

'So I say to all of you, gentlemen, if you want the gov'mint to look after the Coast, cast your vote my way. You all know me. Mayor of Kumara, lay litigant for the miners, storekeeper, publican. Not that I'm 'ere to boast, mind you, just to remind you that in me the coast'll have no more loyal advocate. Just as I spoke up for the lads in the goldfields' warden's court, so I'll speak up in Wellington for the people of Hokitika. But first, gentlemen, I need your votes, I need a mandate – a decent mandate – if I'm to be the voice of the West Coast in the capital. I don't need to remind you that times are getting tough. Men are leaving the Coast because they think the good times are over, that there're no prospects 'ere any more. But I tell you, this is still the greatest province in the dominion. Forests, coal, farmland – it's all here for the taking. But we can't do it all ourselves. We need the gov'mint to pitch in. We need better roads and bridges, more railway lines, deeper ports and longer wharves, if we're to make the most of our potential. Only the gov'mint can give 'em to us, and only Dick Seddon, as Member of Parliament for Hokitika, will put pressure on the gov'mint to do so!'

'You? You couldn't even run a butcher's shop! You're a failed businessman, Seddon, a failed grocer and a failed butcher!'

All eyes turned to the heckler, a slack-shouldered man with a face the colour of saddle leather and a nicotine-stained moustache. A few of the audience laughed, a little tentatively, at the man's audacity. Glaring at him, Dick Seddon bellowed back.

'I'll make mince meat of you, mate, if you care to step outside.'

The retort was greeted with the gales of laughter, but the man with the moustache was undeterred. 'What about last time yuh stood for Hokitika? In '76 yuh come fourth. FOURTH!'

A muttering broke out, occasioned by this reminder. There were derisive laughs now. Someone else called out from the side of the room, 'Yeah, you lost your bloody deposit in '76, Dick. You wanna lose it again?'

Seddon took a step forward. Lowering his head like a bull preparing to charge, he said balefully, 'I might've lost that campaign overall, but I won the vote hands-down where it counted, on the Waimea diggings. I was the miners' man then, and I still am. And I'll tell you why I'm standing again. Because no less a person than Sir George Grey, our great leader, asked me to stand, asked me to stand because he knew a man of principle when he met one. And I gave my word to Sir George that I would stand again. And so, gentlemen, here I stand!' He paused for effect, and when

31

he resumed his voice was several notes lower. 'I'm also standing because I love this coast, and I want this province to develop. I want the Coast to 'ave what only the guv'mint can give it, railways and roads and bridges and wharves and schools and 'ospitals. That's not a privilege, gentlemen. Because we've paid our taxes, that's our RIGHT!'

Applause broke out, but it was not universal. Men were still looking sceptical, still muttering among themselves. Someone else called out from the back: 'How do we know that if you get to Wellington you won't do what all the others've done, forget who put you there!' There was an outbreak of appreciative laughter at this. Instead of replying immediately, Seddon reached for a glass of water from the table beside the dais, then swallowed several mouthfuls from it, as if priming a pump.

From his position by the bar, Luigi followed the unfolding drama in the hotel lounge with fascination. He had never seen a political rally before, had no idea that they were as riotous as this. The big bearded man in the frock-coat looked about thirty-five. With his watch chain looped across his bulging belly and his thumbs tucked into his waistcoat, he was building up a head of steam like a traction engine. Tacked to the wall behind him was a banner with letters in black which read, DICK SEDDON FOR HOKITIKA, and above it was a portrait of England's queen. She was the sole female presence in the room.

Although the campaigner spoke with a strong accent that Luigi found difficult to fully understand, he could follow most of what he was saying. The man had stood for New Zealand's parliament before, without success, he was already the *sindaco* – the mayor – of this little place, and earlier he had lost money with a business.

Now the big man was putting down his glass, glowering, puffing his chest out even further.

'And there's something else I'll do for this magnificent province, gentlemen.' He reduced the volume of his voice even more, and en masse the crowd craned forward to hear. 'I'll rid it of every last alien, of every foreigner oo's sneaked onto the Coast and 'as taken our jobs. Yes, gentlemen, you know 'oo I mean.' A muttering like distant thunder passed through the room. 'The wily Orientals with their untrustworthy ways, the ones 'oo 'ave some'ow persuaded the authorities that they 'ave a right to come and live 'ere, among god-fearing, Christian British folk.' He thrust back his shoulders. 'But we know better, don't we? We know that their ways are not our ways and never will be. So I will rid the Coast of this scourge, gentlemen, I'll see to it that the ones who are here now will be put on a ship back to where they came from, and that no more of 'em will ever set foot in this country. We'll tax the little yellow men so hard they'll never want to set foot in our fair land. Let's keep this province, let's keep our *dominion*, totally British!'

This time the applause was general, and enthusiastic. There were also cries of 'Give it to them, Dick!' and 'We're with you all the way!' 'Out with the Chows!' another man cried, and he was clapped on the back by those around him. Amid the hubbub, another man called out, 'What about the Irish, Dick? I'm from Dublin!' This brought laughter from the crowd, and a swift reply from the campaigner. 'Ireland's as much a part of Britain as the West Coast's part of New Zealand. You're no foreigner, you can stay, friend! But the rest' – his voice took on a sneering tone – 'the Orientals and the Pomeranians and the Austrians and the Bohemians and the Italians, they can pack their bags and get back t'where they belong! Which-is-not-this-country!'

This time the clapping and shouting were thunderous. But Luigi felt as if he had been hauled up on a scaffold. *Italians?* He wanted to send back *Italians*, as well as all those other people from different places? He felt a surge of anger, mixed with bewilderment. Why was this man so against so many people? All they were doing was starting a new life. Why did they not have the right to come here, if they were prepared to work hard? The man was unjust.

Luigi raised his right hand. The speaker, beaming now, eyes roaming the room triumphantly, saw it. Raising his chin, hooking his thumbs in his waistcoat pockets, his voice boomed across the room.

'You've got a question, young man?'

'Yes.' Pausing first to consider how the question should best be phrased, Luigi said, 'I would like to know, why is it that you don't like people like me to come here.'

Seddon looked perplexed. 'Like you? What d'you mean?' All eyes in the room turned to Luigi. Feeling himself colouring, he nevertheless pressed on.

'Immigrant people. You said they should go back to where they came from.'

The campaigner snorted. 'Not all immigrants, my friend. After all, I was born in Lancashire!' A ripple of laughter greeted this. 'Only the aliens will 'ave to go. Not decent people of British blood. Not white, red-headed Englishmen like yourself.'

'I am not English. I am Italian.'

There was a sudden silence, followed by an outbreak of murmuring. The crowd continued to stare at Luigi. Suddenly disconcerted, Seddon raised his fist to his mouth and coughed, loudly. Then he asked, 'And how long 'ave you been in this country, my man?'

'One week.'

More muttering went through the room. There were grunted asides. Luigi heard the man next to him growl to his neighbour, 'Can't throw a man out after a week. Gotta give 'im a fair go.' Another one said, more loudly, 'Man's only just arrived, hasn't had a chance to prove hisself yet.'

What happened next was something that told Luigi everything he ever wanted to know about politicians. He sensed from Seddon's hesitation that the man was slyly reassessing the mood shift in the room, and his own position. What would his reaction be now?

Planting his hands on his hips, Seddon's voice boomed down at him. 'And what's your name, young man?'

'Luigi Galoni.'

'And what do you do?'

'I am a fisherman. And I play the accordion.'

Seddon threw back his head, guffawed, then declared:

'Well, Louie, welcome to the West Coast. Work hard, play your squeeze-box, keep your nose clean, and you can stay.'

A spontaneous shout of acclamation went up from the crowd. People clapped Luigi on the back. Someone shook his hand. He was astonished. What a change, in a matter of moments. Feeling a nudge in the back, he turned. The barman was holding out a glass of beer. 'Here mate,' he said, 'Have this. And good luck.' Although he thanked the man, Luigi was still angry with the politician for the way he had attacked some people who had come to this land, for what he could tell were the man's own selfish purposes. And he was confused, too, by something else the politician had said. What had he meant, 'keep your nose clean'? His was always clean.

The coach reached Hokitika by mid-afternoon, allowing him time to wander through the town before the sun set. It was bigger and more substantial than the other coast towns he had seen, with a wide main street lined with solid buildings: a bank, post office, municipal office and many public houses. But here too were the signs that the rush for the colour was at an end. Men with muddy boots and bowyanged trousers stood about in the street, singly and in groups, their eyes downcast, bags at their feet, idle now and obviously contemplating their exodus.

He walked to the end of the street, to the mouth of the wide river. Here there was a busy port, with two steamers anchored out in the stream and several sailing vessels, rafted together, moored to the wharf. Luigi's fisherman's eyes told him at once that this was no safe haven. The entrance to the harbour was cross-hatched by currents and partially blocked by a bar where the sea and the river's flow conflicted angrily. Great heaps of driftwood were piled on the shore and mist drifted along the sandy coast. After staring at the unruly sea for a time, he returned to the main street. At a shipping office he enquired if there was a sea service to Jackson Bay. The man behind the counter shook his head. 'No jetty there, mate.' Neither was there a regular coach service, there was no road. Again, the options were given to him bluntly – horseback or walk.

Sitting in a public house called the Shovel & Nugget, studying Johann's map, he calculated that the Okuru valley was still well over a hundred miles to the south, and saw that the land between here and there was marked as 'forested mountains'. So he would need more equipment than just new boots.

'Six shillings? For a small axe?'

'That's the price.'

'And for the frying pan?'

'Four shillings and sixpence.'

'That is too much.'

'Take it or leave it.'

'Why do you ask so much for these ordinary things?'

'It's not so much. A year ago everything was double that. Since the rush ended my prices have gone down.'

Turning away, Luigi added up the figures. The cost of the goods he would need came to nearly two pounds! And that was without the food he would need for the journey. It was impossible, he had only fifteen shillings left. He wandered disconsolately along the main street of the town. The gas lights were on, casting eerie shadows over the streets and shop fronts where groups of men stood about aimlessly. Outside the Caledonian Hotel, a chubby, bonneted girl with ruby lips called to him. 'Hello handsome, want your pump primed? I'll work your handle for two bob.' He walked on, head down, her entreaties pursuing him. 'Okay then, a shilling and sixpence!'

What sort of a town is this, he wondered, where the cost of a woman was less than half the price of a frying pan?

He came to the next tavern, the Spade & Cradle. From inside came the sounds of revelry – a piano playing loudly, singing and loud laughter. Pushing open the door, Luigi saw that the bar was indeed crowded, with men gathered around the piano, beer glasses in their hands. The woman at the keyboard finished her jaunty number with a flourish, then jumped up from the piano stool. A man handed her a glass filled with a bright red liquid and she toasted him and drank.

Luigi put his rucksack down in a corner of the bar and bought a glass of beer for tuppence. All around him, men in working clothes were drinking and shouting to each other, or crowding around the three young women who were present. Returning to the corner, Luigi set his glass down on a windowsill and took his accordion from his bag. Very softly, he pumped the bellows, then began to play, nodding his head in time to the beat. He began to sing, softly.

Fente le nane, fentele cantando
finche la popa se va 'ndormenzando,
Nina nana, oh, oh.

La popa se 'ndormenza a poco a poco,
come la legna verda arent al foco.
Nina nana, oh, oh.

The hubbub died away, and curious faces turned towards the accordionist. He played on, a little louder now, pumping the bellows harder, increasing the volume of his voice. Heads began to nod, feet began to tap, other heads began to nod, there was a lusty cheer from the end of the bar. Finishing the song with a flourish, he brought the two ends of the accordion together with a loud '*Ohi* !' There were cries of approval, and someone called out 'Encore!'

Luigi bowed low in acknowledgement, removed his cap and placed it upside down on the floor. In the centre of it he put his Roman silver coin and two pennies, then began to play again, the faster and jollier ...

Jammo, jammo, jammo, jammo ja.
Jammo, jammo, jammo, jammo ja.
Funiculi funicula funiculi funicula
ncoppa jammo ja, funiculi funicula.

Finishing again to loud applause, Luigi bowed once more, set down the accordion and picked up his drink. A man with a handlebar moustache came up, still clapping his hands, and put a threepenny piece in the cap. Another came up, shook Luigi's hand and dropped three pennies in it. Two others did the same. When the fourth brought him another drink and dropped two pennies in his cap, the woman who had been playing the piano approached him.

'I'm Fanny. Fanny Tremble. Who are you?'

'I am Luigi. How do you do?'

'You passing through?'

'I'm sorry?'

'Are you staying in Hokitika?'

'For a little time, yes.'

'Got lodgings?'

'No.'

She leaned forward. Her face was painted, like a mask, her piled blonde hair was dark at the roots.

'*Need* a place to stay?'

'Yes.'

'Board and lodging's available here. Free, if you play every night from seven till late.'

'One frying pan, one billy, one tomahawk. Mug, knife, fork and spoon. Matches. Fish hooks, sinkers and lines, and the cape, hat and groundsheet. Oh, and two yards of muslin. There you are, sir. That'll be one pound, seven shillings and sixpence altogether.'

Luigi passed over the money, the man counted it, then wrapped the equipment in brown paper and tied it with string. Pushing the bundle across the counter, he asked, 'Heading up to the Coromandel, are you?'

'No. I am going to Okuru.'

The man made a low whistling noise. 'Going to be a far downer, then, eh?'

'What is that?'

'What we call the people down there. It's far down, y'see.'

'Oh. Well, yes, I am going to be a far downer, then.'

'Looking for the colour?'

'No, I'm going to see my friend, Leopoldo. I'm going to be a farmer.'

'Well, good luck. How're you getting there, wagon or horse?'

'I am going by shanks's pony.'

'Yeah? Well, good luck again. Where're you from?'

'I am from Italy.'

'Well, you've come a long way already then.'

'Yes. To the end of the Earth, almost.'

The man gave a dry laugh. 'Right.'

Only when Luigi was out of earshot did he add, 'You poor Eye-tie bastard.'

One more look at the map had convinced Luigi that there was only one way to get there, along the coast. He left early in the morning, after finishing the huge breakfast – porridge, toast, bacon and eggs – which Fanny at the Spade & Cradle had prepared for him. Bidding him good luck, the motherly woman hugged him hard, then pressed on him half a pound of sliced bacon and a small flask of brandy, which he added to the pack, along with the rice, salt, flour and cheese he had bought at a general store the day before. He had tried everywhere to buy some pasta, but nowhere in the town was there any. To his amazement, no one had ever heard of pasta. Instead they offered him rice.

'Take care, Luigi! Come back any time, with your squeeze-box!' Fanny called as he headed off towards the bridge over the Hokitika River. He waved to her, then turned and began his journey.

The pack was full but not unduly heavy. The frying pan was tied with twine to one side of the pack, the billy to the other. His oilskins and the muslin cloth that Fanny had insisted he take as protection against flying insects were at the bottom of the pack.

He thought he would aim for twenty miles a day, meaning that he could make Okuru in about week. Day after day he walked, seeing no other human being. Sometimes, when the going was flattish and damp, he removed his boots and went bare-footed, soothing his soles on the sand and in the sea. By day there was usually at least an hour of rain, but by late afternoon it would clear, leaving a sky of pastel blue and the surface of the Tasman Sea like mercury. At this time of the day the swells were shapely and glassy, and lines of stubby sea birds flying at high speed in perfectly straight lines skimmed their crests. But at this time too the flying insects would come, swarms of tiny black flies which invaded his eyes, ears, mouth and nostrils. For every one he killed, another hundred would land on his skin. The only way to cope with them was to put the muslin over his head and body, and trudge the sand like an Arab woman until the time came to choose a site for the night and prepare a fire.

For fuel there was the abundance of driftwood which littered the coast – the trunks and boughs of trees carried down by the rivers – resembling the dried bones of prehistoric monsters. The driftwood fascinated Luigi, he had never seen such flotsam on the Adriatic shore. The wood came in myriad sizes and shapes – thin, thick, truncated, long, straight, bent or curved – and selected pieces made a fine frame for his bivouacs, before he covered it with the oilskin sheet. Dried pieces of the wood burnt well, the bluish flames giving off a good heat, and by banking it up at sunset, the pyre kept away the insects, dried his boots and socks and kept him warm through the night. The sand made a soft mattress, his rucksack a satisfactory pillow. And on the third night the sky cleared completely, the moon was new and the stars seemed bright and close enough to hold in his hand, the constellation they called the Southern Cross hanging low in the western sky like a diamante bracelet.

In this fashion, covering mile after mile of coast through rain and sunshine, wading across streams and river mouths, leaping from shingle bank to shingle bank, he moved closer to the region they called the Far Down. The coastal landforms became more varied. Lagoons and headlands replaced beaches, there were bluffs instead of lowlands. One day he walked to the end of a long sand spit, with the pounding Tasman on his right and a huge tidal lagoon to his left.

As he tramped along the spit, dozens of long-legged white birds rose from the lagoon and floated into the sky, trailing their long legs. Awed by the stork-like creatures and the lagoon, he decided to make his encampment at the very end of the spit. There he made a bivouac from driftwood, lit a fire, boiled his rice and bacon and was enchanted by the hunch-backed birds. Taking little notice of him, they stalked across the lagoon, foraging with their rapier beaks. When they took flight their wings beat gracefully, conducting a slow, silent symphony. And as the sun set over the lonely lagoon, turning its surface golden, Luigi sat with his back to the sea and played his accordion and sang to himself and thought this must surely be one of the most beautiful places on Earth.

But on the sixth day, both weather and terrain abruptly changed. Rock replaced sand; cliff replaced lagoon. A strong wind began to blow in from the sea, driving the high tide against the rocks, making progress impossible. Neither could he go inland, as the cliffs were unclimbable. Instead he found a cave between two headlands and there spent two miserable days, watching the wind forcing the water ever closer to where he crouched. At daybreak, after calculating when the tide would be at its lowest, he wrapped all his belongings in the oilskin, packed them into the rucksack, left the cave and returned to the rocky shore, determined to regain his quota of miles. But his progress was painfully slow, blocked by slippery boulders and the raging sea, overlooked by cliffs as sheer as castle walls. Dodging the waves, scrambling and slithering over the rocks, sliding through bull kelp, he barked his shins and bruised his thighs and in an entire morning made only a few hundred yards. Cursing himself now for not taking the inland way, he inched painfully along the formidable coast, drenched by spray, his billy and pan clanking on his back, palms bleeding from the limpet shells which studded the boulders. Then, just as the rocks seemed unending, he rounded a headland, and, to his immense relief, saw sand again.

The beach was wide and covered with fresh, wet driftwood. In parts there was more wood than sand, suggesting that a large river mouth lay nearby, but from the beach there was no sign of it. In the distance he could see only a sickle of sand, curving away to yet another headland. Now that the gale had died, low white cloud covered the sea, a thick mist obscured the headland, and even at the water's edge the sea was docile. He tramped along the sand, bruised and exhausted, until he came to the headland. There he stopped, gathered what dry wood he could find, and lit a fire. It took half an hour of coaxing before the flames took and began to warm and dry his battered body.

Lying beside the fire, looking up and over at the rocks which lay beyond the high-tide mark, he saw a movement. Blinking, he stared. Yes, something moved. Something living, a dark, moving shape. Then he saw another, and another, awkward, heaving movements among the rocks. Leaving the fire, he moved curiously towards the moving shapes. Then just a few yards from them, he stopped and stared. *Sigillare.* Seals, dozens of them, large and small, sleek, shiny and whiskered, with eyes like black olives. He had seen pictures of them in books, but never before a live one. As he stared, one of the creatures raised his head, opened his mouth and made a honking noise at him. 'Bon giorno!' Luigi called, realising as he did so that it was the first greeting he had made in days. The seal – a large bull by the look of him – honked back. As he came closer the herd watched him warily, standing their ground, flippers braced, mouths open, showing razor-sharp teeth. Their gaping mouths gave off the stench of fish, but it was a smell that caused him no offence, and for some time he stood observing the creatures. They began to ignore him. Some dropped off into a snuffling sleep, heads turned to their sides. A female suckled a pup, which gobbled greedily at the teat. Two young males rose and challenged each another, snorting furiously in a show of bravado but making no physical contact, while the largest male grunted his approval. Luigi watched them for more than half an hour, their presence strangely comforting to him, before returning to his fire.

Another day, another river to cross. This one was braided and shallow, with many shingle banks. As he made his way across one broad channel, he noticed in the shallow, clear, swift-flowing water what appeared to be a moving mass. Peering, he saw that it was actually a large shoal of tiny, wriggling fish, each about the length of his little finger but slender as a worm. He moved closer to the shoal, but as he did so, in an instant it changed course and vanished. Intrigued, he set down his rucksack, sat on the shingle and waited. In minutes the shoal appeared again, swimming upstream against the current in close-packed formation. Luigi untied the frying pan from his pack and slid it carefully into the water behind the shoal. But stealthy as his movements were, the tiny fish evidently detected them, for again, in a split second, they vanished.

Continuing his crossing, Luigi saw more shoals of the wriggling creatures, moving up between the shingle banks. Always, they would scatter and disappear, if they glimpsed as much as his shadow. Hungry again, and with his fisherman's pride challenged, he determined that somehow he would catch one of the shoals. On the far bank of the river he cut a length of the supple vines that dangled like black ropes from the forest trees, and a straight sapling. Bending the vine into a hoop, he lashed it to the sapling with fishing line. Then, using some of the muslin, he fashioned a net, tying it to the hoop with more line and knotting it at the other end. Finding a channel about a yard wide near the river bank, he set the primitive net in the water, anchoring its handle and knotted end with two stones before retiring to the bank to sit and watch.

The shoal appeared as if from nowhere, extending for over a yard as it battled the river's flow. As he watched he saw it steadily progressing, moving closer to the net's mouth. There the shoal paused as if doubtful, then after a minute or so, it crossed the net's threshold. Running to the net, Luigi scooped it up, held it aloft and carried it to the bank. Peering inside, searching the soggy muslin, he was dismayed. Empty! They must move at the speed of an electric current, these fish, he thought. He could have sworn they were in the net. Then he saw a tiny movement in a fold of the muslin, a wriggling. One fish.

Holding it in the palm of his hand, he saw that the creature was as thin as vermicelli, and transparent, with black full stop eyes and a black, thread-like gut that extended the length of its body. So small, perhaps it was the fry of a larger fish, he surmised. Would they be edible? He couldn't see why not, but to obtain a meal of them it would be necessary to catch an entire shoal; just one wouldn't feed a finch. Choosing the same channel, he reset the net and waited. In a few minutes the wriggling shoal appeared again, hugging the side of the channel as they moved towards the net. This time Luigi moved a few yards downstream, and picking up a stick, stepped into the channel and began to move upstream, passing the stick slowly backwards and forwards through the water. As he had hoped, the shoal, frightened by the movements, darted forward en masse and into the net. Leaping after it, Luigi snatched the net up from the water, tilting its mouth upward so that the tiny fish would not spill. Although some did, when he looked inside he saw that at the bottom of the net was a glistening mass, several inches deep.

He ran his hands through the shoal of slippery, writhing fish, his fingers dripping with them. Gradually their wriggling slowed and he poured them from the net into his billy, nearly filling it. Then, on the riverbank, using a little bacon fat, he fried the tiny creatures in his pan, stirring them with his spoon. They cooked quickly, turning opaque as they did so, and he ate them straight from the frying pan. The taste was unlike anything he had experienced before, a sweetish, nutty flavour, with none of the strong smell of mackerel or herring. Delicious!

He cooked a second batch, then a third, filling his stomach with the entire catch, washing it down with black tea. And as he prepared to resume his journey, he did not dismantle the net, instead tying it to the outside of his pack. After all, he reasoned, there would be more rivers, and presumably more of the delectable little fish. Setting off along the coast, he reckoned that there were now only two more days between himself and Okuru. This land may be untamed, he thought, but there could be no excuse for starving here.

Tramping inland now, to find the track that led to Okuru, pushing through scrub and tussock, he made his way slowly up the side of a steep hill. Last night it had rained heavily, the vegetation was dripping and his feet squelched inside his boots. His oilskin leggings provided protection against the rasping undergrowth, but streams of hot sweat poured down his back and chest, making him feel filthy and a little feverish. Glancing up, he saw that the sky was now clear, but the vegetation was too dense for him to estimate accurately where the top of the hill was. Then, gradually, the trees grew more stunted, and twenty minutes later there were no tall trees at all, just stands of tea-tree and the coarse tussock grass that grew in clumps. Minutes later he was standing in open ground. Dropping his rucksack, he stared at the scene before him, drawing breath sharply at the panorama below.

Mountains, forested plain, rivers and the coast. At the foot of the hill he stood upon was a broad, braided river, which he knew from the map must be the Haast. In the centre of the plain, standing alone, resembling a beached whale, was a hump of land, covered entirely in forest. Only where the rivers meandered across the plain was there open land. All the rest was tightly bunched, deep green forest. The great alps, their crests covered in snow, formed a seemingly impassable barrier inland, while to Luigi's right the coastline was a sweeping strip of pale sand, arcing sharply outwards on the far side of one of the river mouths, then inwards to form a great bay. The bay was filled with mist which from this distance looked like white fur. Sitting on a clump of tussock, Luigi consulted Johann's map again. The bay must be Jackson Bay, the hook of land enclosing it Jackson Head. The other rivers were ...he traced them with his forefinger, glancing up, then down again. The Okuru and the Turnbull. Somewhere down there Leopoldo had made his home. Exhilarated by this knowledge, Luigi picked up his rucksack and began to push down through the bush, his first target the nearest of the plain's rivers, the Haast.

At the foot of the hill he came upon a wide track which shadowed the river bank, a few yards above it. Following the track in the direction of the sea, after half an hour he came upon a clearing. Here there was a small board-and-batten building with the sign General Store above the door, a landing and wharf, tied to which was a broad-beamed rowing boat. The store was dingy and disorderly, its shelves crammed with tins and jars and bottles, and it smelt strongly of over-ripe fruit, cheese and the smoked bacon hocks which dangled from the ceiling above the counter. On the counter were a few loaves of bread and a slab of cheddar under a gauze cover. Behind the counter were a middle-aged woman with greying hair and a deeply drawn face, and a small, unsmiling man in a black apron whose gaze followed Luigi suspiciously as he looked over the goods on sale. After buying a tin of tobacco and some bread and cheese, Luigi said to the man, 'I am on my way to Okuru to see my friend, Leopoldo Vitali. Do you know him?' Maintaining his sullen expression, the man shook his head. 'He is Italian. Like me,' he added.

'Italians have all gone, mate.'

'*Gone?* Where to?'

The man shrugged. 'Dunno. Up north maybe.'

'But I have had a letter from Leopoldo. Addressed from Okuru.'

The man turned away. 'Well, best you ask there, then, mate.'

The river was very wide, its waters pale green and icy-looking, divided into myriad channels separated by shingle banks. The ferryman was sitting on a bench outside a small shed by the landing. He was a big-boned man with broad but sagging shoulders and enormous, calloused hands. Luigi paid him sixpence to take him across, then sat and waited on the bank until other passengers arrived. Anxiety was building in his head, causing it to ache. *Italians have all gone, mate.* Gone where? Rolling and lighting a cigarette, he thought that in Okuru they would know.

Two young men emerged from the bush, both carrying packs. They nodded a greeting at Luigi, then paid the ferryman, who beckoned all three men aboard, directing Luigi to the bow seat and the other two to the stern. The ferryman cast off, took the centre thwart and rowed out into the channel. The crossing was no simple procedure, given the river's complex course. It took over half an hour, the rower navigating from braid to braid, the muscles in his forearms bunching as he hauled against the swift currents, then un-tensing as he went with the river downstream. When he reached the relative shallows beside a shingle bank, he got his three passengers to disembark and help haul the boat across the shingle to the next braid. The other two passengers spoke to each other in a language Luigi had not heard before, though some of the words sounded similar to German. The final channel was broad and deep, and the ferryman cut across it at a sharp angle, gritting his teeth fiercely as he dug his oars deep, his vest stained dark with sweat. Then, panting with exertion, he shipped the oars and coasted into the shingly shallows.

The formed track heading south was inland, the ferryman told them, and the other two men headed upriver in that direction. But deciding to maintain his coastal course to the end, Luigi followed the river bank downstream until he came to its wide mouth, pausing there for some time to study the pale green water debouching powerfully into the sea, and the tumultuous zone where the fresh and salt water met.

As he resumed his walking, the anxiety that had come upon him after the storekeeper's revelation began to deepen. If the Italians had indeed gone, what then would he do? How would he find Leopoldo in this wild and unconnected land? What baffled him even more was the reason for the migrants leaving. In his letter Leopoldo had sounded so contented. *I have seven milk cows which graze the land around my house.* Land of his own, a house of his own, why would anyone turn their backs on that? Disconsolate now, Luigi's walking pace began to slow as he followed the shore. A mist was hanging over the bay, pushed landward by a light but cool breeze. Looking inland he saw that the area beyond the foreshore was occupied by a huge swamp whose waters were dark and still, while beyond the swamp was a wall of dense, dark green forest, covering the land and the face of the alps right up to the snowline. So, if the land had been turned to pasture, where was it? After a further hour's walking and brooding, he climbed the shingle bank that lay between the road and the shore, sat down, ate some of his bread and cheese and surveyed the scene before him.

The coast here was almost straight, the foreshore a mixture of sand and shingle, sloping steeply into the sea. Lines of swells moved in from the open sea, then a few hundred yards from shore became white waves which rushed against the shore. The sky was grey, the sea a dull green. He stared down the coast, in the direction of Okuru. *Italians have all gone, mate.* The throbbing in his head grew more insistent. All this way, and likely all for nothing. Standing up, he peered into the misty distance. He could see what seemed to be a lake a little way inland, and from the turbulence he could see just offshore, he judged that there must be the place where the Okuru river flowed into the bay. Four, perhaps five miles further.

As he approached it, he saw that the lake was in fact a small lagoon, connected to the sea by a narrow channel. Skirting around it on the inland side, he saw too that several channels from the great swamp drained across a marshy lowland towards where the river must be. From the slightly elevated foreshore, he could see that the water in the distance was a large estuary. On his side of the estuary, set back a little from the shore, was a handful of corrugated iron buildings, a small wharf and some sort of shed. At first he thought the tiny settlement was deserted, but when he came closer he noticed a man standing on the wharf, leaning against the shed with his back to the road, and two boys sitting on the wharf, holding fishing rods. Luigi's pace quickened. At last, Okuru!

The road ended at the wharf. One of the buildings was a general store, another a pub with a sign above the door, the Excelsior. Long grass grew around both buildings, and a skinny dog was curled up asleep beside the store's entrance. Luigi stepped up onto wharf. On the far side of the river was another cluster of corrugated iron buildings, and between the two halves of the tiny settlement lay the estuary, its waters wide and brown. The tide was low, the banks of the river exposed, their slopes muddy.

Now Luigi saw that the man on the wharf had only one leg, and that he was supporting himself with a pair of rough crutches, fashioned from branches. It was his lower right leg that was missing, and his trouser leg was tied up with string. Luigi unslung his pack. 'Hello,' he announced, and with two stumpy movements, the one-legged man turned around and peered distrustfully at the newcomer.

He wore a flat cap pulled low over his eyes, a worn jacket and waistcoat and had a full black beard and ragged moustache. His age was indeterminate – mid-forties perhaps – and the beard could not hide his hollowed cheeks, the cap the red-rimmed eyes which now looked fixedly at Luigi. For a moment the man swayed heavily on his crutches and he seemed about to fall. Then he managed to correct himself, maintaining a still-stooped but steadier stance. 'Hello,' repeated Luigi.

The man's mouth fell open, revealing missing bottom teeth. In a quick, apparently uncontrollable movement, his head dipped and he swallowed, as if he could not properly catch his breath. Then, raising his head, he emitted a disbelieving cry.

'Luigi. Luigi Galoni …'

He began to topple forward, and as he did so Luigi ran to the man and snatched him up in his arms. The crude crutches clattered onto the planks of the wharf. Hugging the man, Luigi felt his bony frame through his jacket. Now he too held his breath, too shocked for a moment to look. It couldn't be, this old man couldn't be … Relaxing his grip on the wretched figure, holding him at arm's length, he stared into the man's eyes, saw there another person, another life. It was Leopoldo.

THREE

The two men clutched each other. Then, as Luigi stood back and stared into Leopoldo's eyes, he tried to conceal his shock. He looked as old as his father. Yet Leopoldo was three months younger than Luigi. Still holding his friend, he bent down and picked up the crutches. Their cross-pieces were lashed to the uprights with twine, and padded with wads of rags. Leopoldo hunched over his crutches, his jacket riding up around his scrawny neck. Tears were still spilling from his eyes, running down into his beard. In halting Italian, Leopoldo said accusingly, 'Why did you not write and say you were coming? Why did you not tell me you were leaving Pesaro?'

Luigi tried to smile. How could he begin to explain? Instead he fibbed. 'There was no time to write.' He looked around the little settlement. 'There is much we have to talk about. Where is your house? If we go there I will explain.'

Leopoldo opened his mouth to reply, but no words came. His head fell forward, like a bird with a broken neck. Luigi put a hand on his shoulder, gently.

'What is it, Leopoldo? What has happened to you?' He paused, embarrassed at having to ask the question that had to be asked. 'How did you lose your leg?'

The other man lifted his head, opened his mouth wide, breathed in deeply. The skin of his cheeks was yellowed, like a newspaper that had been left out in the sun. But seeming a little calmer now, he shuffled forward, glanced over at the pub and said in a low voice, 'Do you have money?'

'Some, yes.'

'We can talk over there.'

Luigi pushed open the hotel door and held it for Leopoldo, watching his awkward, stumping movements, still dismayed by his piteous appearance. The Excelsior Hotel was one large room with matchwood lining, a sawdust-covered floor and rough-sawn timber tables and bench seats. The room gave off a resinous smell, overlaid with a mixture of tobacco smoke and fried food. Several kerosene lanterns, their glass smeared with soot, hung from chains attached to the ceiling joists. A wooden bar occupied one corner of the room, surrounded by a halo of horseshoes nailed to the wall. A horse collar hung from the wall next to the bar, while above it, in wooden cradles, were three small beer barrels. On the wall behind the bar was a shelf of multi-coloured spirit bottles, and on a side wall hung a large oil painting of a wild-eyed boar at bay in a forest, surrounded by salivating hounds. A stout man with a completely bald head, flaring beard and black rubber apron stood behind the bar, drying glasses.

Only one of the tables in the room was occupied, by two bearded, pipe-smoking men in heavy jerseys and canvas trousers. They stared at Luigi and Leopoldo with undisguised surprise as they entered. When he saw who had entered the room, the man behind the bar raised his chin aggressively. Leopoldo, evading his gaze, hobbled over to a table, Luigi following.

'Just a minute, Leo,' barked the publican.

Leopoldo froze.

'Where d'you think you're going?'

Luigi frowned, aware that all three men in the room were watching them intently, but not comprehending the hostility in the air. Leopoldo brought his left crutch up in one short, sharp movement. 'I am here to talk with my friend,' he said, morosely.

'*Talk*? You can talk outside.' In the same terse tone, he added, 'Talk's free, mate. Food and drink's not.'

With pleading eyes, Leopoldo said, 'We will each have an ale. My friend will pay.'

The publican looked Luigi up and down. 'Let's see your mate's money, first,' he said, gruffly. Luigi took his purse from his pocket and put sixpence on the bar. 'Two glasses of ale,' he ordered. Grunting assent, the man filled two glasses from one of the barrels on the bar and handed them to Luigi, who carried them over to the corner where Leopoldo was shuffling his bum onto a seat, wincing with every movement he made. Taking the glass from Luigi, his eyes showed a flicker of enthusiasm.

Raising it quickly, he said,

'Salute, Luigi.'

'Si, salute, Leopoldo.'

Luigi had seldom seen anyone in such need of a toast to good health. He watched his friend drink greedily, his bony throat convulsing until the glass was half empty. Then, slowly, his breath laboured, eyes downcast, Leopoldo set his glass down on the table and began.

They had left Wellington in July 1877, travelling by steamer to Hokitika, then by pack-horse to Okuru. There were twenty-three of them in all, sixteen men, the rest women and children. Italians mostly, from Livorno – he was the only one from Pesaro – but some Pomeranians too.

'All of us Italians had been working on the railway in the Rimmertuckers. That was very bad work, I think I told you in my letter. None of us was suited to it, and we stopped, walked away from the place, went back to Wellington and complained to the authorities. There our disappointment was overcome when the authorities told us about a special new settlement at Jackson Bay, where land had already been surveyed into blocks. If we went there we were promised a house and government employment for three days a week. We'd be paid eight shillings per man per day, to build the road connecting Haast to Jackson Bay. We knew that work would be hard, but what encouraged us were the other benefits. The government store would provide the goods we needed cheaply, and the purchases would be deducted from our wages.'

Leopoldo paused to finish his ale, then went on.

'Best of all, after seven years living and working here, we'd be granted ownership of our land. We were all excited about this plan. Although again this was not work to which we were suited, we didn't mind greatly, because for the other four days of the week we would be able to develop the land – fell the trees and plant crops. The government had already decided what we Italians would grow. Because the other settlers – especially the ones from England and Ireland – were growing the crops they knew best, like potatoes, the government people decided that we should grow things that were produced back in Italy – grape vines and mulberry trees. From the grapes we would make wine. One of the first things we'd noticed about this country was that the only wine we could get was brought here from other places. The leaves of the mulberry trees we would feed to silkworms and the worms would produce thread for spinning into fine silk. We were not farmers, of course, but we were keen to become men of the land, and grow and harvest these special crops.

'I joined up with four other single men I had worked with on the railway, Aristodemo Frandi, Fortunato Luchesi, Victor Perez and Antonio Lima. The first two had been waiters in Livorno, Victor was an organ grinder, Antonio a cook. I was the only fisherman in the group, but knowing that there was land waiting for us, I, like the others, resolved to become a farmer, growing vines and mulberry trees. Other Italians who had been working on the railway near Wellington had already left for Okuru. Men, women and children, so we knew we wouldn't lack the company of our own kind. But still, all we knew of Westland was that it was "down south", as the New Zealanders say, and that there had been a gold rush there.'

Another film of sadness clouded Leopoldo's eyes.

'You know what we mean when we talk about "the south", back in Italy, Luigi. Calabria, and blue skies and pretty villages. Sunshine day after day, and fields of wheat and vines. But I well remember the day we arrived here in Okuru and saw the land we had been allotted. Each of us was given ten acres, on the north side of the Turnbull River, which joins the Okuru River just over there' – Leopoldo raised one crutch and pointed with it – 'about half a mile away. Houses had been built on the land for us. Aristodemo, Fortunato and Victor shared one, Antonio and I the other. They were rough houses, built of iron, with a wooden floor, chimney and fireplace. I wasn't unhappy with the house. But the land, Luigi, and the weather!

'Although the houses had been built on higher ground, all the land around our houses was swamp. It rained, day after day. I began to keep a record. In our first year here it rained for over three hundred days! But still, although the work wasn't like anything we had done in Italy, we were determined to make the best of it. Especially to develop our land. For three days of the week we worked on the coast road. Very hard work, but we did it without complaint because on the other four days we were free to work on the acres that would one day belong to us. We cut down the trees, burnt the branches, sawed the logs, dug drains to channel the water from the land into the river. Most of the money we were paid for the road work we saved, because we knew we had to pay back the cost of the land and the houses.

'Then, in the spring, we planted our first crops. Seed potatoes were sent to us from Hokitika, along with carrot and turnip seeds. We planted these English crops and a little later, our first grape vines and mulberry trees. The plants were sent to us from the far north of the North Island by Mr Federli, who had come to New Zealand from Venezia and wanted to bring more Italians here to grow grapes for wine and mulberries for silk. When the mulberry trees were mature, we were told that Mr Federli would arrange for silkworms too to be sent to us from the north.

'At first we were excited by the results of all our work. In spite of the rain, or perhaps because of it, everything sprouted quickly. We thought, well, as the land naturally grew tall trees, then it should grow lush vegetables. And it did, at first. Rows and rows of the vegetables shot from the ground, the grape vines sprouted quickly from their root stock and the mulberry trees grew quickly, too. We hoed between the rows of vegetables and vines, making ditches to drain the rainwater away. We cut posts, set them in the ground and put wire between them for the vines to cling to. In our bush clearings there was leafy greenery everywhere. In the evenings, after washing in the river, we would come to this hotel and toast each other with ale and plan how we best we could send our crops to the towns further north. We even planned to build the jetty in the bay that the government had said the settlement would have but which had not yet been made.

'But the promise of that greenery was false. As you know, crops need sunshine as well as rain, and there was too much of the one and not enough of the other. When we took some of our crops from the ground, we saw that the roots were not developing. The carrots were spindly, the potatoes so small they were like marbles, and just as hard. Only the turnips matured, and there were not many of them. As for the grape vines, they were all leaf and tendrils. The flowers budded, then rotted. The mulberry trees drowned in the rain. And as the saying goes, you can't make a silk purse out of a sow's ear. Or, I should say, out of a dead mulberry tree. Imagine our disappointment, Luigi, at seeing that the results of all our labours were fruitless, and knowing that we could do nothing about it. Also knowing that we had no income apart from the wages for the road work, and aware that our debts were growing.

'We decided to try again next spring, this time sowing beans and oats instead of carrots and turnips and ordering white grape vines instead of red – German varieties from Victoria in Australia, because we knew the climate there was cooler and more like this one. We dug deeper drains between the rows. Through that second summer – which was warm but still with rain nearly every day – we kept working on the road for eight shillings a day. But because we had no income from our land, and we needed to pay back our loan for the houses, and buy goods from the government store, we were spending more than we earned. Eight shillings a day didn't cover our costs. Then, when our crops again failed to ripen, the others decided they had had enough. Whatever else we could change here, we couldn't change the weather. Already some of the other Italians had left, abandoned their land and gone back up north. The Resident Agent, Mr Macfarlane, was furious. He tried to get them to pay back the money they owed, but they couldn't. They had nothing. I couldn't blame them for walking off the land, the disappointment was too great. It was so hard too on the women and children. The wives had no comforts whatsoever. It was like slavery for them, living in mud and rain, the washing never drying. They were like lost souls, the poor creatures.'

Leopoldo adjusted his buttocks on the seat, arching his back, then flinching from the pain that the movement caused him. He was silent for some moments, melancholia seeming to overcome him. Studying his friend, Luigi thought again of the letter that had crossed the world from this place to Pesaro. Too proud to admit that his dreams had turned not to dust, but to water, Leopoldo had reported falsely on his life in the new land. Yet now, observing the prematurely aged figure opposite him, Luigi felt only pity for his friend, along with a growing apprehension about his own future in this place. In his purse there was less than two pounds. What would he do now? Trying to set this consideration aside for the moment, he asked, 'Are you hungry, Leopoldo?' Still looking down, his friend nodded.

Luigi got up, went to the man and ordered two meals of beef stew, beans and mashed potatoes from the menu, and had their two glasses refilled. The publican, jovial now at the sight of Luigi's shillings, promised to bring over their meals in a few minutes. While they waited, Leopoldo resumed his story.

By the winter of 1878, he said, most of the settlers wanted to leave.

'The Jackson Bay wharf remained unbuilt, so goods still couldn't be brought in safely by sea. This place stayed cut off from everywhere, even the rest of its own province. As you know, it takes a week to get to Hokitika, even. We urged Macfarlane to persuade the government to build the wharf, and allow us more time to properly drain our land and so grow our crops. But the government had decided that to build the wharf would be too expensive. Then, to show the government what a good businessman he was, Macfarlane decided to sell the government store at Okuru to an Englishman, John Marks. Straight away Marks doubled the price of everything, and all of us fell into worse debt. While that was happening to us, Macfarlane and his family were living like royalty in their huge house at Arawata. 'King Mac' the settlers call him. He started to threaten them, especially the Europeans. For some reason, he hates anyone who is not of British stock. We Italians, and the Pomeranians and Germans. But if you are from Scotland, England or Ireland, he favours you. Yet when a petition was started, to send to the government in Wellington, signed by most of the settlers here, complaining of King Macfarlane's arrogance, Aristodemo, Fortunato, Victor, Antonio and I refused to sign it. We knew that if we did it would only cause more trouble for us. But the petition was sent, anyway. The result was nothing. It wasn't even acknowledged. Then, last December, when our crops failed yet again, my friends turned their backs on the swamp, walked back to Hokitika and took a steamer from there to Wellington. They had heard from Giuseppe Volpicelli, who had worked with us on the railway but stayed in that town, that some Italians were making a reasonable living there, as fishermen. So they went north to join them.'

'Have you had letters from them?'

He shook his head. 'No. Maybe they've gone from there, too.' He took a long draft from his glass. When he set it down again, Luigi asked,

'Why didn't you go with the others, Leopoldo, when they left here?'

Leopoldo stared down into his glass, as if it was some sort of crystal ball in which he saw another, kinder future for himself. Then, still staring down, he said dolefully, 'A man with one leg is only a burden, Luigi. They did invite me to join them, but I knew I would only make things harder for them. I didn't want to be a burden.' He ran his hand down his beard, stroking it slowly, attempting to groom himself. Then he rubbed his eyes. 'Besides, I had a woman here. I loved her, and I thought she loved me.

'She was a Maori woman. Her name was Tui. Her family lived on their tribal land, inland from Jackson Bay. We met while I was working on the road. She spoke no Italian, of course, but it was she who taught me English, and some Maori, after she came to live with me. In spite of all our differences, we were close. We even talked of having children together. We had a house cow – not seven, as I lied to you in my letter – and three goats. Tui was good with these animals, which gave us milk, and she made cheese from it. Her father had taught her these skills; he had a dairy herd on their land. Tui and I had plans to buy more cows, to plant proper pasture when the drains had been dug, and to send the cheese we would make to the towns further north, after the wharf was built. We could see there might be a future in that. But then I had my accident.'

'Accident?' asked Luigi, knowing full well that he must mean his leg.

Leaning back, Leopoldo made little patting movements on his right thigh. Chest rising and falling with the effort of the telling, he continued. 'It happened a year and a half ago. Some kahikatea stumps on my block were too stubborn to dig out, so I decided to use dynamite to blow them away. I had watched others do this work on the road, and was confident that I could do it, too. I took some dynamite and fuses from the supplies we used on the road, bored holes in a big stump with an auger and laid the charges. But instead of burning slowly and allowing me to retreat to a safe distance, the fuse and the dynamite ignited together. The stump blew to pieces and a chunk of it struck my right leg, just below the knee, almost severing it. Tui heard my cries and came running. Using my belt, she tied a tourniquet around my thigh, went back into the house, heated my filleting knife over the fire to sterilise it, returned and sliced the leg right through at the knee. Then she carried me inside, washed and dressed the stump and put me to bed. For the next week she nursed and fed me, and made these crutches out of the tree they call manuka. Then, when I was able to stand again, she walked out and never returned. Went back to her own people.' He paused, sniffed, then continued. 'I suppose she'd worked out, while she was nursing me, that a one-legged man could never provide for her the way she'd hoped I would. Even a *Pakeha* one-legged man.'

'Park…ee…hah?'

'Pakeha. White man. That is what the Maoris call us.' He closed his eyes. 'I never dreamt that a woman could be so cruel.' For some moments he was unable to go on, his shoulders heaving with silent sobs. Luigi, having no words to console him, instead reached out, took his left hand in his and gripped it. Leopoldo, poor Leopoldo, he thought. He knew that this land and its people could be hard, but just how hard he had never imagined. Insecure as Leopoldo's life in Pesaro had been, it could not have been worse than this. There at least he had old friends, family. Here, in this sodden, Godforsaken land, he had no one. No one except Luigi. Gripping his friend's hand harder, he said vehemently, 'I'm here now, Leopoldo. I won't leave you.'

When their meals came Leopoldo ate wolfishly, pausing only to take another mouthful of ale. When he'd cleared his plate, mopping up the last of the gravy with a slab of buttered bread, he sighed with satisfaction, pushed his plate aside and waited for Luigi to finish his meal. When he had done so, he said, a little guardedly, 'You've heard my story, Luigi.' He paused, to wipe his mouth with his hand. 'Now, I want to hear yours. How is it that you're here now? When more than two years ago you could have come with me. Did your father relent and allow you to leave?'

Luigi fell silent, not knowing where to begin. Pesaro now seemed not just a world but an entire universe away. There was no need to tell Leopoldo why he had had to leave so suddenly, he decided. Instead, after waiting until the publican had taken away their empty plates, he said simply, 'I got your letter. I had to come. I decided that my future was mine to make. It was not my father's right to make it.'

Avoiding Luigi's eyes, Leopoldo said remorsefully, 'But I brought you here with falsehoods. I led you to believe I was prospering, and that this shit hole was a paradise.'

Luigi smiled. 'We could still prosper. Together. I want to stay. To help work your land.' He paused. 'With your permission, of course, *signore.*'

Smiling for the first time, Leopoldo nodded. 'Of course you can stay with me. If you can stand it.' He chuckled. 'Do you still play the accordion?'

'Yes. I played for money in Hokitika. It paid quite well.'

'This is not Hokitika, Luigi. There is no music here.'

'Well, I will make some. I will play for the two of us.'

'I would like that.' Leopoldo half closed his eyes as another memory returned. 'How is Violetta?'

'She misses you. There was a letter from her in Hokitika. She sends you her best wishes.'

'If I had stayed, I would have married her.'

'But you didn't stay.'

'No.' Leopoldo struggled to his feet. 'I will take you to my house now.'

The muddy bush track ran inland from the wharfside settlement, following the river bank through a forest of evergreen trees with tall straight trunks, their foliage still dripping from the afternoon's rain. Fine timber trees, Luigi thought, no wonder they built everything of wood in this land. Beside him, Leopoldo limped along silently, the ends of his crutches sinking into the mud. Twenty minutes later, the track opened out onto a large clearing. Leopoldo stopped, lifted his left crutch and pointed. 'My land, my house,' he announced, unable to keep an edge of pride from his voice.

The building stood on the far side of the clearing, enclosed on three sides by bush. It had been built on the one elevated place in the clearing, with the rest of the land sloping away before it. Its piles – round wooden blocks a couple of feet off the ground – were visible, and its roof and walls were made from overlapping, vertical sheets of corrugated iron. On either side of the house's one door were two six-light windows. At one end of the building, on the outside wall, was a large chimney, the iron supported with a rough timber frame on the outside and in places blackened and buckled from the heat of the fire. On a shelf beside the chimney was a washing basin, and a clothes line had been slung from the chimney to the nearest tree. On it hung a ragged towel and a set of 'long johns' underwear. Beside the large flat stone which served as the house's front step was a heap of firewood and an embedded axe, and a lean-to attached to the other end of the house held rounds of sawed wood, shovels, a slasher and other farm tools.

Below the house the clearing sloped away towards the river. The land was covered in weeds and scrub, with a few blackened stumps sticking through the rank foliage. Close to the house was a line of posts, sunk into the ground several yards apart and joined by wires. Several of the posts were leaning crookedly, only the connecting wire preventing them from falling altogether. Bolting grape vines, their tendrils sticking out at crazy angles, covered the wires. Further away from the house the land was visibly wetter, the vegetation denser but more stunted. Patches of swamp were visible among the scrub, shining like ulcerated wounds. Leopoldo waved a crutch wildly at the land, as if trying to frighten a menacing dog.

'You see there the vines, still sprouting like crazy, as they do every spring. But they are all show. All leaf, no fruit. Like they say here sometimes, "All hat, no horse".' Giving a harsh laugh, he pointed again. 'The mulberry trees were planted there, below the vines, then below that were the other crops – potatoes, carrots, turnips. They also grew above the ground but not below. Up there …' Swivelling around, he pointed to an area of grass to the left of the house '… was where the cow and goats grazed.' Another shadow passed across his face, and bitterness soured his voice. 'I had to sell them to pay off some of my debt.' As they surveyed the soggy wasteland, as if mocking him, heavy drops of rain began to fall. Leopoldo swung around and stumped off towards the house. Luigi followed him, removing his boots at the door.

It consisted of one unlined room. A large open fireplace, floored and lined with bricks, occupied almost all of one end wall, leaving only a small space on either side for shelves made of short planks, on which were a few pots, pans and dishes. Logs smouldered in the grate below a blackened iron rod, from which hung an equally sooty pot. At the same end of the room the exposed framing of the house accommodated an assortment of jars, tins and bottles. Beside the rear wall of the house was a refectory table made from slabs of rough-sawn timber, with two upturned butter boxes for seats.

At the other end of the room was a medium-sized, unmade bed, covered in grey blankets. There was a camp stretcher under the wall opposite the table, and three kerosene lanterns hung from wire hooks attached to the building's rafters, one above the dining table, one above the stretcher and the other above the bed. Clothes hung from a wire stretched across the far corner of the room, beside a small latched window, and there was a big grey cabin trunk beside the head of the bed. Several pictures, evidently taken from an old Italian calendar, had been nailed to the walls where space allowed, scenes that Luigi immediately recognised. Positano, Capri, the Piazza San Marco, the Spanish Steps, the Leaning Tower. Their colours had faded and they were curling at the edges. Luigi knew that Leopoldo had been to none of these places, and he hadn't either. But although the small, cluttered room smelt strongly of smoke and grease, to Luigi it felt warm, even homely. Leaning his crutches against the wall, Leopoldo hopped to one of the butter boxes and sat down.

'So, what do you think?'

'It's cosy. But it is too small for two, Leopoldo.'

'Rubbish. Antonio and I were here together for two years. Then Tui after that.' He nodded at the camp stretcher. You will not mind sleeping there?'

'If you do not mind.'

'I told you, I want you to stay.'

'Grazie.'

'So, unpack your bag. Hang your things on any free nail you can find.'

Sitting on the stretcher, his back against the wall, Luigi began to play, the accordion not quite drowning out the clattering of the rain on the iron roof. As he played, he noticed a spark come into Leopoldo's eyes, a spark which seemed to ignite a small flame which spread through his body. He became animated, banging his one foot on the floorboards, then joined in the song, clapping his hands with delight as Luigi pumped the instrument.

'Vit-to-ria, Vit-to-ria, Vit-to-ria, Vit-to-ria, mio cuo – re!
Non la – grimar piu, non la- grimar piu,
E scio – Ita d'A – mo-re la ser – vi –tu,
Vit-to-ria, Vit-to-ria, mio cuo – re!
Non la-grimar piu,
E scio-Ita d'A-mo-re la ser-vi- tu,
E scio – ta d'A – mo – re la ser – vi – tu.
Gia l'empia a tuoi dan – ni fra stuo – lo di sguardi, con vezzi bu –
      giardi di –spo – se
Gl'in – gan ni...'

When Luigi ended the song with a flourish, Leopoldo clapped delightedly. 'Ancora, Luigi, ancora!' he called out. Dipping his head in appreciation, Luigi pumped the accordion harder, sang the next song louder still.

'Co – me raggio di sol,
Mi – te e se – re – no,
Co – me raggio di sol,
Mi – te se – re – no,
Sovra pla – cidi flut – ti si ri – po –sa,
Men – tre del ma – re,
Men – tre del ma – re nel pro fon – do se no
Sta la tem – pe – sta a – sco – sa!'

Leopoldo applauded again, wildly. Putting down his instrument, Luigi rummaged in his rucksack, found the hip flask of brandy, still three-quarters full. He unscrewed the lid and passed it to Leopoldo, who stared at it as if it was nectar. He took a long swig, threw back his head and gasped with pleasure.

'Ah Luigi, Luigi, that tastes so good.' He made a sighing sound. 'You know, sometimes I have such a craving for Italian food. It's three years since I ate an olive, or a plate of pasta. And here they have never heard of olive oil. They cook in mutton fat! Imagine it!' Luigi nodded in sympathy. Then, determined to be positive, he said,

'But the fish must be good, Leopoldo.'

'Yes, the fish is good.' Passing the flask back, Leopoldo said, 'I am so pleased that you are here.' His voice cracked a little. 'It has been lonely, since the others left.'

Luigi drank a little brandy himself. Then he asked,

'How do you live now?'

'I do the only thing I can. I fish. Only with a line, I cannot manage a net.'

'I fished on my way here. Walking along the coast. And I netted tiny fish, in the rivers. Tiny, transparent fish.'

'Whitebait.'

'Whitebait?'

'Si. The Maoris call them inunga. They come up the rivers from the sea. It is their season now, the rivers are full of them. And there are other good fish. Terakihi, groper. What I catch I sell, on the wharf, to the other settlers.' He chuckled. 'It is incredible, Luigi, how few of them know how to catch a fish. They don't even know how to bait a hook. So, I sell the fish fresh, the rest I smoke with manuka sawdust, as Tui taught me. With the little money I get, I buy flour, and sugar, and milk from a neighbour, Joseph Heveldt. That is all I need.' His face darkened. 'But it doesn't pay my debt to the settlement. Twenty-five pounds.'

Accepting the tobacco tin and papers that Luigi offered him, Leopoldo rolled himself a cigarette. Hopping to a shelf, he picked up a box of matches and lit it. Looking at Luigi seriously now, he said, 'So, what do you think you will you do, now that you know the truth of this place?'

Luigi lay back on the camp stretcher. Staring at the ceiling, he said,

'There's still work to be done on the road?'

'Oh yes. It has only reached as far as Hannah's Clearing.'

'And the man in charge of the settlement is…?'

'Macfarlane.'

'He is the one who hires workers for the road?'

'Yes.'

'Then I'll go to see him, and ask him for work.'

Leopoldo's expression grew overcast. 'Macfarlane is a very hard man, Luigi.'

Luigi blew smoke at the ceiling. 'Then I will have to be harder.'

The house was indeed grand, the largest Luigi had seen since arriving in Westland. Set on a knoll between the government store and Robinson's Hotel, it was steeply gabled at each end, with white painted weatherboard walls and a roof of corrugated iron. Two dormer windows protruded from the central section of the house, two cowled brick chimneys extended from the roof-line at each end, and finials stuck up from each gable end, like forefingers pointing at the sky. A verandah ran along the rear wall.

Stepping up onto it, Luigi saw a small boy with a tennis racquet, volleying a ball against the gable wall next to it. Noticing him, the boy stopped his game and squinted at Luigi.

'Yeah?'

'I've come to see Mr Macfarlane.'

'Hang on.'

Dropping his racquet, the boy ran up onto the verandah, past Luigi and into the house. Removing his cap, Luigi gripped it in his hands. A besuited figure emerged from the darkness of the hall and filled the doorway.

'Yes?' the man said, imperiously.

He was tall, with a large moustache and a long spreading beard that covered his chest like a sporran. His forehead was broad, his grey hair clipped short at the sides and brushed up in a wave at the front. He looked about fifty. Luigi said carefully,

'I am Luigi Galoni. I have just arrived in Jackson Bay. I would like to have work building the new road.'

'Galoni? Italian?'

'Yes.'

'You came with the Glynn group?' Luigi found his accent difficult

GRAEME LAY

to decipher. *Glinn Garr-roop.*

'I am sorry. The Glynn?'

'Garr-roop,' the man repeated, his irritability showing. 'From Livorno.'

'Oh, no. No, I did not come with them, I paid for my own passage to New Zealand.'

A puzzled expression spread over the big Scotsman's face. 'So why did you come here?'

Luigi hesitated. Deciding it would not be wise to mention Leopoldo's name, he said, 'I heard there was paid work here. When I was in Hokitika.'

The man tucked a thumb into the pocket of his waistcoat. Pushing his chin out, making his beard flick, he said dismissively, 'We've had enough of Italians in this settlement. More trouble than they're worth. They can't take hard work.'

'I can.'

'How do I know that?'

'By giving me a chance to show you.'

The Scotsman was silent for a moment. He looked Luigi up and down, from his red hair to his newish boots. Then he said, in a voice that was openly scathing, 'Yerr a waiter too, I suppose.'

'No, I am a fisherman.'

'Where are yerr living?'

'At Okuru.'

'How did you get to my place?'

'I walked.'

'What time did you leave?'

'At five o'clock this morning.'

There was a long silence. The Resident Agent continued to appraise Luigi, not bothering to disguise his mistrust as he weighed his offer. Luigi saw why Leopoldo had warned him. This was a man who would hate to not get his own way. At last the Scotsman spoke.

'Well, I'll not pretend we don't need more workers. The road building's long behind schedule, like everything else round here. But it's tough work, make no mistake about that.' He paused. 'What did yerr say yerr name was?'

'Luigi Galoni.'

'Yes Galoni, tough work. But I'll take you on trial, ferr a

62

fortnight.'

Luigi felt a surge of relief. 'Thank you, sir.'

'Hours are eight o'clock till five, six days a week, Monday to Saturday. Pay's eight shillings perr day.'

'Yes.'

'Report to Claude Oliver, the foreman, at eight o'clock termorra, outside the Waiatoto store. I'll send word this afternoon that he's to put you on the payroll.' He paused, meaningfully. 'Only ferr a fortnight, mind. Then I'll ask Claude ferr a report on yerr.'

'I understand.'

The Scotsman stepped back and shut the door.

Walking back along the coastal track, Luigi passed the road gang at work. At the place where the track became a formed road, three men were hacking at the manuka scrub with slashers. Behind them three more men were digging the ground with picks and shovels, two more members of the team were shovelling and barrowing gravel from a dray at the side of the road, another pair was breaking larger rocks up with sledge hammers. A line of surveyor's pegs marked the road's margins. The men were all in shirt sleeves, except the rock breakers, who were naked from the waist up. Beside the newly formed section of the road stood another dray and two horses, munching contently at a heap of hay. Beside this dray was a fire, with a billy dangling over it, attached to an iron spike stuck at an angle into the ground.

As Luigi passed the gang, the men paused in their work and looked at him curiously. 'Hello,' he said, touching the brim of his cap. They dipped their heads in reply, then returned to their labour. Walking along the straight, formed road towards Okuru, Luigi thought, it will be a good thing to do, to help to make a road. Looking back, he could see the head of the new road pushing down the coast like a living creature. A new road is such a useful thing, he thought. And eight shillings a day, six days a week. Two pounds, eight shillings. If he could keep it up, and save a pound a week, after a year he would have paid off Leopoldo's debts.

Claude Oliver was a slab of a man, a tall, balding Yorkshireman of about forty with an enormous paunch. After shaking Luigi's hand, he introduced him to the other members of the gang. They were a mixed lot – English, Irish, Scots, two Germans, three Poles – ranging in age from early twenties to twice that. 'Italian, eh?' Claude had said when Luigi introduced himself. Looking at the newcomer sceptically, he added, 'First time we've had one of your lot on the job. We'll put you on the barrows with Aubrey.'

Aubrey McLeish was a wiry Scotsman of about thirty, with a rubbery face and big, floppy lips. He suffered from some sort of eczema, and when his hands weren't busy working they scratched at his ribs and neck, where Luigi could see the purplish rash creeping up from under his shirt collar. Their duties were to barrow the crushed shingle from the heap beside the road – it was brought down by dray once a week from an inland quarry – to the head of the road. Back and forth Aubrey and Luigi went with the two iron-wheeled barrows, one in one direction, the other going the opposite way, heavy one way, light the other. Shovelling, barrowing, tipping, barrowing, shovelling, tipping.

The full barrows put a strain on muscles which Luigi was unused to extending, his lower back and neck especially. In his determination to show how hard a worker he was, he filled his barrow much higher than Aubrey's, so that he and the barrow staggered under the loads. The formed road over which they pushed the barrows had not yet been rolled and compacted, and Luigi's barrow wheel sank so far down into the soft, slushy topping that it became stuck. Then, as he pulled it backwards, it toppled and spilt its load, just as Claude Oliver was striding past, shovel over his shoulder. Embarrassed, Luigi began scooping up the spilt gravel with his hands. Claude stopped, scowled and threw him the shovel. 'Here mate, use this. And don't try to set a world record for barrowing. Just keep it steady, like Aubrey does.'

Three times a day they stopped for what Claude called 'smoko' – cigarettes and tea made in the billy over the fire by the oldest member of the gang, Bruce, an unhappy lowland Scot with a ginger moustache. As they sat by the side of the road sipping their tea from tin mugs, the other men talked and Luigi mostly listened, conscious that he was on trial in more than one respect, aware that he was the outsider, as well as having to keep his ear attentive to the gang's farrago of accents.

Some of the men had come to Jackson Bay for gold, but now that the area had been shown to have little of the 'colour', the immigrants had had to turn to steadier jobs: bush clearing, pit-sawing timber, quarrying. All his fellow-workers, Luigi realised from their conversations, harboured hopes of owning their own land and property, but all were finding the Jackson Bay settlement considerably less than their expectations. Like Leopoldo, their hopes of becoming farmers had been dashed by the wetness of the place. 'Bloody rain,' Aubrey cursed, scratching at his ribs as the heavens opened yet again, 'this place turns a mun into a bloody frog. Only bloody thing that grows here properly is bloody bulrushes.'

By day Luigi barrowed, back and forth from the gravel pile to the road head, through the slush and mud, aware that Claude Oliver was judging his labours against those of the others. Each morning it took him an hour to walk from Leopoldo's section to the road head, a little longer to return in the evening when the painful stiffness in his back and shoulders had set in. At night his muscles were so sore that it pained him just to turn over on the camp stretcher. But gradually the aching subsided to stiffness, then to just an occasional twinge. Then, towards the end of his second week, Claude told him to stop the barrowing and join short, barrel-chested Irishman Tom McGovern in cutting and clearing the manuka at the road-head. Tom, who had been allocated a swampy section on the Waiatoto River, worked with a ferocious determination as he slashed, explaining to Luigi that, 'Ah just pretend that every manuka tree is a bloody Englishman.'

The smaller manuka they cut with the slashers, the larger kanuka they felled with axes. This work was tougher than the barrow, with the manuka seeds and flaking bark getting inside their vests and trousers, working their way into their body's crevices, causing madding itches. But again, once Luigi had achieved a steady rhythm, he found he could keep up with the tenacious little Irishman. And at the end of his second Saturday on the job, Claude Oliver rode up on his horse and beckoned Luigi aside. Panting, wiping the sweat from his eyes, Luigi looked up at the Yorkshireman. Whatever the decision, he had done his best. Claude leaned down, patting his roan's flanks. 'Well, Louie, how's the job going?'

'It is okay. Not easy, but, okay.' Okay was a useful word, Luigi had discovered. It covered most circumstances that were not actually intolerable.

'"Not easy", hah!' Claude seemed to find this description very amusing. 'Well, I must say, you're a good worker. For an Eye-tie. And I've said so to Mr Macfarlane.' He sat up in the saddle. 'So, if you want the job permanently, it's yours.'

'Thank you, yes, I want to keep this job. Thank you.'

And at the end of that day he queued up with the others by the dray and Claude pressed into his hand a small manila envelope containing two pounds and eight shillings. Luigi signed the pay sheet carefully.

And now that he had obtained paid work, the time had come to carry out an important duty.

Dear Papa,

At last I can write, now that I am settled here in Nuova Zelanda. The fact that I left home without saying goodbye or obtaining your blessing is something that I will always regret, but it could not have been otherwise. I had to leave Pesaro.

The most important thing I have to say is that in spite of our deep differences over the matter of migration, I never ceased loving or respecting you. Through your devotion to our family, and your hard work on the boat and in our garden, the example you set will be with me all my life. If I am ever blessed with children, one of my hopes will be that the example I show them will be as honest as the one you set us. That Mama and the others were taken from us so soon were cruel blows, but those blows never stopped you from always doing what you thought was best for those who remained, Violetta and myself. That you and I disagreed about my future was natural, I suppose. I remembered you saying how although you often quarrelled with your father (over politics, I think it usually was), you still always loved him. So it is with me. Here I will work with Leopoldo and try to make the land fruitful. It is a harsh place, beautiful but still wild. But the people here are determined to make the land productive, and I will do my best to do so as well. The fishing is wonderful, too! If I succeed here, I will become a part of this new land. But believe me when I tell you, I will never forget the Marche, or my family's heritage. And I will never stop loving you, Papa.

I hope you understand now, and will forgive me for leaving without saying goodbye.

Your loving son,

Luigi

And in a separate letter, he wrote to Violetta, telling her what had happened the night he left Pesaro, and concluding, *But say nothing of this to Papa. Nothing at all. He must never know.*

Aubrey went on horseback to Hokitika once a month, to visit his brother, who was a farrier in the town. Luigi gave Aubrey the letters to post. As he did so he felt a mixture of relief and sorrow. Relief that he had done his filial duty, sorrow that he could never tell his father the other reason why he had left Pesaro.

TEMPLES OF THE DEAD

It was a paradox, this place, William thought. Thousands upon thousands of documents on the lives of thousands upon thousands of long-dead people, housed in a building as modern as any in the city. William had heard it said that National Archives claimed that every migrant who had legally come to this land, whether Polynesian, European or Asian, had some sort of record here. The gleaming, modern building was the repository of the nation's human heritage, a temple of the dead. As such, William assumed, it must hold a trace of the man whose origins he sought.

Directed to a large wooden filing cabinet that held the names of all assisted immigrants, he pulled open the 'G' drawer of the card index. As he began to flick through the small white cards, skewered from front to back inside their wooden tomb, his pulse quickened. Date and place of Luigi's arrival, that would be so helpful. Gadburg, Anita, *Herschel*, from Hamburg, 27 June, 1875. Gadstone, Wilfred, *Northern Monarch*, from Liverpool, September 8, 1886; Gerridge, Sarah, *Isle of Bute*, from Southhampton, January 24, 1863. He flicked once more. Gersma, Jonathon, *City Of Quebec*, from Gravesend, February 2, 1873. *Not there*. To make absolutely sure, he checked the Gs again. There was no card bearing the name Galoni.

Next he tried the National Library, where immigrant shipping lists were kept on microfiche. After two hours he had to switch the microfiche off, the intense blue light given off by the screen made his head ache and his eyes sore. He had scrutinised dozens of the lists, for ships arriving at all New Zealand ports during that decade, from Hamburg, Bremen, Rotterdam, Glasgow, Liverpool, Gravesend, Southhampton, Marseilles. The lists were taken from newspapers or hand-written from the ships' manifests. *Ferrani, Pedro, single, 27, Italy, Farm labourer. Jensen, Louise, single, 20, Servant. Sweden. Schultz, Mannfred single, 28, Austria, Engineer. Ludorgsen, Hans, married, 37, Denmark, Farm labourer. Ludorgsen, Maria, married, 40, Maria, Denmark, Farm labourer.*

Hundreds upon hundreds of names, single men, single women, couples, families. All had exchanged the limited horizons of the Old World for the broader ones of the Antipodes. What had happened to them all? William found himself wondering as he scanned the names.

Wandering out onto the library's forecourt, he blinked against the sunlight. No one by the name of Luigi Galoni had appeared on any of the scores of passenger arrivals and shipping lists he had scrutinised. Across the street was Parliament, and the ornate nineteenth century debating chamber, now the General Assembly Library. From the background reading he'd done, William was aware that Prime Minister Julius Vogel had devised a bold scheme in the 1870s, for New Zealand: to borrow on the international money markets and use that capital to create a network of roads and railways, and to populate the burgeoning colony with immigrants, brought in their thousands from Britain, Europe and Scandinavia. That, he presumed, was where Luigi Galoni came in.

After a cup of coffee at a nearby café, William returned to the library, located the next file and switched on the microfiche again. More magnified names sprang into focus. Northern Monarch, *date of arrival March 5, 1879, Lyttelton. Sinclair, Katherine, single, 22, Scotland, Servant. Thompson, Charles, married, 34, London, Carpenter. Thompson, Sarah, married, London, housewife. Thompson, Jennifer, 6 years, London. Thompson, William, 5 years, London. Thompson, Frederick, 4 years ...*

FOUR

Twelve trips a week, back and forth from the house to the road-head; six long days at the road-head itself. Cutting, hacking, digging, barrowing, in the rain three days out of four. On some fine days he took his accordion to work and during the lunch smoko played it for his work-mates as they sat around the billy fire, smoking and yarning. Not knowing the words to his Italian songs, they couldn't join in his soft singing, but while he played, no one ever spoke, and he took this as a sign of approval. Aubrey once remarked, thoughtfully,

'If I could play the squeeze-box like that, I wouldn't be doing a navvy job like this.' Not understanding, Luigi asked him what a navvy was. Tossing the dregs of his tea into the undergrowth, Aubrey replied sadly, 'I'm a navvy, Louie. You're a navvy. The difference is, you can do something else.'

That evening he asked, 'Why do they shorten our names, Leopoldo?'

'Who?'

'The New Zealanders. They call me Louie, they call you Leo. Why don't they use our proper names?'

'I don't know. Maybe they just like short names. Aristodemo was always 'Aris', Victor was 'Vic', Antonio was 'Tony'.'

'I don't really mind being called Louie, but I still wonder why they do it.'

He got up, collected their dinner dishes and spoons and carried them outside. Down at the river bank, he rinsed them, rubbing at the plates with a cloth. Leopoldo had cooked a fish stew, using the remains from their cod dinner of the night before. Looking up, Luigi saw that the sky had cleared and the stars were coming out. Tomorrow was his day off, and he thought he would try some beach fishing. The days were growing longer now, though the winds that blew down from the alps were still bitingly cold, especially in the mornings. Carrying the dishes back up to the house, where the lights from the lanterns glowed at the windows, Luigi thought, this place – where I'm known by no one except Leopoldo – makes a good haven. Although the land was harsh, he felt a growing respect for its defiance and lonely beauty.

On pay-days he passed a third of his wage to Leopoldo, who bought flour and bacon and soap and tobacco from the store, eggs and milk and vegetables from their German neighbour, Joseph Heveldt, who farmed on higher, drier ground. Leopoldo continued to catch fish from the wharf, smoking and selling it to Mr Marks the storekeeper, who Luigi also paid a pound a week, to cover Leopoldo's debt. Although still chronically unwell, Leopoldo was much chirpier in himself, sometimes meeting Luigi on the wharf after he had been rowed across by Adam Nolan the ferryman, and joining him for an ale or two in the Excelsior before they returned through the bush to the house in the clearing.

Then there were the sunsets. On the one-in-four clear days Luigi would watch, captivated, as the setting sun began to shimmer, becoming more radiant as it moved down the sky, touched the horizon briefly, then slipped beneath Jackson Head. Then the sky would flare brilliantly, orange streaks over a pastel background, and he would be spellbound by the sight. At home the sun just disappeared over the Apennines, the sea playing no part in its performance. But here the emptiness of the horizon and the grandeur of the sinking molten ball was hypnotic, like a silent opera starring sun, sky and sea.

A little way along the coast a stream flowed from a lagoon above the shore, then across the beach and into the sea. The course of the stream changed abruptly after every storm. Sometimes it ran parallel to the shore for a few hundred yards before curving sharply and flowing seaward; at other times it flowed more directly into the Tasman. But its waters were always clear and fast-flowing, its bed marked with smooth, round stones. And one day while walking on the beach, Luigi noticed that shoaling whitebait found the stream a handy path to the interior, battling their way gamely between the rocks, unaware that only a lagoon, rather than the headwaters of an alpine river, lay ahead of them. Fascinated by the tiny fish, Luigi made himself a set net with muslin stitched over a supplejack frame, and kept it in the bush beside the lagoon. If the weather was fine on his day off, he would make a race out of the stream's stones, set his net at the side of its flow and wait for the shoals to swim up on the tide. After a few months of fishing there he came to think of it as his own property. He knew that other settlers fished the banks of the big rivers – the Okuru and the Waiatoto – but he preferred the solitude and smallness of the stream. He would sit on the sand, smoking, watching the waves rolling in from the Tasman, studying the sea mists, trying to estimate when they would dissolve into rain. Then, when he saw that one of the struggling shoals had crossed the threshold of the net he would quickly pull it up, let the water drain away, and pour the wriggling mass of bait into a kerosene tin.

After a couple of hours the tin would be half full. Carrying it back to the house, Luigi would then mix the tiny fish in a batter of flour and milk and fry them on a cast-iron griddle over the fire. In this way whitebait fritters became their regular Sunday evening meal, but as there was always more bait than the two of them could eat, the next day Luigi would take the remainder to his fellow-workers at the road-head. Most appreciated this gesture, although the two Germans, Joseph Schmidt and Gottfried Senger, amused the others by pointing out that as each tiny fish must be beheaded and gutted before it was fried, preparation of whitebait was a time-consuming business.

Luigi sat alongside the stream, his net beside him. The tide had turned only a few minutes ago, and it would be another hour before the waves deepened the stream mouth, enabling the shoals to head for its fresh water. He had left the house early – just after dawn – because Leopoldo's coughing had been keeping him awake. It had become worse in the last few weeks, long wracking fits that left him on the point of exhaustion. It was the dampness, Mrs Marks at the Okuru store suggested, that brought on the coughing. Her four children all suffered from it, too. She had sold Luigi a patent remedy, a dark red, syrupy mixture, from the store. Mostly coloured and flavoured alcohol, it made little difference to Leopoldo's coughing, but it did help him sleep. This morning Luigi had brewed strong tea for them both and placed a mug of it beside Leopoldo's bed, urging him to drink it as soon as he was able. Then he had left the house with an empty kerosene tin and made his way up the coast to where he hid the net.

Sitting on the beach beside the stream, the net firmly set, he noticed that the sea was unusually still, its surface filmy. No proper swells were forming, only small, haphazard wavelets which skittered back and forth across the water. Where the sea met the sand there was almost no movement at all. It was as if it had become a lake. The air was utterly still too, the air strangely warm. Luigi had felt no stillness quite like it, it was almost eerie. Then he noticed something else different – the sea birds had disappeared. The oystercatchers and pied stilts, and even the gulls who usually stood on the sand and watched his every movement, were nowhere to be seen. He felt a growing unease. Was there a storm coming? That must be it, such calmness, such absence of birds. Well, if there was a storm approaching, he thought, he'd make sure he got his share of the whitebait first. He stood up, dropped the butt of his cigarette on the sand and ground it out with his boot. And in that instant there came a sound like no other he had heard in his life before.

It was a low rumbling, like thunder, yet the sky was cloudless. And unlike thunder, the sound seemed to completely surround him, coming from a direction he could not determine. His apprehension deepening, he looked up the beach and towards the lagoon, but could see nothing. The rumbling grew louder but still seemed to have no precise origin. Then, abruptly, it stopped. For an instant there was no sound at all, like the pause between lightning and thunder, the same expectant, ominous silence.

A second later, the whole world jolted, as if the bottom had fallen out of it. Luigi dropped to his knees, from fright as much as the ground's sudden instability, and as he did so the beach began to sway. There was a second, harder jolt, followed by another swaying, as if the beach had become a fairground merry-go-round and he was a child tied to it. What had been solid was now liquid, what had been motionless now refused to stop moving. *Terremoto.* Earthquake. The third jolt was stronger still. Now Luigi was on his hands and knees, giddy from the swinging, terrified that the next shake would open the beach up and swallow him. Instead there was no single shock, just a series of smaller spasms, close together, as if the Earth had become a trembling animal, cowering beneath a giant's blows. His heart beating wildly, holding his hands out in an attempt to steady himself, Luigi got to his feet. His hands were quivering uncontrollably, and he felt nauseous. For a moment he thought he would throw up, but as the after-shocks diminished, the queasiness subsided. He'd heard his fellow-workers talk of earthquakes. They were not unusual on this coast, they said. Aubrey had told him of one 'quake that happened a few years back, when he had been part of a camp of miners, working the upper reaches of the Hokitika River. An earthquake in the night had brought down a sluiced hillside, covering half the camp and killing eighteen men. As Aubrey had told Luigi about the horror of it, the memory made his eczema worse, and he began to scratch frantically at his sides, as if he was again digging at the slip for his buried mates. But still, Luigi had no idea that the force of a 'quake could be felt so intensely. Still half-dazed, staring inland, he wondered at what precise place the convulsion had come from, and how far afield it had been felt. In Westport? Nelson? What damage had it caused to the settlement? He looked up at the mountains, with their mantle of snow, and thought they must surely have been altered in some way by the upheaval. Then, turning and looking out to sea, he saw a sight that set his heart stampeding again.

The water in the bay was further out than he had ever seen it, leaving a glistening strip of hard sand, fifty yards wide, littered with stones, driftwood and flapping fish. It was as if some marine fiend had made a gigantic inhalation, sucking the sea back towards its lair. And as he stared, he saw that the fiend was real, and growing higher, darker and more threatening by the second.

Beyond the exposed strip of sand and debris an enormous wall of water had reared up from the sea, as high as a church spire, as dark as midnight, its crest already curving. Trying to suck in air like a man already drowning, Luigi turned his back on the rising wave and began to run, alongside the stream, up the beach and towards the shore. Boots sliding sideways in the sand, legs turning jelly-like, he looked up desperately at the ground ahead, trying to calculate if it would be high enough to provide the sanctuary he sought. Seconds later there was an ear-splitting crash behind him, like a mortar shell exploding. The booming filled his ears, seeming to inundate his fleeing figure before the wall of water itself overtook him, engulfing him in its surging momentum, bowling him forward and hurling him like a piece of flotsam towards the land.

Like a cork upon the tide, he was helpless to stop or control where he was going. The giant wave roared in his ears as it continued to bear him along with its force. He was rolled forward, tumbled twice, flung sideways first one way then the other, striking his left shoulder on what could have been sand, could have been soil. Throwing his head back, gasping for air, knowing that the wave would at some stage suck back, he groped with his right hand for something solid – a bush, a tree, a rock – anything that might hold him to the land. But there was nothing. Instead he was tossed through vegetation, the kanuka trees that grew on the side of the lagoon. Their crowns rasped his arms, the trunks bashed his legs. Arms flailing, he was thrown against a kanuka tree's slender trunk. He grabbed it, wrapped his arms around it and clutched it to his chest. Seeing and feeling the seawater still boiling beneath him, he continued to hug the trunk, saw the wave pause for a few seconds as it reached its zenith, then begin to withdraw, streaming back through the kanuka, its level dropping with dramatic speed, ripping and stripping the undergrowth with a sound like tearing paper. Seconds later, he was marooned in the upper branches of the kanuka. He remained there for several minutes, feet resting on two boughs, head against the twisted trunk, staring down at the ground until he was sure that another wave was not following. The ground below was littered with driftwood and soaked with seawater, and when he climbed down he found that his legs could hardly support him. Sinking to the ground, head on his knees, he found himself instinctively murmuring a prayer of thanks for deliverance.

Out on the beach the entire coast had been scoured. Most of the sand was gone, the rock strata exposed, as if the beach were a filleted carcass. The stream where he had set his net was pouring straight out in a wide fan onto what remained of the beach, while the surface of the sea itself still had an oily sheen. In places its surface was disfigured with rips, which when they met, erupted in ragged lines, like water slopping over the edge of a basin. Beneath his feet Luigi could feel the earth still twitching, like the calf he had once seen in his uncle's back yard, just after it had been pole-axed. Hands shaking, eyes smarting from the salt water, he took off his boots, shirt and trousers and turned his clothes inside out, shaking the bark and seeds from them. Taking off his underclothes, he cleaned them too, then wrung them out and put his long-johns back on. As he did so, he kept looking warily at the sea. At home he had weathered storms at sea, but never had he seen or felt anything like this. Walking unsteadily back up onto the shore, he saw that the lagoon had been inundated, the foliage surrounding it flattened and moulded, like coiffured hair. The wave must have swept half a mile inland before withdrawing. Hearing the cry of birds, he looked up. Gulls, dozens of them, wheeling above the lagoon. A sign of normality, he thought, with relief. Tucking his shirt under his arm, he began to make his way back towards Okuru.

Entering the clearing, he saw that there was a great crack running across the ground, about three feet deep. Water was draining into it from the surrounding land. The house had slipped off its piles in the front right-hand corner and the walls above the corner were sagging, the roof skewed. Inside, jars, tins and bottles had been thrown from the shelves and were strewn about the floor, the earthenware containers shattered. Leopoldo was sitting dismally on the boards, collecting up the shards and sweeping a mess of spilt sugar into a pile with the edges of his hands. The cooking pot had dropped into the ashes and the bricks that lined the chimney sides had fallen in. 'I thought the world was ending, Luigi,' he said, looking up with frightened eyes. 'Other times there have been earth shakes, but never like this.' Luigi helped him restore order to the inside of the house, then the two of them, using a kanuka log as a lever, managed to raise the damaged corner of the house. Then, blocking the lever while they worked, they replaced the corner pile.

They sat on the stone step and smoked while Luigi recounted his escape from the tidal wave. Leopoldo shook his head wearily. 'This place is too much, Luigi. Flood, earthquake, tidal wave. What else can it throw at us?' Laughing, Luigi put a hand on his shoulder. 'They have earthquakes in Italy, too, Leopoldo. I read of one once in Sicily, that caused dozens of villages to collapse. And what about Vesuvius? And Etna and Stromboli?' He grunted. 'At least there're no volcanoes here.' Raising his head, Leopoldo stared ruefully towards the line of snow-capped mountains. 'Well, it wouldn't surprise me if one of those blew up one day, just to give us extra punishment.'

The settlements were severely affected by the 'quake and giant wave. Several brick chimneys were brought down, one killing an infant in its crib at Arawata. The brick store at Waiatoto slipped off its foundations and collapsed like a house of cards. But the very insubstantial nature of other buildings – their corrugated iron walls and chimneys in particular – allowed them to flex with the jolting, so they could be moved back into place without too much difficulty. On the plain the three big rivers had absorbed the tidal wave, channelling its force so that it grew weaker as it moved upriver. At Okuru the locals had watched in awe as the bore moved upriver at high speed, overturning the ferry boat and tossing dinghies aside like toys before fizzling out a couple of hundred yards past the settlement. But further south, three Maori whitebaiters on the banks of the Haast River were unable to scramble for higher ground in time and were washed away. Only one managed to make it back to the bank, the other two were taken out to sea. Their bodies were found on the beach at Waiatoto three days later. Inland, although whole hillsides had collapsed, with mining there now abandoned, the 'quake scarred only the land.

But the road – the new road – suffered grievous damage. Being so close to the foreshore, it had been swamped, and the receding water had sucked greedily at the formed sections, stripping away the shingle topping, tearing at the rock foundation, strewing the stones inland through the bush. Hundreds of yards of the road, the work of months, had been laid waste.

Tipping his cap back on his head, Claude Oliver picked up a large, pointed steel bar used for prising boulders from the earth. Holding the bar up like some tribal chief, he thrust it straight downwards into the soft ground. His road gang was gathered round him, the newly-formed section of road a series of pot-holes, littered with manuka, rocks and driftwood. 'Three months,' Claude averred, 'three months' bloody work, washed away in five bloody minutes.' Luigi and the others, equally glum, said nothing. Screwing his face up into an angry round ball, Claude glared at the sea. Watching his despair, Luigi wondered, as they were all wondering, so will there be any more money to rebuild the road? Will the government pay to start again? Already, the men had been told, the costs of the Jackson Bay settlement had been far greater than first estimated. King Mac would have go again, cap in hand, as the English put it, to Mr Bonar, the Superintendent of Westland, for extra money.

Claude turned back to the others, slapping his hands together. 'Well luds, tidal wave or no tidal wave, I'm not beaten. I'm willing to start again. What d'you say? Do we tell Macfarlane we'll finish the job?'

'Too bloody right!' yelled the Pole, Karl Ziglefski. 'We haven't come this far to give up.'

There was not a man who disagreed.

Visibly heartened, Claude jammed his cap back on his head.

'Thanks, lads. Macfarlane's coming to inspect the damage tomorrow afternoon. And to assess the road's prospects. I reckon if we're all working like chinkies when he gets here, we can show him we mean business.'

The next day, Macfarlane rode up on a chestnut horse at just after four o'clock, head crowned with a black bowler hat, beard flowing over his waistcoat. The men looked up momentarily as he approached, then went back to their labouring. Luigi and Tom McGovern were clearing sodden manuka from the damaged road and heaping it on the inland side, the others were barrowing loads of shingle and filling the many pot-holes. Macfarlane and Claude walked a little way along the ruined stretch of road, heads bowed in conversation, pausing every so often to study the damage. Then they came back to the road-head and Claude called the gang together. His expression was dark. The tall figure of Macfarlane stood beside him, eyes sweeping the assembled group, his expression grim. 'Mr Macfarlane would like to make an announcement, men,' said Claude, disconsolately.

Nodding curtly at the foreman, King Mac took a step forward.

'Yesterday I had a visit from Jim Bonar, the provincial superintendent, regarding the future of this settlement.' He paused, meaningfully. 'I was informed by him that there will be no more money voted by the central government for Jackson Bay. Not a penny more.' The men looked at each other. What else was coming?

'The project was already over-budget, before this …' He waved his hand at the strip of damaged road '… unfortunate occurrence. So, the coffers are empty, I'm afraid.'

'You mean the road's not going to be finished?' Aubrey called out in disbelief.

'Did I say that?' snapped Macfarlane. 'Let me finish, man.' Aubrey looked at him warily as King Mac continued. 'The road *will* be finished. As I said to Bonar, "What good's a settlement without a road?"'

'Or a wharf!' called a voice from the back. It was Tom McGovern.

Throwing a baleful look in his direction, Macfarlane snarled, 'No one knows better than I do how badly this bay needs a wharf, and no one's worked harder to get the money for one than I have. But the truth is, the days of big government spending on public works are over.' He paused. 'As I said before, the coffers are nearly empty.' A muttering went through the gang. 'And how much of the money went on your grand house?' Aubrey said under his breath. Luigi grunted in agreement. Ever since he had visited Macfarlane, he had been wondering the same thing himself. Tucking his hat under his arm, the Resident Agent continued. 'Yes, the road'll be finished. But it'll have to be done with reduced costs. As from today, yerr'll be on half pay. The wage rate'll be four shillings a day.'

Silence. The sudden silence of incredulity. The men stared at Mcfarlane as one. Then, also in unison, their gaze moved to Claude. His head had been hanging, now it came up slowly. His expression pained, he said quietly, 'That goes for me too, luds. All on half pay.'

Luigi's mind churned. That would change everything. Twice as long to pay off Leopoldo's debt, twice as long to be able to buy the equipment they needed to drain the swamp, to clear the land and buy seed. At one stroke, their troubles had doubled. The dumbfounded atmosphere was maintained for some time, each man doing his own mental arithmetic and finding it difficult to add up. Then, from the back of the gang, someone pushed through to the front. It was Tom McGovern. Striding up to King Mac, clenching his fist, he raised it in front of the Resident Agent's face.

'Half pay, eh? And what about you, Macfarlane? Half pay for you too? I think not.' He turned and waved his hand towards the others. 'And how are we meant to manage on four shillings a day? Some of us have got chuldrin t'feed. Aubrey's got four, Frank's got three. We can only just manage on eight shillings a day, given the fact that the land we were given – the land we're supposed to farm – is only fit for bloody croco-dales. How are we meant to survive now?'

Macfarlane didn't flinch. Instead he lowered his gaze, menacingly. 'You're McGovern, right?'

'That's moi name.'

'Well McGovern, we want none of yer Fenian nonsense in this bay. We had enough of that in Hokitika a while back.'

'Who's talkin' Fenian, man? I'm talkin' a fair wage for a job well done! And feedin' wives and kuddies!'

Macfarlane stared at the fiery little Irishman for some moments, his black eyes seeming to disappear into the back of his head. Then he turned to Claude and said in a loud voice, 'Take McGovern off the payroll. As from this afternoon.' His gaze returned to Tom. 'Troublemakers like you are the last thing this settlement needs.' His eyes swept the group with the commanding look of a man who knew he held all the aces. 'Four shillings a day, take it or leave it.' The response was an astonished, disbelieving silence. Tom McGovern turned away from the agent.

'Best of luck, lards,' he said to the rest of them. He began to walk away, then turned back. 'And the worst of luck to you, Macfarlane. May the next bloody earthquake bring that bloody palace of yerrs down on yer bloody Scotch head.' He snatched up his sugar bag and sauntered off down the ruined road.

Without saying a word more, Macfarlane placed his hat back on his head at a jaunty angle, turned on his heel, mounted his horse and cantered off down the track in the opposite direction.

They worked in total silence for the rest of the day, as silent and uncomplaining as scarecrows, but each man reassessing his prospects, reconsidering his options. For Luigi, there were few. He could not desert Leopoldo, that would be unthinkable. But even if they left together, where would they go? Coal mining? The very thought of becoming a human mole revolted him. Timber milling? He knew nothing of that work, except that it was almost as dangerous as mining. He was tied to this place, now, in any event. It would take two years now to pay off the debt at the store, probably another five to get that sodden piece of land productive. He gathered up another armful of manuka. No, he thought gloomily, he could do nothing but accept Macfarlane's grim terms.

That night, after he had passed the news to Leopoldo, the other man sat on the bed, covered his head with his hands and sat in silence for some time. When he spoke he looked straight at the floor. 'You must go, Luigi. Go to Wellington, join the other Italians there. I can survive.'

Luigi went over to him, placed a hand gently on his back. 'No. Things aren't finished here. We'll leave when they are.'

But when he went outside and looked out over the clearing, an island of mud among the dripping bush, he wondered if that could ever be. The great crack that the earthquake had caused had closed up again a day later, and water was once more lying in pools across the clearing. Farming it was out of the question. He got to his feet. But at least, he told himself, I am still here, and safe. And a job on four shillings a day was better than no job at all. Then, turning to go back into the house, he heard a harrowing sound. It was a man, crying.

'The whitebait are running again', Adam Nolan had told Luigi as he ferried him across the Turnbull River after work. The word 'running' always amused Luigi – how could a fish ever run? He hadn't returned to the stream since the day of the earthquake, but he decided that next Sunday he would. When he got to the stream, he saw that it had cut yet another course down the foreshore, pouring at first straight from the land, then swerving sharply to the right, running parallel to the shore for fifty yards before straightening again and flowing down into the sea. The stream water was beautifully clear as it poured down along its rocky bed and into the sea, as if the tumultuous events of weeks before had never happened. But Luigi shuddered as he stood on a low mound above the shore, studied the stream's altered course and recalled the events of that fearful day. Lifting his gaze, he saw that the offshore wind had flattened the sea. A few small waves were rising and falling at the water's edge, and the surface was ruffled only at the place where the stream met the sea.

He walked down to the stream, selected a likely place, arranged a race out of stones and set his new net, anchoring it at the back with a single rock. Then he sat back a little way from the stream and rolled and lit a cigarette. The day was warm and cloudless, and when such a day came to the coast, it was easy to forget all the rainy ones. Round, brown boulders exposed by the tidal wave lay in bunches along the shore, reminding him of the cobblestones in Pesaro's square, and the mist that hung over the sea, and the pale blueness of the sky above the land, was reminiscent too, of the Adriatic in early morning. Perhaps, he also thought, it was the exile's fate to constantly find a likeness of what he had known, in the other land which he had come to. But there were such differences, too. Mainly, there was the emptiness, everywhere. From where he sat he could see not a boat, not a ship, not a person, not a building. It was as if people had taken just a toehold on coast, and could go no further. But now that he was becoming used to the emptiness, he was warming to it. It gave a man the space to think, to be himself, to not have to constantly jostle with others. 'Here there's elbow room', Aubrey had once remarked. He liked that expression, 'elbow room'. Staring down the beach, he saw that the little lapping waves at the mouth of the stream were growing more insistent as the tide rose higher. Another half hour and the tide would rise to meet his net.

He ran his fingers through the sand. Looking down, he saw that the beach had been changed in more than one way by the tidal wave. The scouring had caused the sand to become coarser, its grains were paler in colour, and the fragments of shell which had been mixed with it were no longer there in such numbers. Letting the dry sand trickle through his fingers and fall back to the beach, he saw something glint among the grains. A tiny, golden flake. For a moment, his hand went rigid. Then he reached down and carefully brushed back the surrounding sand. Another of the golden flakes, and another. Pressing his forefinger down carefully, he touched one. It stuck to the end of his finger. Lifting it before his eyes, he examined the little gleaming flake with wonder. *The colour.*

81

Carefully scraping the sand with the edge of his hand, he saw that the flakes were everywhere, just below the surface. Dozens of them, the same golden flecks that he had gazed on in a bottle in the barred window of the Bank of New Zealand in the main street of Hokitika, the Midas flecks that were exchanged for pounds. Hundreds of pounds. Fortunes that turned poor men into rich ones, paupers into princes. Whitebait forgotten, he took his kerosene tin, scooped handfuls of sand into it, then half-filled it with water. Working slowly, he tilted the tin and shuffled it back and forth, so that the sand and water gradually spilled out over the edge. Then, with the same eagerness with which he examined his net when he pulled it from the water, he peered into the bottom of the tin. His heart began to pump. There, clustered in a corner at the bottom of the tin, was a tiny, gleaming, golden triangle. Now he fully understood the meaning of the two magical words, 'the colour', knew at once how men were magnetised by them, why they could leave everything, cross the world and live like ants on the side of a hill to seek it. Putting his cap upsidedown on the sand, he turned the tin up and shook it gently. The little yellow nest slid down the seam of the tin and trickled into his cap, each flake perfect, each one gleaming as if as delighted at being found as their finder was at discovering them.

Reaching out with his finger, he separated the flakes tenderly, then counted them. Eighteen. How much would they be worth? The colour, he had been told, could fetch a price of £40 an ounce. Forty pounds, for the weight of a plug of tobacco! These eighteen flakes would add up to just a fraction of that, but if there was more ...

Staring at the sand, he thought, perhaps it was a fluke, perhaps it was only fool's gold. Perhaps, perhaps.

He peeled off a cigarette paper, transferred the precious yellow flecks to it, then twisted the paper into a tiny parcel. There had been something of a rush on the rivers in these parts, a decade ago, he had been told. But it had never amounted to much, only a fraction of the value of the fields inland from Greymouth and Hokitika. Like a skittering shoal of whitebait, the miners had changed course immediately and moved on to battle the currents elsewhere. But here, on the beach, it seemed that the tidal wave had uncovered a field of the golden flakes. Eyes fixed on the stream, he wondered, was this just a 'flash in the pan', as people called such finds? If not, just how much more lay hidden there? And if there was more, how could he make sure that the discovery remained his and his alone?

FIVE

'And I would like a frying pan, Mrs Marks. A big one.'

The storekeeper looked surprised. 'One of these?' She held the utensil up.

'Yes.'

'They're five shillings.'

'Yes.'

As he took the coins from his wallet, the woman continued to look at him curiously. Handing the pan over, she said,

'Going to have a few fry-ups, then?'

'Yes. Whitebait fritters, especially.'

'Ah, right. The bait are still running, then?'

'Yes, they are still running. Thank you.'

He set the net, walked upstream a little way, then took the frying pan from his sugar bag. Glancing round to see that no one was in sight, he stepped into the stream, slid the frying pan into its gravel bed and scooped up half a panful. Squatting at the edge of the stream, he began to move the pan backwards and forwards, tilting it so that the gravel and water gradually spilled out. It was the gold's weight, they said, that caused it to stay at the bottom. Ounce for ounce it was much heavier than rock. Shuffling the pan, he released all the gravel, then peered into the seam at the bottom of the pan. His heart lurched. There, nestling in the seam, was a tiny streak of yellow. So, it hadn't been a dream! Taking a small earthenware jar with a wire clip lid from his bag, he scraped the flakes into it. He would need some measures, to weigh his findings. But he wouldn't buy them at the store, that might arouse suspicion. In this place everyone watched everyone else so closely. It was essential that his find be kept a secret. If word got out, his claim would be swamped.

Claim? Not, he couldn't call it that. To have a claim you first had to have a prospecting licence, and the nearest assay office was in Hokitika. He had considered asking Aubrey to get him a licence on his next trip north, but decided against it. To ask for such a thing would also lead to awkward questions. So he had decided to mention nothing of his find to anyone, including loose-lipped Leopoldo, who spent much of his time at the landing, talking to everyone who came and went across the Okuru river. If Leopoldo knew of Luigi's find, it was likely that he would boast about it to someone. The very hint of a find brought hundreds of men running, Luigi knew from talking to his work-mates. Although gold fever had been over for a decade now, there was still the occasional outbreak, with the same symptoms – a frenzied rush for the spot, with every man for himself. And Luigi now thought of this as *his* stream, and everything in it as his. Eventually he would share his trove with Leopoldo, but only when the time was right.

Returning to the stream, Luigi scooped up another panful of gravel with the pan.

If he had a miner's cradle and a rocker, the process would be much quicker, but that would make his activities too obvious. After the whitebait stopped running he would come here with a fishing line and cast it off the beach, to keep up his cover. Shuffling the pan slowly backwards and forwards, his eyes were fixed on the little pile of shingle at the bottom, as if magnetised by it. It didn't matter that he could only come here once a week, on his day off. A few hours a week was enough, and time was the one thing he had plenty of.

Months melted into seasons, seasons into years. Not that there were true seasons in this place, he and Leopoldo agreed. The leaves in the forest remained green always and did not fall. The snow on the mountains came and went but never descended to the plain. The rain came for days on end, stopped briefly, then returned, so that the earth was never dry. Throughout the winter months everything turned to a cold sogginess – though there were few frosts – but an endless supply of wood from the surrounding bush kept their fire going twenty-four hours a day. Calendars had little relevance in Jackson Bay. Luigi came to measure months by how far the road had reached. Leopoldo ran the household – cooking, cleaning, washing, tending the fire. Wood chopping was a job that a one-legged man could do better than a two-legged one, he quipped, because

'I have only one foot to keep out the way of the axe'.

Violetta wrote to Luigi every few months, care of the post office in Hokitika. He cherished the news from her, comforted by the understanding she showed towards him, and kept her letters in a big envelope under his bed. The fact that his father never wrote did not surprise Luigi. Ernesto Galoni had never been a man of letters.

In the evenings, after their meal, Luigi would play the accordion to Leopoldo's requests, and they would play cards at the table by lantern light, and talk of home and their plans for the piece of land. 'Potatoes,' Leopoldo declared. 'When the drains are dug, we will plant potatoes. Everyone here eats potatoes.' He also taught Luigi the words that Tui had taught him, for the birds and the fish and the precious stone – pounamu – that the Maori found in the rivers and used for their war clubs and pendants. It was Maori seeking greenstone who had found gold instead, leading to one of the first rushes on the coast, Leopoldo explained. He told him too that the green and white speckled fish that Luigi hooked in the surf and which smoked so well was called kahawai, and the silver-sided one with the small mouth and the sweet flesh that he caught on a set line was the tarakihi. The small shark whose flesh was dry but perfectly edible was known by the Maori as koinge, while the blue cod that lived in the rocky parts of the coast was called raawaru.

The birds he would point out to Luigi as he stumped along beside him through the bush, stopping abruptly and pointing with a crutch into the foliage, where the trees teemed with the beautiful, almost-tame creatures. 'That is the one they call the korimako. Listen!' And the little grey-green bird's lovely, chiming call would ring out through the forest.

'That is the piwakawaka. See its tail, shaped just like a fan? Tui used to say they come out when rain is near. No wonder they are seen everywhere in Okuru.'

'That is the tauhou, the silver eye.'

'Look! Kereru!' And there above them would be a fat native pigeon, squatting on a branch, its belly heavy with berries. 'They are excellent eating, if you have a gun to bring them down.'

'Listen, Luigi, a tui. It sings that strange song, constantly.'

'A weka, look, running there! They are stealers, they come around the house sometimes, looking for food. Once I found one inside, pecking at my potatoes. I killed it and cooked it. It was quite tasty.' Leopoldo laughed, mordantly. 'My woman's name was Tui, but I think she should have been called Weka, she stole so much from me. She even took my belt, the one she used as a tourniquet on my leg, did I tell you?'

When they fished, Leopoldo identified the pied bird with the long red bill as the torea, the oystercatcher, the kawau, the black shag, the big, raucous gull with the black back as the kararo and the iridescent-winged bird which swooped down on the inunga and baby eels in the streams and rivers as the kotare, the kingfisher. Soon Luigi too referred to all these creatures by their Maori names, preferring them to the English ones, savouring the rich vowel sounds of the native language. *Ko*-ta-ray, *ke*-ray-ru, *kaw*-ree-ma-ko.

The coast road pushed slowly south. A rate of a hundred yards a week was considered good going. Most of the family men had given up the work since Macfarlane's pay cut, working instead for the timber millers at Arawata, where contract milling paid ten shillings a day. The settlement was still hungry for timber. But Luigi was content to stay with the road gang. There was companionship there now that he had been accepted, satisfaction in helping convert the track to a proper road, and he and Leopoldo could get by on his reduced wage. Half way through his second year in the bay, Claude put him in charge of the big steel road roller, pulled by an amiable Clydesdale called Rufus, and Luigi knew this was a compliment. Rolling was the final act in road creation, like smoothing the icing on a cake. Leading the big horse by his bridle as the spread shingle was rolled and re-rolled, together he and Luigi compacted it to a hard, nearly permanent surface, one almost resistant to the rains. Although Macfarlane had told them that no bridges would come to this coast for many years, the completed road would become a vital highway, enabling goods and people to be moved much more easily between the isolated little settlements.

On Sunday nights, after a day spent by the whitebait stream, Luigi would add another trickle of golden flakes to the jar, which he kept in a hole in the ground a little way up from the back of the house, covered with a slab of kahikatea and heaped over with wet leaves. Holding the jar in his hand, he could feel its increasing weight, and this reassured him. The hoard represented his future, his life after Okuru. The jar and its golden flecks held promise of things to come: a piece of decent land of his own, a proper house, a new accordion, one with a keyboard, like those he had seen in the mail order catalogues at Marks' store.

But his panning produced wildly uneven results. The gold flakes had evidently been scattered randomly through the stream bed. In some places he panned all day and found none; at other times one panning unearthed a dozen or more of the tiny fragments. He continued to keep his trove a secret. The fact that he didn't share it with Leopoldo made him feel guilty at times. Then he would remind himself that the jar's contents were his discovery, his godsend, his unexpected blessing. The secret of its existence represented a kind of covenant between him and his future, and the worth of the colour would only be redeemed when that future arrived.

Not even in his letters to Violetta did he make mention of the gold. But in these twice-yearly reports to her he was deliberately positive, emphasising the steadiness of his job, the comfort of the house, the contentment of the life that he and Leopoldo were making for themselves in the new land.

Then one day a letter from Violetta brought news which pierced his heart like a stiletto.

Dearest Luigi,

Papa died last week, in the convent hospital. He had been there for three weeks. The cause of death was a tumour on his brain, the doctor told us, and they could do nothing for the affliction. He had begun to suffer from the most terrible headaches, and his eyesight became weaker and weaker. After a few days in the hospital, now blind, he drifted into unconsciousness. The nuns were very kind, and the doctor too. They allowed me to stay in a room next to his for the last week. I spent all day at his bedside, sponging his brow, giving him broth. He died in the afternoon, on 14 September. When the end came, it was peaceful. I was there, with Uncle Franceso and Uncle Mario, when the last rites were given to him. At the funeral, at Sant' Agostino, Uncle Mario spoke on behalf of the family, and he and Uncle Francesco, with Giuseppe Ercolano and Giovanni Falleni, were his pall bearers. His grave lies beside Mama's and the others of our family, near the top of the hill in the town cemetery. It was a time of such sadness, not just for our family, but for our community. I know how much Papa had hoped to live to see his grandchildren born and grow up. As you know, he and our family have been part of Pesaro for so many generations. I know too that you and Papa disagreed over many things, but that did not really affect your love for one another. He said to me not long before he died, after I had read him one of your letters, 'I understand why he left for the new land. And I am pleased that he wrote to me.' So, you see Luigi, he did understand your need to start a new life. I hope you will take comfort from that knowledge.

There is other important news which I must tell you. I am to be married soon. My fiancé is someone you do not know. His name is Antonio Pelacci, and he is from Urbino. His family have a leather working business there. We met at a dance at the Hotel Adriatica when he was on holiday here, with his two sisters, Maria and Isola. I had gone with my friend, Lucia. Antonio is a very kind man, aged 22, tall, with fair hair and brown eyes. I think I fell in love with him from the moment he took me in his arms to dance. We are to be married at Sant' Agostino in December, so by the time you read this, I will be Padrona Pelacci! Uncle Carlo will give me away. So, I too am to leave Pesaro. Urbino, as you know, is a very beautiful town, and we will live in a room above Antonio's family's shop. I think his parents were at first doubtful that he was not marrying a girl from his own town, but after we met and I told them how much I was looking forward to living in Urbino, they seemed much happier. I know I am the happiest I have been in my life. Sometimes I feel that it has eclipsed my sorrow at Papa's death, and this makes me feel guilty. But it is undeniable that I am looking forward so much to being married, and to beginning a family of my own. There has been too much loss in ours. But how sad that you will not be at the wedding, to share our joy and play your accordion for Antonio and me.

Please write soon and give me your news. Have you met a young woman yet, in the new land? Tell me all, Luigi.

Your loving sister,

Violetta

He read the letter by the roadside, at morning smoko. Its mixed messages aroused in him equally varied emotions: sorrow, gladness, regret, hope. Reading of their father's death, he was filled with grief. *Papa, Papa,* he thought, *you should have lived much longer.* Only forty-six. Younger than Ernesto's father had been when he died, he hadn't even lived long enough to see grandchildren born. Eyes filling with tears for his dead father, Luigi turned his face to the sea. In this country a man dared not be seen to cry. Then, wiping his eyes, he read the letter again. But there was hope in it, too. Violetta, marrying. What could he send her as a wedding gift, apart from his blessing? A pendant of pounamu, perhaps.

Looking towards the horizon, he could see a funnel like a top hat and trail of dark smoke streaming from it. A steamship, headed for Westport, probably. Violetta, little Violetta, now a wife and probably soon a mother. It seemed only a handful of years ago since he had read bedtime stories to her. He regretted so much that he would not meet her man, to see if he was worthy of her love. That was his brotherly duty, after all. Yet another price that a migrant had to pay. Getting up, he drained the last of the black tea in his mug. As he did so, he heard Claude Oliver's voice calling from the road.

'Hey, Luigi! Your mate's waiting!'

It was Rufus, the draught horse, impatient to resume their rolling.

'I thought I would come fishing with you today. Help you with the gear.'

Luigi's hand gripped the short stick onto which he was winding fishing cord in figure-of-eight movements. He replied quietly. 'It's all right, Leopoldo, I can manage.'

Leaning heavily on one of his crutches, Leopoldo scowled. 'Why don't you want me to help? Whenever I offer, you refuse.' He looked as reproachful as an unfed cat.

'I already said, I can manage.'

'Well, I might just come for the walk, then.'

'It's a long way to the stream. You'll get even more tired.' Lately Leopoldo had not been sleeping at all well. His coughing had been keeping them both awake at night.

'I like to get out too, you know. Walking to the landing hardly counts.'

Luigi considered this. If Leopoldo came, then panning was out of the question. 'I think it would be better if you stayed. And rested. I'll be back by mid-afternoon.'

'It's almost as if you have something to hide, when you go off on Sundays,' Leopoldo said, a little slyly.

Luigi started. Was it that obvious? 'I don't know what you mean,' he said. 'It's my day off, I go fishing.'

'But why do you always go to the stream? Why don't you come to the landing?'

'Because there are kahawai at the stream mouth.'

'I'm tired of eating kahawai.'

'That's why I'm going to cook pork for dinner.'

'And I will have to stay here and stare at the bush.' His expression was petulant now.

'Leopoldo, I have one day off a week. I like to fish by the stream, alone. I like to have that time to myself. Okay?' The man was becoming as clingy as a cobweb.

'I want to come, Luigi. I *need* to come.'

Staring at the crumpled, downcast figure, Luigi relented. One day's lost pickings wouldn't make much difference. 'All right, then. Do you want to fish, too?'

'No. I just want to come and watch.'

And as Luigi cast his line into the sea and hauled the lure back in through the waves, his eyes kept straying to the stream bed, and he grew resentful. Leopoldo was lying back on the sand, smoking, his crutches beside him. Luigi wondered, how many of the precious flakes had he lost today? Then the line suddenly tightened and pulled hard to the left. Hauling on it, he saw the streak of grey in the wave, felt the continuing tension. A kahawai, a big one. Leopoldo saw it too, and gave a whooping cry. Laughing, Luigi began to haul the fish in, hand over hand.

Claude held up the copy of the *Hokitika Guardian and Evening Star*, and read aloud from page three, to the others, who were clustered around the billy fire at lunch smoko.

Letter from Mr D.Macfarlane, Resident Agent, Jackson Bay, to the Hon. John Hall, Premier of New Zealand, Wellington.

Jackson Bay, 17th June, 1881.

Sir, –

I have the honour to bring under your notice, and crave your favourable consideration of the gravest importance to the inhabitants of the southern part of the Provincial District of Westland, i.e. the construction of a jetty at Jackson Bay. During the last session of Parliament the Government were good enough to recognize our claim to have this work done, by placing the sum of £2,500 upon the estimates; plans were prepared and tenders called for the work, but, owing to a lack of funds, this, as many other works, was held over. The inhabitants of the riding have, by petition through their member, addressed the House on this subject, but, as there are points that could not very well be touched upon therein, I have taken the liberty of addressing you as head of the Government on the subject. In the first place I would point out that a considerable reduction can be made in the cost of construction by doing away with the munz-metal sheathing and bolts specified in Mr Blackett's plans. The object in using metal is to prevent the ravages of *teredo novalis*, which has proved so destructive to the timber used in the wharf and jetty construction in the more northern parts of the colony, but if it can be shown that through local causes their action here is nil, then this expensive item can be struck out; this would materially reduce the cost of the work, without in the least impairing its efficiency. It is a fact known to those who have studied the habits of this destructive worm that a mixture of fresh and salt water is inimical to its existence, and moreover, as we proceed south, the change of temperature has the effect of checking their ravages. The portion of the jetty built three years ago shows no sign of the action of the *teredo*, and I attribute this to the fresh-water creek discharging into the bay almost alongside the jetty, and to the waters of the River Arawata, which, after discharging into the bay, follow the trend of the coast into the bottom of the bay, whence they swing around and meet the tidal inside Jackson's Head, causing a tide rip across the bay. Since my last communication with the Government on this subject, I have found timber (black birch) more easily available than when tenders were called last year; this would also reduce the cost of the work, so that it could be done for £1,500, instead of £2,500, as voted last year. This sum, I hope you will be able to see your way to place on the estimates for the current year. The saw-mill, put up at great expense, and that promised to be the source of profit and employment both to proprietors and employees, has been lying idle two years, and every other industry labours under the same disadvantage. The country is being taken up wherever available for cattle and sheep runs, and in the settlement proper a good many are cultivating with marked success in the way of splendid root and grass crops. The mineral resources of the district are being utilized, but under great difficulties, from the want of facilities for shipping produce, and from the want of assured communication with other parts of the colony.

I have, &c,

D. Macfarlane,
    Resident Agent.

'Well,' declared Claude, 'you have to give the booger full marks for trying.'

'But Christ,' said Aubrey, tipping his cap back on his head, 'what a load of big words. What's that "inimic..."' '...to its what?'

Claude pronounced the words carefully. ' "In-im-ical to its exist-ence". That means the worm doesn't like it. The fresh water.' He sniffed. 'Booger should of said thut.'

Laughing, Luigi said, 'The only bits I understood were the numbers. He says the wharf can be built much cheaper now, is that right?'

'Yes,' said Claude. But even one and half thousand's too much for Hall's government. Tight as a kahawai's arsehole, that sod.' He sniffed. 'Comes from Hull. There's always something fishy about those bastards.'

'Takes one to know one,' observed Aubrey, and they all laughed, Claude included, even though he came from Grimsby himself. 'Least I'm not a wowser, like Hall is,' the foreman added. He made a low whistling sound. 'Well, as I said, it was worth a try on King Mac's part. And he's right, if the jetty'd been finished back in '77, this place'd be doing a lot better. But Macfarlane doesn't seem to realise, the government's money's all spent. The days of special bloody settlements are well and truly over. There's men out of work everywhere. It's a depression we've got in the country now, the paper says. I reckon we might all be down the road soon.' He paused. 'Even if we did build it.'

They were all silent for a time. Luigi felt troubled by the news. If hard times were coming, then they would strike this settlement a body blow. The whole scheme, he saw now, had been a fantasy. Bonar's plan for special towns, Federli's notion of sending Italians here to grow mulberries and grapes. How could they have not realised its futility? It was just Luigi's good fortune, and a rare stroke of it at that, that he had happened upon the colour where he had. The butter jar and its precious contents would be needed sorely at some time, that seemed certain. Lying back in the grass, hands behind his head, he stared at the streaming clouds until he felt giddy, as if the world was upsidedown. Which in a way, it was. In the meantime, jetty or no jetty, this was where he must stay.

'Luigi...'
  'What is it?'
    'I ...can't ....breathe ...'

Springing from his stretcher, Luigi went quickly to Leopoldo's bed. He was lying on his back, his breath coming in quick, desperate bursts. The blankets were thrown back, and he was wearing just pyjama trousers, the legless one in a tangled heap. His hollow chest and thin arms were the colour of whey, and they were quivering. Putting his hand on Leopoldo's brow, Luigi felt hot wetness. For the last few days, after getting caught in the rain without his oilskin on the way back from fishing at the landing, he had been unable to leave his bed. The chill had worsened his hacking cough, clogging his throat with phlegm, causing his nose to stream. His coughing, hoicking and spitting had been constant ever since. But a fever, that was something else. Going to the fireplace, Luigi laid some twigs in the grate and saw them catch on the embers, the rising flames throwing flickering shadows across the walls. He put a pot of water on the grate, soaked a cloth in the water bucket and sponged Leopoldo's face, chest and arms, anxiously watching his chest rising and falling. His eyes were rolled back in his head, his breath bore the smell of over-ripe lemons.

'I ...I ...'

'Don't speak,' Luigi urged. 'Don't waste your breath. I'm preparing an inhalation for you.'

He poured the nearly-boiling water onto the balsam mixture, then carried the mug with its reeking resinous mixture, and a towel, over to the bed. Bringing Leopoldo up into a sitting position, he put the towel over his head and held the mug under his nostrils. 'Breathe it in,' he insisted, 'through your nose.' Leopoldo sniffed, gasped, and retched, his head almost knocking the mug from Luigi's hands. Then he began to cough again, a harsh sound, like wood being sawed. Luigi held him until the racking cough subsided, then tried the inhalation again. Again it only provoked the terrible cough. *This is worse, worse than it has ever been*, Luigi knew, as he carried the elixir called Irish Moss over to the bed. Cradling Leopoldo's head, he spooned the heated syrup between his lips, scooping up the line of crimson dribble which spilled from a corner of his mouth. The coughing subsided, but he was gasping now, and Luigi could feel his body burning, the sweat turning his skin as slippery as an eel's. He is so thin, so feeble, Luigi thought. An old man, at the age of thirty-one.

'I can't ...'

'Don't even try. Say nothing.'

Laying Leopoldo's head back onto the pillow, Luigi picked up the sponge and wiped his face and shoulders again. He was shivering uncontrollably, his teeth making morse code noises, even though his skin was so hot. A doctor, he needs a doctor. But he knew only too well that the nearest doctor was in Hokitika, 200 miles away. People here treated their illnesses themselves, using the potions from Marks' store. The nearest thing to a doctor in Okuru was Joseph Heveldt's wife, Dorothea, a midwife, who lived four miles further up the valley. She had been trained in a hospital in her home town, Hannover.

Luigi dressed quickly, went to Leopoldo and pulled him carefully into an upright position. 'I am going for Mrs Heveldt,' he said into Leopoldo's ear. 'We'll be back as quickly as we can.' He put a hand gently on Leopoldo's forearm. 'If the coughing comes again, take some of the elixir. A little at a time.' Eyes hard closed, wheezing like a bellows, Leopoldo made no reply. Minutes later Luigi was running, kerosene lantern in hand, along the bush track that led towards the Heveldts' 50-acre block.

The house was in darkness. He banged three times on the door and waited for a couple of minutes until it opened. Joseph Heveldt, bald and bearded, in his night-shirt, was holding a lit candle. Luigi told him what had happened and Joseph withdrew, leaving him on the porch. Twenty minutes later Dorothea appeared, in a black crinoline dress and with a medical bag in her hand. Cramming a bonnet on her head, she asked, 'How long has he been ill?' She was a small, bird-like woman with falcon eyes and a mouth as straight and tight as a sutured wound. She listened to Luigi's story as they returned along the bush track, holding her dress clear of the mud with one hand, her bag in the other, eyes on the ground, trying to stay within the pool of light cast by Luigi's lantern. They said little to each other. The only sound was the seething of night insects, coming from the dripping bush, and the ghostly, whoop-whooping call of the bird Leopoldo called ruru.

His head was tipped back, his eyes were closed and his breath was rattling in his chest like dice in a cup. Removing her bonnet, Dorothea laid a hand on his brow for a few minutes, then took a thermometer from a leather case in her bag, shook it hard, and inserted it into a corner of his mouth. 'The lantern,' she ordered, and Luigi brought it over. Withdrawing the glass tube, she squinted at it. 'One hundred and four degrees,' she announced, in her strongly accented voice. 'Very high.' Then she took a rubber instrument with silver cones attached to each end of it, placed one cone on Leopoldo's chest, the other to her right ear, inclined her head and listened, like a bird on a lawn. Leopoldo groaned, then began to cough again, his body racking with the effort. Removing the cones, Dorothea turned to Luigi. 'Fluid. There iss fluid in hiss lungs.'

'That is causing the fever?'

'Yes. I would say the lung tissue iss infected.'

'Pneumonia?' A deadly word. The illness had claimed his grandmother.

'Yes. And possibly, pleurisy.'

Luigi froze. 'What is that?'

'A svelling of the membrane surrounding the lungs.'

Staring at Leopoldo's concave chest, hearing the rattling breath, Luigi felt as if his insides were turning to water. 'Do you have a treatment?' he said, weakly.

Mouth crimping, she turned away. 'Only a linctus. To ease his breathing.'

Feeling his helplessness growing, Luigi said, 'We could make a poultice. With linseed and muslin. Heat it over the fire and place it on his chest.'

'It would not help. The infection iss too deep.'

She took a flat-sided bottle from her bag and withdrew the cork. Luigi fetched a spoon and she filled it with the dark, viscous fluid, tilted Leopoldo's head back and poured it into his mouth. His Adam's apple gave a spasm as the liquid passed down his gullet, and he began to pant like an overheated dog. Standing back, Dorothea said, in a softer voice, 'I will leave more of the linctus with you. Give him one spoonful every hour he iss awake. But if he sleeps, do not wake him.'

They stood outside the door. Sensing the strength and commonsense within the woman's small, wiry frame, he asked her, 'Will he recover?'

Her voice was clipped. 'I am not a doctor, Luigi. I bring children into the world. And zat is not illness. So I cannot say.' He held the lantern up, so that he could see her face, and her pale cheeks turned a creamy shade under its light. 'You should give him plenty of fluids. Sweet tea, hot soup, a mixture of sugar and varm water. That may help to vash the infection away, and give him some strength.'

Declining Luigi's offer to return with her to the house, she asked only that he lend her the lantern for the return journey. Passing it over, he asked her, knowing that pay day was still a week away, 'What is your charge, Mrs Heveldt?'

A small smile unpursed her mouth. 'Joseph has a fondness for smoked fish.'

'I'll bring you smoked kahawai. As soon as I can.'

She nodded, curtly. And with lantern in one hand and bag in the other, the small, darkly-clad figure slipped off back into the bush.

It was just after dawn, three days later, when he breathed for the last time. Luigi held his hand as cool light streamed into the room through the window at the foot of the bed. His breathing had grown more grating during the night, catching on every third inhalation, followed by a deepening clatter in his thorax, and a feeble cry of despair that tore at Luigi's heart. Leopoldo's hands would move over his ribs, as if trying to wipe away some unseen contamination there, while his mouth and nostrils leaked mayonnaise-coloured mucus. Then, abruptly, he went into a spasm, back arching, head falling back, mouth agape as the terrible rattle came. Then there was a long, almost satisfied sigh, and he was still.

Taking both Leopoldo's bony hands in his, Luigi bent his head and murmured the words, 'Subvenite, Sancti Dei, occurrite, Angeli Domini. Suscipientes animam ejus: Offerentes eam in conspectus Altissimi. Suscipiat te Christus, qui vocavit te, et in sinum Abrahae deducant te.'

Although both men had long lost the faith, Luigi well knew that Leopoldo's family – his mother, a brother and sister were still alive – would be comforted by the knowledge that the Latin rite had been performed. Then he brought down the lids, covering the glazed eyes, and with a damp cloth wiped his mouth and nose. Still holding Leopoldo's hands, his own eyes shut fast, he felt tears leaking from the lids and running down his face as the heartbreak that was Leopoldo's life overwhelmed him. The dream that had taken him across the world, the losses and despair that had resulted, the hopes that had been shattered. Would it have been better had he never left Pesaro? Would it then not have come to this? Opening his streaming eyes, Luigi stared at the silent face, his sight blurred as if under water. *No*, he told himself. Leopoldo had done what he had had to do. He had come to the end of the Earth, and in spite of everything, had done what he could to make a new life. And for these last few years he had known a kind of contentment. The two of them had hewn out a rough sort of life here, on this remote but wildly beautiful coast. 'I'm so pleased you came, Luigi,' he once said, soon after he had arrived, when they were traipsing home from a day's fishing. 'It's meant so much to me.' He had said it only once, because there was no need to say it again. Luigi knew, as Leopoldo knew, that together they had fashioned a kind of life which separately they could never have. And now, that dual life was over.

Releasing Leopoldo's hands from his own, Luigi laid them carefully by his side, then drew up the blanket so that it covered the body. Now he thought of practicalities. As well as lacking a doctor, there was no cemetery, church or consecrated ground anywhere in the settlement. The dead were buried wherever the living thought they should be. Luigi knew where this was, but he would still have to notify Macfarlane, and register the passing with him.

Outside the house, with Leopoldo's land still covered in cool shadows, he went to look for timber to build a coffin. As he did so, it began to rain.

He selected a place on higher ground, behind the house, beyond the spread of the swamp. It was necessary to clear the manuka before a decent space could be made, and their roots made digging the grave difficult, cloying the spade so that an axe had to be brought to bear as well. Then he struck yellow clay at about the three foot mark, which stuck to the spade like toffee. But after some hours the pit was finished. He washed, went inside, put on fresh clothes and waited for Joseph and Dorothea Heveldt to arrive. Leopoldo's coffin lay open in the centre of the room, on two butter boxes. Built of kahikatea lengths, he had nailed it together as firmly as he could, trimming the ends with the hand saw and backing the lid with battens so that it would not easily dislodge. And instead of a cross, he had taken a slab of black beech, cut its corners at one end and on it had laboriously routed with Leopoldo's sturdy penknife the words,

Leopoldo Antonio
VITALI
Born Pesaro, Italy, 1857
Died Okuru, Westland, 1888

He took a pot of caulking tar and worked it into the routed letters and numbers with his forefinger, so that the inscription stood out strongly against the pale brown wood. Then he sank the slab deep into the ground at the head of the grave.

Joseph and Dorothea wore their most formal clothing, he in a dark three-piece suit and black tie, she in matching bonnet and dress with

a high white lace collar. Luigi had made himself a tie out of a leftover
piece of black satin which he had used to make curtains for the house
windows, shaved carefully and polished his boots. He and Joseph carried
the coffin outside and set it on the ground beside the grave, then the three
of them stood at its head, hats in hands. Luigi began with the rite, this
time in English, for the sake of Joseph and Dorothea, whom he knew
to be Lutherans.

'Come to his assistance, o saints of God. Meet him o angels of the
Lord, receiving his soul, offering it in the sight of the Most High. May
Christ who has called you receive you, and may the angels conduct you
into the bosom of Abraham.'

He paused for a few moments, relieved to have the formal invocation
dealt with, then added, 'This is to farewell my lifelong friend, Leopoldo
Antonio Vitali, who came to this land in search of a new life. He found
that new life, even though it was hard and short. Too short. But not too
hard. Leopoldo did his best at everything he tried. And he was a loyal
friend, who always shared what he had.' Remembering the secret that he
himself had not shared, the one buried in the ground not a dozen yards
from where he stood, Luigi's voice broke. Looking up, he saw Leopoldo's
gaunt face, heard again his heartfelt words – *I am so glad that you came,
Luigi* – and it was some moments before he could continue. Then he
declared, chokingly, 'Farewell, friend.'

Joseph, bald but handsome, towering over his petite wife, coughed
twice, then said in his thick Pomeranian accent, 'My wife and I knew
Leopoldo since he arrived at Okuru. He vas our neighbour, and a good
man. He worked hard to farm hiss land, and it vass not his fault zat hiss
plants did not grow.' There was a pause, then he intoned, 'Jesus Christ
our Lord, look after Leopoldo for us.' Dorothea's head bobbed as if it was
on a spring, and her lip trembled before she added, 'Yes, Lord, please take
care of our friend and neighbour, Leopoldo. He vass a good man.'

Luigi and Joseph picked up the ropes which were slung beneath the
coffin. Then, holding them at each end, they stood on each side of the
grave and lowered it in, Luigi struggling under its weight, Joseph perfectly
upright and unstraining, as if lowering an empty bucket into a well. Luigi
went inside and fetched his accordion. Standing at the side of the grave,
he pumped air into its bellows, then began to play the tune that seemed
to him doubly suitable, as it was one of Leopoldo's favourites.

'La donna e mobile
qual piuma al vento
muta d'accento
e di pensiero

Sempre unamabile
leggiadro viso
in pianto o in riso
é menzognero ...'

Each of the three witnesses picked up a handful of damp earth and in turn threw it into the grave, murmuring Leopoldo's name as they did so. 'I'll fill the grave later,' Luigi told Joseph and Dorothea. 'For now, come inside and eat.'

He had prepared plates of smoked kahawai and fritters from the whitebait he had caught that morning, scones baked over the fire, apples bought from the store, and a pot of tea. Dorothea had made and brought a duck egg sponge cake, covered in whipped cream and wild blackberries. They sat at the table and talked of Leopoldo, Luigi describing their early life together in Pesaro, Joseph and Dorothea telling of his time with the other Italians, then Tui, as they had all struggled to make a new life for themselves amid the dripping bush.

They sat in a reflective silence for a time, then Joseph said, 'And now, you, Luigi, vot are you going to do? Stay here in Okuru, I think, ja?'

Although Luigi nodded, the gesture was more convincing than he really felt. Leopoldo's death had changed everything.

Later that day, the grave filled, its mound covered with leaves to soften the yellowness of the clay, the headboard firmly in place, Luigi went to where the kahikatea plank was. Brushing aside the leaves that covered it, he lifted the plank and took out the earthenware jar. First weighing it in his hand, feeling its heaviness, he took it inside and unclipped the lid. The golden flecks lay there, almost glowing in the half light. Weighing it in his hand again, he tried to guess the weight. Four ounces? Five perhaps. He tilted the jar and carefully poured some of the flakes into the palm of his left hand. They gleamed back at him, like shining eyes. Four, five ounces. There lay his fortune. His future now lay elsewhere.

The little steamer, *Stella*, was standing off the bay, half a mile out from the shore, dark smoke pouring from its single stack. He was rowed out in a lighter by two crew members, after they had waited for three hours for the wind to ease so that the boat could safely cross the bar at the river mouth. Luigi sat in the stern with a Polish couple who had abandoned their land at Arawata: he brooding and silent, her cheeks rosy, eyes bright at the certainty of their leaving.

Earlier he had farewelled his workmates, Aubrey and Claude and Bruce, over tankards of ale in the Excelsior hotel. Although they slapped his back and shook his hand and wished him good luck, he could tell from their troubled expressions, from the way their eyes slid away from his, that they felt he was abandoning them. 'You write to us, Luigi,' Claude ordered gruffly, as they waited for the lighter to be loaded. 'Let us know where you are.'

'And we'll write back, and tell you how the road's going,' said Aubrey.

'And how the rain's still fallin',' added Bruce.

Then he and the other men fell into an uneasy silence, which clung around them like an odour.

The two rowers were straining against the incoming tide, spray soaking their backs as the boat pitched into the dark blue swells, the rowlocks creaking. Turning, Luigi saw the spindrift streaming from the backs of the waves, saw the gulls wheeling above the estuary. Already the land's features were receding into the mist. He saw the dark green mat of forest, the bush-covered hump that was Mt Mark, the unbroken rampart of snow-capped peaks that shut the rest of the world off from Jackson Bay. Turning up the collar of his oilskin against the chill wind, he wrapped his arms around himself. As he did so he felt the hard lump inside his jacket, and his left arm lingered there, reassured by the bulge and its weight.

S I X

Luigi studied the man's every move. An eye-shade covered his forehead, the mouth below his trimmed moustache was tightly set and his long fingers gripped the jar as he poured its contents onto one of the scales' brass dishes. Then he carefully added weights to the other dish, stacking them up into a tiny, tapered pyramid. As the scales came gradually into equilibrium, Luigi stared at the little yellow cone. Looking intently at the scales' needle, the man scribbled something on a note-pad, then added one more miniscule weight. He looked up at Luigi, his eyes half hidden by the shade above them. The two men's eyes met, and locked. There was mutual but unspoken mistrust there. They both knew what everyone knew, that no one could be fully trusted when the colour came between them. But the assay office was official, its officer a government employee, Luigi reminded himself. If he could not trust this man, who else could he trust? Wetting his lips, he flicked his eyes to the needle. A fraction over five ounces. His mind began to spin so hard so hard he couldn't do the figures. But it was a fortune, that much he realised.

The man raised his head, so that his eyes became fully visible. They were small, green and hard, like pieces of greenstone. 'Five ounces, one dram,' he announced, flatly. Luigi's heart accelerated. *More than he had thought.*

'And what is the price you pay?'

'Forty-five pounds per ounce.'

'Good.' *Higher than he had thought.*

'You want to sell it all?'

'Yes.'

'Very well.'

He took a small canvas bag from under the counter, and a writing pad.

Removing the weights carefully, he said, 'Your claim certificate, please.'

'My claim …'

'Certificate. Your prospecting licence. I need to record its number.'

'I don't have it.'

'Why not?'

'I lost it. At Okuru.'

'Well mate, you don't have your certificate, you can't cash in your colour. That's the law.'

'But I told you, the licence is lost.'

'Where was it issued?'

'Hokitika.'

'When?'

'Seven years ago.'

'From the assay office there?'

'Yes.'

'Then you'll have to get a replacement copy and bring it back here.'

'There is no other way?'

'No.'

'Then I will get another licence.'

'Right-o. Do you want me to hang on to the gold for you? In the meantime?'

'No, no. I'll take it with me. Please, put it back in the jar.'

The Ship & Castle was a two-storeyed hotel at the seaward end of Palmerston Street, the first place Luigi had come across after *Stella* had berthed at the Westport wharf. He had booked into the hotel, then walked up and down the main street of the town. For a time the shops and people and the general busyness of the place had disconcerted him, and he had wandered up and down the street, wondering at it all. People, carriages, horses and carts. Proper shops, with plentiful goods for sale. Leaving Okuru and arriving in Westport was like returning from a long stay on the moon.

Now he sat on the bed in the small upstairs hotel room, holding the priceless, useless jar in his hands. His negligence had rebounded on him. No licence, no payout. He had lied to the man because he had feared for the consequences if his failure to get a licence was known. So now he had a fortune, but one which could not be redeemed. What use was gold on its own? Even if he went to Hokitika and got a licence, the man would see the dates and discover his lie. He remembered as a boy reading the legend of Midas, and how his greed had been his downfall. Now, he too had become a kind of Midas. *Fool*, he told himself, you should have known, you should have told Aubrey you wanted him to get a licence *in case* you ever wanted to prospect.

Unclipping the lid of the jar, he stared at the yellow flakes. Still, gold was gold, and he now knew exactly what it was worth. Somebody would want it, somebody would want to exchange his colour for money. But he would have to be cautious. When the real gold rush was on, anyone holding gold became a target, they had told him back at Okuru. He must be discreet, he must be patient, he must bide his time. At least he had enough cash, saved from his last road gang pay, to keep him for a couple of weeks.

A man in a frock coat and top hat was thumping the piano as Luigi descended the stairs and entered the bar. There were about twenty people in the room, standing about drinking or sitting at tables playing cards. The bar was gas-lit, carpeted and smoke-filled. The patrons were mostly men, although a trio of young women was sitting at a table near the big fireplace, where a coal fire was burning. Luigi bought an ale and began to sip it. Then, striking up a conversation with the barman, he told him he was an accordionist and asked if he could play a tune or two. The man nodded. 'Fine with me, mate, but you'd better ask Henry first.'

'Henry?'

'Henry Rawlinson. The manager. That's him, over there, dealing the cards.'

He waited until the game was over and the manager came across to the bar, then introduced himself and made him the offer. The manager looked him up and down imperiously, frowning as he took in Luigi's well-worn clothes. Henry Rawlinson had black curly hair, a smooth, well-fleshed, slightly florid face and prominent lips. His coal-black beard was neatly trimmed. 'Where're you from?' he said curtly.

'From Italy, then Okuru. I'm staying here. My accordion is in my room, upstairs.'

The manager nodded. Extracting a cigarette from a silver holder, he said a little less tersely, 'Well, you'd better get it then, and show us what you can do.'

He played a couple of songs, without singing the words, then when he noticed the patrons' appreciative looks and tapping toes, broke into song. As the small audience applauded, one of the women brought him a glass of beer. She handed it over, Luigi bowed low, and everyone laughed. Henry Rawlinson approached him, grinning.

'Okay mate, you can play all right. How long are you here for?'

'I am not sure. If I did play, what will you pay me?'

The manager gave him a long look, made a smacking sound with his big lips, then declared, 'Customers'll like your playing. So I'll halve your board. Two and sixpence a week instead of five bob. If you play on Thursdays, Fridays and Saturdays.' He looked at Luigi sternly. 'What d'you say?'

'I will do it.'

The first night he played until nearly midnight. Hearing the strains of his accordion from the street, people walked in, bought drinks and leaned on the bar to listen. Henry Rawlinson, Luigi noticed, watched very closely those who came and went, from his card table. A hearty man, Henry seemed to know everyone in Westport. While he was playing, Luigi observed Henry and his card-playing cronies, all smoking heavily as they dealt and held their hands at the reserved table under the window. Henry laughed and quipped constantly as he played, but when it came to money, Luigi could tell that he knew what he was doing. Invariably it was Henry who wore the biggest grin when the evening was over. And as Luigi played and sang and watched the manager at work, it occurred to him that Henry Rawlinson may be of help in another way.

There was a soft knock on the bedroom door. Turning over, Luigi focused on his watch, hanging by its chain from the bed-head. Six o'clock. He'd been dreaming that he was travelling by train from Pesaro to Bologna, and that Violetta was waving to him from a wheat field. When the knock came again, he sat up, blinking away the vestiges of his dream.

'Yes? Who is it?'

'Your cup of tea, sir.'

'Oh. Just a moment.'

Dashing to the door, he unlocked it, then got back into bed.

'Come in.'

The door opened.

She carried a wooden tray over to the table under the window. On it was a tea pot, a tea cup, a small jug and a sugar bowl. 'Milk and sugar, sir?'

'Please. One sugar.'

He watched her profile as she carefully poured milk into the cup, then picked up the pot and filled it, moving purposefully as she carried out the small domestic task. Her dark brown hair was tied up on top of her head, and crowned with a small white bonnet. There was a frilly white apron over her dark blue dress, which was drawn in tightly at the waist. Then, as she turned to bring the cup over to him, he saw her face more clearly in the half-light. It was oval shaped and pale, with a straight nose and a small, shapely mouth. She was sixteen, seventeen perhaps. Sitting up, tugging at the sleeves of his night-shirt self-consciously, he took the cup from her, and as he did so their eyes met.

Her gaze was direct and confident, her large grey eyes twinkled as she sensed his awkwardness. But as he took the cup, he could not take his eyes from her face. Her eyebrows, though thick, were fair, accentuating the beauty of her eyes. And in some way her face seemed familiar. She turned away. Although not tall, she had a shapely figure and an upright bearing. Moving back to the table under the window, she said, 'I enjoyed your playing, last night.'

'Were you there? I didn't see you.'

'I was in the kitchen, dealing with the dinner dishes. And I looked around the door.' She gave a little laugh, which to him sounded delightful. 'I listened for ages. What language were you singing in?'

'Italian.'

'You are from Italy?'

'Yes. But I left there years ago.'

She was facing him now, straight-backed, gripping the tray in her hands. He still hadn't touched his tea. Instead, he asked her, 'Do you live in the hotel too?'

'No. With my parents.'

'In the town?'

'Yes. My father is a bootmaker.'

In that instant, and as she began to move away, he remembered when he had first seen that face, first felt that directness in her question: *What is your name?* It was her, the woman-like child, the daughter of the churlish bootmaker. He'd never forgotten that face. Now she was truly a woman, and so lovely, so graceful.

'You're Alice.'

She froze. 'How did you know my name?'

'I bought boots, from your father. You were there in his shop.' At her still puzzled look, he added, 'It was some years ago.'

'Fancy remembering that,' she said, frowning now.

'You asked me my name. That is how I remember.'

'Oh.'

Still frowning, deep in thought at this unexpected revelation, she moved towards the door. Tendrils of hair were curling up from the nape of her neck, above the collar of her dress, the only untidy thing about her. When she reached the half-opened door, she paused there and in a brighter voice asked,

'Will you be playing again?'

'Yes. Three nights a week.'

'How long are you here for?'

'I don't know.'

She stood stock still, staring at him for a few moments, appearing to absorb something deeply, the frown once more creasing her forehead. Then she moved through the door, closing it quickly behind her.

By day he fished with a hand-line from the wharf at the seaward end of the town, beyond the area where the railway wagons discharged their loads of coal onto the coastal steamers. Returning to the Ship & Castle, he presented his catch – cod, gurnard and terakihi – to Mrs O'Rourke, who ran the hotel's kitchen. In the evenings on three days a week he played his accordion, alternating with Albert Wells, the man who played the piano. During the daylight hours, Luigi carried everywhere with him, at the bottom of his rucksack, the little jar of gold. At night he slept with it at the foot of the bed, where his toes could touch it, and before the hotel maid, Alice, brought him his tea at daybreak, the jar would be back in the rucksack, hanging from a hook on the back of the door.

'Good morning.'

'Good morning Alice.'

'Raining again.'

'I'm used to it. In Okuru it always rained.'

'What did you do there?'

'I was a road worker.'

'Did you play the accordion there too?'

'Sometimes.'

'I didn't hear you last night, I went home early. My mother is unwell.'

'Oh, I'm sorry.'

'Yes. She has catarrh, the doctor said.'

Her anxiety showed as she handed him his tea. There was a scattering of light freckles across the tops of her cheeks, just below her grey eyes, and her hands were smooth and white, in spite of the kitchen work. Her waist was tightly drawn in, the outline of her breasts obvious. He longed to reach out and touch her face, to stroke her cheeks, to gather in the wisps of hair at the back of her neck, to put his lips on hers. Instead, taking the cup, he said, 'Thank you.'

As she retreated to the end of the bed, he added, 'I hope your mother will be better soon.'

'She's to stay in bed for five days, the doctor said.'

'It's miserable, being sick.'

'Yes.'

She picked up the tray, stood for a moment, looking at him with her unwavering gaze. Thinking of her mother, or him? He could see her chest rising and falling, the lovely contours of her body. He wanted to hold her so much that his own body ached. But he dared not touch her, for fear that she would rebuff his advance. After all, at fourteen years her senior, he must seem closer to her father's age. And yet, each time she appeared in his room, or he saw her watching him play, he could sense something growing between them, a tentative intimacy, a shared but yet undeclared secret.

'Alice …'

'Yes?'

'When is your free day?'

'From here?'

'Yes.'

'Monday is my day off.'

'I wonder. Would you like to walk with me? Next Monday?'

'Walk? Where to?'

'Carter's Beach.'

Knowing a declaration had now been made, feeling his heart accelerating, he held his breath. Her cheeks had coloured very slightly, and she was staring at him, evidently giving the question deep consideration. After what seemed to him a great lapse of time, she said carefully,

'Thank you. I would like to.'

'Shall I come to your house for you?'

'No, no,' she replied, quickly. 'I will meet you here.'

'What time would suit you?'

'Two o'clock in the afternoon. Outside the front door.'

'All right.' He smiled. 'If it isn't raining.'

And he thought, as he watched her leave the room in her usual calm manner, *I have done it. And she did not refuse me.*

'Mr Rawlinson?'

'Henry, to you Luigi. To you and everyone.'

'Henry. I would like to talk to you.'

'Talk away.'

'Somewhere privately.'

'Would my office do?'

'Yes.'

The manager's office was behind the reception counter in the hotel foyer. A small, wood-panelled room, its only embellishment was a gilt-framed oil painting of a scene that Luigi recognised as the Buller River, below Hawks Crag. Beckoning him to a swivel chair in front of a large oak desk, Henry Rawlinson took the seat on the other side, offered Luigi a cigarette from his silver case, which he accepted, then lit it and his own. Smoke billowed around Henry's rubicund face for a few moments, then he said amiably, 'Well, what's the problem, Louie? Not thinking of moving on, I hope. The customers like your playing.'

'No, it is not that. I like it here.' He paused for a moment to allow this small, mutual pledge to settle between them, then continued. 'It is some advice that I need.'

'What about?'

'This.'

Luigi reached inside his jacket and drew out the jar. Unclipping the wire that held the lid in place, he pushed the jar across the desk towards the manager. Henry's head came forward and he peered inside. Luigi saw his jaw drop a little, watched him moisten his lips. He picked the jar up with one hand, then, eyes fixed firmly on it, weighed it up and down.

'How much?'

'Just over five ounces.'

'Where's it from?'

'Jackson Bay.'

'Why are you showing it to me?'

'Because I would like you to buy it.'

'Why not the assay office?'

'Because … I did not have a prospecting licence.'

Looking up quickly, Henry stared at Luigi, his breath making a low whistling sound. A little knot of muscle, like a walnut, formed between his heavy black eyebrows.

'Five ounces, you said.'

'Yes. I have had it weighed.'

'Where?'

'At the assay office.'

'Where?'

'Here in Westport.'

There was a long pause. Henry took a drag on his cigarette, then set it down in the paua shell ash tray. Steepling his fingers, he stared across the desk, his bushy eyebrows crowding in on the walnut between them.

'What rate would you want?'

'The proper rate.'

'What's that?'

'Forty-five pounds an ounce.'

Taking a pencil from the pot on his desk, Henry scribbled on his blotter pad, then looked up.

'Two hundred and twenty-five pounds.'

'Yes.'

'A lot of money, Louie.'

'It is a lot of gold.'

There was another long silence. Henry swivelled his chair around so that it faced the window, then again drew heavily on his cigarette. Smoke enveloped him for a moment, then drifted away. He placed his left hand on the desk and began to thrum on the blotter with his left hand. Luigi watched him intently, saw the profile of the man's prominent lips, the knotted brow. Knew he was calculating carefully, tried to guess which way he would move. At last the chair rotated back the other way and the manager faced him again. His eyes had noticeably hardened.

'I'd be prepared to pay you forty pounds an ounce.'

'The proper rate is forty-five.'

'My rate's forty. Take it or leave it.'

'But then you could sell the gold for forty-five.'

'That's right.' His lips twisted into a smile, but it was a smile that didn't reach his eyes. 'I've got a prospecting licence, though,' Henry said. 'Had one for years.'

Luigi held his gaze. It was not as though this was unexpected. He had observed from the manager's card-playing that he dealt severely to his opponents. That he would strike a hard bargain was to be expected. And in this case he held the much stronger hand. So why should he, Luigi, be greedy? Forty pounds an ounce would still yield two hundred pounds, a sum of money so vast that he couldn't comprehend it. More than his father had earned in his entire lifetime. With it he could buy a house, and furniture, and a horse and trap, and new clothes, and the latest accordion. He could present himself to Alice Harris as a man of means. A gentleman. Looking at Henry levelly, he said,

'I will accept forty pounds an ounce.'

Getting to his feet quickly, Henry extended his hand. He was grinning, in an almost boyish way. As well he might, Luigi thought, with the quick, effortless profit he would make. Taking the proffered hand, Luigi said, 'How long will it take? To get the money?'

The manager waved his hand airily. 'A day or two.' Sitting down again, he gestured at the jar. 'You leave it with me, and I'll get the weight checked.'

Luigi shook his head. There was no way in the world that he was going to let it out of his sight. 'The weight is exact. Five ounces, one dram. I give you my word.'

Henry groomed his beard with one hand, lifted his chin, considered this. He shrugged. 'Very well. Bring the gold here again the day after tomorrow, at three o'clock.'

'One hundred and eighty …' Luigi said slowly '… two hundred, two hundred and one pounds.'

Carefully he gathered up the sheaf of big ten pound notes, with the smaller one pound notes on top, and tapped them together neatly on the desk. Then he took the jar from his rucksack, holding it in both hands, and passed it over. The two men shook hands. Henry's delight at his purchase was all too obvious through his joviality and flushed cheeks. Yet now that the transaction was complete, Luigi felt no regrets. He had the money. The money which was going to change his life. *Two hundred and one pounds.* Carefully placing the notes back inside the manila envelope, he folded it and tucked it into the inside pocket of his jacket. As he did so Henry reached under his desk, brought out a crystal decanter three-quarters filled with amber fluid, and two small goblets, also of crystal.

'Brandy, Louie?'

'Thank you.'

'A toast then. To us, and the colour.'

'To the colour, and us.'

They both laughed, clinked goblets, and drank. Luigi felt the fluid burning a fiery trail as it made its way down to the pit of his stomach.

He bought a new three-piece suit off the peg at F.Sontgens Outfitters for 21 shillings, a pair of braces, three new shirts, four pairs of socks, three sets of underwear and two neck-ties. He had his hair cut and moustache clipped at Wilsons the Barbers and from a catalogue at C. Smiths Music Shop he ordered the latest model Italian piano accordion – a Cremona – from an importer in Christchurch. Then he crossed the street to John Harris Bootmaker.

'Yes?'

'I would like a new pair of boots. The best you have.'

'Work or leisure?'

'Leisure.'

'Size?'

'Nine.'

As he tried the boot on, he was aware of the man watching him closely. His face seemed fixed in a permanent scowl, as if he was the victim of some terrible injustice. His cheeks were hollow, even gaunt, his skin sallow beneath the patchy beard. His hair had receded markedly and his back was stooped. Again Luigi wondered how such a gloom-filled man could have fathered so lovely a daughter as Alice. Pulling the laces tight, flexing his foot, Luigi said,

'They seem a good fit.'

'They're the best.'

'I bought a pair from you once before. They lasted well.'

'I make good boots.'

'What is the price?'

'Eighteen shillings and six pence.'

Handing a pound note over and waiting for the change, Luigi said, 'Is there a photographer's studio in Westport?'

'Yes. Scotts.'

'Where is that?'

'Palmerston Street. On the left. Next to the Post and Telegraph.' His expression darkened. 'Where are you from?'

'Italy.'

'I thought all you buggers had gone home.'

'This is my home.'

Surprised by the reply, the man half turned away. Luigi noticed that his hands trembled slightly. Sniffing unpleasantly, the bootmaker said, 'So why didn't you leave with the others?'

'Because I like it here.'

'Hold it, hold it. Sit as still as you can, please.' The young man's head disappeared under the black cloth, but his muffled voice continued. 'As still as you can. Oh, just a minute.' He reappeared, dashed to where Luigi was sitting, picked up the dampened brush with which he had already groomed his subject's hair, then carefully stroked the side of his head with it. 'That's better, that's better.' He passed the brush slowly along both sides of Luigi's moustache, then vanished under the black hood once more. 'Yes, yes, that's good, hold it there, just there.' Luigi sat rigid, feeling foolish, but he had promised Violetta he would have it done. On either side of him, on top of plaster pedestals, were hanging ferns in large brass pots; the background was a mural of the Acropolis. Below him, away from the platform, was a mess of cases and boxes and packets.

There was a *woomph!* as the magnesium exploded. Although expecting it, Luigi was still startled by the brilliance. Closing, then re-opening his eyes hard, he said to the photographer, 'I think I blinked.'

Charles Scott's head emerged. Laughing, he said, 'Just after the flash, not during it. Now, stay there – nice and still – and I'll take three more.'

The photographs would be ready by Friday, he was told. Descending the stairs from the upper floor studio, Luigi walked out into the bright sunlight and the main street of the town. Everything he was wearing – from the collar of his shirt to the toes of his new boots – was entirely new. He almost felt like a new man, a man who could confidently court a beautiful young woman. Returning to his hotel room, he placed the manila envelope carefully in the leather pouch below one of his accordion's hand-straps. It was meant to hold sheet music, now it held the balance of his fortune. There was a Bank of New Zealand in Westport's main street, but Luigi didn't wish to open an account there. 'Never trust banks', his father had always said. Not that his father had ever had enough money to deposit any, but it was true that in Italy during and after the revolution, many people had lost their entire savings when the banks had collapsed, causing riots in the major cities. Clipping the pouch closed with its row of domes, Luigi pushed the accordion under the bed, then debated with himself which tie he should wear, the blue or the red.

'Your father seems very unhappy.'

'Yes. My mother worries about him. We all do.'

'It is not my business, really, but I wonder, what is the reason for his unhappiness?'

Alice plucked at the long sleeves of her emerald green, satin dress. As she turned her face into the wind and lifted her chin, he thought yet again how lovely she was. Her face was entirely unpainted, unlike other women he had known, and the only jewellery she wore was a small cameo brooch, pinned to the neck of her dress. Looking down at the sand, she made little patting movements on it with one hand.

'He's very disappointed with his business.'

'But he's the only bootmaker in Westport, isn't he?'

'Yes. But now that there are so many men out of work, he doesn't sell many boots.'

'Times will change. Things will improve, I think.'

'Perhaps.'

There was a sudden gust of wind from the sea, and she quickly put her hand hard down on the top of her straw boater to hold it there until it passed. Then she went on.

'A few years ago he had the chance to go into partnership with another bootmaker. A man from Ireland who'd been a gold miner here on the coast. He moved to Wellington and opened a boot factory and a shop. He wrote to my father and asked him to be his partner in the business. It was already growing, he said. My mother urged father to, but he wouldn't.'

'Why not?'

'He preferred to stay on his own, to be his own boss. He didn't want to work with anyone else.' She tugged at a clump of seagrass. 'The other man's making a lot of money now, everyone says. He's got several shops already.'

'What's his name?'

'Robert Hannah.' She smiled. 'Before he went to Wellington, he married a woman from here called Hannah.' She giggled delightedly. 'So now she's Hannah Hannah.'

They strolled along the beach. Apart from a man galloping a horse in the distance, and a troop of oyster catchers fussing at the water's edge, they had the beach to themselves. It was spring now, but the mountains which loomed above the plain were still coated with snow. Alice stopped, took a green ribbon from her bag and tied it over the top of her hat and under her chin. Still feeling a little awkward in his new clothes, Luigi tugged at the collar of his shirt, which kept riding up around his neck. But it was wonderful to be with her, to talk to her away from the hotel, to listen to her voice and her stories.

As they walked he told her about Pesaro, and the voyage to New Zealand, and the way he and Leopoldo had tried to make a go of things at Jackson Bay. She gave him her full attention as he spoke, only interrupting to ask serious questions. ('Is Italy as beautiful as they say it is?' 'Had your family always lived in Pesaro?' 'Were you the first of your family to migrate?')

More and more he felt himself being drawn to her. It was so long since he had enjoyed this kind of company. He loved the thoughtful way she replied to his questions, her inquisitiveness, her femininity, her sincerity. She seemed much older than sixteen. As they walked on into the wind, she said,

'So why did you leave Pesaro?'

'To start a new life.'

'Was it so bad there?'

'People were very poor, yes.'

'Your family too?'

'Yes. None of my family ever owned a house, or any land.'

'But you had land at Okuru, you said.'

'With Leopoldo, yes. But it was not good land. I want something much better.'

'Italy is a very old country, I know. I read an encyclopaedia of mother's. About the Romans. They built fine roads. And theatres. Outdoor theatres, of stone.'

'Yes. Amphitheatres. There was one in the hills behind Pesaro. Ruined now, but you could still see how grand it had been.'

'How old was it?'

'Probably over two thousand years.'

'I cannot imagine anything as old as that.'

'This might help you to.'

From his waistcoat pocket he took out his Roman coin and handed it to her. 'This is nearly two thousand years old. From the Roman Empire.'

She held it in the palm of her hand, bent her face closer to it, turned it over. 'Is it really that old?'

'Yes. The likeness is of an emperor. Caesar Octavianus. He ruled Rome before the birth of Christ.'

Her mouth hung open, her eyes were staring. After he told her that he had dug it up in their rented garden plot, and that such finds were not uncommon in Italy, and seeing her captivated look, he said, 'You can keep it, Alice.'

Looking up quickly, she shook her head. 'No, I couldn't. It must be very precious to you.'

'I want you to have it.' *Because you are precious to me*, he wanted to add.

'Oh, thank you. Thank you so much.'

Gripping the coin in her hand, she reached up, put her arms around his neck and kissed him lightly on the cheek. Thrilled by the gesture, he longed to take her in his arms and return her kiss, but didn't. It was too soon. Instead, feeling clumsy and embarrassed, he said, 'We had better be going back. Did you tell your parents where you were going?'

'No. I said I was going to see my friend Emily.'

'Why?'

'My father.'

Without warning, she tore off her shoes, threw her head back and broke into a run, hitching up her skirt as she headed towards the low dunes and tussocks above the beach. He watched the bustling, energetic figure for some moments. Then, walking briskly, followed. He found her sitting on a dune, plucking at a tussock flower. She looked anxious, upset even.

'What's wrong, Alice?'

'You're Catholic?'

'Everyone in Italy is Catholic. Why?'

'He hates Catholics.'

'Your father?'

'Yes.'

'I haven't been to mass for years. I have nothing to do with the Catholic church.'

'But you were born Catholic.'

'Yes.'

'Then he will hate you for it.'

'Why?'

'I don't really know the reason. "Papists", he calls them. "Popery", the way they worship.' Her brow became knitted. 'Years ago, here on the coast, there were troubles. Riots, mother told me. Between Protestants and Catholics. The Fenians. He was part of that, on the Protestant side. He was injured by a Fenian. We're Wesleyans, you see. All our family are.'

'The Fenians are Irish, I think. I am not Irish.'

'It wouldn't matter. It's enough that you're from a Catholic country.'

Luigi sat down beside her. The sun had gone behind a cloud and the sea had turned the colour of old pewter. From the endless rows of waves, veils of spray were being torn back seaward.

'Alice, your father need not worry. I have no love for the Roman church, and the Pope has no hold over me.' He had no intention of telling her more. That was the truth of the matter, and it was enough.

But when she turned to look at him her mouth was still crimped, concern still clouding her eyes. He thought she was going to cry. Instead she looked down, and began brushing the sand from her dress with quick little flicking strokes.

'We'd best be getting back. Father will be home from work soon.'

Luigi put his hand over hers and held it there. 'Would it help if I talked to him? If I asked his permission to walk out with you again?'

'*No,*' she said, her eyes filled with alarm. 'Seeing you must stay a secret.'

'Westport is not a good place to keep a secret, I think.'

'That's true.'

As her eyes stared into his, her expression softened. He had a sense then, as he had had before, of the strength and determination which lay behind those eyes. This girl was her own person.

'I like being with you, Luigi. Talking with you.'

Gripping her hand, he allowed a long pause before he said, 'I can't help being born what I was, Alice.' He laughed, sardonically. 'It was not my choice.'

Taking a small handkerchief from inside her sleeve, she dabbed at her nose. 'I understand that. But he won't. It seems that he hates anyone who is not just like himself. Catholics, Maoris, foreigners. He is so bitter.'

'And your mother?'

'She stays silent, mostly. His bitterness frightens her, I think.'

Both of them fell into a long silence as they allowed the hurtful truth to sink in. The differences between them were so great. Religion, nationality, age. Too great? Certainly. After a time Alice got to her feet, smoothed the front of her dress, then stood rigid, inhaling deeply as she stared out to sea. Watching her chest rising and falling, he so much wanted to hold her, to tell her honestly how much she was coming to mean to him. But he felt also that his love for her was hopeless. There was just too much between them.

When at last she turned to him again, her eyes were glistening. 'I must be getting back now,' she said.

She walked quickly down the slope of the dunes and onto the damp sand, Luigi following, his heart like a lump of lead in his chest.

THE DIRECTORIES

From time to time in the evenings, William returned to the laser copy he had had made of Gina's photograph of Luigi Galoni. The handsome, thoughtful young man in the suit and tie stared back at him enigmatically. There was no clue as to the subject's time or place. Then he remembered, there *was* one. Opening his notebook, he found the reference he'd made. Scotts Photography. Was it possible, he wondered, to find the location of a nineteenth century business, if one had only its name?

'You could try the Wises Directories,' a woman at the National Library suggested, and showed him where they were shelved. Hard-bound books published biennially, they listed names and occupations, by districts, of nineteenth century citizens. But William had no idea in which island – let alone which town – the photograph might have been taken. He would have to go through them all.

Starting with the 1879-80 Directory, William went through the alphabetical lists of places and names, working his way from Auckland to Whangarei and all towns in between. The same male occupations kept recurring: farmer, farm labourer, millhand, storekeeper, bootmaker, carpenter, clerk. The few women listed had only two: clerical assistant or nurse. How simple society must have been at that time, he thought. As for the name Scott, well, it was far from uncommon. Three cropped up in the first directory, one in Taihape ('bank clerk'), one in Oamaru ('stone mason') and one in Nelson ('farm labourer'). Moving through the rest of the 1880s directories, he found no Scott listed as 'Photographer'. The last volume on the shelf was 1888-89.

He worked his way through the thick, hard-back book, starting with Auckland and moving on through the alphabet. Again the towns were peppered with Scotts. In Motueka there was a 'Scott, Gabriel, hotelkeeper', in Taupo there was a 'Scott, Anthony, labourer', in Wanganui a 'Scott, Wilfred, railway worker', and in Westport ...

He stopped, peered, placed his forefinger under a name. 'Scott, Charles, photographer'. Palmerston Street, Westport. That must be it, there was no other. But to make sure, he moved on quickly to 'Whangarei' and scrolled down the names.

There was no Scott, photographer, listed there.

As he noted down the name and place, William felt a surge of hope. Luigi Galoni had been in Westport, some time in the 1880s. Checking to see if 'Galoni, Luigi', appeared in Westport's list, he found that it didn't. Whatever occupation he may have had, Wises hadn't listed it. And when he checked the Westland electoral rolls, Luigi's name was not listed there, either. Did that mean he'd just been visiting Westport? And if so, why? In this game, it seemed, a clue didn't lead to the solution, only more questions.

SEVEN

The soft knock on his door came twice, three times. He turned, opened his eyes. Darkness, broken only by the faintest glimmer of light, coming through the little gap between the brocade curtains. He closed his eyes again. He had imagined the sound, daylight was still some time away. Then he heard it again. Two low knocks. Reaching for his watch, he brought it close to his face. A quarter past five. Much too early for his morning cup of tea. So? He got out of bed, went to the door, drew back the bolt.

'Alice, what?'

'Shhh.'

Moving swiftly, she slipped into the room, closed the door behind her and slid home the bolt. There was no tray in her hands, no tea pot or cup. The bonnet she was wearing was tied under her chin, and came well over her forehead and eyes. She untied it hurriedly, threw it aside, then stood before him, face upraised, looking up into his eyes. Then she came forward, put her arms around him, laid her head on his chest and began to cry, softly, almost soundlessly. He held her against him, feeling through his nightshirt her body shuddering against his. Bending his face to her ear, he said in a whisper, 'What is it, Alice?'

She drew back for a few moments, searching his face again, blinking away tears. Swallowing hard, eyes burning, defiant. 'I need you,' she said, almost angrily. 'I want to love you. I want to *be with you* ...'

Later, among all the other recollections, he was to recall that time – after he undressed her and led her to the bed – as a series of opposites. Fierce and gentle, hard and soft, clumsy and dextrous, swift and slow, all-consuming, all-giving. All the time he lay above her, feeling her body moving with him and against him, he was aware of her eyes staring into his, and commanding, whenever his own gaze wavered, '*Look at me! Look at me!* And when the first time he entered her and caused her to cry out and he hesitated then, not wishing to hurt her more, she urged him again, '*No!* Stay there. *Stay there!* It'll be all right, it'll be all right! Oh, Luigi, Luigi …'

Until at last, their naked bodies streaming, exhausted but elated, they lay side by side, covered with a single sheet, inhaling the fragrance they had themselves created, listening to each other's slow breathing, watching the light behind the curtains grow stronger, as if the wick of a gigantic lamp was being turned up on their world.

'How old are you?' she murmured, her inclined head on his chest. It was something they had never talked about till now.

'Thirty. And you?'

'Seventeen.' She paused. 'Well, almost seventeen. In three months' time.'

He ran his finger down her cheek, collecting tiny beads of sweat as it moved across her warm skin.

'Is there an English word which means floating on air?'

'I don't know of such a word. Why?'

'Because I am floating on air. Like a gull. Or a falcon.'

'I think a falcon is nicer. Gulls are vulgar.'

'A falcon, then. Alice ...'

Propping himself up on one elbow, he stared down at her. Her hair was loose and damp at the edges, her eyes shining, the pupils still dilated, her entire expression calmly radiant. And as he looked at her, it was as if their minds as well as their bodies had become one. He felt the way she looked. Now, he could read her thoughts. It was as if they were the very first to have found so much in each other, the first to have given to each other so utterly, the first to have ever loved. Gently stroking the wet hair away from her forehead, he put his lips there. 'I didn't think there could ever be such happiness.' Drawing the sheet back, he gazed with wonder on her pale body, then lovingly anointed each of her still-firm nipples with his lips. He loved her entirely, utterly, he could not exist without her.

She reached up, put her arms around his neck and drew him down to her. '*I want to stay with you, Luigi*,' she whispered, more resolutely than he had ever heard another human speak. Her lips were on his face, his neck, his chest. Then, to his consternation, her hold on him suddenly relaxed. 'I have to go now,' she said. She slipped from the bed, and while he watched, speechless with awe, she collected up her clothing, dressed quickly, and a minute later was gone.

'Louie!'

He turned. It was Henry Rawlinson, walking briskly along the street towards him. His face was flushed, his bowler hat at a rakish angle. Taking the hat off, he fell into step with Luigi. 'How's the fishing?' he asked.

'It is good.' Luigi held up the sugar-bag. 'Seven gurnard, three terakihi.'

'Excellent. Mrs O'Rourke'll have it on the menu tonight.' Then, looking up towards the distant mountains, he said nonchalantly, 'Are you doing anything this Wednesday evening?'

'No. I don't play on Wednesdays. That is Albert's night on the piano.'

'Ah, yes, of course.' He set his hat back on his head. 'Well, as you're not working, I'd like to invite you to be my guest at a special evening.'

'What sort of evening?'

'A few friends of mine, talking and drinking. The drinks are on me.'

'Where?'

'In the billiards saloon.'

'Oh.'

He had heard the staff talking about Mr Rawlinson's gentlemen's evenings, held in his private billiards room at the rear of the hotel's ground floor, but he'd never expected to be invited to one of them. The people invited were a group of the town's businessmen, the same ones Henry played cards with in the lounge on other evenings of the week. The manager clapped his hand on Luigi's shoulder. 'Now you're a man of means, you've earned the right to join us.' In a lowered voice, he said, 'Have you decided yet how to invest your capital?'

Feeling a little foolish in having to admit it, Luigi replied shortly, 'No.'

'All the more reason to come along. My friends are influential men. They could help you invest it.' He kept his hand on Luigi's shoulder.

Feeling a little abashed now about his fish bag and the smell coming from it, Luigi considered the offer. He couldn't deny that the invitation flattered him. The men who met in the billiards room were a select group, everyone attached to the Ship & Castle knew that. Even the mayor of the town – Joseph Carter – sometimes went. So, if Alice's father heard that he, Luigi Galoni, had been invited to socialise in that company, he could be impressed. An elevation like that might begin to remove some of the obstacles to his and Alice's relationship. Already Luigi was planning to ask for her hand in marriage, regardless of John Harris's prejudices. And there was the matter of the money. Henry was right, he needed to think about investing it, he couldn't just keep it hidden in his accordion for much longer. He'd been thinking he might buy a fishing boat, or an investment in one of the timber mills along the coast.

'So, what do you think?'

'Thank you, Henry,' he said, 'I will be there.'

'Luigi Galoni – Albert Cartwright, Dermot O'Connor, Oliver Chetwin, Edward Smithers, George Anderson, Charles Dalgety, Marcus Coulston ...'

Luigi shook hands with them all, relieved that he had decided to wear his new suit. The men were dressed in frock coats, smoking the small cigars that Henry had handed around, and sipping brandy from crystal goblets. The room had a coal fire burning in one corner and, in the middle, a billiards table, its baize top lit by a gas lamp dangling from the pressed-zinc ceiling directly above it. There was a door in the wall next to the fireplace, and a brandy decanter and more crystal goblets standing on an oak sideboard under the room's one window, which looked out to the yard and stables at the rear of the hotel. Adorning the walls were several oil paintings with heavy gilt frames, of semi-naked voluptuous women, reclining on beds in extravagantly decorated bedrooms.

The soiree was informal, in spite of the frock coats. Two men were engaged in a game of billiards, and while they waited their turn the others stood around smoking, drinking, chatting, or contemplating the nudes on the walls. None of the women in the paintings, Luigi noted, were as lovely as Alice. But he felt encouraged by the way the others talked to him and made enquiries as to his plans. It was as if his presence in the room, and the knowledge that it had been sanctioned by Henry Rawlinson, had automatically conveyed social acceptance upon him. Clearly too, the well-established prosperity of these businessmen had been little dented by the end of the good economic times for the general population.

Warmed on the inside by the brandy and on the outside by the coal fire, Luigi felt his confidence growing. Although he made no direct reference to his capital, he did raise the question of investments in a general way with George Anderson, who ran the town's printery. Anderson was about 40, a lanky, affable fellow with fluffy sideburns. He ground his teeth with concentration as Luigi spoke of his plans.

'I am thinking of buying a fishing boat. Steam-powered, so I can fish well off the coast. With a crew of two, to help me with the lines.'

Anderson considered this for a moment, looking doubtful. 'Too risky, if you ask me. The coast's so exposed to the south-westerlies.' He plucked at a sideburn. 'I'd say milling's the way to go. When the depression's over, there'll be a big demand for rimu, in Christchurch and Nelson. Wellington, too. Timber's there for the taking, thousands of acres of it. Cheap right now, too.' Sipping his brandy, he added thoughtfully, 'Mind you, the expense of shipping it out's still there. But a railway'll solve that problem. When it comes.'

Luigi had not found himself in such company before, and these businessmen of Westport intrigued him. Along with their heartiness, their 'hail-fellow-well-met' manner, there was something else they possessed in common, something he thought gainsaid their bonhomie – wariness, alertness, calculation. Throughout all the chortling and the back-slapping, the men watched one another guardedly, like seagulls on a beach waiting for picnic food. Noticing this watchfulness, Luigi thought it probably explained the success of these self-made men. Self-made men. He liked that English expression, because he, Luigi Galoni, was a self-made man too.

'Gentlemen, gentlemen, your attention please.'

Henry's fleshy face was even more florid than usual. Exuding joviality, he raised his glass to the others, then announced loudly, 'At this stage of the evening, I'd like to bring in the wheel of fortune. Any objections?'

The question caused an outbreak of mirth and animation among the men. Along with the guffaws were cries of 'About time', and 'Bring it on, Henry'.

Wheel? What wheel? Luigi wondered. Then he saw Henry open the door next to the fireplace. Behind it was a storeroom, from which he trundled out a simple metal structure on a set of four casters. About a yard in diameter, the wheel had thirty-two steel spokes, each numbered in white lettering on its wooden rim. Bright steel nails driven into the rim, their heads protruding about an inch, marked the precise divisions between the numbers. Two of the spokes had a zero at each end. Painted on the hub of the wheel was a large golden £ sign, while hanging above it, at the equivalent of 12 o'clock on its dial, a silver arrow pointed directly downwards.

Henry manoeuvred the wheel into the space between the fireplace and the billiards table, took its rim in one hand and pulled lightly downwards. It spun smoothly for about sixty seconds before slowly coming to a halt – the silver arrow was long enough for the nails to brush against it, gently impeding its rotation – with the number 5 directly under the pointer. While it had been spinning Henry fetched a large folded board from the storeroom, opened it and laid it on the billiards table. On the board, each with its own rectangular space, were painted the numbers one to thirty. Drawing hard on his cigar, Henry tipped his head back, blew out a stream of smoke, then announced jocularly, 'When you're ready gentlemen, place your bets for the first round. Odds are as usual, thirty to one.'

Luigi nudged the man next to him, Dermot O'Connor, and said in a low voice, 'Why are there two zeros on the wheel?'

'If the arrow points to one of those, all bets are forfeited to the bank.' Dermot was staring at the board. 'And the bank also collects when a winning number hasn't had a wager put on it.'

Luigi watched, absorbed, as the men dipped into their pockets and placed their bets on the board. Henry wrote down the amounts of the bets and the bettors' nominated numbers one by one as they came forward. Soon the board was covered in money – half crowns, ten shilling notes, even a couple of one pound notes – and only Luigi had not placed a bet. He had occasionally gambled at cards at Okuru, but just for a few pence. He wasn't going to start now. But Henry was looking at him expectantly.

'You're not joining in, Louie?'

'No, I'll just watch, thank you.'

'Fair enough. The only rule is, whoever spins the wheel doesn't place a bet. So, you can be the first to turn it. All bets in? Right-o, gentlemen, we're away. One spin, Louie, hard as you can.'

Gripping the wooden rim with his right hand, Luigi gave it a firm downward tug. The wheel spun fast and easily – he realised by its smoothness that there must be a set of bearings inside its hub – turning the numbers on its rim to a white blur. There was a faint *click-click-click-click* as the nails touched the pointer, then the wheel began to slow. The men craned forward, the clicking grew louder, and there were sharp

125

intakes of breath as the numbers began to pass under the pointer with agonising slowness.

...25, 26, 27 ...

When the wheel stopped at last the arrow was directly above number 28. Chortling triumphantly, Albert Cartwright came forward. Henry gathered up the losing bets and handed Albert three £5 notes. He promptly placed one of them on number 14 on the board. The others too came forward and made their next choices.

Luigi had a few coins in his pocket, and two one pound notes inside his wallet. He stared at the board. He could hardly put just a shilling on a number, not in this company. A pound was a lot of money, though. But there was plenty more, up in his room, in the pocket of the accordion. Thinking it unsociable not to join in, buoyed by the good-humoured company of the other men, he took a £1 note from his wallet. He stared at the board. Which number to choose? The ninth of March being his mother's birthday, he placed the note on number 9. As he did so the others cheered.

This time George Anderson handled the wheel. As it began to spin, the men made cries of encouragement, as if urging on horses in a race. Then, as the wheel slowed, they fell silent. *Click-click-click-click.* Luigi felt his heartbeat racing as he watched the wheel rotate even more slowly, saw the white numbers gliding beneath the arrow.

.... 5, 6, 7, 8, 0, 9.

The wheel stopped. *Nine.* Someone – he thought it was George – called out, 'Well done Lou!' Others muttered, and Oliver Chetwin, who had bet on number ten, swore loudly. Luigi was still staring, entranced, at the wheel and the arrow pointing to the magic number. Henry handed him thirty, one pound notes, nodding thoughtfully as he did so.

Luigi stared at the bundle of pounds. *Twenty-nine quid profit, just like that!* He thought of his gold, and how many months it had taken to glean one ounce. Six months perhaps? And for six months' work, £40. But with the wheel, £30 had taken just two minutes. He stuffed all the notes except one into the side pocket of his jacket.

'Your bets please gentlemen,' called Henry.

Luigi hesitated. The chance of number nine coming up again being so unlikely, this time he chose his own birthday, number 15. He placed the purple note on the board.

...22, 23, 24, 0, 25.

The wheel stopped.

Watching Henry gather up the losing bets, Luigi considered his position. He'd lost a quid, but was still flush. He'd stick with his birthday. Again he placed a pound on number 15.

The wheel spun, blurred, clicked, slowed, stopped at number 20. There being no bets on it, Henry collected all wagers, amid loud grumbling. Luigi drew a deep breath. Slipping his left hand into his jacket pocket, his felt the comforting scrunch of his winnings. That, combined with his gold money upstairs, amounted to a fortune. He could well afford to keep going, so he would. After all, it was all for Alice and their future together. With what he could make here, and the rest, he could buy Alice a diamond ring, and a gown. He could raise a mortgage and have a villa built for them.

Around him, the other men seemed equally undeterred. If anything, they appeared even more determined to beat the bank. Eyes bright and fixed on the board, they drew hard on their cigars as they considered their next bets. Now there were no coins on the board, only notes. Purple notes, green notes, red notes, all bearing the portrait of the English queen. Henry offered Luigi a cigar, which he accepted gratefully, and Henry lit it for him.

'Another brandy, Louie?'

'Thank you.'

'Spinning now.'

He bet on Violetta's birthday, his father's, and – on his fifth bet – Leopoldo's. None of the numbers came up. But the bank had also lost three times in a row, and Luigi estimated that Henry had now forfeited a huge amount, over eighty pounds. How could he keep paying out that amount of money? But the hotelier's expression remained impassive as he paid out the winnings. Only a baring of his teeth, still clamped on his cigar, suggested a frustration with the way the evening was developing. His teeth were slightly discoloured and widely spaced, like a picket fence.

Around the table, the other men remained in a state of jocularity. Eyes fixed, laughing easily, they didn't miss a bet, excepting the one whose turn it was to spin the wheel. George Chetwin placed every bet on number 13, and it paid out twice. Excusing himself, Luigi went quickly upstairs for more money. He was still ahead, but he needed to win again, and handsomely, if he was to finish the evening flush.

Number nine, he'd go back to number nine.

Hands slid into jacket pockets, wallets were opened. Hand trembling, Luigi placed one of his five pound notes on number 9, then held out his glass for another shot of brandy from Henry's decanter.

...31, 32, 0, 1, 2, 3, 4, 5, 6. The wheel stopped. Another win for the bank.

A small voice somewhere in his head was saying, *Stop now Luigi, stop now, that's enough.* But a louder, more insistent, brandied voice was drowning it out: *Go on, you can win again, there's every chance, you can be richer still.* After the bank won three times in a row, the mood of the gamblers became more subdued. Fortune, it seemed to Luigi, must now be favouring Henry. But still the hotelier betrayed no emotion. He collected, he lit more cigars, he topped up the goblets, as if he was merely a hotel waiter. A new round was called and Luigi placed another £5 on number 15. The wheel spun, slowed, stopped on number 13.

It was Edward Smithers who took him aside. His hand on Luigi's shoulder, he put his mouth close to his ear and said, 'Look mate, I know you're having a dud run.' Edward's breath reeked of smoke and brandy. 'And when that happens, there's only one way to go.' Luigi turned. Edward's eyes were glazy, his cheeks aglow through his patchy black beard. 'Double up on your losing stake. Then you're bound to get your money back, and more besides.'

It was nearly midnight and the board was littered with multi-coloured bank notes. A pall of cigar smoke enveloped the table. The wheel spun again and again. Luigi didn't miss a turn, each time following Edward's advice and doubling up on his losses, certain that eventually his number would come up. There could be no going back now.

Setting his brandy glass down, he placed four £5 notes – double what he had lost on the last spin – on number 9. When it came up, he would win six hundred quid. Three times what he worked for years for to get from his gold.

Luigi put his hand up to his brow. Number 10. An inch away, just an inch away. He watched the yet-expressionless Henry collect up the sheaf of notes and make a payout to a gleeful and now-reeling Edward Smithers. Once more Luigi's hand reached inside his jacket for his wallet. One last bet, one last chance not only to recover his lost capital, but to multiply it. He placed the wad of £5 notes on number 15.

The only movement in the room was the blurred wheel, spinning, spinning. And as it spun on, so did his mind, whirling, turning, faster,

faster. With his winnings he would marry Alice and live with her in their villa. She would grow flowers, he would raise vegetables. They would have a carriage and four, they would travel to Christchurch and Nelson. He would buy a fishing boat and pay others to work it. They would have several children, and they would all take a voyage to Italy. Once there, he and Alice would take Violetta, her husband and their children to the grandest restaurant in Urbino. All paid for by the gold and the wheel. The room, as well as the wheel, was spinning now.

The men in the room had turned to stone. Transfixed, their heads were craning forward, eyes only on the wheel. Luigi could hear his own breathing, could feel his heart ricocheting against his rib cage. One hand clutched the stem of his brandy goblet, the other was balled tightly in his pocket. *Click-click-click*-click. As the wheel began to slow the numbers emerged from the blur, like stars coming out on a dark night.

…12, 13, 14, 15 – Luigi's heart was set to leap from his chest – 16, 0.

There it stopped. A collective groan came from the men. The bank had done it.

Henry stepped forward. 'Tough luck gentlemen,' he said, nonchalantly, as if remarking on a kahawai that had thrown the hook. Picking up the money, eyebrows knitted with concentration, he began to shuffle the notes through his fingers. Aghast, Luigi watched Henry fold the thick wad of notes and tuck it into the inside pocket of his jacket. He went over, clutched the manager's arm.

'Henry, I didn't mean to do that. Not all of it. Please, give me a chance to start again.'

The hotelier's face had a greasy sheen, like salami left out in the sun. He gave a laugh as harsh as breaking glass.

'You win some, you lose some, Louie. No second chances.'

Turning his back, he announced to the others. 'Right, that's it for tonight, gentlemen. Same time, same place, next Wednesday.'

Sitting up in bed, staring into the blackness. His head was throbbing like a threshing machine, his mouth felt like old fishbait. But far worse than that was the shame of it. Of losing it all, in front of the others. That was the worst of it, the shame of his stupidity, the notion – the delusion – that he could have won against the wheel. Over and over in his mind, sitting in the darkness, he saw the cursed wheel spinning, slowing, stopping, pointing always to the wrong number, whirling his fortune away. And at the same time spinning away his future as if it was a dry leaf in the wind. Now, there was only one thing he could do. Moving like a drugged man, he got up, lit the lamp, took out his pad and pen.

Dear Alice,

By the time you read this I will be gone. I cannot tell you the reason I am leaving, I can only say that I have been more foolish than any man ever was, and as a result I have nothing left to offer you. That I will never see you again is a thought I can hardly begin to imagine, but I have no choice. You are so young, the best years of your life lie before you. Many of mine have been wasted. But not all, for with you, over these past weeks, I found a love that brought me more happiness than I had ever known. Now, though, I must leave. I go in the hope that you may in time find your own true happiness, with someone more worthy of your love.

Yours,
Luigi Galoni

He put the single sheet of writing paper in an envelope, wrote on it, 'Alice Harris, c/o The Ship & Castle Hotel, Westport', and left it at the reception desk in the foyer. Two hours later he was on the early morning Newman Brothers coach, being driven through the Buller Gorge, this time in a northerly direction.

As Luigi wandered along Lambton Quay, his eyes kept straying upwards, to the top levels of the three and four-storeyed stone buildings that lined the street. A real city, with fine shops, offices, hotels and heavy traffic. It was so strange to be in one again. The street itself was wide, muddy and crowded with carriages, carts and horses, and although it was late afternoon, the gas lamps had not yet been lit. Boardwalks lined both sides of the quay, and as Luigi made his way through the crowds of pedestrians, hawkers holding trays called out to the passers-by, beseeching them to buy their products: tobacco and matches, apples and oranges, buns, biscuits and confectionery. He bought an apple and munched it as he walked along.

Wellington seemed a city on the move. A good place, he decided, to put his past behind him yet again. Totally unknown here, this was where he might be able to make another fresh start. Banish all memories of Alice. Yet as soon as he thought this, her face appeared again in his mind's eye. Everywhere he looked, every minute of the day and night, he saw her lovely face. Look at me! Look at me! He would never forget her. But he had to. Fool, he told himself, look only ahead, not back.

Pausing at the corner of Lambton Quay and Wakefield Street, by the corner of the triangulated Bank of New Zealand building, he waited for a uniformed pointsman on a dais at the intersection to permit the pedestrians to cross. When the horses and carriages were signalled to halt, Luigi crossed the quay and walked down Wakefield Street in the direction of the Clarendon Hotel. Wakefield Street was narrower than Lambton Quay and congested with pedestrians and carts, particularly at the intersections, where horses, carts, traps and carriages became tangled. He'd been told that the municipal fish market was near the entrance to Queens Wharf, on the seaward side of Customhouse Quay. So if the other Italians were still in Wellington, he guessed someone at the fish market would know where. But first he needed to call at the hotel to collect his jacket. It was early winter, and a strong southerly was blowing through the streets, turning the day cool.

As he made his way along Wakefield Street, he heard a sound both familiar and strange, coming from further down the boardwalk. Familiar in that the tune sounded Italian, strange inasmuch as it was not one that he knew. Moving closer to the source of the sound, he realised it was coming from an organ, being played directly in front of the Clarendon Hotel. When closer still, he saw that a crowd had gathered around the place where the organ was being played. Luigi joined the throng, peering over their heads to see the source of the sound.

The organ grinder was a slim, dark-haired man in his early thirties with a long moustache, dressed in a black suit edged with red braid and matching bow tie. He was nodding in time to the music and singing in Italian as he turned the handle of the small organ, which stood on a tripod in front of him.

The crowd – men mostly, with a few women holding the hands of small children – were standing around the organ watching the man curiously, the object of their curiosity not so much the organ or the man grinding it, but a small grey monkey perched on his left shoulder. There was a collar around the monkey's neck and a light chain connected it to the lapel of its master's suit. Its tail was in the shape of a question mark, and it had in its paws an inverted bowler hat. As its master played, the monkey bared its tiny teeth, clicking them rapidly as it looked around at the audience. Some among them were laughing and pointing, a reaction which seemed to annoy the monkey, which glared in the direction of those who laughed. As this scene was being played out, the organ grinder continued to sing, his head swaying from side to side, his eyes closed, his expression mournful.

After listening for a few minutes, Luigi pushed through the crowd and put a sixpence in the bowler hat, adding the coin to a few others already there. The monkey bared his teeth at Luigi in what could have been a grin. 'Grazie, grazie,' the organ grinder said, nodding his head, then, at Luigi's reply of 'Prego, amico,' lifting his head in delight.

'Italiano?' he asked.

'Si,' said Luigi, grinning, before going to the rear of the crowd to carry on listening.

What happened next occurred so quickly that later he found it difficult to put it into a precise sequence. From the other side of the crowd a stout young man in grey overalls and with a stick in his hands pushed through to the front, stood just in front of the organ and scowled at the monkey. Momentarily disconcerted by this intrusion, the organ grinder then recovered and went on playing. But the monkey now became agitated at the close presence of the man, baring his teeth at him and making a series of squealing sounds. The man in the overalls moved closer still, thrusting his face towards the monkey and baring his own teeth. This sent the little creature into a frenzy. Dropping the hat, it began to do a furious dance on the organ grinder's shoulder. Coins rolled from the hat and dropped between the gaps in the boardwalk. The organ grinder stopped his turning and said loudly, 'Why did you do that? You are frightening him! Go away, please!'

The man ignored the request, instead thrusting his stick like a sword at the monkey and saying, in a menacing tone, 'You cheeky little shit …' The monkey leapt aside and the stick missed. Drawing its lips right back, the monkey shrieked at the man, who raised his stick to thrust at it again. But before he could do so the organ grinder tore the stick from the man's hand and began to beat him over the head and shoulders with it. The crowd started to shout, pushing the women and children aside as they surged forward. The hurdy-gurdy fell to the boardwalk with a crash and the monkey leapt onto the organ grinder's head, where it grabbed handfuls of his hair and hung onto them as if they were reins. The man in the overalls began swinging punches at the organ grinder, but as he was still under attack from the stick, none of them landed.

Desperately sorry for his compatriot, Luigi began to force his way through to the front of the crowd to offer help. As he did so he heard a whistle sounding shrilly in the distance. Reaching the man in overalls, Luigi grabbed his hands and pinned them to the sides of his body, at the same time yelling in Italian to the organ grinder to put his stick down. The man turned and snarled a curse at Luigi, who caught the stink of alcohol on his breath. The fracas continued for some moments, with the organ grinder – still with the monkey clutching his hair – continuing to rain down blows on his would-be assailant, and Luigi holding the man's arms and shouting for the organ grinder to stop. Seconds later two burly, helmeted policemen burst through the crowd, one carrying a truncheon, the other a pair of handcuffs.

'Your name again?'

'Vincenzo Labronico.'

'Jesus. How do you spell that?'

The organ grinder told him.

'Nationality?'

'Italian.'

'And your name?'

'Frank Wilson.'

'Nationality?'

'Australian.'

'Well, I'm charging you both with assault and disorderly behaviour. You're remanded in custody until a court hearing tomorrow morning.'

'What about Jacko?' The organ grinder was stroking the monkey's back.

'He'll be in the cells too.'

The Australian raised his head, sneered at the monkey but said nothing.

'Please, officer.' Luigi came forward.

'Who are you?'

'I am Luigi Galoni. I saw everything that happened. I can tell you now that this monkey business was not Vincenzo's fault.'

'Can you now.' The officer looked at him suspiciously. 'You Italian too?'

'Yes.'

'A friend of his, I s'pose.'

'No. I never met him before. But I saw the whole business, so I know what happened on the street.'

The constable's expression turned thoughtful. He looked from Luigi to Vincenzo, then back at Luigi, but still said nothing.

'So, will you let me tell you what happened?' asked Luigi.

Still with the pen in his hands, poised above the charge sheet on the desk before him, the officer gave Luigi another considered look. Then he grunted assent. 'All right then, tell me. How did it all start?'

'I cannot thank you enough, Luigi. I thought I was going to wake up in prison.'

'It was no trouble. You'll have to go to court, though, to give evidence against him.'

'That is all right, I will do it.'

They were sitting in the small lounge at the front of the Clarendon Hotel, drinking milky coffee. At first they spoke in Italian, but laughed when each realised how much of their mother tongue he had forgotten. After that, they spoke mainly in English. The monkey, now off its chain, was curled up in a corner of the sofa, fast asleep, and Vincenzo's organ was parked in one corner. When Luigi told him that he had just arrived in the city from the West Coast, Vincenzo nodded, knowingly.

'Were you at Jackson Bay?'

'Near there. Okuru.'

'I was, too. From '76 to '77.'

'You came with the Livorno group?'

'Yes. We tried to grow vines on the land they gave us, but it was hopeless. Raining, always raining. The vines rotted.'

'Did you come to Wellington after that?'

'Not directly. Some of us went to Goldsborough, near Hokitika. But that was nearly as bad, there was no gold left. So I came here. Now I make my living on the streets, with my organ and Jacko.'

Luigi looked over at the slumbering monkey. 'Where did you get him?'

'From a circus that came to Hokitika. And went broke. I paid five shillings for him. The hurdy-gurdy I brought from Livorno.'

'Is it a good living, organ grinding?'

'Better than you might expect. In New Zealand, there is not much life after dark.'

'I know.' Luigi finished his coffee. Putting down his cup, he said, 'Did you ever know a man there called Leopoldo Vitali?'

'Yes. The one who lost his leg. He stayed after we left. Did you know him?'

'I did.'

After he told Vincenzo the story of Leopoldo's demise, the other man's expression grew sorrowful. 'That's so sad. Poor Leopoldo. We tried to get him to leave with us, but he refused.' He frowned. 'Is that why you left the coast?'

Not wishing to say anything about losing both his capital and Alice, Luigi just nodded. Then he said, 'Leopoldo told me that some of the others came to live here in Wellington, after they walked away from the settlement.'

'We did.' He shrugged. 'We didn't have much choice.'

'Are the rest still here?'

'Most of them are, yes.'

'What do they do?'

'They are fishermen.'

'Where?'

'At Makara.'

'Where is that?'

The day was cloudy and mild with a moderate wind, the road quiet apart from the occasional coach and farm dray. It took him half a day to walk up through Kelburn's hills and valleys and across the farmland to where the hill country began. From there a rough track rose steeply, winding its way up to the summit. There a sign pointing north said, 'Makara 2 miles, Makara Beach, 4 miles'. Luigi stopped by the sign, put down his rucksack and studied the wide view. Before him, to the west and north, was range upon range of rolling, bush-covered hills. Each range had valleys creased into its side, and was separated from the next by deep valleys. Beyond the most distant range to the west, dark and glittering, lay the sea. Cook Strait. Lowering his gaze a little, Luigi saw a valley which ran from south to north, and a stream running through it, gleaming like a snail's trail. Feeling parched, he picked up his rucksack, made his way down the steep hill, lay on the banks of the stream and drank the numbingly cold but crystal-clear water. He ate the mutton pie he had bought from a bakery in the city, then carried on along the valley.

The track shadowed the stream. The going was much easier in the valley, and he covered the ground steadily. The calls of bellbirds and tuis came to him as he walked, and the iridescence of kingfishers flashed like mirrors among the willows.

The valley broadened, and divided, one branch veering west, towards the coast, the other continuing north. Taking the western fork, he saw that the stream meandered across flat land, then merged with an expanse of swamp. The track ran along the edge of the swamp, following the foot of a high escarpment. Fifteen minutes later, he walked out onto the shore of a broad bay.

A sweep of shingle covered the foreshore, sloping down to the sea, which was a beige colour. Heaps of dark brown seaweed and scatterings of driftwood marked the high tide mark. The bay itself was enclosed by two high, rounded headlands. Where the land met the sea it was raked sharply from top to bottom, as if it had been violently tilted, and at the right-hand end of the shingly beach a stream emerged from the swamp, passing through a narrow channel before running into the bay. Where the sea met the sky, there were hazy shapes of more land. The South Island, Luigi guessed.

But where, he wondered, was the fishing village that Vincenzo had told him about? There was not a building in sight, just hills and cliffs and rocks. Then, looking to his left, he saw that the track continued, following the rocky shelf at the foot of the hills towards an intermediary headland about half a mile away. Beyond the headland smoke could be seen rising, before it was whipped away by the wind. Picking up his rucksack, he walked on in the direction of the smoke, and after rounding a rocky point, came to the Italian village.

THE MUSEUM

He met Abigail in a wine bar in Woodward Street, off Lambton Quay. She was looking better, William thought. Probate had been granted for their father's will, she told him. Then, sipping her merlot, she eyed him levelly over the rim of her glass and in a tone of voice suggesting that she considered his project somewhat less than important, said, 'How's the ancestor sleuthing?'

William just said, 'Painstaking.'

'Well, there must be clues somewhere in Wellington. Tried Te Papa?'

'Yes. But you know what it's like, just a big amusement park, really.' He smiled. 'Nothing helpful for *serious* ancestor sleuths.'

Abigail swirled her wine. 'Chloe was taken to that other museum by their teacher last week, the one on Customhouse Quay. She's doing a project on Wellington's history. It was "cool", she said. High praise from an eleven-year-old. Have you been there?'

'No. I've driven past it often enough, but I've never been inside.'

'Why don't you? It's got heaps about Wellington's history, Chloe said. So you might find something helpful there.'

Unlike Te Papa with its mismatched planes, the Museum of Wellington City & Sea was a handsome, late Victorian, two-storeyed brick building.

Entering the museum, William felt as if he had stepped into a time capsule. There was a convincing recreation of a bond store, then displays of paintings, photographs, maps, artefacts and dioramas of the harbour and the colonial town that had grown up around its shores. Wellington had indeed been sired by the sea.

Absorbed by the displays, William's imagination was stirred. Could this have been the place where Luigi Galoni first came ashore?

He made his way upstairs to the next floor. More historic photographs, maps and displays. Among the exhibits was a cubicle, above it a sign. Wellington's Fishing Communities. 'Many of Wellington's early fishermen were Italian immigrants', a notice among the photographs stated. 'They came from Italy from the 1870s onwards, settled in Paremata, Eastbourne, Makara and Island Bay and lived and worked there in close communities'.

There was a photographic montage, of clinker-built fishing boats drawn up on a rocky shore, and groups of fishermen standing proudly beside their catches, men with thick moustaches wearing boots and seamen's jerseys. There was a shot of a cart laden with fish for the market, another of a row of small houses, huddled alongside each other beside the sea.

William stared at the photographs and the other exhibits. He peered at the faces of the men in the photographs, searching for one who may have been Luigi, but they were too unclear for him to tell. But William felt sure that Luigi would have sought the company of fellow-Italians, and so may well have been part of one of these communities. But which one? And what had brought him from Westport to Wellington?

EIGHT

The little houses – twenty or so of them – had been built directly onto the rocky shelf at the foot of the cliff, extending in a line a few hundred yards long. Luigi could immediately see the sense in this. This smaller bay, though it had jagged reefs close in-shore, was far more sheltered than the other. Here the water was calm, lapping at the rocks and the curve of shingle beach, where a dozen or so clinker-built boats were pulled up safely. Beyond the row of cottages a small stream tumbled down through a fold in the hill, flowed across the track and into the cove.

The track ran across the front of the row of houses, like a crude main street. On its seaward side, just in front of the beached boats, fishing nets were hanging out to dry on driftwood frames. Approaching the cottages, Luigi saw that most of them were rudimentary, some no more than shacks, built of corrugated iron, tar paper and lengths of rough-sawn timber. Every dwelling had an external chimney, also made of sheets of corrugated iron, attached to one end of the building. Smoke was coming from all the chimneys and beside several of the cottages, washing hung in lines stretched between manuka poles. Two of the houses, Luigi was startled to see, also flew the green, white and red flag of the Kingdom of Italy, with the gold crown of Savoy in the centre.

Two young men were plucking seaweed from one of the suspended nets. Both wore heavy navy blue jerseys, coarse trousers, boots and caps and one was smoking a pipe. As Luigi greeted them in English, they looked up, their expressions incurious.

'I am looking for a man called Giuseppe Volpicelli,' he said. The shorter man took the pipe from his mouth.

'He is not here.'

'Where is he?'

'Gone.'

'Where to?'

'Paremata.'

The man turned away and went back to his net cleaning. The other one, after looking guardedly at Luigi for a few more moments, did the same. Annoyed by their attitude, Luigi tried again, this time speaking in Italian.

'What about the men who were at Jackson Bay? The ones who came from Livorno. Aristodemo, Fortunato, Victor and Antonio.'

This time the men showed more interest. The man with the pipe said gruffly, 'You are from Italy?'

'Yes. And Jackson Bay.'

'Aristodemo and Fortunato have gone to Paremata, too. Victor and Antonio are still here.'

'Where can I find them?'

'Their house is second from the end. By the stream.'

'Grazie.' He paused. 'I am Luigi. I was from Pesaro.'

The pair nodded, then returned to their work. Luigi walked to the other end of the 'street'.

There was a man sitting on the front step of the cottage, lashing a gaff hook to a long manuka pole. There was a pair of boots on the step beside him and his feet were encased in thick grey socks. He looked up at the newcomer, his expression cordial.

'Are you Victor?' enquired Luigi, in Italian.

'No, I am Antonio. Victor has gone to the farm to get milk.' He had a leathery, weather-beaten face, heavy black eyebrows and a bushy moustache. His trousers were held up with braces.

'I am a friend of Leopoldo Vitali,' Luigi said. 'I lived with him at Okuru.'

The man's jaw dropped. Getting to his feet hastily, he held out his hand and Luigi shook it. 'You have news of Leopoldo?'

'Yes.'

'Please, come inside.'

The building was one unlined room containing two beds and an open fire, burning driftwood. A woven flax mat covered the floor and there were two battered chairs in front of the fire. Antonio gestured for Luigi to take one of them.

'Would you like some tea?'

'Yes, thank you.'

'It will have to be black, until Victor returns with the milk.'

He made two tin mugs of tea, using water from a billy suspended over the fire, handed one to Luigi, then sat down again. 'So, when did you last see Leopoldo?'

'A few months ago.'

'And how was he?'

It took some time to tell the story, and as he told it he saw the light in the other man's eyes going slowly out. When he had finished, Antonio's eyes were dull. 'Poor Leopoldo. We wanted him to come with us, but he would not move from Okuru.' He paused. 'How long were you together?'

'Eight years.'

Antonio made a low whistling sound, accompanied by a slow, sorrowful shaking of his head. Then he brightened.

'And now you have come to Makara to live?'

'Yes.'

'To fish?'

'Yes.'

'Do you have money for a boat?'

'No. I'll have to just help. Until I can afford my own.'

'We have a boat, Victor and me. You could share the work with us. And the money from the fish.' He shrugged. 'Such as it is.'

'I would like that.'

'Good. And you will need somewhere to live.'

'I will.'

'Aristodemo and Fortunato's house is empty, since they went to Paremata. You could use that.'

'How much will it cost?'

Antonio burst out laughing. 'Luigi, you are now at Makara. Everything here is free.'

So he became a part of this tiny outpost of Italy. The cottage he inherited was primitive: walls of rough-sawn timber, covered with tar paper, the roof and chimney corrugated iron sheets. The bed was a palliasse on a driftwood frame, the chairs half-barrels, the table an upturned tea chest. But being warm and dry, it was all he needed. His toilet was the same as all the others, a bucket behind the cottage, emptied daily into the outgoing tide; his bathroom the little stream at the end of the settlement.

Driftwood and manuka fuelled the cottages' fires, a nearby farm supplied meat, milk, butter, eggs, cheese and fruit in exchange for fish.

The place they called Fisherman's Bay, and which the Maoris called Warehou, was tucked away out of the prevailing winds, so that only the on-shore nor-westerlies drove into it directly. During these times, when fishing was impossible, the men stayed in the cottages and played cards or sang the songs of their homeland. The southerly, Luigi quickly learned, was both the best and the worst of Makara's winds. It howled over the hills above the settlement, missing the houses completely and flattening the sea in the larger bay. Rowing out under these conditions, when the wind was on the boat's beam, was easy, but it was crucial to turn every few minutes and check the sea conditions further out, where the sea ceased to be in the lee of the land. At that point and all parts beyond, the waves were whipped into whitecaps, the foam flew and a small boat – whether under sail or oar – became well-nigh uncontrollable. The trick was to judge the zone where the southerly struck the sea, and not go beyond it.

But what fishing there was off this coast! A fifty-hook line baited with kahawai, trevally or paua and set by mid-morning would produce nearly every time at least twenty-five groper – some as heavy as forty pounds – as well as large numbers of blue cod, ling and warehou. When their net was pulled up, it took two of them to do it, so bountiful was the haul. Often when he was bringing up his line, and every hook bore a fat groper, Luigi would think back to Pesaro, and the basketful of scrawny mackerel and herrings he and his father would be lucky to catch in a day. But here he would sit in the boat at anchor and look back at the cliffs rising abruptly from the sea and think, this land, and this sea, they have so much to give. If he kept working hard, maybe he could still save enough money to buy a piece of land. Some land near the sea, where he could garden as well as fish.

All this he described in his next letter to Violetta – instructing her from now on to send her letters to him care of the post office in Johnsonville, the nearest settlement to Makara. He concluded,

So, I am contented enough here. The company is mainly good, and we can talk of the Old Country (that is how I now think of it now), and visit the city from time to time. But I must tell you too how much I miss a woman's loving company. The one I loved, the one I lost, I can never forget or replace. It seems my fate to always lose the people I love. A melancholy thought, and one I express to you and you only. But there is little sense in dwelling on what might have been. I will not be in Makara forever, I hope, so while I am I must make the most of things as they are.

Write soon and tell me more of your new life, Violetta.

Your loving brother,

Luigi

'Where did the wood for the houses come from?' Luigi asked Victor. 'There's no mill round here, is there?' They were sitting on the beach, mending their net.

'The wood is another gift of the sea,' laughed Victor. He was short and rotund, and although illiterate, knew the libretto and tunes of every popular Italian opera, had a fine tenor voice, and often broke into song as he worked. He and Luigi had already formed an informal duo, Luigi providing the accordion music, Victor the vocals.

'Ships bring sawn timber from the Manawatu, out of the port at Wanganui, to Wellington,' Victor explained. 'The timber in their holds is covered with other timber, to stop the salt spray getting onto it. There is an English word for this ...' He stared skyward, as if he would find it there. '*Dunnage*, they call this wood. And when the ships reach here ...' he pointed out into the strait '...they throw the dunnage overboard, and presto! It comes into the bay on the tide.'

'And the corrugated iron?'

'Oh, everywhere in New Zealand there is this iron. The whole country is made of corrugated iron. Ours comes from old farm sheds, up the valley. The Kiwi farmers throw it away, the Italian fishermen pick it up.' He broke into song.

Che bella cosa e na jurnata 'e sole,
N'aria serena doppo na tempesta!
Pe'll'aria fresca pare gia na festa...
Che bella cosa na jurnata 'e sole.

Ma n'atu sole
Cchiu bello, oje ne'.

O sole mio
Sta 'nfronte a te!

Victor and Antonio shared with Luigi the proceeds of their catch, which was taken over the Makara hill by the village's horse and cart every Thursday, to be sold at the Municipal Fish Market in the city. The men took turns to take the laden cart on its half-day journey to the city's waterfront. There the fish would be weighed and a price agreed on according to demand, before the return trip was made. But first there would be visits to suppliers for essential goods: a hardware shop in Taranaki Street for replacement hooks, lines, nets, glass floats and anchors; brandy from a liquor store in Manners Street, tobacco and papers from the barber's shop next door, groceries from a store in Willis Street. Some of the men thought this journey to the city and back tedious, but Luigi enjoyed it, urging the gelding, Maestro, over the hills, the load of fish on the cart behind him covered in wet sacks to keep it as fresh as possible.

He spent little, saved hard. After five months he had enough cash for his own boat, a second-hand, fourteen footer bought from Gino Bianca, who was moving on to Island Bay, where there was another Italian fishing settlement. Luigi gave his boat a fresh coat of white paint, screwed a name-plate to her stern and into it routed a single word, Laetitia, his mother's name, in accordance with a Marche tradition. She was a robust craft, built of Coromandel kauri, and came with two sets of oars and a canvas sail, so could be rigged if the conditions were right. With the sail up and the wind from the right quarter, he could be at the groper grounds in fifteen minutes.

In this way he came to relish the independence and self-sufficiency of the little settlement. They wove pots out of the supplejack vines that grew among the bush in the hills, baited them with fish-heads and brought up crayfish by the dozen. They prised fat paua from the rocks at low tide, hammered them tender and fried them over their fires. They split and smoked fish in smoke-houses behind their cottages, using manuka sawdust, they baked their own bread and brewed their own beer. The winds were often bitter, but there was plenty of wood to keep the little houses warm, and the rain did not come nearly as often as it had down south.

The little community was not free from divisions, however, Luigi soon learned. There was a line drawn between those from the south of

Italy – from in and around Massalubrense, in the Bay of Naples – and those from the north, like Antonio and Victor and himself. Each found the other's accents difficult to understand, each of the two groups kept largely to itself. Occasionally quarrels broke out, over the areas fished and tangled lines and payments for their catches. Some of these could have become serious, were it not for if the presence of French Louis.

His real name, Luigi was told, was Victor Leopold Haupois. He'd been born in a fishing village in Normandy, in 1853. After leaving home to go to sea at the age of ten and sailing the world, he became the first Pakeha to settle on the Makara coast. A tall, immensely strong man in his fifties, with a white beard which came half-way down his chest, French Louis could handle a fishing boat better than any man Luigi had known. He could row his boat for half a day into the wind without stopping, and had once rowed across the strait to the Marlborough Sounds, then rowed back the next day, with two sacks of blue cod aboard. Even though he was not Italian, the Makara fishermen all considered him their community's patriarch. And he was the enforcer of law and order. Whenever quarrels threatened to turn serious, word would quickly reach French Louis. Then he would stride down onto the beach and in booming, heavily-accented, mangled English, reproach the arguing parties.

'Hey! Giovanni! If I must to tell you once more to stop your bloody complaining, I will take you by the neck of your shirt and throw you over the bay!'

'He catch my line with his net, then he cut my line. He doan even ask me first, he just cut it ...'

'Shit, man, what are you, a fisherman or a baby? Did your bloody line never get caught in any another's net? Yes! In mine, often times! When you are the perfect fisherman, you can tell him on. But not yet, Giovanni, not yet.'

And French Louis would aim a kick with his knee-length boots at the hapless one, causing him to slink away and provoking mirth in the men who were watching. In this way disputes were defused, and seldom simmered.

In spite of their different regional backgrounds the fishermen worked communally, helping one another to maintain or add to their cottages, taking turns to fetch produce from the Makara farms and using a roster system to deliver their fish to the city. For most of the men, this was a completely new experience. As Antonio remarked to Luigi one day after they'd returned from Wellington and divvied up the proceeds among the fishermen, 'You know, back in Italy we never helped each other like this. We didn't share. Apart from family, there it was every man for himself.'

Luigi knew what he meant. Living this way was different. It was mainly their exile status which helped to unify them. Pride in their homeland was upheld. News in letters from Italy was read out and discussed, and the Italian flag flew proudly from several of the little houses. Paradoxically, however, their émigré status also helped bind them to the new land. There was the sense, never declared but well understood throughout the little community, that they were all in it together, and together they would make a success of the migration business. They all had a yearning to succeed, to prove themselves, to make their mark in the new land. And by supporting one another, they would.

On Sundays no one fished. Once a month a priest came on horseback from Johnsonville to hear confessions and administer the sacraments in the house of the pious one, Francesco Alighieri, who had a Maori wife, Miriama, and three young children. All the villagers were invited to the mass, and Victor and Antonio usually attended, but Luigi never went. The very sight of the black-clad cleric riding around the rocks to Fisherman's Bay made him turn away.

The rest of Sunday he enjoyed, however, because in the afternoons visitors would descend on Makara, arriving in carriages from the city or from Johnsonville. These men, women and children would be dressed in their Sunday best, promenading around the bay and, if weather permitted, taking their picnic lunches at the top of the hill. French Louis would act as a guide for the visitors, putting on a top hat, escorting them graciously through the village and introducing them to the fishermen. Luigi would scrub the fish from his hands with sand soap, put on his suit and greet the day-trippers as they passed through the village. The city folk would buy fresh fish, then stop and talk, and he would enjoy these chats. He would show young boys his boat, or the jaw of a shark he had caught, or an octopus which lived in a rock pool.

He especially admired the young city women in their bonnets and tight-waisted crinoline dresses, who carried bright parasols whether the weather was fine or not. Observing these elegant young women, and the couples and families, listening to their laughter and their chat, he thought how companionable it would be to have a wife to share his life with, and children of his own, and a proper place to house them. But he knew that this couldn't be. Visiting Makara for half a day was all very well, but what woman would want to come and live in a shack on the rocks with only coarse fishermen for company? Francesco's wife lived in the village, but she'd been raised in a pa at Palliser Bay, so had known no other life. All the other men were single, but most were saving their money, hoping to move on to another community where they could find a wife, preferably an Italian one. Island Bay, Eastbourne, Paremata. A woman could not be expected to live in a place like Makara. Especially a woman like Alice.

Alice, Alice …

Although the months passed and he settled well enough into his new life, he never spent a day on land or sea without wondering where she might be and what she might be doing. Having no photograph of her, he tried to picture in his mind every detail of her face, her eyes, her mouth, her hair. Sometimes at night he dreamed of her in the Ship & Castle, bringing another man tea and biscuits, then entering his bed. He would wake shaking and anguished then, as if someone was physically tormenting him, and reproach himself, reminding himself that she had to live her own life and had a perfect right to do so. That he had lost Alice forever was no one's fault except his own; that he could ever find another woman that he would love as much was impossible.

He woke at dawn, started the fire, cooked himself porridge, drank two mugs of black tea and went outside. The air was still and mild. Staring up at the sky, he saw that it was a very pale blue. It would be another two hours before the sun climbed above the hills and its rays reached the waters of the bay. By then he would be at the groper grounds. Already he could see, down on the foreshore, Victor and Antonio and some of the others, baiting their lines and loading their boats for the day's fishing. He doused the fire, washed in the stream, collected his tackle from behind the cottage and went across to where *Laetitia* was drawn up on the shingle.

It was not yet six o'clock when he dragged his boat into the water and began to row out from the bay. He had left the mast and sail back behind the house, as the clear sky and settled conditions suggested that this would be, like yesterday, a windless one. It was summer now, and after the blustery conditions that spring had brought, the days were longer, the weather much more predictable. Pulling steadily on the oars, he felt the boat moving smoothly through the water with barely a swell beneath her. The tide was ebbing, helping *Laetitia* on her way. In her stern was the coiled long-line, already baited, in the bow a sugar bag in which was a flask of water, mutton sandwiches, a block of cheese wrapped in newspaper, and three apples. High overhead, a trio of gulls had him in their sights, gliding, circling, watchful. In conditions like these, he could stay out until sunset.

As he rowed, with his back to the sea, the bay gradually opened out and he could see the expanse of tilted cliffs, the broad gap between the hills where the road came through alongside the swamp and the lumpy green ranges inland. In front of the main bay he could make out the humps of swells moving beachward and see the spray rising where they broke, and he appreciated again how sheltered their bay was, and what a sensible choice it had been to build the houses there. After half an hour of rowing, the cottages of Fisherman's Bay had shrunk to doll's-house size.

Pausing for breath, he shipped his oars. Three other boats were being rowed across the bay, in a line, with fifty or so yards separating them. But they were heading in the opposite direction, north. To fish off Smiths Bay, he guessed. Already Luigi had decided to row south today, in the direction of Opau Bay. It was further away, but the water there was deeper, the groper bigger. Good blue cod, there too. Pulling hard with his left arm, he altered course slightly and ten minutes later was rounding the point.

In another twenty minutes he was off the next rocky point, which stuck out from the coast like a sprocket. There he anchored, paid out and set his line, marking the end with a netting-covered glass float.

The land before him rose up steeply from the water to a high, level crest. Still in shadow, the face of the land was like a long, forbidding wall between the sea and the ranges behind them. As Luigi sat in *Laetitia*'s stern munching a sandwich, he saw the sun come up over the crest like a ball of gold. And at the exact moment it did so, he saw a breeze ruffle the smooth waters of the strait. The boat promptly swung round to the north-west, the direction from where the gust had come, then dragged against the anchor rope.

Minutes later, the sea had been transformed, first turning choppy, then rough. Swells rose and began to stream in from the north, causing *Laetitia* to strain at the anchor rope. At first Luigi was not overly concerned. He'd experienced the nor-westerly before, although admittedly when he was not this far south. Usually when the wind came from this quarter he'd head north to Smiths Bay, rowing out into the wind, then sailing back with it. But now, without the sail, when the time came to return he'd be rowing into it. Tough going. He'd better allow extra time for the return trip. He moved to the centre thwart, to distribute his weight more evenly.

Ten minutes later he was surrounded by whitecaps. Driven by the still-rising wind, the swells were coming at him quickly across the open water. *Laetitia* bucked against the swells, some of which were breaking over the bow and slopping into the boat. Using the tin baler, he scooped out as much of it as he could, then, taking off his oilskin cape, he stretched it across the bow of the boat and lashed it in place with a rope. This stopped some of the water coming in, but now the wind was growing stronger, the swells streaming across the dark blue water towards him like the ranks of an attacking army. Looking over towards the land, he wondered if he should try to take *Laetitia* ashore, but quickly realised that to try to beach the boat on the lee shore – where the driving sea met the land – would be impossible. The surf would make a landing suicidal. His only option was to row back, into the wind. Looking at the land, he could tell too that the anchor had begun to drag. The coast was coming closer, the features of the slanting cliff face more distinct. He must row back, and he must start now.

When he hauled up his line there were seven groper on it, three of them more than ten pounders. Removing the hooks from the fishes' thick lips, he threw them all back. The less weight in the boat the better. He rewound the line, placed it in the sugar-bag in the stern, then moved to the bow and pulled up the anchor. As it emerged from the water *Laetitia* swung to port and began to drift quickly towards the land. Just as rapidly, Luigi sat down on the centre thwart, grabbed the oars and began to row, digging as deep as he could into the swells, his back quickly drenched by the spray being whipped from their crests.

Twenty minutes later, he could tell that he had made almost no progress. For every yard he moved the boat forward, the gaps between the swells meant that the oars struck only air. Without making consistent purchase with them, he could at best only expect to stay in the same place. At worst, he would be driven shorewards. Bracing the heels of his boots against the ribs of the boat, he dug deeper, pulled harder. The boat rose, dropped sharply into a trough, then rose into the next swell. When it broke against the bow, water sloshed over the cape and kept on coming, into the for'ard section of the boat. Shipping the oars for a few moments, he bailed as much of it as he could over the side, then grabbed the oars again. But in just those few seconds *Laetitia* was pushed back ten yards or more.

Bunches of white clouds, driven like him before the wind, were streaming overhead, then merging and darkening over the ranges. Now, the land loomed huge and threatening, the rocks at the foot of the cliffs like bared teeth. But still he kept rowing, the thought of *Laetitia* being dashed to pieces as horrifying as the thought of himself meeting the same fate. Back and shoulders straining, he rowed on, pushing with his legs, pulling as hard as he could with his arms. But the boat remained in the same place. Wiping the spray away from his face, he corrected himself. No, not the same place. He was losing ground, or, rather, losing water. The rocky shore was now only fifty yards away. He could see the swells becoming waves, the waves breaking against the rocks, the spray hanging like a curtain along the coast. What if he rowed outwards and went with the wind? For a few minutes he attempted to, but quickly returned to his former course. What he had glimpsed frightened him even more: by heading south he would be taken straight into the bay they called Te Ikaamaru, where the waves were being concentrated with furious force.

Lungs burning, his rowing began to slow. He cursed himself. Why hadn't he gone north with the others, to Smiths Bay? Why had he come south, on this day of all days? Because he wanted to be alone, because he wanted to catch bigger fish. And by making that stupid decision, he had sealed his own fate. He could not hope to survive a landing anywhere along this coast. So he kept rowing, into the wind and the raging sea, though more slowly now. The boat rose and fell, pitching and bucking as he attempted to keep it under control. The day which had begun so benignly had become wicked. If only it was possible to predict what the weather was going to do, he thought bitterly, if only he had been warned of this fatal change.

Then, through the howling wind, he thought he heard a cry. Turning, he heard it again. It *was* a human call. Half closing his eyes against the spray, he peered ahead, across the driving swells. Then he saw it. A sail, beige against the dark blue, flopping up and down among the swells like a moth in daylight. A boat, its boom extended, sailing fast before the wind. Seconds later, there came another call across the water. '*Luigi! Hey, Luigi!*' He recognised the white hull wallowing towards him, and the white-bearded man in the stern, clutching the tiller. It was French Louis, and *Antoinette*. Moving closer, the old man called across the swells.

'What the hell you doing here, you dumb bastard!'

'Trying to get back.'

'Against a nor-westerly? Jesus …'

When he was ten or so yards away from *Laetitia*, the Frenchman turned his boat into the wind. Its sail became a flag, flapping madly against the mast. He quickly lowered the sail and lashed it to the boom, bracing himself against the mast. Then he grabbed his boat's painter, steadied himself and tossed it across to *Laetitia*. Luigi joined the rope with a reef knot to his own painter. Yoked now, both boats began drifting backwards together. As French Louis brought *Antoinette* alongside, he called out. 'Okay, you listen to me good! Together we row out.' He waved his left hand towards the strait. 'Then, when we get so good enough away from the land, I put z'sail up again. So we come back home by wind. The tide, by then she comes in too, so she helps us. You understand me?'

Exhausted but grateful, Luigi nodded. But how on earth could the two of them make headway against this sea? And across the wind? French Louis was already sitting in the centre of *Antoinette*, on either side of the mast, hauling on his oars. And in minutes the two boats began to move, in tandem, out into the raging strait.

Later, Luigi would describe with astonishment French Louis' Neptune-like strength. Every time he glanced around, he saw the Frenchman hauling on his oars, ignoring the swells, seemingly unconcerned as to whether he went through them or over them. And the older man's strength and example lent Luigi fresh energy too. The knowledge that not to keep up with the other boat would imperil them both, led him to dig deeper and more strongly with his own oars. Whenever he felt his strokes falter, a jerk a few seconds later on *Laetitia*'s painter would remind him that Louis was still pulling his weight.

Although both boats slewed drunkenly down the swells, gradually the pair began to make erratic progress. Staring back at the land as he rowed, Luigi saw that it was beginning to retreat. Encouraged, he dug deeper, battling every swell as if it was a foe which must be vanquished. Then, after three-quarters of an hour, and with the coast now a long wall in the distance, French Louis stopped rowing and waited for Luigi to draw up alongside him. The Frenchman was sitting with shoulders slumped, mouth open, panting. Then, squinting at the sky, he called, 'Right, far enough. Now we sail.'

'What do you want me to do?' asked Luigi.

'Sit on your arse. Except if your boat gets too close for mine. If it do that, you take your oar and push it away.' He raised his fist. 'You hit my boat, I break your bloody neck.'

Slowly the sail came up the mast. Louis made fast the downhaul, then as the wind filled the sail, hastily grabbed the tiller and let out the mainsheet. The boom swung out wide and his boat surged forward. Seconds later, *Laetitia* followed, rocking wildly for a few moments until their course steadied, then sliding across the swells in pursuit of *Antoinette*. A few minutes later, left hand on the tiller, working the sheet with his right, Louis let his headsail unfurl. When the sheet was cleated and the jib filled with wind, both boats began to move faster. Cutting across the swells, rolling heavily, both took on water, but by bailing as they went, Louis and Luigi kept the intake manageable. And although the swells were still large, with the wind on their beams, three-quarters of an hour later the duo was making its way into Fisherman's Bay.

'Louis, thank you. You saved my life, I think.'

Still shaking Luigi's proffered hand, the Frenchman clapped his other hand on Luigi's shoulder. 'No problem. Just doan do that again, uh? A nor-westerly is very bad wind for here.'

'I can see that now.' Stretching his racked shoulders, Luigi asked, 'How did you know where I was?'

'The others they come back when the wind starts up. They tell me they see you go south. So I sail around the point.' He gave his gravelly laugh. 'And there I find you.'

'You're a great sailor.'

French Louis shrugged. 'Well, I have fifty years of practice.'

'Luigi, hey, Luigi!'

He looked up. Victor was running down the beach towards them, barefooted. When he reached them he was puffing. 'Luigi,' he announced breathlessly. 'You got a visitor. At your place.'

'Who?'

Victor grinned like a panting dog. 'Go and see.'

Puzzled, Luigi walked up the beach, his boots squelching as he went. Soaked from head to foot, he shivered in spite of the afternoon sun. Wiping the water from his face with his arm, he went across the track and into the house.

He went inside. And froze. Sitting on the bed, a suitcase on the floor in front of her, was Alice.

NINE

'Alice, Alice ...how did you get here? How did you know where I was?'

He held up his hands in bewilderment. But he could not take his eyes from her. And she was staring up at him, eyes shining through her tears. She was wearing a navy blue dress and matching laced boots, there was a bonnet on the bed beside her and her hair was untidy at the edges, just the way he remembered it.

Mouth open a little, she was breathing deeply, her upper body rising and falling, rising and falling. At last she was able to speak.

'I had to find you.'

'But how?'

'I remembered, you talked about the other Italians going to Wellington.'

Her expression darkened. Voice filled with reproach, she demanded, '*Why did you not tell me you were leaving? Why didn't you write to me?*'

Dropping to his knees, taking her hands in his, he said, 'I can explain. I will explain.' Her hands were so warm, so soft. He clasped them. 'Alice, Alice, I have thought of you constantly.'

Her expression remained distraught. 'But you vanished. And you never wrote.'

He hung his head. 'Yes.'

'*Why not?*'

'I had to.'

Tears streaming from her eyes, without taking her eyes from his face, she took his right hand and placed it over her belly. He felt, then saw the bulge there. When she found her voice again it was just a whisper. 'I am with child, Luigi.'

He stared into her face, realisation breaking over him like a dumping

153

wave. 'I didn't know, I couldn't know.'

Her expression became fierce again. 'Because you didn't write and tell me where you were.' Through the tears, her eyes blazed. 'That was so cruel of you, Luigi. To go, with no explanation. *Why did you do that?*'

'Because I had done something unforgivable.'

'What do you *mean?*'

Still clasping her hands, he said, 'I will tell you. Soon. But first, tell me how you found me.'

She looked away, tilting her chin upwards, reproving still. Then she took a deep breath, held it for a few seconds, exhaled, returned her eyes to his. The struggle to gain composure partly won, she began to speak.

'I thought at first that you may have gone back to Okuru. So I wrote to you there, care of the post office at Hokitika. Weeks later, the letter came back. It had 'Not Known Here' written across it. By then I knew I was pregnant. But I told no one, not even my sister Evie. I saved every penny I earned at the hotel, until I had the fare to Wellington. I took a berth on a collier, leaving a note for my parents, telling them I was going there to find better paid work. I stayed in the city for three weeks, working as a domestic in a boarding house in Cuba Street. I asked people where in Wellington the Italians lived, and they said in a fishing village at a place called Island Bay. So I took a coach to that place. There were lots of Italians there, but not you.' Tears flowing again, she paused to stem them with a handkerchief. 'I became desperate then. An old lady at the village said I could stay with her while they asked others if anyone knew of you. One of the Italian men, someone called Gino, came to the house. He told me that he had sold a boat to Luigi Galoni, and that it was at a place called Makara. He said I could get a ride there on the fish cart that left the market on Thursdays.' Putting the soaked handerchief to her eyes again, she added. 'So I did. This afternoon.' She tried to smile. 'And here I am.'

'Alice, Alice. My poor Alice.'

She stared at him with her intent, unwavering gaze. 'I am *not* poor Alice. I am here, to be with you. To have our child.'

Their eyes both went to her expanded waist. He was struck with the wonder of it. A child. Their child.

'When?'

'February. Early February. I went to a doctor when I was at the boarding house.'

There was a long silence. Then, seized with the need for practicalities, he got to his feet, waved his hand around the room. 'This place is nothing like what you are used to. It is not fit for you. Or a child.'

She smiled, tightly. 'As long as you are here, and I am with you, it is all I need.'

He strode to the other end of the room. His mind still in turmoil, he took a towel from the line above the fire and wiped his face and neck. Then he went back and sat on the bed next to her.

'I could improve it. Make it bigger. Add another room.'

'Are you a builder?' She was smiling properly now.

'I've watched men building. It isn't so hard. I can borrow tools. Wood comes in on the tide.' He put his arm around her shoulder. 'I will turn this place into a palace, Alice.'

She laughed, in the way he remembered and loved, the laugh itself preceded by a quick, delighted little intake of breath. They stood then, and held each other, and he felt the pressing of the child between them. Drawing back a little, she said, 'You're so wet. You'll catch a chill. Why are your clothes wet?'

'I nearly drowned today. But I was rescued. And now you're here.' He planted a kiss on her forehead. 'So I have regained my life, twice, in one day.' He stared down at her. 'Will you stay with me?'

'Yes.'

'Will you marry me?'

'Yes. I love you, Luigi. You must know that, now.'

'I know it. And I have never stopped loving you. So we must marry. Soon.'

'Yes, we must.'

She went to her suitcase, opened it and rummaged through the contents. She withdrew a small object, wrapped in tissue paper, opened it and held it out to him in the palm of her hand.

'I brought this with me, hoping against hope that I would need it. It belonged to my grandmother.'

Luigi stared at it, awed by its beauty. A gold ring, studded with tiny rubies.

That night, as they lay in each other's arms, he explained to her how he had made, then lost, a fortune, trying to make clear that it was for that reason alone that he had left so suddenly without telling her.

'I had gambled away my future, I had no prospects. I was so ashamed.'

'But I didn't care about the money. I didn't even know about it. I loved you for what you were, not for what you had.' There was a pause. 'Although if I had known you'd been invited to that billiards room, I would have warned you. Henry Rawlinson's a ruthless man. He is known to have bankrupted others.'

'But I was so *stupid*. I should have realised he only bought the gold from me because he knew that somehow he would get the money back again.'

'Luigi, don't fret about it. We're together now, that's all that counts.'

In the long, wondrous silence that followed, she stroked his brow and he held her hand tightly. Their fingers entwined, and in the flickering light of the fire, he saw her smiling.

'When did you first know that you loved me?' she asked, her voice almost a whisper.

'When you brought me tea and biscuits. You moved with such grace. Such loveliness.'

'Such tea, such biscuits.'

'Don't mock me, Alice.'

'I'm not mocking. It's just that it sounded strange. To fall in love for so humble a reason.'

'Not so humble, really.' He drew her closer to him. 'And so, I will turn your question around. When did you fall in love with me?'

She paused, then said, 'I think, when you played that love song on your accordion. At the hotel.'

'Which one?'

'The one about the secret tear. What is it called in Italian?'

'Una furtive lagrima. Donizetti.' He shrugged. 'But it is such a sad song.'

'Yes, but beautiful, too. I watched you playing, and singing, from the kitchen door. And by the time you had finished, I was in love with you.' She laid her head on his bare chest. 'I've shed so many tears, Luigi, since you left. Secret tears.'

'No more tears, Alice. We are together now. That is all that matters.'

'Yes, I know. I know.'

And as they lay and watched the fire burn and talked of what they must do to prepare for the child, without saying so each knew that a double miracle had occurred in their lives. The first, that the two of them had been brought together from opposite sides of the world, the second, that they were now reunited in this wild place beside the sea.

Next day they took a lift to Paremata on the dray of Alfred Morgan, who supplied the Makara fishermen with farm produce. They travelled up through the twisting Takarau gorge, along the Ohariu valley road and across the Porirua plain. Both wore their best clothes, he his Westport suit, cap and blue tie, she a loose-fitting primrose cotton dress, with matching bonnet and gloves. The plan was for them to be married at Paremata, then to stay the night in Flanagans Hotel, beside the harbour. French Louis had recommended the place to Luigi. There were two churches in the village, he also told them, one Roman Catholic, the other Church of England. When Alfred took a break at Johnsonville to water and feed his horse, they sat on a bench outside the farrier's there and talked again of which church they should be married in.

'You would prefer a Catholic service, I suppose,' Alice suggested.

Luigi considered this for some moments. He said soberly, 'It is the only church I have known. But I belong to no church now. You would prefer the English church?'

'It does not matter to me.'

'If it was the Catholic church, what would your family say?'

'My father would be enraged.' Her expression hardened. 'But I don't care. So long as we are married, I don't mind. My father need never know.'

'And your mother?'

She looked away. 'I will tell her. In time.'

'If it is the Catholic church, they will make the child be Catholic.'

'Like its father,' she rejoined.

Laughing, they climbed back onto the dray.

The Catholic church was beside the main Plimmerton road, opposite the railway station, a solid, red-brick building with a shingled steeple topped with a large concrete cross. 'St Theresas', a sign on the lawn in front of the building stated. Next door was a double-storeyed house in matching brick, and it was there that they first called. A wimpled nun with a pallid face answered the rectory door, and after they told her what they needed, went inside to get the priest.

He was a short, thickset man in his forties, clean-shaven, with a waxen face and cropped, greying hair. His cassock reached to the ground, his white collar to the underside of his chin. Around his neck was a large black and silver crucifix. Although he was barely five and a half feet high, by standing on the top step of the rectory he was able to look down on them both. Luigi stared at the figure for a moment, then removed his cap and spoke.

'Good afternoon, father. I am Luigi Galoni and this is my fiancée, Alice Harris. We wish to be married in your church.'

The priest inclined his head to Luigi, then turned to Alice. His examination began at her face, went to her breasts, moved quickly to her feet, then travelled slowly upwards. When they reached half-way, they stopped, then lingered on her bulging midriff. Flicking his eyes upwards, he said coldly, 'You are with child.'

'Yes,' said Alice, her face colouring.

The priest switched his gaze to Luigi. 'Your child?'

'*Our* child, yes.' Luigi took Alice's hand. 'We love each other. We wish to be married. So our child is born in wedlock.'

'You are Catholic?' the priest demanded.

'I was born so,' said Luigi, warily. His cheeks prickled. He felt anger rising, thick and hot as lava, from the depths of his belly.

The priest's gaze drifted downwards again. When it reached Alice's stomach one side of his mouth went up. Looking over their heads, he enmeshed his fingers and held his hands together tightly in front of him. In an arid tone he pronounced,

'You must be married in the Catholic church, but you cannot be married in mine. Not at the high altar. If there was a side altar, it would be possible, but there is not one here. I suggest you go to the city, to St Marys in Boulcott Street. There is a side altar there. For couples such as you.'

Luigi took a step forward. His instinct was to take this little man by the throat and hit his head against the brick wall of his own rectory. But Alice's hand restrained him.

'Luigi, no.'

He glared at the priest for a few more moments, clenching his fists, then turned away.

They sat on a seat above the estuary. The Paremata inlet had the appearance of a lake, but sinewy currents streaming under the bridge next to the seat showed that the tide was flowing into it. Further out in the harbour a man was rowing a dinghy with slow strokes, while another man in the stern paid out a net. Alice had stopped crying now, but her voice still quavered.

'He made me feel… like a criminal.'

Luigi, his arm around her shoulder, hugged her harder. 'He made me feel like behaving like one. Like punching him. The little pig. I hate him, and I hate his church.'

'Looking me up and down like that. It seemed like he was trying to make us feel dirty.'

'Yes. As if he was saying, "I will never be married, I will never have a wife or child, so you can go to hell." '

'I thought that too.' But when she turned to face him, her expression was desolate. 'What are we to do now? I want to be married. I want our child to have parents who are married.'

He stared out over the water. 'There's another church here, French Louis told me. The English church.'

'And if they refuse too?'

'We will take a coach into the city, and go to a registry office.'

'I'd rather it was a church.'

St Thomas's of Paremata was a board and batten, imitative Gothic building with a crossless steeple. By the time they found it, it was late afternoon and the heat was draining out of the day. Holding one hand to the small of her back, Alice walked along the footpath in her sailor's rolling gait. Their boots covered in dust, tired and dispirited now, they went first to the vicarage alongside the church, where there was no answer to Luigi's knocking, then to the church itself. As they approached the entrance, a man wearing a minister's collar, black shirt and dark grey trousers emerged.

He was about fifty, tall and balding, with a pouchy face, large dewlaps and broad sideburns. Luigi greeted him and introduced himself and Alice. The minister shook his hand. 'And I'm Charles Swindon, vicar of this parish.' He had a booming, basso profundo voice. 'How can I help you?'

'We would like to be married here,' Luigi declared.

'Ah.' The minister gave a little cough. 'What did you say your surname was?'

'Galoni.'

'An Italian name, am I correct?'

'Yes, I am Italian.'

Glancing first at Alice, the minister looked back to Luigi. 'So, are you not a member of the church of Rome?'

Luigi hesitated. What was the honest answer to that question? He looked the minister in the eye. 'I was brought up as a Catholic,' he admitted.

The minister's brow ruckled. 'So shouldn't you be married in a Catholic church? St Theresa's is further along the road. Towards the bridge.'

'We have already been there,' Alice put in, plaintively.

Trying to stay calm, Luigi said, 'The priest refused to marry us in his church. Because there is no side altar.' Gesturing towards Alice, he added, 'My fiancée is with child.'

The minister tipped his head right back, opened his mouth wide and said 'Aaaaah,' loudly, as if gargling salt water. He inclined his head, glanced at Alice's figure, then quickly looked away again. 'I see, I see. So, when would you like the marriage to take place?'

'Today. Now.'

The minister's eyes bulged. 'Now? Well, goodness me. Such a hurry.'

'Is it possible?' Luigi's voice was more insistent than he had intended it to be. If they were rejected again Alice would be distraught. Again he reached for her hand.

The vicar made a rumbling noise as he cleared his throat, then clapped his big hands together. 'It is possible, certainly.' He intoned, 'St John, chapter iii: "In my Father's house there are many mansions".' In a lowered voice he added, 'Although not at St Theresa's, obviously.' Then he smiled in a kindly way. 'You both live in this area?'

'I am from Makara,' said Luigi. 'We will be living there.'

'Right. Near enough.' His attention turned to Alice. 'And you, my child, are of age?'

'I'm seventeen.'

'Good, good.' As he was struck by another consideration, his expression turned serious. 'Have you brought a witness?'

Luigi looked at Alice blankly, then back at the minister.

'What is that?

'Someone to witness the ceremony, and your signing of the

register.'

'We didn't bring another person,' Alice confessed, frowning. 'We didn't know we had to.'

The minister's eyes twinkled. 'Well, in that case, we'll ask Thomas Burgess.'

'Who is he?' asked Luigi, even more puzzled. Why should it be so hard to get married?

The minister pointed to the railway station across the road. 'Paremata's station master. A most reliable fellow. You two go on inside the church and wait, and I'll fetch him.' His eyes twinkled again. 'Say a prayer or two if you like, while you're waiting.'

'Alice Galoni, now I am Alice Galoni.'

'It is a very nice name, Alice Galoni.' He stroked the hair from the sides of her face, then placed a kiss in the centre of her forehead. 'I am the luckiest man in the world.'

'Even though I am so blown up?' She held her hands over her bulge, which was as round and tight as a white balloon. Her breasts too were swollen, and pale blue veins radiated from her nipples. Staring at her ripened body, Luigi thought it one of the most beautiful sights he had ever seen. She watched him staring for a time, then took his hand and held it over her navel. 'He moves, now, often.'

'He?'

'Yes. I am sure it is a he.'

'Then we must call him Ernesto.'

'Why?'

'That was my father's name.'

Alice nodded. 'He could be Ernesto William. William was my mother's father's name. He was from England. A carpenter. He died when I was nine.'

'Ernesto William Galoni. Yes, I like that. It is a fine name.'

Their room was on the upper level of the two-storeyed hotel, overlooking the main road. The double bed had a brass head, there was a wash basin on a pedestal beside it and opposite the end of the bed was a double wardrobe with a pair of long, bevelled mirrors set into its doors.

Earlier in the evening they had dined downstairs on roast beef and Yorkshire pudding, kumara, carrots and silver beet, and celebrated with a bottle of Madeira which they couldn't finish because just two glasses made their heads spin. Then, after dessert they went upstairs and bathed together in the claw-footed bath in the bathroom at the end of the passage. There they explored each other's bodies tenderly, and sponged one another until the water became too cool. Then they ran back to their room, dripping and giggling, towels wrapped around themselves. And in the big bed Alice stroked him slowly and lovingly until he came with a cry, then she cleaned him again and they sat side by side in the bed, staring at each other's reflections in the wardrobe's mirrors, having no need of words.

Gradually Alice slipped further and further down in the bed, closed her eyes and fell asleep. Luigi turned down the gas-lamp and studied her face. Her lips were slightly parted, the dampened edges of her hair dark, her curlicue lashes long. There were tiny veins in her eyelids and a scattering of light freckles across her high cheek-bones. He touched the little cleft in her chin, and she stirred. After a time of staring at her he got up, put on his night-shirt, rolled and lit a cigarette, went to the window, leaned on the sill and smoked. Across the now-quiet road, beyond the entrance to the harbour, the sea between the headlands was velvet black and still. Drawing deeply on his cigarette, his thoughts turned inward. That he should be here, with a wife and child-to-be. What responsibilities he now had. Taking care of Alice and the child would use all the resources he would be able to get together at Makara. The little house must be enlarged as soon as possible. He couldn't expect Alice to wash herself or the baby's clothes in the stream like the men did. He would have to make a crib. And get a water tank and taps, and a bath, and a proper food safe. He would manage, but how would she? How would *they*? Turning, he looked back across the room. In the half-darkness Alice was fast asleep, her face turned towards him. As he watched she stirred again, sighed heavily and turned over to face the other way.

A wife, and child, he thought. You have a wife, and soon, a child. And suddenly he was fearful. For all of them.

Three large groper, a dozen tarakihi and six crayfish were swapped for one of Alfred Morgan's geese, which came with a bag of new potatoes, some onions and carrots. Alice began cooking the goose the day before Christmas, stuffing the bird with seasoned bread crumbs and wrapping it in grease-proof paper before putting it in the big roasting pan over the fire. Already she had reorganised the household, rigging a hessian curtain between the sleeping and the cooking end of the cottage, doubling the fishing cord washing line and sweeping the sand from the floor every day.

Luigi chopped down a little pine tree from the hill above the bay and stood it in sand in a bucket next to the fire. Victor carved an angel from macrocarpa wood for them, Luigi painted it with silver paint and they stuck it atop the tree. There was no money for presents, but Antonio brought beer and port wine back from his last pre-Christmas delivery trip to the city, and French Louis invited him, Victor, Luigi and Alice for drinks at his place on Christmas Eve.

The evening was warm, and as the sun wasn't setting until after eight-thirty, they sat outside Louis' cottage and drank their wine. After darkness fell, further round the bay the other fishermen lit a driftwood bonfire and sat around it drinking their home-brewed beer. Flames from the fire cast tongues of orange light over the dark water of Fisherman's Bay, and from time to time a burst of sparks showered into the sky like fireworks.

Luigi and Alice, he with his arm around her shoulder, sat on a rug on the foreshore, admiring the flames and the sparks and the way the lights turned the bay beautiful. The advent of Alice was a great novelty in the little Italian community, her advanced pregnancy at this time prompting many wry observations of the Madonna similarity. She hadn't yet met all of them officially, only French Louis, Antonio, Victor, Francesco and his wife Miriama, but they all knew who she was and the significance of her arrival. Later in the evening the Johnsonville priest was coming to celebrate midnight mass on the shore outside Francesco's house, but Luigi had already decided not to attend. When he told French Louis this, the old man guffawed.

'So, what are you Luigi, a heathen or a Mohammedan? It's Christmas, for Christ's sake. Even an old sinner like me takes the sacraments on Christmas Eve.'

'Call me whatever you like, Louis, I don't care. By the time the priest comes, Alice and I will be fast asleep.'

Glancing at Alice's midriff, French Louis nodded approvingly, refilled Luigi's glass, then did the same for Victor. The Frenchman swallowed more wine, then announced gruffly, 'The child cannot be born here.'

Alice's eyes darted. 'Why not?'

'If there are difficulties, who will help?'

'Miriama has said she will,' Alice said. Her tone was defensive. She and Luigi had been through this already.

'She's not a midwife, ma petite,' said Louis, gently.

'She has borne three children,' Luigi put in, with more conviction than he felt. He'd become increasingly doubtful, too, lately. This was hardly the best place for Alice to bear her first child. No running water, no sterile equipment, no midwife.

Victor said keenly, 'We will all help.'

French Louis glowered at him. 'You're a good singer, Victor, but you'll never be a midwife.' He swallowed some more wine, then said, 'I know one, in Petone. You could stay with her, have the baby there.'

'Where is Petone?' asked Alice.

'In the Hutt Valley. Mrs Delgarno could help you with the birth, and the baby. Until you're able to bring it back here.'

'Delgarno,' said Luigi. 'She is Italian?'

'Yes. From Stromboli. I met her and her husband when I lived in the valley. She's a widow, now, no children of her own.' He looked at Alice in an almost fatherly way. 'With your understanding of what I do, I will write to her. Ask if you can both stay at her house, until after the baby is born.'

Alice looked at Luigi, confusion in her eyes. 'But Luigi and I had agreed. That the baby would be born here.'

Luigi put his hand on her arm and gripped it, reassuringly. He knew Louis' suggestion made sense. There was only one problem. Hesitant, embarrassed, he said to the Frenchman, 'The woman would charge. And while I was away there would be no fish caught. So, no income.'

French Louis lit a match, put it to the bowl of his hooked pipe and sucked hard. His face was enveloped in smoke for a few moments. When it cleared he said gruffly, 'The charge won't be great, when she learns you are from Italy. And I can lend you money. Catch some crayfish before you go, and take them to Mrs Delgarno.' He raised his glass. 'Now, it's nearly Christmas. So go and get your accordion, Luigi, and play us a tune. An Italian Christmas tune.'

Alice put her hand over her mouth, stifling a yawn. Getting to her feet, she announced, 'I'm sorry, but I'll have to go now. I'm very tired. And the goose ...'

French Louis leapt to his feet, took her hand and kissed it, at the same time bowing low. 'Of course. Good night, and merry Christmas

Eve.' He gave Luigi a mock glare. 'You escort your wife to your home now, you hear? She must to get her sleep.' Laughing, Luigi stood up too. Taking Alice's arm, they wished the others good night, then walked back along the track to the cottage, their way partly illuminated by the still-blazing bonfire.

They left Makara on the fish cart on the last day of January, with Victor taking the reins. From the city market they took the short walk to the railway station, Luigi with four crayfish wrapped in newspaper in one hand, a suitcase in the other, and caught the train to Petone. It was very hot in the carriage, and Alice was asleep even before they reached the first stop at Kaiwharawhara. As they pulled into the Petone station, Luigi woke Alice gently and they walked down into the suburb's main thoroughfare, Jackson Street. French Louis had given them directions to Mrs Delgarno's house and they found her street without difficulty, running to the left off the main street.

Nelson Street was long, very straight and lined on both sides with small villas only an arm's length apart, built of weatherboard and corrugated iron and with picket fences along their frontages. Alice, rolling along, her steps becoming slower and slower, counted off the house numbers as they trudged along. 'One hundred and eighty-two, one hundred and eighty-four …'

At last they came to number 390. It was another villa, verandahed at the front like all the others, with red geraniums and orange canna lilies growing in its small front garden. Lace curtains covered the sash windows on either side of the front door. Luigi rapped three times on the iron knocker.

'Mrs Delgarno?'

'Yes.'

'We are Mr and Mrs Galoni.'

'From Makara?'

'Yes. I am Luigi and this is my wife, Alice.'

'Come in, please.'

She was about forty, short and dumpy, with a round face and an olive complexion. Her English was heavily accented, her manner brisk but considerate. She showed them into the front bedroom, which was opposite the parlour on the left-hand side of a narrow passage which ran down the centre of the house. The bedroom was small but comfortable, carpeted, with a double bed and a wash-stand. As she took Alice's case and placed it on a stool under the window, Luigi realised that the decision to come here had been the right one: as Mrs Delgarno showed them the rest of the house and explained the procedure for the confinement, he could see gratitude shining in his young wife's eyes.

They ate Mrs Delgarno's scones and drank tea in the small, cluttered front parlour. She told them how she had left her village in Stromboli in 1883, one of the very few young women to emigrate alone. She met her husband on the voyage out, married and settled in the Hutt Valley. There, at the cottage hospital, she trained as a midwife and he grew vegetables for the Wellington market on half an acre of land. Then, five years ago, he had been thrown from his horse and died of a fractured skull. The couple had been unable to have children.

'So, I sell his land to other Italian people, and buy my house here.' Sadness glazed her eyes. 'Is nice house, but lonely too. So when ladies have babies, they come to stay. You will be all right here, Alicia.' She looked across at Luigi. 'And I have arranged a room for you, at the boarding house.'

Startled, Luigi said, 'You mean, I cannot stay here too?' French Louis had mentioned nothing of this.

Mrs Delgarno shook her head firmly. 'No, no. No men stay here. When babies come, men are no use.'

Luigi looked at Alice, who smiled weakly and gave him a look that said, What else can we do? Frowning at the woman, he asked, 'Where is this boarding house?'

'Esplanade.' She got up. 'I explain to you. It is only half an hour walk from here.'

He strolled out onto the beach, disturbing a black-backed gull tearing at a fish carcass. The bird glared at him, then cawed accusingly as it rose into the evening air. The wind had dropped and the harbour was still, Somes Island in shadow. Tiny waves advanced, licked at the sand, then retreated, as if not liking the taste.

Picking up a pine cone from the tideline, Luigi hurled it out into the water. He was still smarting from the woman's dismissal. Of course men had no part to play in childbirth, he was fully aware of that. It was women's business. But he wanted at least to be there when things began, to comfort Alice in any way he could. That was his responsibility. She was so young, so vulnerable, her family hundreds of miles away. When their child came into the world, he had at least expected to be in the same building. Banishment to a gloomy boarding house was the last thing he'd expected. Every room in the place stank of boiled cabbage and fried fat, most of the occupants seemed to be derelict alcoholic men, and the woman in charge was a slattern. Sitting on the sand, he rolled and lit a cigarette. He'd seldom felt so useless.

'Luigi Galoni?'

He opened his eyes. It was as dark as a mine in the room.

'LUIGI GALONI?' The man's voice came again, booming up the stairs.

He opened the door. 'Yes?'

'Message for you.'

Still in his nightshirt, he went quickly down the stairs. The husband of the woman who ran the boarding house handed him a small, folded note. 'This came for you. A kid brought it here, a few minutes ago.'

Holding it up to the low gas lamp at the foot of the stairs, Luigi opened the piece of paper. The words on it were printed. Yor wife is in laber. Do not cum until the morning.

He took out his watch. Three thirty-five. *He had to be there for her.* After dressing quickly and pulling on his boots, he went downstairs to the communal bathroom, dashed water onto his face and brushed his hair. He walked up to Jackson Street and through the deserted town centre to Nelson Street. The identical, side-by-side villas were dark, closed and silent and the only light came from a gibbous moon, high in the sky above the hills, the only sound the wind moaning as it swept down from them. He walked on, as quickly as he could, hot sweat turning his body clammy. *Yor wife is in laber.* He had to get to her.

He saw light glowing in the front window of number 390 when he was still over a hundred yards away. Panting, he reached the front gate. There he hesitated, and stopped. From behind the lighted window he heard a ghastly sound. A scream, rising into the night. He stared at the curtained window and the rectangle of yellow light. The curtains were drawn tightly, but he could see two dark shapes behind them, standing, bending, moving this way and that. The scream died away slowly, followed by a few seconds' silence. Then it came again, with the same intensity and a rising pitch. The sweat on his body turned cold. Suddenly and uncontrollably giddy, he reached out and put his hands around the gate pickets. *Alice, Alice*, he said aloud, gripping the pickets. The screaming continued for perhaps a quarter of a minute, then subsided, followed by a sobbing which could have been relief, then a series of just-audible whimpers. Sinking to the ground, Luigi turned his back to the gate. Something must be wrong, he thought, to cause her to cry like that. His mind began to reel. What if the child died? How could he atone for bringing that upon her? What if *both* died? He put his face in his hands. The screaming came once more, rising steadily to bursting point, before again falling away, slowly and agonisingly. He closed his eyes, put his hands over his ears, but the cries still reached him, as from the depths of a forest which he could not enter.

A last, silence descended upon the house. An utter, but equally terrifying silence. He stood up, staring at the lighted window, inclining his head to catch any sound. There was none. Behind the curtain, shadows were still moving. Unable to stand not knowing any longer, he unlatched the gate, went to the front door and rapped on it several times. A minute later, the door opened. A young woman he hadn't seen before, wearing a striped nurse's uniform, long white smock, rubber gloves and a head scarf. The apron was smeared with blood. 'Yes?' Her face was knotted with irritation.

'Where is Mrs Delgarno?'

The young woman turned away, half closing the door behind her. Seconds later, it opened wide again. Mrs Delgarno, her face wet with sweat, was also wearing rubber gloves and a long white smock that covered the entire front of her body. It too was covered in blood. Her brow wrinkled. 'Mr Galoni, what are you doing here?'

'Alice. Is she …?'

His sentence remained unfinished, interrupted by another cry from the room to the left of the passage. First reedy and mewing, it grew quickly in strength until in seconds it was a lusty bawling. Luigi turned his head. Not Alice. His eyes flicked back to Mrs Delgarno's.

'The child?'

She swallowed, then passed the back of her gloved hand across her brow. 'It had to be turned. A breech birth. Very difficult.' She heaved a great sigh. 'There was much bleeding. But your wife is young and healthy. She will recover.'

'And the child?'

Her face broke into a weary smile. 'The child is fine. Seven pounds, 12 ounces. A fine, healthy daughter.'

Luigi found himself unable to take his eyes from the baby's face, its pink complexion, the rosebud mouth, the delicate strands of pale hair which came over its perfect ears. And as he stared he felt an emotion quite unlike any he had ever felt before, a jubilance, a sense of wonder which transcended every feeling he had ever experienced.

'Your face, Luigi.'

'What?'

'You should see yourself.'

'Why?'

'You look so …struck.'

'What do you mean?'

'Astonished. As if you think she is not real.'

He turned to her, lying in the bed, her hair unloosed and spread over the pillow. Her face was blotchy, her eyes bloodshot and half focused. But there was radiance too, beaming through her exhaustion, as she stared at him. She held the child out.

Reaching for the baby's minute hand, feeling its response, an amazingly strong grip on his finger, he said quietly, 'I *am* astonished.' A wave of love and wonder surged through him again. 'She is so perfect.'

Looking down at the swaddled, crimson-cheeked child, watching its gums working, its eyelids flickering, Alice smiled. 'You do not mind that she is not Ernesto William?'

'No, no.'

'So, what shall we call her?'

'Violetta.'

CERTIFICATES

That evening, after calling at the Leighton family's engineering works in Porirua, William drove on to Paremata, turned off busy State Highway 1 and parked beside the harbour. Getting out, he walked to the edge of the water and sat down on the shingle shore. The sun was setting, lending a lovely blush to the water. A few launches were anchored in the harbour, their shapes mirrored by the still water. Had Luigi lived here? he wondered. The museum's display had told him that there had been a community of Italian fishermen here, so he may have walked this shore, fished these waters. And were his children born here, or elsewhere in Wellington? Birth certificates would say. If the trail of one generation went cold, it might warm up for the next. Marriage and birth documents, that was the next way to go. Gina would remember the Christian names of those concerned.

You could request them over the phone, William learnt from the Births Deaths and Marriages Registry. After a woman there took down the name and approximate dates, read them back to him to check that the details were correct, he supplied her with his credit card number and address. A few days later, photocopies of the certificates arrived in the post. Taking them to his desk under the window, he studied the two sheets.

1888   **Marriages in the District of Wellington**

No.	When and Where Married	Names and Surnames of the Parties	Ages	Rank or Profession
113				
	22 December	Luigi Galoni	31	Fisherman
	St Thomas's	Alice Maud Harris	17	Spinster
	Church, Paremata			

170

Condition of Parties	Birthplace	Residence	Father's Name & Surname and his Rank or Profession
Bachelor	Italy	Wellington	1. Ernesto Galoni
			2. Fisherman
Spinster	Westport	Wellington	1. John Harris
			2. Boot-maker

Mother's Name and Maiden Surname

1   Laetitia Maria

2   Varonetta

1   Edith Harris

2   Hunter

I certify that the above is a true copy of the entry in the Register-book of Marriages kept by me,

In the presence of us,
(Reverend) Charles Swindon, Paremata
Thomas Burgess, Station-master, Paremata

C.J.Swindon
Officiating Minister

The implications of the certicate touched William. Their age difference, the fact that they were from opposite sides of the world. Had they had a big family wedding? Where did they honeymoon? *Did* people honeymoon, in those days?

He looked again at the date of Luigi and Alice's marriage. December 22, 1888. Three days before Christmas. A strange time for a wedding. People didn't usually get married at Christmas. Puzzled, he turned to the other photocopied sheet, their first child's – his father's mother's – birth certificate. Its facts were also recorded in sloped, looping longhand.

Given name and surname: Violetta Laetitia Galoni. Date of birth: 9 February, 1889

Place of birth: 390 Nelson Street, Wellington

His eyes flicked from one certificate to the other, from the first set of dates to the second. Then, as the significance of their timing brought realisation, his mind tumbled. He studied the two sets of dates again.

Between the two life-transforming events there were just over six weeks.

TEN

He added another room to the cottage, a lean-to which doubled as a bathroom and wash-house. Framed and weatherboarded with more dunnage timber, the extension's roof was covered with farmers' cast-off corrugated iron and lined with tar paper. Behind it, hard up against the hill, he made a dunny out of more sheets of iron, the pan a bucket with a wooden seat on top. Alice carried water in a bucket from the stream to the basin in the lean-to, and Violetta slept in a cot made of butter-box wood beside their bed, on a little mattress made of kapok.

By the time Luigi finished building the lean-to, Alice was pregnant again. The following spring, when Violetta began to crawl, Alice insisted that the property be cordoned off to keep her away from the sea, so he made a fence out of wire netting along the frontage and sides, using lengths of galvanised pipe for posts. The gate he made out of trimmed driftwood, the latch was a loop of number 8 wire.

In the early summer of 1890 they again made the trek over the hills to the city, leaving Violetta in the care of Alice's young sister, Evie, who had come north to work as a domestic help for a well-to-do family in Kelburn. Like Alice, she did so against her father's wishes. In the first week of December, at Mrs Delgarno's Petone villa, Edith Mary Galoni was born.

They sat together on the driftwood seat in the little front yard. After yet another toiling day, there was at last time for relaxation and reflection. It was high summer, the evening was light, the air warm. Luigi rolled a cigarette and lit it; Alice was letting down the hem of Violetta's skirt. Down on the shore, Victor and Antonio were hanging their net on a driftwood frame to dry. Inside the fence, Violetta was putting a doll, that

Alf Morgan's wife had passed on to her, to bed in a miniature cradle that French Louis had made. Edith was asleep in Alice and Luigi's bed. As they watched, greatly amused at little Violetta busying herself with the doll, Luigi said, 'I should become naturalised, Alice.'

'Why?'

'So I really belong here.'

'You've lived here over eleven years, does that not that make you a New Zealander?'

'Not in the eyes of the government.'

'But you've got a New Zealand wife and two children. All born here.'

'But I wasn't. People still think of me as an immigrant.'

'Lots of people are immigrants.'

'But they are mostly from England. Everyone accepts them. But if you are Italian, you are still an alien. Antonio and I were talking about it with French Louis. He's naturalised, and he advised us that we should be. For our own protection. That politician, Seddon, is always talking about aliens and how they don't belong here.'

'He is a wind-bag.'

'But he is powerful, too. And they say he might be Premier one day. For our own protection, I should become a New Zealander.'

'How do you do that?'

'Appear before a Justice of the Peace, declare that I am a good citizen and always will be. And pay a fee of two and sixpence.'

'*Two and six*? Luigi, we cannot afford that!'

'It will be worth it. After that, no one can tell me I am not a New Zealander.' He put his arm around her shoulder. 'So I will always be here for you and the children.'

There was a long silence. Violetta began to rock her doll in the little cradle, and murmur the lullaby Alice sang her to sleep with. Alice put her head on Luigi's shoulder.

'Well, if you get your naturalisation certificate, I might get the right to vote.'

'Why would you want to do that?'

'The Women's Temperance Union is saying that New Zealand women are helping to build this country, so they should be able to help say who runs it, too.'

'They are the women who don't want anyone to drink. "Wowsers",

French Louis calls them.'

'But they are right about voting, I think.'

'Perhaps,' Luigi mused. There was a pause. 'Will you come to Paremata and see us naturalised? Victor and Antonio and me?'

'When?'

'Friday afternoon.'

'I'd like to. But the children ...'

'Of course.'

So, in the company of Victor and Antonio, along with Charles Merveldt, a German bushman from Kumara, and Theodore Belong, a Dutch fisherman from Paramata, he took his Declaration of Verification, in the council chambers at Paremata. Afterwards the three Italians lunched together at Flanagan's Hotel, before returning to Makara on the cart before darkness fell, the new New Zealanders all with their precious certificates in their jacket pockets. On the way back Luigi played his accordion, accompanying the trio's tipsy singing of Italian songs and the New Zealand anthem, God Save the Queen. And three weeks after Luigi officially became a New Zealander, Alice found she was pregnant again.

Alicia Lydia Galoni was born in the summer of 1891. Eighteen months later, Esther Eveline arrived. All four girls were delivered in the front room at 390 Nelson Street while their father stayed in the Petone boarding house. Their different personalities were evident almost from the beginning. Violetta, serious and responsible, Edith fun-loving and mischievous, Alicia the beauty, with the soulful eyes and fretful manner, Esther slow and withdrawn. Only Alicia inherited her father's flaming auburn hair. Violetta and Edith were fair-haired, like Alice, Esther dark-haired, like Alice's mother.

After each child arrived, Luigi enlarged the Makara cottage yet again, adding a lean-to to the lean-to, then another wash-house with copper and tubs behind the building. To support them all, he spent longer and longer hours at sea, rowing out to the fishing grounds at daybreak, at times in conditions that were threatening. But there was no choice. The growing family demanded food, clothing, shoes, beds, linen. Their needs seemed insatiable; the more fish he caught and sold, the more his family consumed. He and Victor made the trip to the municipal fish market twice a week now, with almost all the Galonis' share of the proceeds going on groceries – tea, coffee, baking powder, flour, sugar – and off-cuts of material from a Dixon Street drapery which Alice cut and sewed by hand into dresses for the girls. Clothes, boots and shoes were handed down, Violetta being the only one who ever wore anything new. There was no time for leisure, for both Alice and Luigi, work was unending.

But whenever he rowed back into the bay, hauling hard on the oars, his boat half-filled with fish, whenever he glanced over his shoulder and saw the little house by the bay drawing closer and the girls rushing down the beach to meet him, he always felt a glow of pride and love. A wife and children, a family of his own.

Yet hard as Luigi worked, for Alice life was harder. She cooked and washed and cleaned and sewed from dawn until nightfall, stoking and lighting the fire in the house, bucketing water from the stream to the wash-house, boiling water in the copper tub and scrubbing nappies, underwear and other clothing on the wash-board, hanging the washing on the lines beside the house, emptying the chamber-pots into the pit above the bay, mixing dough, baking bread and biscuits, preparing breakfasts, lunches and dinners, heating more water to wash the dishes. She chopped wood for the fires, made soap from boiled tallow, hand-sewed clothes and bed-linen, stewed and bottled apples, pears and plums from the valley farms, and tried to keep the flies from the bacon and mutton they obtained from the same source. Her work continued unabated, seventeen hours a day, seven days a week. Young Evie came over from Kelburn sometimes, on her day off, and was a great help with the children. She slept in the bed with Alice, while Luigi slept on a camp stretcher in the wash-house, waking before sun-rise to prepare his nets, baits and lines.

And when the Sunday visitors from the city promenaded around the bay in their fine clothes, Alice stayed indoors, not wanting them to see her faded dresses, worn shoes, cracked hands or other evidence of her life of relentless toil.

It was not long after Esther's birth that the first sign of trouble between them began.

'Alice, Alice …'

'Luigi, no. I can't, I can't.'

'Do you not love me then, is that what this means?'

'I *do* love you, you know that.'

'Then why don't you come to me any more?'

'I *can't* fall pregnant again. We can only just manage as it is.'

'Alice, *I want a son*. The girls will grow up and marry. My sister is married. So my family's name will vanish.'

'It seems that I can only conceive daughters.'

'But let us try again and see.'

'And if we have another daughter?'

'Then we can try once more.'

'No. *No.*'

And she turned away, tearful with fatigue and frustration.

Saddened but resigned, Luigi asked French Louis how one could still make love to one's wife and not make her pregnant. The Frenchman – who for years had visited a Cuba Street brothel once a fortnight – gave him the name of a pharmacist in the same district of the city who supplied Luigi with a sheath. It was made of vulcanised rubber. Although he found it distasteful – 'Like swimming with my oilskin on', as he put it – using it was better than not making love at all. And rinsed in the tide after use, one sheath could be made to last for three months before it showed signs of perishing.

After they discussed the ways Alice's domestic drudgery might be eased, they invited Evie to stay more often. Pretty and jolly, and the only single woman at Fisherman's Bay, Evie soon began to attract the attention of the unmarried men.

When Stephano Bartolli, a 20-year-old newcomer to the community, set eyes on Evie he immediately came to the Galoni cottage and asked Luigi for permission to walk her along the cliffs with him. Luigi refused. Stephano was one of the Massalubrensians, a raffish young man with a lustful look. Protective of his sister-in-law's virtue, Luigi told him that if he wanted a wife, to go over to Island Bay and find an Italian one there. Shortly afterwards, Stephano did.

The years seemed to race by. By the time Violetta turned four and Esther was walking, the house became less and less adequate for their needs. During the winter months the wind often turned to the south, turning the sea furious, so for days on end it wasn't safe for Luigi to take his boat out. In these conditions they were all confined within the little house's walls. Usually just big enough for four, at such times it became almost impossible for six. Then, after the storm, the shore would be strewn with jellyfish and heaps of rotting seaweed, whose briny stench was overpowering. And as Violetta moved into her fifth year, other concerns pressed in on them.

'She must go to school, Luigi. She's a bright child.'

'I know that. They must all go to school.'

'But, how? There's no school here, and Karori's eight miles away.'

'Alf Morgan told me the government has plans to build a school in Makara.'

'Not at the beach, surely.'

'No, in the valley.'

'So the girls would have to walk. Three miles there and three miles back.'

'I could get a horse. Violetta could ride to the school.'

'You talk as if there was one already there.' She scowled. 'When will this school be built, did Alf Morgan tell you that, too?'

'No. But they must do it before long, now that all children have to be schooled.'

'It could take *years*.'

Picking up the poker, she stirred the fire's embers fiercely. 'We should move, to where there's already a school. To Johnsonville.'

'How could I fish if we lived at Johnsonville?'

'To Paremata, then.'

'I have enquired already about Paremata. It is too expensive. Sections there cost twenty pounds.'

Alice banged the poker against the grate. 'I want Violetta to go to school. I want *all of them* to go to school.'

From the lean-to, they heard the sound of little Esther crying. Tight-mouthed, bristling with anger, Alice set the poker down and went to her.

Luigi walked outside. He hated these exchanges, firstly because he knew she was right, and secondly because they exposed his shortcomings as a provider. Even with Alice's strict economising, the proceeds from his fish only just covered their cost of living. He could save nothing. Even a deposit on a piece of land in Paremata was beyond their resources. But he too fervently wanted the girls to receive an education. Times were changing, women were training for work other than domestic service. Their girls could learn to be nurses, clerks, schoolteachers even. But it was true, a Makara school could still be years off. He walked down to the water and rinsed the clinging fish scales from his hands. All he could do was fish and play the accordion, and there was little money in either. Dejected by this thought, recalling yet again what had happened that night in Westport, for the thousandth time he cursed himself. If only, if only …

'Papa! Papa!'

Looking up, he saw Violetta and Edith running along the beach towards him, their long hair flying. When they reached him, they flung themselves into his arms. Edith was crying, Violetta breathless.

'Papa, there's a monster!'

'Yes, a terrible monster!'

'It roared at us!'

'Roared at us like …

'…like a horrid monster!'

'Hey, hey, little ones, get your breath back, then tell me. Where is this monster?'

'Past Mr Ercolano's house, by Indian Rock. Come, quickly!'

They ran on ahead and he followed, along the path to the point. There they stopped, waited for him to catch up, then made him go first. A few yards further on, around the point, they stopped. Violetta pointed, Edith put her hands over her face and peeped through her fingers.

The huge creature lay slumped and slobbering on the rocks. When it saw them it opened its mouth, showing a cavernous pink hole. Its nose was lumpy and hung down over its mouth, its whiskers were long and drooping.

'It's so *ugly*, Papa,' whispered Violetta, her eyes on stalks.

'And it makes a *terrible* noise,' added Edith, clutching her father's arm.

As if it heard, the creature raised its blubbery body, flopped forward towards them on its flippers and gave an enormous, throaty bellow which echoed around the bay. Glaring at them, it roared again. Screaming, the girls turned away, and Luigi held them both close to him.

'It's all right, little ones. It's just a sea lion.'

'A sea *lion*?' cried Edith, tearfully. 'Will it eat us, then?'

'No. It only eats fish.'

'But it's looking at us, as if it's going to attack. How can we get it to go away, Papa?'

'I think it will go away when it gets hungry.'

And although it took some days, it did.

Yet there were compensations to life by the bay. At night the stones on the shore shushed in and out on the tide with a consoling sound which lulled the children to sleep. And apart from an occasional cough and sniffle, the girls were fit and healthy. The beach and rocks on their front doorstep and the valley and hills behind the bay, were playgrounds where they roamed freely and happily. At low tide they explored rock pools for hours on end, bringing home hermit crabs, starfish, sucker fish, and once, a baby octopus which Edith kept in a bucket and fed on shrimps.

In the winter of 1893 Violetta found a little blue penguin with a damaged leg, washed up by Indian Rock, and carried it home wrapped in a cloth. Alice bound its wounded leg, Luigi fed it fish scraps and the girls made a nest of straw for it under the house, where it stayed for weeks. By the spring it was able to hobble, and although it tottered down the beach every day and flopped into the water, in the evenings it would return to the house and sleep in the nest. The girls named it Benny, and when one day it left and did not return, they were heartbroken. Until Luigi explained that it had probably found a mate, and was even happier now. Then French Louis' terrier bitch had a litter of three puppies, and although they didn't have room in the house to take one for themselves, they put ropes around their necks and took the little dogs for walks along Makara beach and gave them rides in Alicia's dolly's pram, which Miriama had handed on to her. There were, Luigi often thought – as he watched them making pebble houses on the shore or exploring the rock pools – many worse places for children to grow up.

And over those Makara years, his love and respect for Alice deepened. He loved her for her forbearance, her industriousness, her resourcefulness, her devotion to their daughters, her commonsense understanding of what they needed and wanted. He loved her too, for her love of him. He was aware that in turning her back on her parents and following him, she had gone beyond a point of no return, but not once did he hear her express regret for making that choice. Knowledge of her sacrifice brought them closer, manifesting itself in a love for their children which made all hardship bearable. But Luigi was aware too that Alice was becoming overburdened by the relentless drudgery that was her lot in life beside the remote, rocky bay, and he yearned to provide something better for them all.

But how, he wondered constantly. *How?*

It was just after ten in the morning when he reached the summit of Makara Hill. There he rested the horse and allowed it to graze for twenty minutes before continuing the journey. Under the wet sugar sacks behind him were more than 200 groper, blue cod and ling, as well as 50 crayfish

– the result of two days' work for the fishermen. He flicked the reins and Cristina broke into a trot, relishing the fact that the road, although still rough, was now downhill. By ten-thirty they reached the main road and Cristina was trotting steadily alongside a row of pine trees which formed a shelter belt for the farm paddocks on the other side.

As usual, the thought that preoccupied him was what return this load would fetch at the market. Lately prices had been pushed very low, mainly as a result of the Island Bay Italians getting there first. It was becoming harder and harder for the Makara men to keep up. At the most, he and Victor and Antonio could expect no more than ten shillings as their share of the cartload. Of that, half would go on essential supplies from the city shops, written on the list that Alice had given him. The usual things – sugar, salt, flour, rolled oats, yeast – but also more expensive items. Violetta had already outgrown the boots they had bought her just four months ago, and Esther was badly in need of a new jacket. Last in line for the hand-me-downs, the clothes were always patched and mended by the time they eventually reached little Essie.

Perhaps they would be better off living in the city, he thought. Remembering Vincenzo, the hurdy-gurdy man he'd once helped, he wondered if he too could make a living on the streets, with his accordion. There were always crowds in Lambton Quay, Willis Street and Manners Street, around the hotels and stores especially. But he quickly dismissed this idea: if they moved to the city they would have to rent a house, and that would be costly. And there would be no fish and no cheap farm produce to feed the family. At least at Makara he and Alice paid no rent.

At that moment, from behind the pine trees to his left, he heard a sound which struck him like a lightning bolt, the high-pitched scream of a child. Stopping the cart, he heard it come again, a cry of utter terror. Jumping down from the cart, he pulled Cristina to the verge, flicked the reins over her head and ran in the direction of the sound. As he did so the scream came again, a cry of such intensity and dread that it sent a flush of fear through him, too. Who or what could be tormenting the child? In front of the line of pine trees was a barbed wire fence. Scrambling over it, he ran between the trees and out the other side. And there, looking to his right, he saw the source of the screaming.

The girl was about five years old. She was crouching on her hands and knees on top of a pile of logs, evidently one of the pines which had been felled, trimmed and sawn into lengths. And in front of the pile, pawing at the long grass of the paddock, was a young jersey bull. Its bulky shoulders were grey, its flanks black, its horns curved and sharp, its ball bag orange and dangling. Atop the pile of logs, wearing a red velvet dress and with a scarlet ribbon in her long brown hair, the little girl was transfixed with terror. As Luigi sized up the situation, the bull lowered its head and tore at the turf with its horns, flicking them first one way, then the other and grunting furiously, saliva drooling from its mouth.

A second later, the bull lowered its head and charged at the logs, twisting its head quickly as it did so. Just high enough to evade the horns' flicking, the child screamed again, turned away, then scrambled higher up the log. As she did so it rocked heavily, and she just managed to cling to the bark and stop herself being pitched from it and into the bull's path. Bellowing with frustration, the creature backed away a few feet, then began to paw the ground again with its left hoof, sending divots of earth flying as it prepared to charge again. The little girl began to sob hysterically, clutching the log as if it was a pony's mane, and in that instant Luigi realised what he must do.

He pulled off his oilskin cape. Then, recalling the pictures of matadors he had seen in magazines, he ran towards the incensed creature, waving his cape wildly as he went, shouting at the top of his voice, using instinctively the Italian command for 'Go away.' '*Andare via! Andare via!*'

The bull stopped its pawing, turned its head and stared at him balefully. Gobbets of snot hung from its nostrils, the saliva dribbled from its mouth. For a few seconds Luigi and the bull stared at each other, both standing stock still, no more than six feet apart. Without taking his eyes from the bull's, Luigi called out to the child. 'Climb down. To the other side. Then run to the fence and climb over it. *As quickly as you can.*' But from the corner of his eye he could see that she had become petrified, crouched rigid, stock still. The bull began to paw the ground again, its horns flicking menacingly, its tail swinging.

When he called to the child again his voice was as loud as he could make it. 'CLIMB DOWN. THE OTHER SIDE. THEN RUN AND CLIMB THE FENCE. *GO ON*,' he urged. '*NOW!*'

His commands jolted her from her trance. She began to scramble down from the pile, but her long dress snagged on the stump of a trimmed branch. She screamed again but kept moving, tearing the dress from the branch, then dropping from the log pile to the ground on the other side.

At the same moment the bull lowered its head and charged Luigi.

Holding the oilskin in his right hand, he stepped as far as he could to the left, extended his arm, then waved the cape up and down. Distracted by the unexpected movement, the bull altered its course a fraction, turning its head and flicking at the oilskin with its right horn. The tip of the horn passed under the cape, tearing it from Luigi's hand. The bull stopped abruptly, then jerked its head upwards. The cape fell down over its eyes. Bellowing in frustration, it began to toss its head up and down in an attempt to dislodge the cape from its horns. And as it did so Luigi too ran for the line of trees.

Reaching them in seconds, he sprinted across the bed of brown needles beneath the tree line. Emerging on the other side, he saw that the little girl was there. But instead of climbing the fence she had tried to get between the strands of wire, and the back of her dress had become caught on a barb. Sobbing uncontrollably, she could go neither forward nor back. Luigi turned. Through the trees, he saw the cape fly from the bull's horns and the animal looking their way. Returning his attention to the little girl, he disentangled the back of her dress from the wire, then, standing on the lower strand, pushed her through to the other side. 'Run! Run!' he urged her again. Still crying loudly, she stumbled, got to her feet and made for the road.

On the other side of the trees, he saw the bull lower its head, then come rampaging towards him, bawling with fury. Seconds before it reached him, Luigi ran to the nearest fence post, put his foot on one of the wire strands and vaulted the fence. Safe on the other side, he turned his back on the steaming, still-roaring bull and looked around for the child.

She was sitting on the grass at the side of the road, not far from where Cristina and the cart were drawn up, the mare munching contentedly at the verge. The child was still crying, but in a more subdued way, holding one hand over her left eye. Luigi went to her.

'What is your name, child?'

Dropping her hand, she sniffed deeply, then stared up at him miserably. Her plump cheeks were flushed and streaked with tears, her eyes red-rimmed, her hair bedraggled and damp. There were two rips in her dress, one on the hem and the other on her left sleeve, which was nearly torn completely away. Her red ribbon was dangling from the left side of her head and her right shoe was missing.

'Kathleen.'

'Where do you live?

She pointed up the road, then gave another huge sniff. A fresh stream of tears sprang from her eyes.

'I'll take you home on the cart.' Taking her hand, he helped her to her feet.

'I hated that horrid bull.'

'So did I.'

She gave him a sharp look, frowned, then declared, 'You saved me.'

'It was very lucky that I heard you.'

Lifting her up onto the seat, he said in an effort to distract her, 'My horse is called Cristina.'

Climbing up beside her, he flicked the reins and the cart moved off. As it did so he sensed the child silently observing him. There was only one house in sight, a large building in the distance, on the left-hand side of the road.

'Is that where you live?'

'Yes.'

'How old are you?'

'Nearly five.'

'I'm Luigi. I'm thirty-five.'

There was silence for a few moments, then she asked:

'Where do you come from?'

'Makara.'

'Yes, but you speak differently.'

'Before that I came from Italy.'

'Oh.'

Another, longer silence. Then, 'Where are you going?'

After he told her she turned and said, 'Are the fish under those sacks?'

'Yes.'

'I can smell them. Pooh!'

'That's why I have to get them to the market soon. If I don't, they will smell much worse.'

She gave a little giggle, then fell silent again. To distract her from her ordeal, he told her he had four daughters, gave her their names, explained that the eldest was the same age as her. Glancing at her as he spoke, he saw that her shoulders were hunched, and that she was frowning. As they approached the house, the girl took off her remaining shoe, then said sombrely, 'Mother will be angry when she sees me like this.'

It was an imposing house, two-storeyed, with walls of shiplap board, painted dark brown and with white framed, double-hung sash windows. There was a portico at the front, hanging from which was a sign with the name 'Chesney Wold' painted on it, in Gothic lettering.

A driveway covered in crushed white shells curved around the entrance to the building. There were some large oak trees in fresh spring leaf to the left of the house and some blossoming orchard trees – apples and pears – to the right, separated from the house by a driveway which led to the stables. Behind the stables, fenced farm paddocks stretched away to a line of bush-covered hills in the distance.

Luigi drew the cart up, he and the child got down and Kathleen ran to the panelled front door, opened it and went inside. Luigi stood on the step and waited, knowing that he would have to provide an adult version of what had happened. Standing there, he also realised that somewhere along the way he had lost his cap as well as his cape.

'Kathleen has told me what happened. What a dreadful experience. We've told her not to wander as far as that farm, but ...' she gave the girl a stern look '... she has not yet learned of the dangers.' The woman clicked her tongue in frustration. 'And to think we moved here from the city so we could enjoy a peaceful life in the countryside.'

In her early thirties, she was wearing a navy blue dress with a high white collar. Her hair – brown like her daughter's – was piled high on top of her head, and she had a sensitive, even-featured face and large, expressive eyes. Beside her, holding her hand, Kathleen was now chattering non-stop.

'And after the bull tried to kill me and I was stuck up on the pile of logs he took off his cape and waved it at the bull and the bull charged him instead of me and ...'

'Keep quiet, child, and let Mr ...'

'Galoni.'

'... let Mr Galoni tell me what happened.'

With Kathleen silent and pouting beside her mother, Luigi summarised the events. Although he tried to minimise the drama that had occurred, the woman's hand went up to her mouth in dismay at the facts of the story. When Luigi had finished, the woman looked down at

Kathleen, who batted her long lashes and announced, theatrically,

'You see, it is true Mama, the bull did try to murder me.'

Unable to refrain from smiling at her performance, Luigi concluded, 'So, madam, she must keep away from that paddock, from now on.'

'Indeed she will, I'll never let her wander again!' Clasping her hands in front of her, her anxiety still obvious, she said. 'And now Mr Galoni, you must come inside and rest. I'll get Vera to make you tea. And sandwiches, if you wish.'

'Thank you, but I must be on my way.'

'He's taking his fish to the city,' Kathleen put in. 'To sell at the market.'

'But do please come in. You've done such a brave thing.'

'I won't, thank you.' He looked down at the child and smiled. 'I was glad to be of help.' He looked back at her mother. 'I have daughters too, madam. I know how precious they are.' Reaching down, he patted her head softly. 'Goodbye, Kathleen.'

'Goodbye. And thank you so much for rescuing me.' Drawing a very deep breath, she braced her little shoulders. 'I shall write a story about this.'

He looked at her mother and they both laughed. What an extraordinary child she was, Luigi thought. Nearly frightened to death one minute, chirpy as a canary the next.

It was late morning the following Sunday when French Louis came along the track at Fisherman's Bay, accompanied by a tall man of about forty years of age. Hatless but wearing a suit and tie, he had a beard and a drooping moustache, and although his beard was black, his hair was greying and receding. Luigi and Alice were sitting on the seat at the front of the cottage, peeling potatoes for Sunday dinner. Down on the shore, the girls were making a pyramid out of rounded stones and several of the other fishermen were pottering about with their boats. French Louis stopped at the gate.

'You have a visitor, Mr and Mrs Galoni.'

Luigi went to the gate, opened it and admitted the man into the small yard. French Louis stood outside the fence, watching curiously.

'You are Luigi Galoni?' said the newcomer.

'Yes. And this is my wife, Alice.'

The man inclined his head, respectfully. 'My name is Beauchamp, Harold Beauchamp. I'm the father of Kathleen, whom you saved from a bull last Thursday.' His manner and voice were those of a man of authority.

'Oh,' said Luigi, taken by surprise to see a man of such obvious substance visiting this place. 'How did you know where I lived?'

'Kathleen told me you came from Makara, and Italy. I realised you must be one of the Italians of Fisherman's Bay.'

'His carriage is back at the beach,' French Louis put in eagerly, over the fence. 'A carriage and four. The driver is there waiting for him.'

Wishing that Louis would go away, Luigi asked, 'How is Kathleen?'

'She is fine, all things considered. And she's told her mother and me everything you did for her on Thursday.' He gave a quick little nod of admiration. 'In spite of my daughter's predilection for romanticising events, there's no doubt in our minds that you saved her life.'

Luigi looked away, abashed. Then, pointing towards the beach, he laughed to cover his embarrassment. 'I have daughters too. It was a natural thing to do.'

The man turned, saw the girls and smiled understandingly. 'Perhaps. But it was also courageous, and my family and I will be eternally grateful to you.' Slipping his hand inside his suit jacket, he took out a long white envelope and passed it to Luigi.

'So, I would like you to accept this.'

Confused, Luigi took the envelope, then held it awkwardly.

'But, I don't expect …'

Kathleen's father held up his hand. 'Keep it, please. I insist.' His grey eyes flicked past Luigi and Alice to the cottage, alighting briefly on the tar paper flashing, the lean-tos, the battered corrugated iron chimney, the dunny, the row of wet washing on the line, before returning to the couple. 'It comes with our heartfelt thanks. I hope it will prove useful to you and your family.'

Then it was his turn to look embarrassed. Taking another envelope from his jacket pocket, he cleared his throat loudly, then also handed this one to Luigi. 'And Kathleen insisted that I give you this.' After a pause, he said, 'Thank you again from my family.' His eyes sparkled. 'And good luck for the future.'

After Luigi took the second envelope, the visitor inclined his head first to Alice, then Luigi, turned, walked briskly through the gate and back along the path, with French Louis following.

Luigi opened the first envelope and withdrew a single sheet of heavy cream paper. The words on it were typed and it was headed:

The Chairman,
The Bank of New Zealand,
Lambton Quay, Wellington.
November 28, 1894.

Dear Mr Galoni,

Enclosed is a promissory note, made out to yourself, for the sum of Two Hundred and Fifty Pounds. This amount consists of an interest-free loan from the Bank of New Zealand, underwritten by myself. The loan is to be repaid within a maximum period of 25 years, at a minimum rate of two pounds per calendar month, from the date of this letter. I respectfully suggest that this sum could be used for the purchase of land or other property in the district of Wellington, best suited to you and your family's needs.

If you are agreeable to such a loan being issued, please call at the office of the Bank of New Zealand in Lambton Quay at your earliest convenience, bringing this letter with you, so that the funds can be lodged into your bank account and suitable arrangements made for the repayments of the loan, under the terms described above.

Yours faithfully,
Harold Beauchamp

Luigi felt as if he had been tossed from a horse. Speechless, he handed the letter to Alice. When she read it, her hand went up to her mouth. Holding it there, she turned to Luigi.

'Two hundred and fifty pounds …' Still unable to speak, he just nodded. Alice's eyes returned to the letter. 'And interest-free.'

At last Luigi found he could speak. 'We cannot accept it, Alice.'

She looked up in astonishment. 'Why ever not?'

'He is doing this out of pity.'

'*Pity?* Why do you say that?'

'He has seen how we live. And he pities us.'

'He had *not* seen how we live. Until a minute ago.' She gripped the letter. 'He means to thank us.'

'It is charity. And no Galoni ever accepted charity. In Pesaro or in

Makara.'

'It is *not* charity, Luigi, it is gratitude.'

Luigi shrugged. 'To me, it seems like charity.'

He held out his hand for the letter and she passed it back. Studying the figures again, he added, 'Besides, repayments of two pounds a month. How could we afford that, just from my fishing?'

'I will help. I will take in sewing. Do alterations. Piece-work perhaps. I could do it.' Her voice carried a steely reesolve. 'So if you do not accept his offer, then I will.'

'The letter is addressed to me,' he pointed out, and immediately regretted doing so. Alice's eyes blazed.

'It is our chance, don't you see? Our only chance, to escape from …from …' She waved her hand at the ramshackle cottage. '*All this*. We can buy land, and a house. One with everything we need for a family with four children.' Tears of frustration sprang into her eyes. 'Do you think I haven't dreamed of living in a proper house? *Don't you know what we all need?*

'I know it. Of course I know it. But …'

Alice's eyes became hooded, in a way he had never seen them appear before. 'You have already lost one fortune, remember.'

'It is hurtful to me, Alice, for you to say that.'

'*And so is what you say, to me.* You would turn down a sum that would allow our children to be properly housed and schooled.' When Luigi made no reply to this, she added, in a quieter tone, 'It is out of gratitude. You were brave, you saved his daughter's life. You heard him say that.'

'But not for money. It was what any man would have done.'

'You are not *any man*. You are my husband. You acted bravely and and he is thanking you for it. In the best way he can.' Her voice was as threatening as a knife held to his throat. 'So you will go to the city, and accept the loan. Tomorrow!' She turned, strode into the house and slammed the door behind her.

His mind still reeling, Luigi opened the second envelope. It was hand-written in black pencil, on a single sheet of lined paper, with a frieze of hand-drawn red roses around the margins of the page.

The Bull

That morning the girl went further from her house than she was suppose to. She climbed a fence and walked through a paddock of long grass. After she walked for a little while she saw a bull eating the grass. The bull was ugly, with big grey shoulders and curvy horns. The girl hated bulls, and she turned and ran back towards the fence. But the bull began to chase her, and she was very frightened. She climbed on top of a pile of wood, because she knew that bulls have hoofs and cannot climb. But the bull began to charge the wood and the girl started to scream, as loud as she could. Then a man with red hair came running from the trees. He took off his coat and waved it at the bull. The bull charged at the man, and the girl ran away and was safe. Then the man escaped from the bull too. And the man took the girl home on his horse and cart and the girl never went near that paddock ever again.

Smiling to himself, Luigi folded the page, then went inside. Alice was sitting by the fire, pushing at the embers with the poker. As he entered she looked up, her expression still livid. Going to her, he took both her hands in his. Then, looking down at her, he said quietly,

'You are right, Alice. It is our chance. And we must take it.'

THE DISAPPEARING STREET

William looked again at the place of birth of Violetta Laetitia Galoni, as recorded on her birth certificate. Nelson Street. He had lived in Wellington most of his life, but he'd never heard it. Yet with the street numbers reaching nearly 400, it was obviously a long one. He took down the book of city street maps from a shelf, looked it up. It was at the southern end of the Hutt Valley, in Petone, a suburb he'd only been to a couple of times.

Lately he'd read in the real estate supplements that the once thoroughly working class suburb had become fashionable. Sure enough, the main street's verandahed shops had brightly-painted frontages, and there were café tables on the pavement. He turned off the main thoroughfare and into Nelson Street, wondering again how it was that Luigi and Alice's first child had been born here, ten kilometres from the central city. Had Petone too been a fishing village once?

Nelson Street was long and straight. Its nature changed noticeably as William drove along it. Shops, businesses and industrial workshops were replaced by small colonial-era villas. Most were in poor condition, with peeling paint and rusting iron over their front verandahs. Some had had their small front yards concreted over, others had ugly carports grafted onto the yard. Few had gardens. Nelson Street was yet to be gentrified.

The even numbers were on the right. Noting them on the gates as he drove slowly along, he reached 100, then 200, 260. He stopped. After 280, Nelson Street rose, veered left and…ended. At a high wire fence, on the other side of which was the Hutt Valley railway line. Puzzled, William parked the car and got out. Across the other side of the tracks was the four-laned Hutt Road, along which cars, trucks and trailer units were moving rapidly in both directions. Taking the birth certificate from his satchel, William checked the number. 390. Yet there was no 390. There was not even a number 290. What had happened to the rest of the street? And to the house where his grandmother had been born?

Walking up to the fence, he stared across the railway and the motorway. Realisation dawned. Nelson Street must have once reached to the foot of the Korokoro Hills. But with the coming of the railway and the widening of the road, the top end of the street had been obliterated, along with the houses which had lined it. Staring into the distance, he tried to calculate where number 390 must have been. A kilometre away, perhaps? Where there was now a motorway and speeding vehicles. He tried to imagine what the destroyed end of the street must once have looked like. A pretty colonial villa, perhaps with a picket fence and a verandah, a flower garden at the front and vegetables growing at the back. Now all he could see were grimy railway lines, a motorway and racing traffic.

Another dead end.

Then, driving back into the city, William remembered another approach, suggested by one of the women at National Archives. If Luigi had become a naturalised New Zealander, there would be a certificate to prove it.

ELEVEN

'Country Land. Quiet rural retreat, Paraparaumu. Thirty-three miles from Wellington, this property features a cottage of six rooms, with a stable, and stands on two acres of land, adjoining a pleasant country village. Climate and scenery unsurpassed. The land is fenced, with one acre in grass and one in garden and orchard. School, church and post office handy. Close to the Wellington-Manawatu railway line. Price £175.'

Alice looked up. 'Paraparaumu? That is beyond Paremata, isn't it?'

'Yes.' He re-read the newspaper advertisement. 'Two acres. Huge. '

'Handy to a school.'

'With an orchard.'

'And a stable.'

'But we don't have a horse.'

'We could get one.'

'And how many rooms, did you say?'

'Six.'

'*Six!*'

'How far from the sea, I wonder.'

'Paraparaumu is near the coast.'

'But there's no road there, I've heard.'

'There is the railway, though.'

'We could take a train and look.'

'There's no harm in looking.'

'No.'

'So, shall we?'

'Yes.'

'Close to the railway', was no exaggeration. The Wellington-Manawatu line ran, arrow-straight, to points north and south, across the back boundary of the property, and just a hundred yard from the house. A track from the little Paraparaumu station wound its way among the district's low-lying fields, market gardens and orchards to the house. The land agent, Theo Webber, was waiting there when they arrived and showed them through the property. The vendor, the agent explained, a widow, had bought a small retirement cottage in Otaki and the property had been vacant since October. Twelve years old and of board and batten construction, the house had three bedrooms with board floors, a carpeted parlour, a kitchen-dining area and a wide verandah along its front, north-facing wall. Agapanthas sprouted from the ground around the verandah, along with hollyhocks and black-eyed susans, and a wisteria vine with mauve blooms wound its way up one of the verandah's corner posts. At the rear of the house was a water tank, a long-drop toilet and separate wash-house, complete with copper, taps and twin tubs, a small stable in a large overgrown paddock, then the railway line. The orchard – also overgrown – was on the western side of the house, where there were several mature apple, cherry, peach and pear trees, all coming into fruit. Beyond the railway line, a green wall of hills rose abruptly from the plain. Covered in stands of native bush, the range would provide good shelter from the southerly winds, Luigi noted.

He and Alice wandered through the house, still scarcely able to believe that if they wanted it, it could be theirs. But as Harold Beauchamp had promised, two hundred and fifty pounds had been lodged in Luigi's new Bank of New Zealand account one week ago. Alice paused again in the kitchen, where she turned on the tap above the sink. 'Running water,' she said, still close to disbelief. The agent smiled. 'And a recent model Shacklock coal range, madam,' he added, pointing to it. He adjusted his tie, self-importantly. 'There is a coal merchant next to the railway station. He delivers weekly.'

'How far is it to the sea?' asked Luigi.

The agent waved his hand, airily. 'There is a track along the Tikotu Creek, a walk of no more than fifteen minutes.' He smiled in the ingratiating way which Luigi was finding annoying. 'You are fond of sea bathing, Mr Galoni?'

'No. I am a fisherman.'

As the train back chugged past Paekakariki, close to the slate-grey waters of the strait, they discussed what they should do.

'It's *just* what we want, Luigi.'

'But it is the first property we've looked at. There will be others. We should look more widely before we decide.'

'Why, though, when it is exactly what we need?'

Doubts about the magnitude of such a purchase were gnawing at Luigi. Everything was happening so fast, it was unnerving. 'One hundred and seventy-five pounds. It is so much money.'

'Mr Beauchamp's loan will cover it easily.'

'But we will need to buy new furniture, too. And wardrobes for the bedrooms. And I will need another boat.'

'There will be enough. Let's write to Mr Webber, and offer him one hundred and sixty pounds for the property.'

'The asking price is a hundred and seventy-five.'

'Yes, but I think the seller will accept that. You saw the long grass, it's been on the market for months. And besides …'

'Besides what?'

'With the extra money, you could buy something else you need.'

'What?'

'A new accordion.'

The Sunday before they left, they held a lunch for all the others. After their last fish delivery trip to the city together, Luigi and Victor called at the Club Garibaldi in Courtenay Place, where they bought Italian wine, olives and olive oil, prosciutto, salamis, cheese and dried tomatoes from the syndicate that ran the club and imported foods from Italy. Back at Makara, Luigi, Victor and Antonio prepared a frittata of barbecued vegetables, mussels in tomato broth, fish parcels with olives, pork chops with rosemary, baby chickens wrapped in the prosciutto and salads of peas, carrots and shallots. Evie came over from the city and helped Alice prepare the salads, Alf Morgan and his wife brought a leg of home-cured ham and strawberries from the farm and French Louis brought a small barrel of his home-brewed beer, chilled in the Makara stream.

By the shore, in the warmth of early summer, they ate and drank. Luigi played his squeeze-box and Victor sang, and the children paddled and played on the beach, and by the time the sun was starting to go down they were all bursting with food and drink. Then they built up the bonfire and as darkness fell, all sat around it and French Louis, by now scarcely able to stand, called for order.

'Mes amis! Quiet now!' A kind of silence settled over the people sitting or lying around the fire, which threw a flickering light over Louis' face and beard.

'I must like to prepare a toast. But first I need say that how much we will all miss Luigi and Alice Galoni and their four sweet daughters who have carried such laughter and games to Makara.' He bowed, then blew a series of kisses at the girls, sitting in a row beside their parents, and they dissolved into giggles. French Louis continued. 'You came to here, Luigi, knowing no one. You leave as our great friend of us all. Alice, too, came from nowhere. But now you are all such a part of us, such a part of Fisherman's Bay, and so we will miss all the family Galoni so much. So much.' The old man paused, to draw a deep breath. Tears began to run from his eyes. His voice faltering now, he continued. 'So, so, goodbye to you all.' He bowed his head for a few moments, recovered, looked up. 'And now everyone, fill your glasses again and drink the toast. To Luigi, Alice, Violetta, Edith, Alicia, and little Esther... Oh and not to forget the beautiful Evie...buona fortuna to you all!'

As Luigi got to his feet and thanked each one by name for their many kindnesses, he could still not quite believe that this night would be the last they would spend at the bay. His eyes kept straying to the little house along the track, the building where he and Alice had rediscovered each other, the shack they had turned into a home, where three of their children had been conceived and where each of the girls had been brought to spend their first days and years, the shelter where they'd spent four winters, hearing the south wind howling like wolves in the hills behind them, and the waves crashing angrily on the rocks, only yards away. Memories of Makara would remain lodged in his heart forever.

Luigi raised his wine glass.

'To all of you, friends from the old country and the new, my family and I thank you from the bottom of our hearts. Grazie, grazie, grazie!'

And by the light of the dying fire, he and Victor played and sang Verdi together for the last time, Victor with his head tipped back, his hands crossed over his chest.

'La donna é mobile
qual piuma al vento
muta d'accento
e di pensier

e di pensier
e di pensier…'

Antonio drove them to the city in the cart, with everything they owned packed into two suitcases, four bags and three tea chests, the children sitting in the back in the dresses that Alice had sewn especially for the journey. As the cart left the beach the girls stared back at the bay and fell silent. Little Esther with her thumb in her mouth, holding her piece of soft cloth to her cheek, Violetta tight-faced, trying to be brave, gripping Edith's hand, Alicia with tears running down her cheeks. They were leaving the only home they had ever known. Last night, when he had tucked Alicia and Esther into the bed they shared in the first lean-to, Esther had whispered to Luigi, 'I don't want to go to the new house, Papa.' Then Alicia had thrown her arms around his neck and said, 'Me too. Both of us don't want to go.' Kissing them in turn, he said softly, 'It'll be all right, little ones, we will all still be together. And one day we'll come back to Makara. For a holiday, perhaps. Now, buona notte, sleep well. We have a very long way to go tomorrow.'

'There's the island, see? Kapiti, it's called.'
    'It's *huge*. Like a whale,' said Alicia.
    'A *green* whale,' Edith put in.
    'Can we go there, Mama?' asked Violetta.
    'When you're older, perhaps,' Alice replied.
    'Do people live on the island, Papa?' asked Edith.
    'I don't know. We will find out, soon.'
    Little Esther was fast asleep, her head on her oldest sister's shoulder. It was mid-afternoon, they had been travelling most of the day and the thrill of their first train trip was wearing thin. It was very hot in the carriage, with the windows beside them only opening a few inches from the top, but wide enough to admit drifts of smoke that made them all feel grubby. As the train puffed and chugged along the coast, the girls all fell silent, eyes on the forested island whose features were becoming clearer by the minute. Soon Kapiti looked close enough to throw a stone at. Between the railway line and the shore was a wide area of swamp from which white plumes of toi toi stuck up. The shore was marked by a ridge of sand-dunes, covered in tussock grass, and above the beach flocks of gulls rose and fell lazily in the sea breeze.

He hauled the boat into the shallows, then pushed her through the small waves. As soon as buoyancy lifted the boat, he leapt into it, picked up the oars and began to row. Minutes later he was beyond the lines of waves and rowing hard into the Otaheke Strait, his back to the island. He'd bought the boat for £9 from Frank Donovan, another fisherman who had a house on the bank of the Waikanae River. Fourteen feet long and with a beam of five feet, the new boat had a covered bow and a roomy hatch beneath it. He'd decided to keep her near the mouth of the Tikotu Creek, rather than the Waikanae River. In fair weather the river mouth with its neighbouring lagoon was more sheltered, but after rain the river would rise quickly, Luigi reckoned.

As he moved further away from the shore, the coastal plain and the hills behind it came more clearly into view. Dark smoke signals were rising into the air and moving steadily across the land. The ten-thirty train from Wellington. Already the railway had become part of their lives, its distinctive sounds drifting across the paddock behind the house: the shrill whistle marking the train's arrivals and departures, the engine's panting as it gathered speed, the rapid click-clacking of its wheels. Quickly too the girls had become railway children, loving the train's noisy comings and goings, sitting on the fence above the line and waving to the passengers and the uniformed guard who stood, flag in hand, at the last van's taffrail.

Violetta and Edith were both attending Mr Foster's one-room school near the station, and enjoying it, bringing home their readers and sharing them with the other two. And Alice loved the house and its grounds. 'It's like getting a new life, Luigi,' she had said to him just yesterday. Only then did he fully realise what she had had to put up with at Makara. Now they all had space to roam, to harvest their own fruit and vegetables, to milk their own cow and ride their own horse, Bella. Alice made jam from the plums and bottled the peaches, filling the kitchen cupboards with her preserves. Every second day Luigi put his fish on the afternoon train to the city and every other week he received a payment for it in the post from the fish market accountant.

Because repayments on the loan were manageable, they could afford some luxuries. Alice now had a Singer sewing machine; he had a new accordion. Made by Mariano Dallape in Stradella, Italy, it had a right-hand keyboard of three octaves and no fewer than 112 left-hand brass buttons. Although it was difficult to master after the simple old one, it had a beautiful tone and most evenings he played it for Alice and the girls. As Alice had hoped, her seamstress skills were bringing in a few shillings a month, contributing to their loan repayments. Skillfully she let out waistbands, lowered hems and nipped and tucked bustlines for local customers.

The one cloud hovering over their lives was the fact that Alice remained estranged from her parents. Evie – still in the city – was now betrothed to Alex McIntosh, a builder from Glasgow, and the couple visited the Galonis once a month, but Alice's father refused to communicate with them. Her mother wrote, and asked after the children, but from John Harris there was no communication. And last week there had been a letter from Mrs Harris, informing them that her husband had developed tuberculosis. Alice wept at the news, knowing this was a death sentence, suspecting she would never see him again. At 43, her father was only eight years older than Luigi.

He rowed on, steadily. Luigi had given his sympathy to Alice, but still struggled to feel pity for John Harris. His refusal to acknowledge Luigi as his son-in-law, or communicate with his daughter or his grand-daughters, Luigi considered unforgivable.

Resting the oars, he turned to assess the wind and water ahead. The strait's waters were sheltered by Kapiti from the westerlies and northerlies, but the island tended to funnel the southerlies, making conditions flukey, especially along its south coast. The fishermen here were less community-minded than at Makara, seeming reluctant to share their knowledge of the best spots, so that Luigi was having to experiment to find the areas favoured by the big fish. As he would this morning.

But gradually the Galonis were becoming part of the small community. The girls were making friends at school, storekeepers like the baker and the butcher delivered their goods to the door, and what vegetables they couldn't grow they bought from three Chinese men who ran a market garden by the Wharemakau stream. Apart from the district's terrible roads – which were 'not roads at all, just stream beds', as Alice described them – it was an agreeable little settlement to be part of.

The Wellington-Manawatu railway was the artery which had brought life-blood coursing through Paraparaumu. Opened nine years before the Galonis arrived, it now connected the little coastal settlements and the city in ways long-time residents found almost unbelievable. So often local women – while chatting outside Mr Foster's school, Howell's butchery or Sherring's bakery – would preface a remark to Alice with the words,

'Before the railway came …' then follow with an anecdote of anguish
caused by Paraparaumu's isolation. A whole day's walk through the swamp
to get to the doctor in Paekakariki, becoming cut off from the post office
in Waikanae for days because rain had flooded the pathways. The stories
would invariably end with the jubilant words, 'Now we've got the railway,
though, we can be there in less than half an hour. No matter what the
weather. It's like a miracle, Mrs Galoni.'

'Alice. Please, call me Alice.'

When Luigi wrote to Harold Beauchamp, thanking him again for
his generous gesture, reporting on the purchase of their property and the
way it was changing their lives, he'd received a prompt reply.

Dear Mr Galoni,

My wife and I were delighted to receive your letter of February 22, in
which you describe your family's satisfaction with your new Paraparaumu
property. The Kapiti coast has an equable climate, I believe, and so will
constitute a healthy location for the raising of your children. No doubt
you are relishing the markedly increased size of your property. Being so
close to the new railway, I have no doubt that it will also appreciate in
value over the years.

You ask after Kathleen. She began school in Karori village three weeks
ago, and appears to be enjoying the experience. It would not have been the
school her mother and I would have chosen for her, but as it is the only
one in this area, there was no choice. However she appears in the main
to be enjoying her schooling. Last week she contracted a chill and was
confined to bed for two days. When I reported to her that I had received
your letter, she instructed me to say 'Hello' from her, and to inform you
that she has been keeping away from the bull paddock. She also requested
that I send you a copy of a poem she had recently written. Accordingly, I
enclose it here, although it seems to me to be a trifle self-pitying.

My best wishes to yourself and your good wife. My wife too wishes
me to convey her regards to you all. May you and Mrs Galoni, along with
your daughters, continue to enjoy your new property and prospects.

Yours sincerely,

Harold Beauchamp

Luigi read the enclosed, hand-written poem, decorated around its margins with coloured daisies.

A Day in Bed

I wish I had not got a cold;
The wind is big and wild;
I wish that I was very old,
Not just a little child.

Somehow the day is very long,
Just keeping here alone,
I do not like the big wind's song,
He's growling for a bone.

I'm sitting up, and Nurse has made
Me wear a woolly shawl –
I wish I was not so afraid:
It's horrid to be small.

It really feels quite like a day
Since I have had my tea;
P'raps everybody's gone away,
And just forgotten me.

And, oh, I cannot go to sleep,
Although I am in bed;
The wind keeps going "creepy creep"
And waiting to be fed.

By Kathleen Beauchamp

He read the poem to the girls, who loved it. Violetta learnt it off by heart, and wrote a note to Kathleen to let her know that she had done so.

Although the tide was flowing, the boat moved easily into the channel, propelled by his steady strokes. Behind Luigi the island loomed larger, its great flanks creased with gullies. A cluster of smaller islands was in sight now too, near the southern end of Kapiti. Resting the oars again, he let *Laetitia II* drift for a few minutes. Today he wanted to try fishing the waters near an outcrop they called Passage Rocks. Taking a large mullet from the bait box, he filleted it and sliced it into chunks before resuming his rowing.

Tethered by the anchor rope, the boat rocked gently in the swell. The sun was climbing the sky, brightening the Mataihuka Range, and an inconstant little breeze was scuffing the surface of the channel. He began to draw in his line, feeling only slight resistance as he did so. The chunks of mullet spun as he lifted them free of the water. They were untouched, but he was not unduly concerned. There were three good-sized warehou in the sack. It seemed likely that the nearest groper ground lay elsewhere, though.

Bringing up the anchor, he placed it in the bow, then turned and reached for the oars, which he had lain lengthways in the boat so they wouldn't become entangled with the line. Half crouching, and with his left hand on the gunwale, he grasped both oars with the other, but as he did so the boat, now free from the anchor's restraint, pitched, causing him to stumble against the thwart. For a second he groped at air, then fell forward, thrusting the oars in front of him as he did so. The instinctive move was partly successful – the oars broke his fall – but as he lifted his head he saw one of the rowlocks sliding down the shaft of one oar. He lunged over the stern for it, but being still off balance, could only stare as the rowlock slipped from the end of the oar and into the water.

He took his watch from his pocket. Eleven-forty-five. The breeze was a wind now, a north-easterly, coming directly across the channel from the land. He let his head fall forward. His hands were very sore. Sitting up, he flexed his fingers and arms, slowly. For over an hour now he had been trying to row with one oar against the tide. What a simple device a rowlock was, he thought bitterly. Simple, but essential. The ones he had made from a length of fishing line had frayed quickly, lasting only a few strokes before friction wore them through. He stared around, from the beach across to the island and back. Now there was no doubt where the tide and wind were taking him. Straight towards the rocky coast of Kapiti, at surprising speed, and he could do nothing but go along with it.

But he had a plan. He would land on the island, walk around the shore – there was a track at the foot of the cliffs, he'd been told – to Waterfall Bay, where he'd also been told that a fisherman lived. He'd borrow a rowlock from him, then row back to the mainland when the tide turned.

As he came closer to the rocks he began to study the island. Strange that after seeing it every day since they had moved to Paraparaumu, and fishing the strait at least every other day, he hadn't yet set foot on it. Now he could see that it was much larger than he had thought – its spine very high – and that it was forested right down to the shoreline. The gullies which ran down its eastern slopes were deep, ending abruptly in a series of triangular headlands, at the foot of which were shelves of black rocks.

The bottom of the boat scraped rock. He stood up, took one of the oars and poled *Laetitia* into a channel between two boulders, through which the sea was surging. Throwing out the anchor, he hauled the boat by its rope to the head of the channel. There he made the boat fast fore and aft, using the anchor rope and another length of rope at the stern. The tide was almost high now, and the boat would go no further. He took off his jacket and cap, folded them together and placed them in the boat's for'ard hatch. Then he rolled up his trousers, took off his boots and stepped into the knee-deep water.

Gingerly, boots in hand, he began to wade towards the rocky shelf in the distance, his toes feeling for flat surfaces beneath the surging, kelpy water. Minutes later he climbed up on to the rocks, put his boots back on and began to make his way carefully across the promontory.

A movement in the sky caught his attention, and he looked up. A black-backed gull, gliding backwards and forwards some way ahead of him. There was something odd about the bird's flight, and he stared at it for a moment until he realised what it was that was unusual. The bird was flying in a strangely limited orbit, in unusually tight circles. As he stared the bird was joined in its wheeling flight by a second gull, then a third. Lowering his gaze, Luigi carried on, picking his way awkwardly across the rocks towards the shore proper.

Soon he realised that his progress would be much slower than he had estimated. The rocks were a bloody inconvenient size, he concluded ruefully, too big to walk over, not big enough to jump on. Then, only a little later, he stopped altogether.

His way was blocked by a deep channel in the rock shelf, five or six feet wide. He paused for a few minutes on the edge, looking one way, then the other. If he followed the channel along it might close and that way he would avoid having to jump. But that would take too much time. He braced himself, then leaped at the other side of the channel.

He did not misjudge the distance, neither was the gap too wide, but as his right boot landed on the rock he had aimed for, it moved under his weight and he fell forward on to his outstretched hands and knees.

For what seemed quite some time he felt no pain at all, only a thick numbness on his palms and his legs. But as he scrambled to his feet the bruised skin stretched, and the numbness was replaced by a thudding pain. He held his hands up, cursing the fall which had bruised his hands and legs to the bone. Closing his eyes against the pain, at the same moment the silence of the island was shattered as the trio of gulls above him burst into discordant protest, about forty feet above his head. *Arr! Arr!* And the echo *Arr! Arr!,* as if he was an object of revulsion to the birds.

He set off again, letting his arms swing loosely at his sides as he walked, so that the moving air passed over his hands and soothed them a little. What worried him now was that he still couldn't see any sign of a track among the trees and rocks ahead. He turned and looked back. He had come about a quarter of a mile. There was no point in going back to the boat, he had to keep going. He stared up ahead again. The track *must* be somewhere up there. He limped on.

Arr! Arr! The cries of the gulls were constant and clamorous now. The noise of their raucous calling was causing an ache, just behind his eyes. Perhaps the birds were hungry, he thought. He should have brought the fish, and diverted them with it. *Arr! Arr!* The noise was coming closer. As he focused his eyes on the rocks up ahead, he saw the reason for the gulls' anger.

The young bird looked, from where he stood, like a ball of grey down, squatting between two rocks. He squinted. There was another, just over to the right, and a third, and a fourth. Half a dozen fledglings, huddling among the rocks.

He stared up at the sky. He couldn't count the black-backed sentinels now, there were too many, and they were changing direction too quickly, the smaller females rising in a shrieking flock as he approached their young, their cries berating him as he stumbled across the nesting ground. *Arr! Arr!* Yet he thought they wouldn't touch him as long as he made no move to harm the chicks. If he could just keep going as straight as he could he must come to the track. But as he stumbled on he could tell from their cries that the birds above had dropped still lower in the sky.

His head throbbed, his chest was burning. Sweat was streaming into the corners of his eyes, and the cries of the birds were deafening now, and so close.

For an instant the ball of down cushioned the sole of his right boot, then he felt the softness yield and heard a strangled cry. Lifting his boot, he looked down to see the chick's small wings rising and falling feebly as it tried to move its crushed body. And at the same moment two of the black shapes above plummeted, backs arched, legs dangling, backstaying with their wings as their beaks thrust at his face.

Lifting his arms to protect his eyes from the flashing beaks, he spun round, keeping his eyes shut hard as the wings beat about his head and shoulders. He felt a stab in his scalp as a beak found its target, and with the pain of the wound came a sudden, blinding anger. He whirled his arms about, striking one of the soft white bodies with a clenched fist, screaming, cursing. He was a man, how dare these creatures attack him!

The flailing counter-attack worked. The squadron of gulls withdrew, rising, crying. He stood, fists still clenched, yelling at the sky, but his shouts were drowned by the derisive cawing of his attackers.

He looked about for a stick, but the platform of rock was beyond the tide's reach, and there was no driftwood. He stumbled forward again, blind with pain and sweat, the cries from the birds becoming louder and louder. And before he'd covered another twenty yards, the gulls rallied and attacked again.

This time they came singly, swooping, pecking, then rising again so that those behind could take their place. He dropped to his knees and hid his face – all he could think of now was his eyes – but in so doing he exposed his scalp and the nape of his neck. One after another the attackers found their target, the stiletto beaks driving at him again and again. Groping among the rocks, his hands touched a piece of wood. A broken branch. He staggered to his feet and struck out with the stick, but the bruising on his palms was too great, and as he whirled about he felt it fly from his hands. Weeping with pain and anger, he staggered forward once more, the cries of the gulls taunting him, the great wings flapping about his face, the beaks slashing. He moved in a shuffling, stumbling travesty of a run, his eyes closed, his head a mass of throbbing pain, sweat and something thicker trickling down into his brows. Touching it, he held his fingers up to his eyes. Blood.

This time as he fell he was conscious of another noise mixing with the cries of the birds, a very different sound, a human call. Then it stopped, abruptly, and he could hear his own breathing, louder than the fading cries of the birds. He began to rub at his scalp, and as he did so he heard the scuffing of boots on rock. He tried to lift his head, but could only turn it to one side. A voice.

'Hey, mate, you all right?'

'All right, yes.'

He realised he was now on flat ground. Dirt, not rock. Hands slid under his arms, and he felt himself being turned over, heard the sound of a breath drawn quickly inward.

'Jesus, mate.' A pause, then, 'You'll be okay, you'll be okay.'

A handkerchief, dabbing at his scalp.

He opened his eyes, slowly. Brightness, dissolving into blue. He closed his eyes, hard, opened them again. Sunlight, streaming down. And silence, perfect silence. He closed his eyes again, blinked hard, opened them once more. A short, dark-skinned man.

'G'day. I'm Percy. Percy Watene.'

'Luigi. Luigi Galoni.'

'Where've you come from? Para'pram?'

'Yes.'

'Where's your boat?'

'Back there. On the rocks.'

'Okay. Good thing I came along. I was going to get some paua. Can you stand up?'

'I think so.'

Putting his hand under Luigi's right arm, the man helped him to his feet. He was about forty, short and round as a barrel, with a crinkled face, flat brown nose and short black hair. The tip of a very pink tongue showed between his prominent lips.

'You live here?' Luigi asked.

'Yeah. Waterfall Bay. How you're feeling now?'

'Better, thanks. But the birds ...'

'Yeah, it's nesting season, they're nasty bastards right now.' He looked again at Luigi's head, and winced. 'You'd better come back to my whare, get washed up.'

'But my boat.'

'You made it fast?'

'Yes, but ...'

'Tide'll start to drop soon, it'll be okay. The nor-easterly'll die down by mid-afternoon. It's usually followed by a westerly, that'll help blow you back to the beach.'

'Are you sure?'

'Lived round here all me life, mate. I know what the wind'll do. I'll row you back round to your boat when the nor-easterly drops.'

'Have you got a spare rowlock I can borrow?'

'Got half a dozen, mate.'

They walked along the narrow track, Luigi limping, holding his bruised hands out in front of him, his rescuer taking quick little steps beside him. To their left bush-clad cliffs rose steeply, to their right the high tide lapped at the rocks. A chorus of birdsong came from the bush. Glossy tuis swooped from rata branch to rata branch, chiming as they went, and fat pigeons eyed them curiously from the boughs of karaka trees, seemingly unafraid of the men's presence. As they went, Percy told Luigi about himself.

'I use to be a bushman. In the Muaupoko Valley. After the missus died, five years back, I came to the island t'live. Family own land over here. I fish outa the bay, take it over to the Waikanae to sell it. You new round here?'

'I've lived here two months.'

'Where y'from?'

'Makara. Before that, the West Coast. Before that, Italy.'

'Italy, eh?' Percy paused. 'Who's got the pub there now?'

'What?'

'Joke, mate. Maori joke.' He coughed, and his throat rattled like stones rolling in the tide. 'I met some other fullas from Italy one time, at the fish market in town. From Island Bay, they were. Not bad fullas, either.'

They reached a small clearing, a niche in the coast, surrounded on three sides by forested slopes. Drawn up above the pebbly shoreline was a cream-coloured fishing boat. Set back about twenty yards from the sea was a small board and batten house with a smoking, corrugated iron chimney. There was a vegetable garden plot at one side of the house, an iron shed on the other. A washing line ran from the chimney to the shed, around which were scattered glass floats, nets and bamboo rods. Further around the bay, a waterfall tumbled down a rock face and into a dark pool at the foot of the cliff.

Inside the whare, Percy stoked the fire and put a billy over it. Caps, jackets, jerseys and oilskins hung from nails in the unlined walls, along with a small rifle on a rack above the table. Across one corner of the hut, beside the open fireplace, was a wire from which hung the plucked bodies of half a dozen small birds, their legs bound to the wire with string.

'Kereru?' Luigi guessed.

'Yeah, bush pigeons.'

'Did you shoot them?'

'Yeah.'

'They are good eating. We had them in Okuru sometimes.'

'Great kai all right.' Suddenly he scowled. 'Bloody government's talking about making Kapiti a reserve. Protecting all the birds. Bugger that, I say. I can't live just on fish.' He tossed some tea leaves into the boiling billy, took it from the fire and stirred it with a spoon. 'My family's Ngati Toa, we've had this land since the 1820s. No politician's going to stop me shooting pigeons.'

There was a loud 'meow' and a large tabby cat with only half a tail came in the door. As it purred and rubbed its side against Percy's trouser leg, Luigi was startled to see that its eyes were entirely white.

'What happened to your cat?'

'One day I dragged up an old whaler's harpoon in my net. I thought it'd look good by the fireplace, so I put it there. A few days later, while Kingi – the cat – was sleeping by it, the harpoon blew up. Must've still had explosives in it. They got dried out and set off by the fire. Good thing I was out in the garden at the time.' He chuckled. 'Bloody thing blew the back out of the fireplace and the cat right out the door. Didn't see 'im for a few days after that. Then he came limping back, blind and with half 'is tail blown away.' He began to stroke the cat fondly. 'But you recovered, didn't you, e hoa? And he might not be able to see, but the bugger can smell all right. Still catches rats and mice.'

He poured some of the hot water into an enamel bowl, added some salt, stirred it, dunked his handkerchief in it and began to dab the beak wounds on Luigi's head.

Flinching, he asked Percy, 'Does it look bad?'

'You'll live. Get your missus to put iodine on it tonight, though. Bloody gulls. They raid my bait box some times.'

He rinsed the handkerchief and squeezed it dry, then poured tea into two tin mugs, added some condensed milk from a small tin and handed one to Luigi. 'There you go, mate, that'll take your mind off the holes in yer head.'

As they sat smoking, sipping their tea, Percy looked hard at Luigi. 'How long've you been in New Zealand, Louie?'

'Sixteen years.'

'You speak good English, for an Eye-tie.'

'Thank you.'

'Like it here?'

'Yes. It is my home, now.'

Percy nodded, clearly pleased. Then he said, 'What d'you think of King Dick?'

'Mr Seddon?'

'Yeah.'

'Not much.'

He told Percy the story of his encounter with the future Premier in Westland. The other man chuckled.

'That's him all right.' Percy sipped more of the brew, then asked Luigi, 'You met a Chinese fulla called Young Lee yet? In Para'pram?'

'The vegetable grower?'

'That's the one.'

'Yes. He is a very hard-working man.'

'He is. But the poor bastard's still paying off the poll tax the government put on the Chinese immigrants. A hundred quid, Young Lee, Wong Sun and the other market gardeners have to pay off. *A hundred quid!*' Percy snarled. 'Blimmin' unfair.'

'Yes. I am pleased I am not a Chinaman.' Touching his scalp gingerly, Luigi asked, 'How often do you come over to the mainland?'

''Bout twice a week. To sell my fish and get supplies. And sometimes, when there's a dance at Wise's Hall, I play the piano there.'

'Is that so?'

'Yeah. Great fun, those dances.'

'I play the accordion.'

'That right?'

'Maybe we could play together one night.'

'Maybe we could.'

And so began a friendship that was to last for seventeen years.

THE MEMORIALIST

The woman smiled as she handed William a sheet of A4 paper. 'He *was* naturalised', she said. 'Here's a copy of the certificate.'

He ran his eyes over it.

Addressed To His Excellency the Governor of New Zealand, it stated that —

The Memorial of *Luigi Galoni* of *Makara*, in the colony of New Zealand, Occupation *Fisherman*, made in conformity with the provisions of 'The Aliens Act, 1880,'

Humbly Showeth:

1. That the name of your Memorialist is *Luigi Galoni*
2. That your Memorialist is *33* years of age.
3. That your Memorialist was born at *Italy.*
4. That your Memorialist resides in *Makara.*
5. That your Memorialist has been residing in the Colony of New Zealand for *11*
   years, and is desirous of settling therein.

And your Memorialist prays that Letters of Naturalisation may be granted to him.

Signature of Memorialist: *Luigi Galoni*

The lower half of the certificate consisted of a verification.

DECLARATION OF VERIFICATION

I, <u>*Luigi Galoni* ,</u> the above-named Memorialist, do solemnly and sincerely declare that all the above-stated facts relating to myself are true as I have stated them, and I make this solemn declaration conscientiously believing the same to be true, and by virtue of an Act of the General Assembly of New Zealand entitled "The Justices of the Act, 1882."

Declared at *Paremata*
this <u>*3ʳᵈ*</u> day of *November 1890*
before me —
Thomas Smith J.P.

I, the undersigned *Thomas Smith*
do hereby certify that I know *Luigi Galoni*
the Memorialist named in the foregoing Memorial, and that, to the best of my knowledge and belief, he is a person of good repute.

Thomas Smith
A Justice of the Peace for the
Colony of New Zealand.

Place: *Paremata*
Date: *November 3/1890*

Thanking the woman, William took the sheet into the reading room and examined it line by line. Its quaintly archaic, legal wording intrigued him. The word 'Memorialist' was one he was unfamiliar with. But at last, he had something official, confirmation of his great-grandfather's residency, and his year of arrival in this country. He did a quick subtraction. 1879. The naturalisation ceremony would have been gazetted, too, the Archives woman had told him, also telling him where he could find the details. In another section of Archives he took from a row of identical volumes *The New Zealand Gazette* for 1890. Checking the date on Luigi's certificate, he found on page 1324 of that year a small notice. His eyes zoomed in on it.

Letters of Naturalisation Issued

Colonial Secretary's Office
Wellington, 7th November, 1890

His Excellency the Governor has been pleased to issue Letters of Naturalisation, under "The Aliens Act, 1880," in favour of the under-mentioned persons:-

Name	Occupation	Residence
Victor Perez	Fisherman	Makara
Antonio Lima	Fisherman	Makara
Luigi Galoni	Fisherman	Makara
Theodore Belong	Fisherman	Paremata
Charles Merveldt	Bushman	Kumara

So, he had lived as a fisherman, had become a New Zealander in the company of three other fishermen. Most, by the look of the names, Italian as well. At Paremata, where he and Alice had been married. But he had been living then at Makara. God, what a place to live. No wonder none of the children had been born there. Petone must have seemed like paradise by comparison.

Holding his photocopies of the documents, William walked from the building with a spring in his step. Slowly, fragment by fragment, the pieces of the Luigi puzzle were falling into place.

TWELVE

'Papa, the Premier is coming!'

Breathless, Edith dropped her school bag on the kitchen floor. Luigi looked up from his newspaper.

'Coming where?'

'Here. To Para'pram.'

Then Violetta rushed in the door. She had wanted to be the first one to announce the news to their parents, but Edith was a faster runner and had beaten her home by half a minute. But all the same, Violetta made her own announcement. 'Mr Seddon's coming here. The Premier of *all* New Zealand.'

Alice walked into the kitchen from the scullery, having overheard the announcements. With a doubtful tone in her voice, she said, 'Who told you this, girls?'

'Mr Howell,' the girls announced, together. William Howell was the chairman of the local school committee, a man of great self-importance.

'He's … Mr Seddon's coming on Friday,' said Edith, shooting Vi a triumphant look. Lately the rivalry between them had become more noticeable.

'But what is he coming here *for*?' asked their father.

'To open the new Technical School,' said Violetta, quickly.

'Good gracious,' said Alice, sinking down onto one of the kitchen chairs. 'The Premier.'

The news went through the district like a whirlwind. Richard John Seddon was coming to declare open Paraparaumu's nearly-completed, grandly-titled Technical School. This consisted of a single-roomed workshop in which carpentry would be taught to adults in the community by Edward Davis, a skilled woodworker, on Saturday mornings. Next day, talking to other local men at the railway station, Luigi learned that it was the children's school headmaster, William Foster, who had pressed the Education Department in Wellington for the technical school to be built, who had also had the audacity to write to the Premier of New Zealand and invite him to formally open it. And to the district's astonishment, the Hon. Richard John Seddon had accepted.

There had been nothing like it in the little community's half century of existence. Plans quickly got under way for a reception for the dominion's leader, who was to arrive in a special train at ten in the morning and leave again at mid-afternoon. A meeting was quickly arranged at Wise's Hall, where all community events involving more than ten people were held.

Luigi decided to attend the meeting. At Wise's Hall he took a seat in the second row, next to Percy Watene, who had rowed over from Kapiti for the night. Under the chairmanship of William Foster, a tentative schedule was agreed on by the meeting. As the Technical School was close to the school, that would be the focus for the Premier's reception. A welcome banner and the national flag would be hoisted above the entrance to the school grounds and bunting strung between the flag-pole and the school-house. All forty-two children would parade and join the adult community in singing "God Save the Queen". There would be speeches from William and the Premier, then Mr Seddon would cut a ribbon across the door of the school and declare it open. A luncheon to which everyone in the community would be invited would follow, with every lady in Paraparaumu contributing a plate.

There remained one problem, however. The luncheon would be over by 1.30pm. What to do with the nation's leader for the remaining one and a half hours, when his train would return from the capital to fetch him?

William Foster sat behind a table on the small stage. A slightly-built man of twenty-nine with an enormous black moustache, this was the cricket-loving headmaster's finest hour. 'One and a half hours to fill in,' repeated William. 'Do we have any suggestions as to how we could best entertain the Premier?'

'What about a cricket match, Will?' someone called out from the back. 'Between Para'pram and Pae-kok?'

'One and a half hours,' William replied, scathingly, 'Hardly time for a cricket match.'

'A rugby match, then.'

'In February?'

There was a pause, then Percy Watene shouted,

'Take 'im down to the Otaihanga swamp and show 'im how badly it needs draining.' A ripple of laughter went through the crowd.

'Give him a tour of Young Lee's market garden!' someone else yelled.

There were hoots of glee at this. Seddon's anti-Chinese statements had become more virulent in recent months.

Listening to these responses, it was confirmed in Luigi's mind that, Premier or no Premier, there was no great love for the government in this district. Apart from the railway, completed before Seddon's elevation, Wellington seemed to regard Paraparaumu as an insignificant backwater. The roads were atrocious, the local school had only been built after years of agitating by William Foster and others, and the nearest hospital was in Wellington city.

And in Luigi's case, there was another, more personal grievance. He raised his hand.

'You have a suggestion, Luigi?' said William.

'I would like to take the Premier on a tour.'

'What sort of tour?'

'Of our district. Around the roads of Paraparaumu.'

There was murmuring through the hall, then, as realisation dawned, outbreaks of appreciative laughter. William nodded, thoughtfully, then said, 'What does the meeting think of that idea?'

'Yeah, why not?'

'Hear, hear!'

Stroking his huge moustaches, William said, 'But would it make a difference?

'There's an election in December, don't forget!' Percy called out. This was received with gales of laughter. Sensing the mood of the meeting, William said carefully:

'Are we in agreement, then, that the Premier is given a special tour of the district?'

Cries of 'Too right!' and 'Hear! Hear!' came from the meeting. Then Luigi stood up.

'I will volunteer to drive the Premier.' He paused. 'If someone will lend me a block dray to take him in.'

William frowned. 'Don't you think a two-horse carriage would be more suitable for the Premier?'

'In his case, not a carriage,' said Luigi. He turned to the others. 'Can anyone lend me a block dray?'

'You can use mine,' called Tom Pudney, who used his rough wagon for delivering coal from the station to the district's houses.

'Thank you Tom,' said Luigi.

The following day, William, Luigi and Percy carefully planned the Premier's itinerary.

The morning of February 29 dawned very hot. A strong wind was blowing across the coast from the north-west, raising the temperature even more, and the sky was streaked with high, feathery clouds. It was a special day in another way too, Alice explained to the girls as she supervised them getting into their best dresses and shoes, a date that only happened every four years. Leap Year day. The evening before, she and the girls had baked sponge cakes and afghan biscuits and cooked little meat pies in the coal range, while Luigi walked to Tom Pudney's depot to collect his block dray and horse, returning with them before dark.

Now, as Luigi stood and watched the Premier step down from the carriage, followed by an entourage of officials from the Education Department, he saw how much the years had inflated the man. A head taller than everyone else, the Premier had a chest like an ale keg and a voice like a megaphone. He must weigh nearly twenty stone, thought Luigi. His beard had turned grey, but that was not surprising, Luigi thought, having read in the paper that the Premier had recently turned 51. Today he was wearing a black frock coat, matching bow tie, white waistcoat, baggy pale calico trousers and a top hat that added another foot to his already commanding height. His big arms hung down as he cast an imperious eye over the waiting crowd, then he began to shake hands and speak with the local notables. Even after all these years, Luigi well remembered that domineering style and grating English accent.

He watched the Premier and his followers stride through the gate, under the WELCOME TO PARAPARAUMU banner and into the school grounds, then Luigi went over to the verge opposite the station, where Tom's dray and draught horse, Sybil, were waiting. He had no wish to join the luncheon, his role in the ministerial visit was more important than that.

At just after 1.30pm the Premier, William Foster, William Howell,

Charles Mills and Henry Field emerged from the school compound, all in jovial mood. Before they took their seats on the dray, William Foster introduced Luigi to the Premier. As he shook the leader's hand, Luigi looked directly at him. This had the effect of catching the politician's full attention. But it was held only for an instant, before it slid back to the others. And in that instant Luigi noted the politician's judgement, and divined his thoughts. It was not a look of disdain, merely dismissal. *You are no use to me*, the momentary glance from those dull grey eyes said, *there is no need for us to speak further.* But still it stirred something like ire in Luigi, and underscored the contempt he felt for men like him. He would continue not to bother even to enrol for voting.

As the Premier took his seat at the front of the dray, next to William Foster, he took a large handkerchief from his coat pocket and began to brush the breadcrumbs from his beard. Before he had finished doing so Luigi had given Sybil's reins a firm flick, the big horse began to jog off and the cart moved down the slope, still watched by a sizeable crowd, adults only now, as the children were back in their classroom.

The tour that Luigi and the others had devised formed a circuit. In the following hour and a half he was taken through the swamp land to Otaihanga, back up the poorly-formed track to the saddle that led to the Muaupoko valley and stream, and along the rough track which had been cut through the standing bush. At first voluble and full of bonhomie, the Premier became increasingly subdued. As the dray slowly climbed up towards the Muaupoko saddle, Seddon removed his top hat and placed it firmly between his feet. Then, half-way across the saddle, with the dray lurching first one way, then the other, and Sybil baulking at some of the tight bends, Luigi overheard the Premier ask in a low voice, 'When do we reach the main road, William?' And he heard William's truthful reply. 'This *is* the main road, Mr Seddon.'

Holding tight to the reins, not really listening to the commentary which William was providing for the Premier, Luigi concentrated instead on taking care not to miss any of the large rocks, deep mud holes and protruding tree roots along the way. But he caught snippets of William's observations as they bumped and ground and thudded along on the dray's unyielding wheels.

'Overflow from the Otaihanga stream causes this swamp, Premier. A stop-bank would help, but council's never bothered to build one.'

'That's the quarry over there, Premier. When we get a proper road, that's where the shingle will come from.'

'Oh, hang on very tight here sir, the track's extra steep from now on.'

'Luigi'll have to take us across the stream, Premier. We've been requesting a bridge, but no one's done a thing about it.'

And throughout the long, uncomfortable excursion, Luigi sat silently, smiling to himself as he guided Sybil towards another pothole or tree root.

Back at the school, William helped the Premier down from the dray. There was only a handful of people gathered at the station now, curiously watching their leader's return. Visibly weary and shaken, he looked at the ground as he attempted to brush the spots of mud from his pale trousers. Then, still without looking at his host, he said gruffly, 'Thank you, William. That was a most interesting excursion. There is obviously great potential for further development in this district.' Placing his top hat back on his head, he added, 'Although it is obvious to me, too, that the district's roading is in need of some attention.'

He pulled down hard on the brim of his top hat and walked off unsteadily towards the now-opened Technical School, where he was to be reunited with his departmental officials.

As Luigi drove away the now-empty dray, he saw Percy Watene standing by the railway station entrance, clutching his sides, convulsing with silent mirth.

It was exactly a week later that Paraparaumu residents read with great interest an announcement reported in the *Dominion*, in which the New Zealand Minister of Public Works stated that: 'A survey of the Paraparaumu district will shortly be undertaken, preparatory to a comprehensive, first-grade roading scheme being implemented, to connect the settlement of Paraparaumu with Paekakariki to the south and Waikanae to the north'.

The New Zealand Minister of Public Works was the same Richard John Seddon who also happened to be Premier of the Dominion.

It was a few weeks after this memorable day when Luigi came in from a day's fishing to find Alice sitting at the kitchen table, weeping. There was an opened letter on the table. Going quickly to her, he asked.

'What is it?'

'Father died. On the seventeenth of March.'

'Oh Alice …'

Taking the chair next to her, he put his arms around her. Sobs racked her body and her tears soaked his shirt. When she looked up her expression was distraught.

'I know he was …a difficult man, but he was my father.'

Luigi nodded, understanding all too well, remembering the thoughts that had rushed in upon him at the news of his father's death. So many memories, so many regrets.

'Yes, yes.'

'But we never made our peace.'

'The fault wasn't yours, Alice,' he said, as gently as he could. 'He could have written, at any time. He could have visited us, any time. It was his choice not to.'

She nodded. Then said, in a more hopeful voice, 'Can I invite Mother to come and stay? I'm sure she would, now.'

'Of course. Of course.'

He put his arms around her again and held her close, putting his face in her hair, smelling the fragrance of lavender there. Cruelties, he thought, there are so many cruelties in families. And, he determined, there must be no such vindictiveness in his.

That summer the heat grew more and more intense. Even as March drifted into April it continued, and each day seemed hotter than the one before, as if the sun was moving closer to the Earth. The landscape took on a different appearance. Wherever the bush had been felled and grass planted, it was burnt by the sun and seared by the hot winds, so that the hills above Paraparaumu took on the appearance of a brown and green chequerboard. Streams dwindled to a trickle, then died altogether. Sluggish pools formed on the Waikanae River bed and the mud in the swamps cracked and curled until it looked like squares of freshly-tanned leather. Water levels in the settlement's corrugated iron tanks dropped lower and lower, until it dribbled ginger in the taps.

In the Galonis' garden, tomatoes and runner beans withered on the vine, lettuces turned brown and the soil turned to a fine dust that blew in the front door, through the kitchen and scullery and out the back, coating cupboards, clothes and furniture as it went. Violetta and Edith would arrive home from school at three-thirty exhausted and fractious from their ten-minute walk, while at home Alicia and Esther fretted and quarrelled until Alice told them crossly, 'Please, *go outside*. Play in the garden. Or watch for the train, if you can't think of anything better to do!' And as the heat of the afternoon sun began at last to wane, the girls would pull off their dark stockings, track off along the dry creek to the beach, change into their bathing costumes in the dunes, then run gratefully across the sand and into the tepid sea.

The heat brought other changes, too. As the sea turned unusually warm, some species of fish moved closer towards the shore and others retreated from it. Luigi could hardly move through the shallows without treading on large slippery flounders as he pushed his boat out, and when he rowed *Laetitia* out into the strait, schools of hammerhead sharks would be floating lazily, just beneath the surface. Schooling snapper became plentiful inshore, but all he seemed able to catch on his deepwater long lines were sting rays, which were unsellable, and dogfish, which fetched the poorest of prices at market. The tarakihi, evidently seeking cooler water, had moved much further out, beyond any small boat fisherman's reach. So in the evenings, by lantern light, Luigi and Percy speared the flounder, slipped flax ties through their gills and sold them in the village for sixpence a dozen.

But despite the remorseless heat, a pair of words that brought a chill into every parent's heart also became common that late, baking summer. Infantile paralysis.

The first reported case was of a seven-year-old boy at Waikanae. After suddenly developing a sore throat and a fever, a paralysis developed in both his legs. A few hours after being rushed to Wellington Hospital on the train, he fell into a coma and died. The cause at that stage was unknown. Then a second child from the same area, a boy of five, was struck with similar symptoms. He died in the night, before he could be admitted to hospital. Then a third child developed the fever, and a fourth, all in the Waikanae district. In the fourth case it was the young girl's breathing that was affected, and despite being given respiratory treatment, the patient died. Now the medical authorities, on full alert, pronounced that the disease which was striking the young was highly infectious, and that it attacked the nerves of movement at the point where they left the spinal cord. Thus its name, 'infantile paralysis', was cruelly accurate. An epidemic threatened and there was no known cure. Desperate to prevent the disease spreading, the schools in Waikanae, Paraparaumu and Paekakariki were all closed, indefinitely. Work was sent home by teachers for the children to do, under parental supervision.

'I wonder, Luigi, if it could be something to do with this heat,' Alice remarked. It was a week since the schools had been closed.

'You've heard what they're saying. It is infectious.'

'But why now? There's never been such a thing before.' Brushing the flour from her hands, she said, now a little defensively, 'Just as there's never been anything like this bakingly hot weather, the old people are saying.'

'Well, perhaps. Percy told me he's never known anything like it.'

He got up and went to the open door. Even the leaves of the wisteria which climbed along the verandah had turned yellow, weeks before they usually did. In the front garden the girls were playing on the swing in the peach tree, Edith pushing a squealing Esther and Alicia while Violetta busied herself by arranging fallen camellia petals in a pattern in the sand-pit. Luigi felt a rush of love for them all. They were growing so quickly, so strongly. His heart went out to the parents of the children afflicted by the paralysis. And he thought too, how could any man regret fathering daughters? They were so loving and so loyal to one another. As he watched he saw the swing slow, then stop. The girls went into a huddle, then Edith rushed inside.

'Papa, can we go for a swim? It is *so* hot.' She passed the back of her hand over her brow, like the little actress she was.

Her mother looked up from her scone mixture. 'Where?'

'In the stream.'

'The Titoku's dry,' said Luigi.

'Not that one, the other one. The Wharemauku. There's a pool there.'

'All right then.' Alice paused. 'As long as Vi's with you. And you *must* watch little Esther. Every minute.'

'Yes, Vi's coming too. And I promise to watch Esther.'

'And you must be home by …' Luigi took out his watch. 'Five-thirty.'

'Yes.'

Alice smiled at him, indulgently. 'How will they know when it's five-thirty?'

'Violetta can take my watch,' Luigi announced.

Edith rushed out again. 'We can go! Get togs and towels!'

They were home at exactly the appointed time, but hadn't changed out of their swimming togs. Instead they had wrapped themselves in their towels and carried their dresses under their arms. Their long hair was wet and loose, their bare feet muddy, and Alice insisted that they rinse off under the outside tap, water shortage or no water shortage, and dry themselves in the garden.

As they ate their tea that night, as the others chatted about the pool and how they had seen a giant eel there, Esther said little. Instead she began to shiver, her little shoulders quivering as she nibbled at her meat. Her face took on a bluish hue. One by one, the others paused in their eating. Although she had dried herself with her sisters, and was now wearing a dress, the shivering was becoming more noticeable. Feeling their gaze upon her, Esther turned her eyes slowly towards her parents. Her eyes were glazed and unfocused. 'I don't feel well, Mother,' she said, feebly. The fork slipped from her hand, and she closed her eyes. Alice looked quickly at Luigi, then at Violetta.

'Did she get cold at the creek?' she demanded.

Vi shook her head, quickly. 'No. When she got out I wrapped the towel around her. Straight away.'

'She didn't get cold, mother,' affirmed Edith.

'No, we didn't let her,' Alicia echoed.

Alice got up from the table and put the palm of her right hand to Esther's brow. When she looked back at Luigi, there was a flash of fear in her eyes. But instead of speaking, she helped Esther down from the table and led her by the arm away to the bedroom that she shared with Alicia. The other girls stared down at their plates, Luigi's eyes were fixed on the bedroom door. A fearful silence descended on the table. Then Luigi got up and went to the bedroom.

Esther was under the covers, her hair spread out on the pillow, her eyes closed. Alice was sitting on a chair beside the bed, her hand held on the child's forehead. Even from the doorway, Luigi could see Esther's jaw trembling, see the bedclothes making sudden little jumping movements. Without taking her eyes from the child's face, Alice said grimly, 'It's a fever.'

'It's probably just a chill. She probably got cold coming home.'

When Alice turned to look at him, her expression was stony. 'It's *not* just a chill. *It is a fever.*' She turned back to the bed.

As she did so, Esther opened her eyes wide and murmured. 'My leg.

My leg's hurting, mother. It's so sore.' Closing her eyes, she screwed up her face against the pain, then held her eyes shut.

This time when Alice looked back at Luigi and spoke, her voice was urgent, and more forceful than he had ever heard it.

'Go for Dr Wakeham. Take the horse. *Straight away.*'

It was half an hour's ride to Waikanae, along the rough track that crossed the swamp and the ford in the river. By the time he reached the doctor's house it was dusk and a crescent moon was rising above Kapiti Island. Dr Wakeham, a clean-shaven man in his late thirties, answered the door. He was in shirt sleeves and socks. As Luigi described Esther's symptoms, his face darkened.

'A fever?'

'Yes.'

'Has her temperature been taken?'

'No. Not yet.'

'Then how do you know it is a fever?'

'She trembles. And her brow is hot.'

'Has she been suffering from a cold?'

'No. Not at all.'

'Any difficulty in breathing?'

'Not when I left.'

'But she has pains in her leg?'

'The right leg, yes. Bad pains.'

The man was silent for a moment, staring past Luigi, his face tight with concern. Then, turning away, he announced, 'I'll come now. In my trap. You lead the way.'

The doctor turned the thermometer over carefully, squinting at the thread of silver liquid. Then he shook it and slipped it back into its tube. His face was grave, and even before he spoke, they both knew what he was going to say. The symptoms were now familar to every parent in the district. But still his words lanced them to the heart.

'It is what I thought, Mr and Mrs Galoni. Infantile paralysis. If we're to save her we must get her to Wellington Hospital on the morning train.'

It was a sight and sound that neither Luigi nor Alice was ever to forget. The way little Esther's right leg began to twist, like a board warping in the sun, the way the leg stayed twisted and the muscles wasted, and worst of all, her agonised cries as it did so. It was as if the diseased limb had developed a mind of its own, a wayward mind heedful of nothing else in Esther's tiny body, including her pain. As they sat beside her bed in the isolation ward, the sight and sound of her suffering was a torment to them. Slow, hushed, trusting little Esther, who followed her big sisters like a pet lamb in everything they did, and until this terrible time had never been ill in her life.

As the paralysis held her in its grip, her only relief came from the spoonfuls of laudanum that the nurses administered. During the night, when the pain seemed worse, it took two nurses to hold her down while the sedative was spooned into her, and even then its effects were limited, and as they wore off there would be a fresh outbreak of pain. When a Catholic priest called at the ward one evening and suggested they pray together for Esther, Luigi sent him away in a cold fury. If there was any kind of God, if He could allow a child to suffer the way little Esther was suffering, then Luigi had no wish to have anything to do with Him. Instead, he and Alice took it in turns to sit with her beside the bed, departing afterwards, exhausted, for the Newtown boarding house where they were staying, a block away from the hospital. There they found it almost impossible to sleep, their thoughts haunted by Esther's crying and the knowledge that her right leg would be, as the hospital doctor informed them solemnly, 'crippled for life'. Although the fever had passed and her life was out of danger, weeks, possibly months of recuperation lay ahead.

Back at the house, Evie was looking after the others and writing to Alice and Luigi every day. As well as their anxieties over Esther, there was the continuing fear that the other girls, having been exposed to the ghastly infection, would also succumb to paralysis. They dreaded opening Evie's letters for the news that it might contain, but as the weeks passed, no symptoms were reported in the others. There had been seven more cases of the disease in the district, and five had died. The schools remained closed. But it seemed that the Galoni family had been struck only once by the lightning bolt that had come from nowhere.

Late in May they brought Esther home on the train, wrapped in a hospital blanket, a pair of small wooden crutches on the seat beside her. Gradually, over the months that followed, their life resumed a kind of normality. In June the schools reopened, the authorities having announced that the epidemic was over. The heat wave had long passed, and winter rains began to soak the coast. But for the Galonis, nothing was the same. On fine days, when Esther was at last able to go outside, she could go no further than the garden on her crutches, and when she used them they chaffed at her tender armpits until she cried. It was months before she could walk without the crutches, and when she did, her limp caused people – not just other children – to stare, and comment in whispers as she passed. Once Vi came home from school red-eyed and crying. Tommy Cruikshanks had called out to her and Edith in the playground, 'How's your sister, the little hobbly-wobbly horse?' Furious, Vi had run up to him and kicked him, hard, on the knee. After Tommy had gone howling and complaining to Mrs Elliot, her response was to admonish Vi publicly. 'That was a *very* unladylike thing to do, Violetta,' she reproached. 'Young ladies *never* behave like that.' That night Vi tearfully repeated this story to Luigi, who hugged her and promised, 'I will talk to your teacher about it.'

He did, and although there was no more public teasing, the stares continued.

Esther tired easily, the limp draining her energy. Sometimes she fell asleep at the dinner table. And from the day she arrived home, as she realised that she would never be like other children, or other adults, her expression assumed a shadow of sadness that never left her. Lines had formed at the side of Alice's face, too, which from that time onwards deepened.

When the day came that Esther was to begin school, they discussed what they should do.

'She can't walk there, Luigi, it's too far.'

'She could go on the horse, perhaps.'

'She's much too young.'

'I could take her on the horse.'

'How can you? When you are out in the boat at dawn most days.'

'Vi or Edith could go with her, then, on the horse.'

'No, that would be too dangerous.'

'I've an idea.'

'What?'

'We could get her a bicycle.'

They chose the latest model from Hethington's Mail Order Catalogue, sending a postal order for £2-10- 9d to the company in Wellington. A week later, when it came on the train, Luigi collected it from the guard's van and wheeled it home. A 'Junior Junior Ladies Model', its frame was painted green with thin white stripes, and it had pneumatic tyres, a leather seat, and a bell and a wicker basket at the front. When Esther saw it, her eyes popped and her mouth fell open with delight. For a few moments she was speechless, then she said, 'But Papa, I can't ride a bicycle.'

'But you can learn, little one.'

While the others all stood around and watched, he held the machine upright and she climbed keenly up onto the saddle. Then immediately burst into tears. The foot on her withered and shortened right leg was well short of the pedal. 'I can't reach, I can't reach!' she cried, dismounting and limping inside, sobbing, Alice striding after her. Violetta, Edith and Alicia stared dismally at the bicycle, close to tears themselves.

Still holding the gleaming little machine, Luigi had an idea. Going to the woodshed in the garden, he selected a small block of macrocarpa and after measuring the pedal, cut it to size with his handsaw, drilled two holes through the block with his brace and bit, and secured it to the right pedal with a pair of nuts and bolts.

Half an hour later Esther was back on the bicycle and riding it in wobbly fashion around the garden, her face gleeful, Luigi trotting along beside her in case she fell.

'You've done it, Esie!' called Violetta.

'Keep going, keep going!' urged Alicia.

'You're the Para'pram champion!' Edith shouted.

From that day on, little Esther Galoni and her bicycle became as familiar a sight around Paraparaumu as Len Howell with his butcher's cart or Tom Pudney with his coal dray. She would coast down the hill to school on it in the mornings, share it with her special friends at play-times, then push herself back home again in the afternoons, usually beating the others back by five minutes. At weekends on fine days she rode it along the track to the beach, and once went as far along the beachfront as Raumati and back. The strenuous daily exercise of cycling helped her right leg become stronger. Although the limp indeed proved permanent, her calf and ankle muscles strengthened too, so that she could walk as fast as anyone else her age, and when she gamely entered the three-legged race with Polly Drewitt at the school sports in 1898 and the pair came third, all the spectators got to their feet and cheered.

As the century drew to a close, although changes came to the Kapiti Coast, one upon another in quick succession, it seemed that they had lived in the house by the railway line forever. Luigi fished whenever the conditions were favourable, or even marginal – usually on two days out of three – and Alice made firm friends with the other women in the district. Their girls were safe roaming the countryside, the sand dunes and the beach. The Galonis' garden flourished, fertilised liberally with the fish that Luigi could not sell: hammerhead sharks, sting rays and surplus flounder.

Luigi became firm friends with the only other Italian man in the district, Mario Monopoli, who had an orchard just outside Paraparaumu. Like Luigi, Mario had come as an unassisted migrant, in his case in 1886, after five years as a seaman on Italian merchant vessels, then sent for his fiancée, Claudia, and married her in Waikanae. The Monopolis were both from Genoa. Once a month, on Sundays, the Galoni and Monopoli families shared long Italian lunches outside, under the fruit trees whenever possible, and when they were alone Luigi and Mario enjoyed speaking the old language together. Mario's orchard began to prosper, and soon local people were choosing to hold their wedding celebrations there, beneath the apple, pear and cherry trees.

And as always, there was the music. Not long after they met, Luigi and Percy Watene became a duo, playing accordion and piano at the monthly Saturday night dances at Wise's Hall, above Billy Wise's boarding house in the centre of Paraparaumu. Percy was a self-taught pianist, and like Luigi, played by ear. They quickly reached a close musical understanding. To Luigi's surprise, there was something about the rythmns of Maori songs that were similar to Italian tunes, and his and Percy's Italian tunes, and their mix of waltzes, marches, valittas, polkas and quicksteps became favourites with the locals. Percy's *Ake Ake Waltz*, *Moa March* and *Maori Haka Rondeletto* happily alternated with Luigi's *Santa Lucia*, *Addio Mio Bella Napoli*. Yet the song they would sing together with most feeling was *Violetta*, when tears would invariably spring into Luigi's eyes as he pumped his accordion and thought of his sister and his homeland:

'Hear my song....Vio-let-ta!
Hear my song, beneath the moo...oon.

Come to me... in my gon...dola,
Waiting on the old la...goo...oon.

Serenade, across the wa...ter...
Can you hear it, soft and low...
A tale of love, and lovers sing...ing...
Long....long... ago...

Hear my song, Vio-lett-ta!
When the dawn is breaking through...
Still with me, in my gon-do-la!
Where we've been, the whole...
Night throu...oo!

Hear my song....Vio-let-ta!
Hear my song, beneath the moo...oon...

Two years after Richard Seddon's rough ride, the Paekakariki to Paraparaumu road was completed along the foothills, and a wooden ramp built over the railway line, only a few hundred yards from Alice and Luigi's home. Coaches could now move at a fast clip along the coastal plain, and although it was often slushy, the road began to rival the railway as a means of getting from one settlement to the next. In 1897 Seddon's government passed the Kapiti Island Reserve Act, which reserved all the Crown-owned areas of the island. Most of Kapiti was to be returned to its natural state. The farmers leasing Crown land were paid compensation and given until November 1900 to vacate the island. Percy continued to grumble about this, but his family land remained unaffected. He gardened at Waterfall Bay without interference, and continued to shoot the kereru that roosted in the trees around his house.

The changes to the island in no way affected Luigi's livelihood. Whenever the weather was favourable he dragged *Laetitia II* down the sand, then rowed steadily across the strait to set his lines, with the forested slopes of Kapiti, pleated and tucked like the green velvet dresses Alice sewed for the girls, overlooking him, as familiar now as the hills that formed the backdrop to Paraparaumu itself.

But as Luigi moved into his fifth decade, hauling the boat across the beach to the tideline, rowing out to the fishing grounds, then hauling her back to the dunes became more and more difficult. Often now he was obliged to pause from time to time while rowing, to regain his breath, something which never used to interrupt his regular rhythm. His lower back muscles sometimes gave stabs of pain when he stood up, and while digging the garden in particular, he would sometimes flinch as parts of his spine protested. Alice noticed this, and from time to time would ask when he planned to give up fishing. He treated such enquiries as a poor joke. Give up fishing? He might as well give up breathing.

But when in the spring of 1897 Frank Donovan's boat overturned in the surf and struck him on the head, causing his death, Alice's anxieties deepened. Whenever Luigi came in the back door, weary after a long day's work in the strait, he would see her face light up with relief. And when he went to her and held her, she would whisper in his ear, 'I was worried when the wind got up. I worry about you being out there, Luigi.' And he would laugh and reply, 'You have no need to, my darling, I always take care.'

In 1898 the English Queen celebrated her diamond jubilee and Premier Seddon led an outpouring of nationwide acclaim for the distant monarch. Although the children's school entered into this with fervour – it seemed the girls were making cardboard crowns with cotton wool ermine and sewing little Union Jacks on Alice's machine for weeks – Luigi was moved very little by all the carry-on. It appeared to him to be just another opportunity for Richard John Seddon to fill the news pages of the papers and weeklies.

A few months after the jubilee the South African War broke out, and there was another outburst of patriotism. Two local lads, Maurice Lynch's only son Richard and Fred Davies' eldest boy, Alfred, volunteered, and although Luigi went to the station to join in their send-off, as he watched them waving from the train to the crowd, he felt little enthusiasm for the far-off cause of Imperial Britain, and blessed relief that he and Alice had had only daughters.

The end of the century, on the other hand, was no occasion for misgivings. A huge bonfire was built on Paraparaumu beach and there was a firework display more spectacular than any other anyone had ever witnessed. It lit up the forested slopes of Kapiti more clearly than daylight, and was accompanied by a beach party which every citizen of the settlement – from babes in arms to the elderly – attended. This was followed by a Welcome The New Century Ball at Wise's Hall, where Auld Lang Syne was sung joyously at the midnight hour to the accompaniment of Luigi's accordion and Percy's piano. Friends and neighbours shook hands and embraced, and Luigi and Alice had never before felt such community joy and optimism. The twentieth century had arrived, greeted by almost boundless goodwill and confidence.

As if in confirmation of this zest, the year 1900 became notable for further national celebrations. February 28 was declared a nationwide holiday after the Boer leader, Cronje, surrendered. The relief of Ladysmith produced a half-day holiday on March 8 and that of Mafeking on May 22 was worth a whole day of rejoicing. Overhearing his daughters chatting about the conflicts and triumphs in South Africa, taught to them exhaustively at school, Luigi was bemused by the fact that the girls now seemed to know far more about that war-torn, foreign land than they did about their own.

In January 1901 the Queen of England and all her colonies died, after having seemed to have ruled forever. The school again closed for the day, and in the mourning period that followed, Premier Seddon led the nation's grieving.

In the second year of the new century, at the age of twelve, Violetta left school and was apprenticed as a seamstress to a Mrs Crowder, who lived in Waikanae, travelling back and forth to the woman's home-based cutting shop on the train. Already a skilled sewer – Alice had had several of her immaculately stitched samplers framed and hung from the walls at home – Violetta revelled in the work. The following year, Edith left school too. Lacking Vi's dexterity, but always willing to help the less fortunate, she obtained work as a nurse aid at the newly-opened Otaki Cottage Hospital, also travelling to work on the train. Alicia, beautiful, dreamy Alicia, took part-time clerical work at the Paraparaumu Post Office when she left school. And in the summer of 1905 something happened which was to ensure that she, of all the girls, became in a way, immortal.

THIRTEEN

'I *hate* my hair,' Alicia said yet again, brushing it with long, aggressive strokes. 'Why did *I* have to be the one to get hair like father's?'

Alice smiled. How many times had she heard her third daughter voice this sentiment? And her response to Alicia's grievance was always the same.

'Lots of girls would envy you your hair, dear.'

'Not *this* girl. *Red* hair. Ooooh.'

As she continued to brush it in front of the hall mirror, Alice watched her admiringly. Tall for her fourteen years, and with perfectly upright bearing, her long auburn hair was her single most striking feature. So glossy it almost seemed burnished, the hair came down to her narrow waist, falling in a thick, reddish-brown mane which shone as it caught the light, contrasting strikingly with her creamy complexion. With her mother still watching, Alicia swept her hair up on to the top of her head, twirled and pinned it, picked up her bonnet and crammed it on top of her head. 'There,' she exclaimed, 'gone!'

She flounced into the kitchen, where Luigi was reading the paper, having his first day's break from fishing for a week. The two eldest girls were at work, Esther was at school and it was a beautiful May day, clear, fresh and still. As Alicia filled the kettle, Luigi said, 'You're not working today, then?'

'No. Mrs Oakes doesn't need me on Tuesdays.'

'So, do you have any plans?'

'Not really. I may walk to the beach, later, with my friend Josephine.' She placed the kettle on the coal range. 'Would you like tea, Papa?'

'Yes, thank you.'

There was a knock on the front door and Luigi got up and answered it.

Standing side-by-side on the verandah were two women, one tall and thin and about forty, the other short, sturdy and a few years younger. Both were dressed in white, high-necked blouses and dark skirts. The taller woman had a brown sports jacket over her blouse and a wide-brimmed straw hat over her greying, tightly-drawn-back hair; the shorter one a small boater perched on top of her dark hair. The taller one had an amused expression and lively eyes; the other woman's expression was rather downcast. At their feet were two wooden cases and a pair of large easels. The taller woman said, in a clear, confident voice,

'Good morning. I'm Dorothy Richmond, and this is my friend Frances.'

'Good morning. I am Luigi Galoni.'

'Frances and I are here on holiday from Wellington, staying at Pudney's guest house.' She gestured towards the other woman. 'Frances's sister Isabel is married to Will Field. You know the Fields, I presume?'

'I do, yes.' Everyone in Paraparaumu knew the Fields. Will Field was a Member of Parliament, and as the wife of a parliamentarian, Isabel moved in fashionable circles, giving herself airs these days when she moved among the local people.

The tall woman waved a hand at the cases, then gave a dry little laugh. 'We're on our way to the beach, to paint, but we can't manage to carry all this equipment that distance. We wondered if there was anyone here who might be able to help.'

Luigi was about to offer his own services when he remembered that he'd promised to help Mario Monopoli scythe the grass in his orchard this morning.

'I will be busy, but Alicia may be able to help.'

'Alicia?'

'My daughter.' He turned, called to her, and she came to the door. Again the tall woman explained what she needed. Although she seemed a trifle surprised at the request, Alicia nodded.

'Yes, I'll help. I was going to walk down to the beach anyway. I'll just go and get my other hat.'

The two women beamed gratefully, and Luigi stood back. When Alicia reappeared, wearing her straw beach hat instead of her bonnet, the short woman – Frances – looked at her intently. The woman had a large undershot jaw and a mouth that turned down at the corners, emphasising her unhappy appearance.

When Alicia picked up a painting case in each hand, Frances asked earnestly, 'Are you sure you can manage both, dear?'

'Yes, they're not really heavy,' Alicia replied cheerily.

The women picked up an easel each, and the trio walked off towards the gate. When Alice came into the kitchen and Luigi had told her where Alicia had gone, Alice said thoughtfully, 'They are both painters?'

'Yes.'

'And one is Isabel Field's sister?'

'Yes, the taller one. Dorothy.'

'Isabel's landscapes are lovely. The Monopolis have one of Kapiti in their lounge, remember?' She smiled. 'The talent must run in the family.'

It was nearly lunchtime when Alicia returned from the beach, half an hour after her father had finished working in the orchard. Flushed and breathless, she sank down onto one of the kitchen chairs.

'Papa, you'll never guess.'

'Guess what?'

'What happened at the beach.' She took a deep breath. 'Well, not at the beach, in the sand dunes.'

'What d'you mean?'

Alicia paused to regain her breath.

'When we got to the sand dunes – just by the creek mouth – I put down the ladies' painting cases. And I was hot from the walk, so I took off my hat and let down my hair. Let it right down.'

Luigi looked at her sharply. He knew full well what Alicia's feelings were about her hair, and who was responsible for bequeathing it to her. He had always been secretly proud of it, delighted in fact that this Galoni trait had been passed on to one of his children in such striking fashion. His name may not be passed on, but at least his hair would be. Alicia continued.

'When the short woman – Miss Hodgkins – saw my hair, she gasped. Like this …' Alicia put her hand up to her mouth and went, "Oh, oh, oh." *Then*, the woman – Miss Hodgkins – said, "Your hair is so beautiful. *You* are so beautiful. I must paint your portrait, child". 'And she's going to. At the Pudney's. Starting tomorrow.'

She sat and stared at Luigi, her big eyes aflame. 'Imagine, me having my portrait painted.'

'That is wonderful.' He called past her, into the scullery. 'Alice, come and hear the news.'

And he laughed then, as he realised something else. For once, Alicia was not wearing a hat, and her hair – long, glossy and auburn – was falling over her left shoulder like the tail of a spirited chestnut filly.

The sittings began. Every afternoon Alicia would walk from the post office to Pudney's guest house, and spend two hours in the front parlour there while Miss Hodgkins, her easel propped up before her, sketched and frowned and dabbed and stroked. 'It's hard to keep still for so long,' Alicia told her parents, 'especially when Miss Hodgkins insists that I keep my hand up here, like this, the whole time.' She placed her left hand across her left breast, with the two middle fingers pointing directly at her throat. 'And I must look down the whole time, like this ...' She cast her eyes downward, and slightly to the right. 'And another thing. She won't show me what the painting's like. I'm *dying* to see, but she refuses. "Not until it's finished", she keeps saying, "Not until it's finished, my dear". It's in water-colours, that's all I know.'

Then Alicia brightened. 'But Miss Hodgkins has had *such* an interesting life. She's from Dunedin, but she's travelled to London and Belgium and Holland and France and Italy and *Morocco*.' Looking up, she blinked. 'Where *is* Morocco, Papa?'

'In North Africa. Not very far from Italy.'

'Oh. I didn't like to say I didn't know where it was. Anyway, her paintings have been exhibited in London, so she must be a *very* good artist, then she came back to live in Wellington and ...' Alicia's face fell '... this is very sad. She was engaged to be married, to an Englishman, but the engagement was broken off. Just last month.'

Alice put her hand up to her mouth. 'Oh, no.' Every woman's dread.

'Yes. She met him on the ship coming home, but he got off in Egypt or somewhere. She was going to go back to England and marry him there, but he wrote and broke it off.' Alicia stared out the window, pensively. 'I think that's why she's so sad most of the time. She told me this, while she was painting.' Alicia brightened. 'She's amazing the way she manages to talk and paint at the same time, all the time moving her eyes from me to the easel and back. Anyway, after she got the letter from the man, breaking the engagement off, her friend Miss Richmond persuaded her to come and have a holiday here, to help her forget what happened. Miss

Richmond tries to jolly her along, I can tell, but Miss Hodgkins still seems *very* sad.' Alicia flicked her hair with one hand. 'I can't *wait* to see the finished painting.'

The whole family assembled to see the unveiling, in the parlour of the guest house. Mrs Pudney made tea and Miss Richmond had bought a sponge at the bakery and they gathered in the room with their cups of tea and plates of cake late on Saturday afternoon and Miss Hodgkins – wearing a dark jacket and matching dress and looking, the girls agreed later, the very image of a rejected spinster – drew back the sheet from the easel, glancing anxiously at Miss Richmond as she did so.

There was a spontaneous, collective intake of breath from everyone in the room. The water colour was about three feet high and two feet wide. It portrayed a young girl from the waist up, dressed in a plain white, high-necked blouse. Her left hand was held up, the extended fingers over her left breast, her brown eyes looking downward demurely, a blush colouring her cheeks. But it was the feature which had captivated Miss Hodgkins so forcefully – her subject's long auburn hair – which was the painting's most arresting trait. The hair was so radiant it was almost luminous. Parted in the middle, drawn down around both sides of her head, the hair had a burning intensity. Yet it also seemed entirely natural, mainly because the way it was tied was slightly disorderly. A wisp stood out from the left side of her head, exposing one ear lobe, and the tail of hair which fell over the front of her left shoulder was also ungroomed.

The second feature which mesmerised the small audience was the girl's expression. Wistful and innocent, it was also not quite unknowing, as if the subject was beginning to be aware of her own allure, but hadn't in any way succumbed to it. The enormous brown eyes were looking down slightly, and contemplatively. The portrait was unmistakably Alicia, but it was also not Alicia. The forehead was much higher, the hand disproportionately large, the nose too strong, the expression uncharacteristic. But the painting's beauty and power was undeniable, it was not just a portrait of a girl, it was a portrait of girlhood. And the entire effect was of such hypnotic attraction that some moments passed before anyone in the parlour could break the silence which had descended upon the room.

Dorothy was the first to speak. Putting a hand gently on her friend's shoulder, she said, 'It's one of the best things you've ever done, Frances.' She gave a sardonic little laugh. 'Now they won't dare say you can't draw the human face.'

Then Alice spoke. 'It's beautiful,' she murmured. 'So beautiful.'

'Yes,' said Luigi, unable to take his eyes from the painting, at the same time wondering just who Dorothy's 'they' might be. 'The hair, it seems to …' his voice wavered as he sought the right word, then found it. '… *shimmer*.'

'It's as if she were alive,' said Mrs Pudney, almost to herself.

Then, together, they all looked at Alicia. She was holding her right hand up to her mouth, staring at the portrait that was herself but at the same time not herself, looking perplexed, as if seeing herself for the first time and finding the image impossible to fully comprehend. Violetta, Edith and Esther continued to stare at the portrait, awe-struck into silence.

At last Frances spoke. Tea cup in hand, shoulders slumped as if very tired, she allowed herself a little smile. 'I have called it "Babette"', she said quietly. She swallowed, hard, as if her throat was constricted, then said, 'I'm going to give it to you, Dorothy.'

With a jolt, Luigi realised then that the painting would not be theirs. Without ever raising the subject with the artist, he had somehow gained the impression that it would be. Glancing at Alice, he saw from her startled expression that she had been similarly struck by Frances's announcement. Then he saw the appreciative expression on Dorothy's face, the look of subdued satisfaction on Frances's, and he thought again. Of course the portrait must be the painter's to dispose of as she wished. It was her creation, her hours of work which had gone into it. Alicia had merely inspired her, then sat for her. He and Alice had the living Alicia, who was beyond price. But as his eyes returned to the painting, and lingered on its alluring beauty, he still wished that it could be his family's to have. Now, where would it be hung? To whom would it be passed? And why had Miss Hodgkins called it "Babette", when it was really Alicia?

Luigi and Percy sat on the breast of the sand dunes, just above where their boats were lying, waiting for the machine's arrival. Percy had rowed over from Kapiti especially to see it. Further along the beach a large crowd had gathered near the mouth of the Waikanae River, having been told that the machine would be coming at twelve-thirty, when the tide was at its lowest. Below Luigi and Percy was a wide expanse of flat, black sand, with scatterings of ginger seaweed and jumbles of driftwood sticks marking the tideline. Both men rolled cigarettes and lit them. 'A good day for it, anyway,' remarked Luigi, looking up at the clear spring sky. 'Yeah,' said Percy, 'He'll have a good run if he starts at Raumati.'

They heard it before it appeared, a loud put-put-put-put-putting, interrupted by several explosions, coming from somewhere inland, sounding like small arms fire. Then it appeared, rolling down through the gap in the dunes where the Raumati fishermen launched their boats, before veering right and heading towards them.

Moving at the speed of a horse and trap, it had four solid rubber tyres, mudguards and a bench seat for the driver, Harold Vaughan, who was steering the machine with some sort of tiller arrangement. Next to Harold, also wearing an oilskin cape and hat, was his friend Wilfred Moult. Both men also wore goggles. Behind them, facing the way they had come from, were Harold's wife and one of his daughters, both wearing thick jackets and hats secured by scarves tied under their chin.

As the motor car came closer, Luigi and Percy both stared at it in fascination. They had seen photographs of the horseless carriages in papers and magazines, but this was the first to be owned by a Paraparaumu resident. As it raced along the beach, spray rose from its wheels and drifted up into Harold and Wilfred's faces, so that every few seconds they had to wipe their goggles. As it came opposite Luigi and Percy the motor back-fired, making a noise like an enormous fart. A flock of gulls standing in the shallow water at the mouth of the Tikotu Creek rose into the air in alarm, then flew away towards Kapiti. The vehicle faltered, lurched forward, farted again, then continued on its way north, towards the mouth of the river.

'What do they call it?' asked Percy, drawing hard on his cigarette.

'An "Oldsmobile"', replied Luigi.

'"Oldsmobile", eh?' Percy stared after the departing motor car, whose engine could still be heard clearly. 'Don't reckon the things'll ever catch on. That noise'd terrify the horses.'

Half an hour later, after they had checked their gear and stowed it in the lockers of their boats, they began to drag the vessels across the beach towards where small waves were lapping at the damp sand. As they did so, Percy asked, 'Where you heading for today, Lou?'

Luigi looked up, briefly. 'Wharekohu Point,' he said. 'Off the reef there.'

Percy grunted. 'I'm heading up the other way. Rangatira Bay. Closer to home.'

'All right then,' said Luigi. 'I'll see you tomorrow.'

'Okay, mate.'

And so began Luigi Galoni's last fishing trip.

FOURTEEN

For twenty minutes the two men's courses ran parallel as they rowed out into the strait. Then, a quarter-mile from the shore, they began to diverge, Luigi heading south, Percy turning north. As they did so they waved to each other, then concentrated on their rowing. As he moved further out, Luigi saw the sand-dunes become a low grey wall, the tussocks sprouting from them looking like urchins' spiky hair. It was a completely still day, unusual for September, when the equinoctial winds often kept him and his boat on land. But today the water in the strait was satiny, the incoming tide offering little resistance to the hull. The boat moved cleanly through the water, but as he rowed, slowly and mechanically, Luigi felt the now-familiar twinges in his lower back begin again. Lately there had been other pains too; twinges in his groin when he rowed, a cramping in his gut at night. Neither lasted long, but when they came they caused him to wonder if this was what growing old was about, a slow accumulation of discomforts, then aches, merging into permanent pain. Already he had lived for a decade longer than his father. Did that mean he was now on borrowed time? This was such a dire thought, he tried to drive it from his mind, but couldn't. Of his various aches, the ones in his back were the most persistent. In the evenings after he had bathed, Alice sometimes rubbed his back and shoulders with lavender oil. This eased the discomfort, but the way she reproached him as she massaged irked him so much that at times he would have preferred to be left alone.

'How much longer do you mean to do it?'
'You're over fifty, for goodness' sake.'
'You can't go on rowing out there for much longer.'
'I worry so much about you, especially when the wind gets up.'
'When will you stop?'

Then he would fall into a sullen silence, rather than go over the old arguments. Fishing was his livelihood, the sea was his life and always had been. He would never give it up. He loved the sea's changing moods, its small and huge beauties, its salty scent, its mystery, the fact that when his line was hauled up, he was never quite sure what its depths had yielded. He wasn't incautious, either, he respected the sea as much as he loved it. And he knew this strait as well as his front garden.

Today, as conditions were so favourable, he would anchor some way off Wharekohu Point. That would leave him clear of the island's sheltering range, but as there was so little wind, it'd be quite safe to do so. And he knew, from having fished there once before, that there was a reef extending south of the point, followed by a drop-off into very deep water. Good cod, ling and groper territory. He rowed on, watching the early afternoon sun highlighting the dark blue water, turning it to mats of flashing diamonds, with yet more diamonds dripping from the blades of his oars every time they emerged from the water. If this weather kept up, the girls would soon be swimming again. Or at least collecting tuatuas from the shallow water, and hunting for the toheroas that hid just under the surface of the sand. They loved that.

He reached the fishing ground, half a mile from the end of the point, and slipped the anchor overboard. As the coils of rope continued to spin out, they confirmed that he was above deep water. Almost to the end of the line, over a hundred feet. A slight breeze had sprung up, and the water here beyond Kapiti's shelter was a little choppy, but as he scanned the sky and saw the high cloud it seemed as if the day was overflowing with sunlight. After years of fishing these waters he could now predict the weather as accurately as Percy could. The favourable conditions would persist, he felt sure.

He baited the line's ten hooks with lumps of trevally and mullet and cast it over the side. First letting plenty of slack run out, he left the rest of the line coiled in the bottom of the boat, then made fast the end of the line with figure-of-eight turns to the cleat inside the port gunwale. Settling into the bottom of the boat just in front of the for'ard hatch, he took the lunch that Alice had packed for him out of his rucksack. Cheddar sandwiches, pickled onions, home-baked biscuits and a corked bottle of raspberry cordial. As he ate and drank, his gaze was on the distant plain and the bush-covered range rising behind it. How he had come to love this place, both land and sea. Percy sometimes talked of his affinity with his family's land as if this was unique because he was a Maori. But Luigi understood Percy's feelings perfectly, because he too felt that way, even though he was a settler. One did not have to be born in a place in order to love it.

This was a subject he and Percy disagreed on.

'I'm what we call here tangata whenua, Lou, my people have lived here for ten generations. When I look at Kapiti I know it holds the bones of my ancestors, and it'll hold mine. You haven't even lived here for one generation, you Eye-tie bugger.'

'But I love the land no less for that, Perce. My body will be buried here. And my children, and their children, will be tongue-utta whatever-you-call-yourself, too. Remember, I *chose* this country to live in, over my place of birth. Now I love it more than Italy. It's like the love a man has for a woman. He meets her, and if she is the right one, he falls in love. And if that love is right, it lasts forever. It doesn't matter at all where she is from, or what her colour is.'

Percy would have no answer to that. Instead, he would chuckle, open a bottle of his home brew and they would drink each other's and their young nation's health.

Yes, Luigi thought, he'd achieved in this land a contentment and prosperity he could never have in the old one. He had had his share of misfortune, it was true, but then who hadn't? On balance, the scales had certainly tipped in his favour. And what had tipped them more than anything else, much more than saving the banker's daughter, he had come to appreciate more than ever, was meeting and loving Alice. Without her, and her fortitude, and the love that she returned, his life could never have become what it had. With each year that passed, she seemed to become stronger and more capable. She was a marvel. Raising the cordial bottle to his mouth, he drank gratefully.

If he had a regret, it was the lingering one that they hadn't had a son, so that here in this country, as far from Italy as an Italian could get, his family's name would die out. But the fact that he and Alice had had only daughters was an uncontrollable thing, a matter of fate. Anyway, what was a name? Only a kind of label stuck upon a person. There were far more important things in life: family, friendship, love, laughter, music. And the Galoni blood-lines – if not the name itself – would still flow on, through their children's children.

As his thoughts meandered in this way, he saw the coiled fishing cord line at his feet begin to move, snaking over the gunwale and into the water. Quickly he bent down, grabbed the line, held it. There was tension on the line, mighty tension, and he could not stop it moving out without it cutting his palms. Instead, working as rapidly as he could, he paid out the remaining slack, at the same time checking that the end was still made fast to the cleat. The line tightened, then held, but whatever was on the other end was so strong that the boat's bow immediately slewed round one hundred and eighty degrees. Could the line be snagged on a reef rock? The boat was starting to move through the water, so it couldn't be. Now he had to move quickly again – with the anchor still down, the line could be snapped by opposing pressures. Grabbing the anchor rope, he hauled it up quickly, first feeling the anchor dislodge from the sediment on the bottom. He dropped the yards of dripping rope into the bottom of the boat, then as the anchor came up, laid it on top of the coils of rope, and returned his attention to the fishing line. Still taut, it was angled into the water ten feet from the boat's prow. Now there was no doubt about it, *Laetitia* was being pulled strongly through the water by a creature on the other end of his line.

Moving for'ard, bracing his thighs against the bow cover, he took the line in both hands and pulled on it. For a few seconds it yielded, then quickly jerked away again. The boat was still moving steadily, dipping up and down as it passed through the slight chop. Placing the line inside the metal anchor rope guide on the top of the bow cover, Luigi moved back to the centre thwart, removed the oars and rowlocks from the gunwales and placed them in the bottom of the boat. Then he returned to the line and tried again to pull it in. The resistance was too great. Whatever was on the end of the line was so big, he couldn't bring it up. Yet. He would let the fish run, and so tire itself out. No fish could drag a boat of this boat's weight, with a man inside it, for very long. So he sat facing the bow and watched the line cutting through the water, taking him and *Laetitia* in a southerly direction, away from Kapiti. And as they moved, his thoughts were dominated by speculation about what it could be. A shark? But one of that size would have bitten through the line with its razor teeth by now. A sting ray? Could be, although he had never before hooked a ray in such deep water. A marlin? But surely one of those would have broached by now. As he stared at the sharply angled, moving line, his resolve strengthened. Never before had he hooked anything so powerful. It was pulling the boat at a speed he estimated to be two to three knots.

But he would win, eventually. Whatever creature was down there, he would bring it to boat.

Half an hour later, he and the boat were still moving. From time to time he picked up the line from the anchor guide and pulled on it. Always, the line would initially yield to the pull, but just as he began to draw it in, it would resist again, as strongly as ever. Looking over towards the land, he saw that the fish was pulling him roughly parallel to the shore, and that by his reckoning – after glancing back at Kapiti, now in a grey haze in the distance – he must be almost opposite Raumati. Getting further from home. No matter, when the fish was in the boat, he would row ashore there and ask a local fisherman for help to get the boat and his catch back to Paraparaumu. The main thing was, to bring the fish in.

Suddenly, without warning, the line went slack. The boat carried on for a few yards under its own momentum, then stopped and began to drift. Cursing, Luigi reached for the line. The fish had thrown the hook. Now he would never know what had been on the end of it. Furious, he began to pull the line in, and as he did so was astonished to feel that the tension had returned. Tension, but less resistance. The fish was exhausted. He continued to haul in the line, slowly, letting the dripping cord fall at his feet. The line cut into his palms, the ache in his back intensified. What a weight it was! As he hauled, occasionally he felt a convulsion travelling up the line, as the fish made another effort to resist, but the intensity of each spasm grew less and less, until after ten more minutes he knew he was hauling up a dead weight. Then the line gave another spasm, lasting several seconds. No, not dead. It was still fighting. But as much as he admired it for that, he was more determined still to get it aboard.

Realising from the amount of line covering his boots that the fish must now be close to the surface, he reached for his gaff and laid it on the aft thwart, then hauled again, hand over hand, bracing himself against the gunwale. Moments later the fish appeared, a few feet below the surface.

Luigi's heart stopped. It was not a fish, it was a monster. He saw the huge body roll, exposing its bright white belly to the sunlight. As it did so its mouth fell open, its saucer-sized eyes rolled back in its head and its tail made threshing movements. The line jerked across his hands, painfully, and he gripped the line and pushed his knees against the gunwale. A groper. But a groper of such a size that it almost defied belief. Staring at its body, he began to make comparisons. Two-thirds the length of his boat, the girth three times that of a man, the gaping mouth capable of accommodating an ox's head, the lips as thick as bicycle tyres. Surely over two hundred pounds in weight. Never had he set eyes on such a fish. Back at Makara, Victor had once landed a groper of ninety pounds, and fish of the same species weighing sixty or seventy pounds were not uncommon there, either. French Louis had told Luigi of a groper he had once caught that weighed one hundred and twenty. But this …

Now he began to plan just how he could get the creature into the boat. To avoid capsizing *Laetitia*, it would have to be brought aboard over the stern. He stepped carefully over the thwarts to the back, then brought the fish in as close as he could to the stern. As he did so he found himself staring into its still-open maw, and saw that his hook had caught the fish at the side of its mouth, where it had lodged in a strip of muscle-covered bone. It could not possibly throw the hook. More worrying was the likelihood that the line would snap once the fish was free of the water, its breaking strain incapable of holding such a weight. *The gaff, Luigi, the gaff.* Gripping the line in his left hand, he picked it up in his right, slipped the barbless hook over the stern and into the water, carefully placed it in the groper's gaping mouth and with one firm tug pulled it through the side of its jaw. Immediately the fish's tail began to thrash the water, jerking Luigi forward so suddenly that he only stopped himself from tumbling overboard by dropping the line and bracing himself against the stern with both knees. Jamming his boot on the line, he steadied himself, and using all his remaining strength, began to pull on the gaff with both hands.

As the great blue-black head came over the stern Luigi lost his footing on the draining board, stumbled and fell backwards, striking his lower back against the aft thwart. For a few seconds the fish, still only half inside the boat, lay on top of him. With its body still atop the stern, water began to pour in over the back of the boat. Scrambling out from under the fish, Luigi hauled it right into the boat, then reached for the bailing bucket, which was tied to the centre thwart. He began to bail, quickly, scooping up the water in half-bucketfuls and hurling it over the side.

Gradually the boat steadied. His breath coming in gasps, his back feeling as if something had been snapped across it, Luigi staggered for'ard, then sank to the bottom of the boat. Alongside him, the fish's body took up over half the width and almost the entire length of the boat. Its belly was the size of a horse's. Turning his head, he found himself looking straight into its vast mouth and at its shovel-sized tongue, its muscular white throat and pads of emery board teeth. From deep in its gullet came a wheezing noise, interspersed with an almost human groaning. The leading edge of its gills – nearly a yard long – were quivering, and where the hook had penetrated, a tear an inch long had developed. The fish's side fins were as large as a small snapper, its still-extended, webbed dorsal over two feet high. And as he watched, he saw too that its big red eyes were beginning to become glazed.

He lay there for some minutes, unable to move, staring up at the cloud-strewn sky. The ragged white shapes were moving very quickly, he realised. Turning to check the boat's position, he winced from the pain in his back. He wasn't cold, at least he wasn't cold. But his clothes were wet through, his boots full of water. So he would certainly become cold, once the sun was lower in the sky. Because conditions had been so favourable, he had not brought his oilskins. Bringing himself carefully but still painfully into a sitting position, he looked towards the shore. The shapes of the hills were unfamiliar, the fish had pulled him much further south than he'd realised. He looked in the direction of Kapiti. The island was just a blur now. Turning the other way, he saw a headland in the distance, realised it must be the one that enclosed the bay they called Pukerua. Slowly, painfully, he got to his feet.

He drove his filleting knife straight and hard into the centre of the fish's head. It convulsed, twice, its throat emitted a low moan, then it lay still. He withdrew the knife, then, leaving the hook in the fish's jaw, he looped the line three times around its body and secured the line to the port cleat, to prevent it rolling overboard. Now he had to get it, and himself, ashore. But he couldn't possibly row back to Paraparaumu, instead he would head for Pukerua Bay, get there before the daylight faded. The tide was still flowing in the direction of the headland, that would help. He would row with the tide's flow, land inside the headland, then walk home. Tomorrow he would borrow Tom Pudney's dray and return for the fish. Staring at it again, still amazed at its size, he thought they would need a cross-cut saw, not a knife, to cut it into steaks. It could feed the whole of Paraparaumu for a week.

But first, he must make land.

Easy to say, much more difficult to do. The fish's size and weight, equal to that of two men, made *Laetitia* list heavily, so that trying to row her was like rowing a boat half-full of water. Also, the bruising on his back was now so painful that he could hardly pull the oars for more than half a dozen strokes at a time. After an hour of sporadic rowing, his progress towards the bay was minimal. Away to the west, the sun had begun its slow slide down the sky, and although its rays were still dazzling, there was now little warmth in them. Forcing himself to continue, he picked up the oars and began to row once more, in the direction of the still-distant bay.

One summer he, Alice and the girls had made a day trip to Pukerua Bay, for a picnic. It was quite different from Paraparaumu, because there were rocks there, and at low tide, rock pools. Like Makara. But in the midst of the rocks was a small beach, he seemed to remember, because Violetta and Edith had swum, while Alicia and Esther explored the pools. He seemed to remember that they had all had a bacon and egg pie and cordial on the beach. Letting his head fall forward, he shipped the oars yet again. Now he scarcely had the strength to turn round, to see if any progress was being made. Instead he kept his head down, his mind becoming giddy as he tried to recall the details of that day. How had they got to Pukerua Bay? It was such a distance from Paraparaumu. The Monopolis had taken them, that was right, in their trap. February, it must have been, because it was very, very hot. Dropped them off at the bottom of the hill, then collected them in the afternoon on their way back from Paremata. Not all the Monopolis, just Mario. No, Claudia had been there too. Yes, and there *had* been a beach at the bay. But where, and how big was it? He tried again to row, but his strokes were feeble, the oars scarcely gaining any purchase. His head dropped onto his knees. He should get rid of the fish, push it overboard, then he'd be able to get the boat moving again. He glanced at its great blue and white body, lying still and shiny in the boat. It would take only a few seconds to cut the line, unloop it and roll the groper over the side. But as he imagined doing it, the thought appalled him. *No, never*! He must get it back, to show Percy and the other fishermen. The giant fish was evidence, proof even, that he, Luigi Galoni, had beaten the sea, and that his claim to belong here was as strong as anyone's. Including Percy Watene's. He *would* get it back, *had* to get it back. But his arms stayed still, refusing to move, and his spine was a pole of pain. He would rest some more, and gain the strength to carry on. Head still down, he blinked, several times. Something was wrong with his eyes, too, he was unable to focus properly. Dimly, he was aware that the sun had disappeared.

Now, although he had stopped rowing, he had an odd sensation.

That the boat was still moving. Lifting his head, he looked at the water. It *was* still moving. How? Half-turning, he saw in the low light the backs of waves, heard the distant rush of sea on shore. Squinting at the water beyond the stern, he saw a swell rise, then move towards him. Seconds later he felt it pass beneath the boat, causing it to buck, then fall, as the swell moved on. *Waves.* Picking up the oars again, he tried to gain some purchase with them on the water. But only the right oar dug in, the other merely flailed at the surface. *Laetitia* began to turn sluggishly to starboard. As she did so another, larger swell approached, rose and swept beneath the hull. The boat slewed, then listed heavily with the weight of the fish.

A third wave followed closely, and this time broke. Striking *Laetitia* in her broached position, it crashed over the starboard gunwale and water poured into the boat. Dropping the oars, Luigi scrambled for the bailer, but it was too late. Under the combined weight of man, water and fish, *Laetitia* capsized to starboard. Luigi fell across the fish and together they were hurled into the dark water. But in the second before he was engulfed, he had an instant of clarity. A succession of faces, female faces, flickered across his mind's eye. Then the hull came down, the boat was struck by another wave, and the whole world turned black.

FIFTEEN

He opened his eyes. Sand. Everywhere. In his eyes, his mouth, his hair. Beneath him, too. Cold, so very cold, and darkness now, all around him. He shuffled to his knees, and as he did so a wave struck him from behind, covering him, carrying on up the sand, then sliding back and engulfing him again. Pushing down on the sand, he staggered to his feet. They were bare, his boots had gone. Turning, he saw a sloping beach, and in the shadowy distance, rocks. Pukerua Bay? Soaked and shivering, he wiped the sand from his eyes and strained them, seeking any sign of *Laetitia*. Further along the sand, half in the water, he could make out a low shape. Feet sinking into the sand, he lurched towards it. The shape became more distinct. *Laetitia*! Still upturned, she was at right-angles to the shore. As he approached her a wave broke, swept up the sand, struck the boat's prow and cascaded over the hull. Ignoring the pain in his back, he gripped her gunwale and heaved. The boat didn't budge. He stood up, waiting for another wave. When it came, sliding over and under the boat, he heaved again, his back and shoulders muscles screaming in protest. *Laetitia* came up a little. He heaved again and she came over slowly, then crashed down onto the sand. Luigi stared into the boat. The anchor was still in the for'ard compartment, but the oars and rowlocks, fishing tackle and rucksack were all gone. But none of that mattered. The fish, the hook still in its jaw, the line still looped around its body, was still there, its body slumped over the thwarts, its huge head in the for'ard compartment, its tail dangling over the stern. *His great fish, landed*!

Unable to tell whether the tide was now ebbing or flowing, he had to assume that it was coming in. He uncleated the line, slid his hands inside the groper's gills on both sides, dragged it from the boat and down onto the sand. Waiting for some minutes to regain what strength he had left, he took the fish by the tail and dragged it up the beach, a couple of feet at a time, beyond where he estimated the tideline to be. Returning to the boat, he tried to haul it up too, but was soon defeated. Too weak, too cold, too sore, he could barely move it a yard. Instead he took the anchor from the for'ard compartment, carried it up the beach and dug its flukes deep into the sand on the foreshore.

Staring up at the plain, he saw that it was covered with lupins and backed by a high cliff. There was little moonlight, and he could see nothing more. Did anyone live here? Pushing through the lupin bushes, he emerged on to a narrow track. Knowing that the main road must be somewhere off to the left, he began to walk in that direction, picking his way tenderly on his bare feet over the track's sharp stones. It widened, and so did the plain. A few minutes later the glow of a lantern appeared through the gloom. Approaching the buttery light, he saw a curtainless window and the outline of a corrugated iron hut, set back from the track on a small patch of cleared land. Walking unsteadily up to the front door, he slapped on it twice with the flat of his hand.

'Luigi! Oh my God, where've you been?'

'Alice …'

'The men have been searching the beach all night. They're still searching. *Where were you?*'

Instead of replying, he fell into her arms. They clutched each other. All he could say was her name, over and over again. Through her dress, he could feel her whole body shaking, and his neck turning wet with her tears. From the rear of the house he heard a squeal, and seconds later all the girls appeared, still in their nightwear, hair loose, mouths agape. They stood staring at him as if seeing an apparition.

Alice drew back.

'Thank God, thank God you've come back.'

He held her at arms' length, stared into her swollen, red-rimmed eyes. Her face was blotchy, the lines on the side of it had deepened, and strands of her fair hair flew out from where she must have hastily tied it. Tears flooded into his own eyes then, and once more he held her hard against him. As he did so the girls ran forward, and he tried to embrace them all, at once.

'*What happened? Where were you? Whose clothes are these?*'

Releasing her, he sank down onto a kitchen chair, clutching his back.

Back, shoulders, groin, thighs – his body was in pain from head to foot. Alice and the girls clustered around the chair, wide-eyed and speechless. Then little Esther began to cry, and he held his arms out for her. At last they all took seats around the big table. Violetta made tea and they drank it, while he told them the story. When he'd finished, Alice began to fire questions at him.

'How did you get home?'

'With Thomas Duggan.'

'Who's he?'

'The man whose hut I went to. Where I stayed last night.'

'Are those his clothes?'

'Yes. Mine are still soaking. They're in his dray.'

'Where is the man now?'

'Gone to get ice from the store.'

'Ice? What for?'

'To pack the fish in.'

'*You brought the fish back too?*'

'Yes. I wanted you all to see it.'

Alice rolled her eyes, incredulous. 'You thought we wanted to see *your fish?*'

'I did, yes.'

'Oh, Luigi …'

Seeing her mother's expression of disbelief, Violetta began to giggle. The others joined in, and soon all were laughing. Except Luigi. He looked at them in turn, not comprehending. Tears were rolling down Alice's cheeks, tears of laughter and despair. Luigi shrugged, feeling outnumbered. Stroking his moustache, he looked from one to another of his four daughters.

'It is a very big fish,' he pleaded. 'The biggest anyone from here has ever caught, I think.'

'Mother,' said Edith suddenly, 'the men will still be searching the beach. We'll have to let them know Papa is safe.'

Alice got to her feet. 'Yes, yes.'

'I'll go,' said Luigi quickly. 'I'll tell them.'

Alice put her hand firmly on his arm. 'No. You're not leaving here.'

'I'll go, mother,' piped up Esther. 'On my bike.' Her eyes shone at the prospect.

Luigi smiled. 'That's a good idea, Esther. But take care, all right?'

'Find Mr Watene, darling, he's the one in charge,' Alice instructed.

Almost before they had issued their orders, she was running out the door.

'It was the worst night of my life, Luigi. The worst night for all of us.'

'I am sorry. Truly sorry.' He put his arm around her shoulders and brought her closer to him. The lamp was out and there was little light in the bedroom. 'But I am safe now. I'm home.'

'You mustn't go out there again. I want you to stop.'

The only sound was her hesitant breathing. He knew she was again close to tears. But although he'd been expecting this, he'd prepared no proper response. He knew how close he'd come to death, closer than he had yet told – than he would ever tell – Alice. And he knew how terrible it would have been for them all had he not returned, had his body been found on the rocks or the beach. Or even worse, not found at all. Leaving them without a husband and father's love. And a husband and father's livelihood. Hearing her stuttering breathing, he put his face against her neck. Feeling her familiar, her wonderful softness, he said:

'When the boat overturned, just before it struck me, I had a vision.'

'What do you mean?'

'I saw faces. You, our daughters, my mother, my sister. One after the other. Laughing, loving faces, as clearly as if you were there in front of me. It must have been only in the instant before I was struck, but I saw you all.' He paused. 'It was so strange.'

'Doesn't that tell you something?'

'Yes.' He held her more tightly. 'That you are all the most precious things in life to me.'

There was a long silence before Alice replied. Turning her face to his, speaking in a voice that was a strange mixture of wistfulness and resolve, she said,

'You must not go in the boat any more, Luigi.'

'I know.'

Drawing away suddenly, she sat up.

'You *will* stop?'

'Yes. I know how close I came to being lost. And losing you all.' He flexed his still-painful shoulders. 'I will sell the boat.'

'When?'

'Soon.'

She gave a long, low sigh, then ran her fingers lightly over his brow. 'You'll be able to get other work. Safe work. On land.'

'I know. There's the railway. And the roads.'

'You worked on the road at Jackson Bay.'

'Yes. And I can do it again.'

'Luigi …'

'What is it now?'

Sensing her hesitation, knowing that something else momentous was coming but having no inkling of what it might be, he waited for her to speak again. Always, with Alice, there was some new possibility to be pondered and discussed. Sometimes practical, often not. When she spoke again her voice had an edge of excitement to it.

'I thought, we could have another child.'

'*What?* But you have always said …'

'I mean, not ourselves.' After a hesitation, she added quickly, 'An adoption.'

For some moments he couldn't reply. *Adoption?* This was the last thing he would have expected. 'Alice …' he began, patiently, 'Where did this idea come from?'

'I was coming back from Otaki on the train yesterday. I sat next to the matron of the home there for unwed mothers, the Deliverance Home. Mrs Buckley said they're forever looking for foster parents for the babies.' When Luigi made no reply, Alice went on. 'We have the room here in the house, and the section.'

Still he didn't reply. Sitting up straight, she said, 'Why don't you say something?'

'This comes as a shock to me, that's why. I had no idea you were thinking of adoption.'

She gave a defensive little laugh. 'It isn't something I've been harbouring. It came to me only after I spoke to Mrs Buckley.' Her voice now just above a whisper, she added, 'The girls would love a brother.'

'A boy?'

'Yes.'

'He would be a Galoni.'

'Yes.'

In that way the name would live on, in the new land. Even though the child would not really be theirs. But when he grew up and had sons, his children would bear the name. Then it would never die out.

'I haven't even *mentioned* it to the girls. I wanted to ask you first. We must decide together.'

'We must, yes.' His mind still trying to take in the enormity of it, he said, 'What would we need to do?'

'Visit the home. Talk to Mrs Buckley.' There was a pause. 'Ask to see a boy baby.'

Silence, for some moments, then he said, 'We could do that.'

'So, shall we?'

Arm still around her, he stared through the half-light towards the bedroom window, the one that faced the sea. The sea that he had just promised he would forgo. His life was about to be transformed, in a way that he had never intended. A decision made for him, not by him. And now, this as well. Another child. An adopted son. Could they manage such a change, such responsibility? He thought then of Makara, where they had raised four babies in what was little more than a tin shack. This house was a mansion by comparison. So they had the space. Esther was eleven now, the other three girls approaching marriageable age. Violetta had already talked to Alice of the young railwayman she had met at the dance at Wise's Hall last month, although she hadn't mentioned it to Luigi. A well-mannered young man called George, an Australian, Alice had reported. There would be others too, surely, Luigi knew. Alicia drew men to her like gurnard to berley. Always had. So, probably, there would be other beginnings before much longer. Courtings, marriages, grandchildren probably. Looking at their girls now sometimes amazed him. Where had the years gone? It was like planting a grove of trees and letting them grow. One day you looked up and were astonished to realise that the trees were taller than you were. So, soon the girls would be marrying and leaving home. But still, another child for Alice and himself? At his age? After all, he was nearly fifty. But still, this country had blessed him in so many ways. Given him Alice, and their daughters, and a house and land of their own. In return, he and Alice could give an otherwise unwanted child new chances, a proper beginning. It'd be hard work, but neither of them had ever been afraid of that.

Continuing to stare towards the window, he could hear the sighing of the sea and a wind's low moaning. A westerly, if the sea sounds were as clear as this.

'Luigi?'
'Yes?'
'What are you thinking?'
'That we should go to the children's home. Together.'

SIXTEEN

'Soup, Luigi?'

'What kind is it?'

'Pea and ham.'

'A little, please.'

Alice put her arms under his, brought him fully upright, placed the tray on his lap, sat on the chair beside the bed. 'Shall I give it to you?'

'No, I can manage.' Carefully he picked up the spoon, took a mouthful. 'It's good, Alice. Tasty.'

She smiled, tightly, as she watched him, unable to conceal the sorrow in her grey eyes. Then, taking the tray away, she said, 'I'm going to the post office. To send a letter to Evie. Will you be all right here for an hour or so?'

'Yes. Ronaldo is here?'

'He's in the orchard. If you need him, ring the bell.'

'Yes.'

He watched her walk through the gate and out onto the road, basket over her arm. She was, as well as everything else, a fine nurse. Loving, caring, considerate. When they had given him the option of hospital or home, there was no question of where he preferred to be.

He drew himself up a little higher, so he could see the sea. This was the best time of day, out here on the porch, watching the sun go down the sky behind the island. Still warm enough to be outside. Mario and Percy had fixed casters to his bed, and built a little ramp over the front door step, so Alice could wheel the bed in and out of the house. He picked up the tumbler from the table beside his bed and sipped some water. As he did so the pain came again, from deep in his belly. He pulled his legs up hard against his stomach. Each day the pain became more intense, the spasms longer and harder. Catching his breath, he waited for it to pass, and after some minutes it did. He picked up the flask from the table, shot some brandy into the water and swallowed the mixture. It moved down his throat and inside him, making a warm, strong path. So good, it was. No wonder the French called it eau-de-vie. Edith brought him a bottle every week, when she visited from Otaki.

What day was it? Hard to tell now, when one was much like another. Friday, he thought. No, Thursday. Alicia came yesterday, and she always came on Wednesday. He swallowed some more of the brandy. But every day was precious. How much longer now? he wondered, as he wondered every hour of every day. A month, perhaps, the doctor had said the last time he came. 'Perhaps'. Doctor McLennan was a kindly man, but he could do nothing. At the hospital another doctor whose name he didn't even know had shown Luigi the glass plate that held the photograph of his stomach, pointed out what lay coiled there inside it like a serpent. Then delivered his death sentence, in a matter-of-fact tone. And despite the horror of it, Luigi felt a kind of fascination, too, that they could take a photograph that could see right *through* a person. Right through himself. It was a wonder, one of the many he had lived to see come to pass.

As he drank again he heard a horn honk and seconds later saw an automobile pass by, raising dust from the road. They were everywhere now, the automobiles, almost more of them than horses and carriages. But that was one invention he didn't like. Too noisy, too fast. Everything seemed to be speeding up, leaving him behind. Last year he and Alice and all the children had gone down to the beach to watch a flying machine land there. It had come dipping and wobbling out of the sky, bouncing several times on the hard sand before sliding to a halt. Everyone was astonished. It had taken only forty minutes to get there from Palmerston North. *Forty minutes.* And now, Percy had reported, they were talking about building a special place at Paraparaumu for the flying machines to land regularly, on the land where the swamp had been. An *aerodrome*, they were going to call it. Flying machines, dropping out of the sky, then soaring back into it. What would his father have thought of that? Ernesto Galoni had refused to even board a train, when they came to the Marche.

'Hello, Papa.'

Ronaldo, twirling a rope.

'Hello, son.'

'Can I get anything for you?'

'No, thank you, I'm fine.'

'I'm going to make a swing, in the oak tree. For Esther and me.'

'Good, you do that.'

The boy began to throw a rope over the lowest branch of the oak tree, the one by the gate, which had grown from the acorn Luigi had planted in…in…. 1896. Now the tree towered above the gate. He watched Ronaldo secure the rope around the branch. Nearly nine years old now, he was an appreciative, considerate boy. It seemed that he had always been part of their family. And, although Luigi never made as much of this as he once did, Ronaldo would ensure that the Galoni name would not die out with him.

'Make sure it is tied properly, son, before you swing on it.'

'Yes, Papa.'

Since the adoption Ronaldo had become particularly close to Esther, who mothered him as much as Alice did. They were always in each other's company. The one thing that bothered Luigi was that none of the others would let him cut the boy's hair, which now grew down to his shoulders, so that people often mistook him for a girl. Although Luigi was annoyed by this, it didn't seem to bother Ronaldo at all. The boy was proud of his hair, brushing it as much as the girls did. Strange. Pulling the sheets up higher, Luigi closed his eyes. He felt so tired. He did nothing, and still he felt so tired. All the time. So tired.

'Luigi.'

'Yes?'

'There is something I need to ask you. Something very important.'

'Is it about my will? I showed you my will.'

'No.' He could see how deeply concerned Alice was. Even more so than she usually was. She sat down beside the bed, a handkerchief in her hands. Squeezing it hard, she said, softly, 'When the time comes, will you want a priest to be here?'

Luigi stared at her.

'*No.*'

Alice looked away, fighting distress. 'I know you have never been to church here, but I thought, since you were baptised a Catholic, you might want… the rites.'

'You should know, Alice, I long ago ceased to be a believer.'

'Yes, but I thought perhaps …'

Summoning what strength he had left, he said fiercely, '*No priest.*

No rites.'

Leaning forward, she wiped his forehead with the handkerchief, then sat back again. Alice still looked upset, even anguished.

'Luigi, you never told me why. Why you have this feeling.' She slipped the handkerchief under her sleeve. 'Can you tell me now?'

Luigi closed his eyes and kept them shut for some time. He could hear Alice's steady breathing, could sense her expectation hanging between them. He thought, it was only right that she knew. Now. Opening his eyes, looking into her troubled face, he said,

'I will tell you.' He put out his hand, found one of hers, gripped it. 'But you must promise me you will never tell the children. Or anyone else. No one.'

She nodded. 'I give you my word.' Getting up, she went to the door, shut it, returned to the chair beside the bed. Slowly, carefully, he began. And as he told her, he was amazed at how clearly he remembered. Every scene, every incident, every movement. Although he had stayed silent, he had never forgotten.

'When I was young, before I left Pesaro, I played my accordion and sang in a trattoria in the town once a week. Emilio's, on Friday nights. Emilio paid me a few lire to play, and gave me a meal. I enjoyed it, it wasn't really like work …'

> *Piscatore 'e 'stu mare 'e Pusilleco*
> *ch'ogne notte me sient' 'e canta,*
> *piscato sti pparole so' llagreme*
> *pe' Maria ca luntuna me sta!*

Although few people in the trattoria watched him as he played, he could tell from the boots tapping in time to the music they that were appreciating his efforts. And at the end of each song there were bursts of applause and shouts of 'Bis!' which pleased him. The customers were nearly all men, sitting at the round wooden tables with their tumblers of wine in front of them, talking volubly, laughing loudly, rolling and smoking their rough-cut tobacco.

At nine o'clock one of the serving girls brought Luigi over a plate of pasta and prawns and a tumbler of red wine. It had been eight hours since he had eaten lunch, and he ate and drank gratefully, the accordion set down on the floor beside him.

The air in the little restaurant was so thick with cigarette smoke that at first he didn't see the tall figure standing at the bar. Then, when he had finished playing the always-popular *Funiculi, funicular,* there was applause from the man in the cassock and white collar. It was Father Benassi, their family's priest. Luigi waved to him and played the tune again, watching Emilio hand the priest a glass of wine and bowing respectfully to him as he did so. Then, as the cassocked figure began to engage in conversation with two other men at the bar, Luigi resumed playing, putting as much effort into it as he could, noting again the booted feet, thumping even harder on the trattoria's floor.

He played another tune, then took his grandfather's watch from his fob pocket. Nearly half-past nine. In ones and twos the customers began to don their caps and drift off, tipsily, into the night. A few minutes later Father Benassi left too, beaming his appreciation at Luigi as he went out the door, and by the time he played his final number at just after ten o'clock, the place was almost deserted. Squeezing the last breath from the bellows, he squashed the two ends of the accordion together, clipped them into place and pushed the instrument into his rucksack.

As he collected his pay from the trattoria owner, Emilio handed him a blue envelope. 'Father Benassi asked me to give you this, Luigi.'

'Oh, thank you.'

The envelope contained a single sheet of paper, on which was written a short message in pencil.

Dear Luigi,

Your playing and singing were wonderful. Please call in at Sant' Agostino on your way home. I have something important there for you.

Giovanni Benassi

Luigi was surprised when he saw the first name, having never known him as anything else but Father Benassi. But of course, he thought, everyone had been given a name, even priests and nuns.

Sant' Agostino was near one corner of the town square, and as Luigi approached he could see a faint light inside through the open double doors. Entering the church, he saw a figure sitting on a pew near the front, opposite the side altar. The high altar and pulpit were in darkness, the stained glass windows above the altar tall blank shapes. Candles in a wall bracket above the side altar shed a pale light over the solitary figure. Luigi went up the aisle. The figure on the pew was leaning forward, his left hand pressed to his temple.

'Father?'

The priest started.

'Luigi …'

'Emilio gave me your note.'

'Yes, yes.'

He stepped out into the aisle. Eyes fixed on Luigi's face, Father Benassi smiled, then announced, 'I had to say how much I enjoyed your music tonight.'

'Oh, thank you Father. But it was nothing special. A few folk tunes, that's all.'

'You are too modest, my son. You have music in your blood, I can tell.'

Luigi shrugged. 'My grandfather taught me. He was a very good musician.'

'And a good teacher, it seems.'

'Yes. Yes, he was.'

The priest turned away, abruptly. 'Let's not talk here. Come into the sacristy. I've got something for you. In appreciation of your fine playing.'

His chasuble brushing the stone floor, he led the way towards a door next to the side altar, opened it, beckoned Luigi to enter, then closed the door behind them. Inside, three candles in an iron bracket on the wall cast a flickering light over the small room. Embarrassed, Luigi said,

'Father, Emilio has already paid me. I cannot accept anything from you.'

Smiling, Father Benassi said gently, 'Emilio does not pay you nearly what you are worth.'

Turning away, he went to a table against the back wall of the small room. It was covered with a heavy white cloth, and on it were a pair of brass candlesticks and another blue envelope. Father Benassi picked up the envelope and handed it to Luigi. Still smiling, he said, 'This is for you.'

This envelope was bulky. Puzzled, Luigi looked up at the priest.

'Open it,' Father Benassi urged. 'Go on.'

Luigi did so. Banknotes, dozens of red banknotes. A wad of lire, in

1000 lire denominations. Luigi gulped. He'd never seen so much money. But it wasn't right. Passing the envelope back, he said firmly,

'I cannot take this, Father.'

'Emilio may not pay you enough, Luigi, but I can.'

'But …'

'It is for you, my son. There'll be more, too, later.'

He came closer, holding his hands out wide as if preparing to administer a blessing. Then, slowly, the priest reached down with both hands and drew up his vestments. There were no undergarments, just long white shanks, a sagging belly, and jutting up like a purple eel, a rigid cock. Luigi felt as if he had been turned to stone. Averting his eyes from the hideous sight, he found them looking up into the priest's still-smiling face.

'Now, Luigi, I want you to pray for me.'

'No, no …'

Dropping the envelope, he turned to flee, but it was too late. Moving with surprising swiftness, the priest grabbed his arms and pinioned him. He felt the priest's hardness thrusting into his groin, a wet mouth on his neck. Then one hand released him and began to grope between his legs. Luigi twisted, trying to free his arms, but the priest was so tall and his arms were so long he felt as though he was grappling an octopus. Pawing at Luigi's crotch with his hands, the priest went on pushing his wet mouth into his neck.

Nearly blind with horror, but able to free his left arm a little, Luigi thrust his elbow up hard into the priest's belly. His body yielded slightly. Luigi repeated the blow, this time harder, but now the priest was pushing down on the back of Luigi's head with his right hand. Twisting his body as hard as he could, Luigi felt the other man turn with him. Desperate now, Luigi twisted harder still. As their entwined bodies turned, Luigi again thrust his left elbow into the priest's side and he stumbled backwards against the edge of the table, toppling one of the brass candlesticks.

For a moment the pair came apart and stood perfectly still. The priest's face was crumpled, his mouth agape, his greying hair sticking out from the sides of his head. He began to sob.

'Luigi, please, pray for me. Pray for me, please.'

Looking past him, Luigi saw the other candlestick on the table. Lunging forward, he snatched it up and brandished it. 'Release me,' he warned. *'Release me.'*

With a cry the priest launched himself at Luigi. Glimpsing for a second the whites of his eyes, Luigi saw that all reason had left him. Gripping the candlestick in both hands, he swung it round and into the side of the priest's head. The head recoiled, the eyes snapped shut, the legs buckled. As the priest's legs went from under him Luigi raised the candlestick and this time brought it down on the top of his head. There was a sound like the snapping of a stick before the priest's head dropped forward, his legs folded and he slumped at Luigi's feet.

Hands shaking, Luigi stared down at the fallen figure. Although his eyes were closed and blood was oozing from his temple, the legs were writhing. Still alive. Turning for the door, Luigi saw an object on the floor beside the prone figure. The envelope. He snatched it up, threw open the door, picked up his rucksack and ran down the aisle, his boot-plates reverberating against the stone. As he ran he glanced up at the walls of the church, where the figures in the stations of the cross seemed to mock him.

Sprinting across the deserted town square and the marketplace, he reached the alley that led to the Galonis' tenement flat. There he stopped, leaned against the wall and dropped his rucksack. The sky began to reel, then spin. Pushing the palms of his hands against the wall, he tried to stop the spinning. But it continued until he felt the bile in his throat well up, then overflow. Head hanging forward, he felt his stomach heave, then a torrent began to flow, spilling from his mouth and down the wall. And as it did so, there came another kind of release. Through the revulsion there came another, even stronger thought. A determination, a certainty, a kind of absolution.

Now I must leave. Now I can leave. Now no one will stop me.

Alice was sitting rigid, hands clasped, tears coursing down her face. She got up, went to him, put her arms around him, held him, saying nothing. He felt again her warmth, her strength, her understanding. Her love. Now he did not fear death. All that he feared was leaving Alice.

EPILOGUE

'William?'

'Yes?'

'This is Gina.'

'Oh. Hello. How are you?'

'As well as can be expected.' She made a little wheezing noise. 'How's your research going?'

'I've done what I can.'

'What have you found?'

'Fragments. That's all.'

There was a pause before she said, 'I've been going through my mother's old suitcase. From the storeroom. I came across a few things.'

'What sort of things?'

'Odds and ends. To do with the family.'

'With Luigi?'

'Yes. Would you like to see them?'

'I would.'

'When could you come?'

'Tomorrow morning. Would 11 o'clock suit?'

'Yes.'

After ushering him in the front door and out onto the sun porch, she peered up at him querulously. 'Tea? Coffee?'

'Not for me, thanks.'

There was a foolscap manila envelope on the coffee table, creased and worn with age. In her fussing, slightly confused manner, Gina gestured at one of the old lounge chairs in front of the table.

'Well, I won't have any either, in that case. So, you sit there, and I'll sit here. The sun gets in my eyes if I sit on that side.' She panted. 'Hasn't it been hot?'

'Yes, very. This summer's going on and on.'

His eyes were on the envelope. What could it possibly hold that he hadn't been able to find after months of searching?

'As I told you on the phone, I was going through the cases, looking for my wedding photo. Sophie, my great-grand-daughter is doing some sort of history project. Never thought I'd be history. Anyway, I came across this envelope.' She picked it up. Opening the flap, she drew out some sheets of paper. 'There's this newspaper clipping. She passed it over to William.

It was a faded photocopy. Hand-written at the top were the words, '*Dominion*, October 12, 1907'. He read it.

The largest bass groper ever recorded in the Wellington area was caught three days ago by a Paraparaumu fisherman, Luigi Galoni. The fish, which weighed 234 pounds, was caught on a line from a boat in the Rauoterangi Channel, just south of Kapiti Island. Galoni, an Italian migrant, managed single-handedly, after some hours, to bring the fish ashore at Pukerua Bay, although in the process his fourteen foot boat was capsized. Fortunate to escape with his life, the Italian was rescued by a Pukerua Bay fisherman, Thomas Duggan, and he and his giant groper were returned to his house in Paraparaumu, where the out-sized creature was weighed and preserved in ice. An authority from the Department of Fisheries in Wellington, after being given notification of the size of the fish, visited the Italian the next day and confirmed that it is the largest of its species ever recorded in this region. Accordingly, he is arranging for it to be transported to Wellington, where it will be preserved and mounted for display in the National Museum.

Smiling, William passed back the sheet of paper. 'He must've been a good fisherman, then.' But really, he thought, this told him little. A fish was just a fish, however big.

'Yes, he must've been. And there's this.'

Another photocopy, another newspaper story.

31.3.1910 Social and Personal
Wedding at Paraparaumu

A wedding of great local interest took place in St Paul's Church, Paraparaumu, on Wednesday afternoon, when Mr George Howard

Leighton was married to Miss Violetta Galoni. The sisters of the bride, the Misses Edith, Alicia and Esther Galoni acted as her bridesmaids. The ceremony was performed by the Rev. J. Edwin Jones, vicar of the parish. After the ceremony Mr and Mrs Galoni held a reception at Mr Monopoli's beautiful orchard, where various toasts were honoured and the bride's father entertained the guests with his accordion playing. The bridal pair left by the 5.05pm train for a visit to Auckland.

'Violetta. My grandmother?'

'Yes. Your father's mother. She was Alice and Luigi's first-born.'

'I can't remember her. She died when I was five or six, I think.'

Gina fiddled again with the envelope. This time a sepia photograph fell out, along with some slips of paper. Picking the photograph up, she said, 'This was taken in a studio. Most of them were in those days, I suppose.' She handed it over.

An Edwardian family group, posing in their best clothes. Two parents, five children, all unsmiling. But only one was really a child, the four young women looked more like adults. Eighteen, nineteen years old, perhaps? They were standing at the back, all of similar height, with their long hair piled up high on their heads. The one in the middle – the most attractive of the three – also had hers trailing down over her shoulders. All three were wearing frilly blouses with high tight collars and tight-waisted skirts. The fourth girl, the one at the front and obviously the youngest, was clasping her hands over one knee. She had a straight mouth and a downcast expression.

The mother and father were seated separately, she on an upholstered chair, he on one made of cane. The mother had shapely cheekbones and a serene, sensitive face. The father was sitting rigidly upright. Dressed in a three-piece suit, white shirt and tie, his short greying hair was parted and brushed firmly into place. His large moustache came down over the sides of his mouth and a watch and chain dangled from his waistcoat. He was frowning, and there was weariness in his expression.

Standing in the front, between the mother and the father, was a plump-faced child of about five, in short trousers and velvet smock, with long thick hair almost reaching his shoulders, and a straight fringe.

William's eyes lingered on the man. It was Luigi, unmistakably. Much older, much more careworn, and noticeably much older than his wife. But then, he remembered, there were sixteen years between them.

Unable to take his eyes from the group, he said to Gina:

'When was it taken?'

'About 1908, I would say.' She picked up the piece of paper which had fallen from the envelope and began to read. 'Back: Edith (17), Alicia (16) and Violetta (18). Front: Esther (14), Alice (36), Ronaldo (4) and Luigi (52).'

'Ronaldo?'

He stared at the small boy in the photograph. 'So they had a son, too.' Suddenly puzzled, he looked up. 'So why is the name Galoni nowhere? I've been through all the electoral rolls. There's no one by that name in this country.' His eyes returned to the small boy. 'Did Ronaldo not marry?'

Gina looked away, making clicking noises with her tongue.

'He did marry. A girl from Palmerston North.'

'So, did they have only daughters?'

'No.' There was a pause. 'There was no issue from the marriage. They were divorced, sometime in the 1940s.' In a distasteful tone, as if eating something rotten, she said, 'It turned out that he was a *homo-sex-ual.*' Then she added quickly, 'He wasn't really Alice and Luigi's child, he was adopted.'

'Oh.'

William's eyes dwelt on the small boy. The long hair, the smock. How many sadnesses were awaiting him, in that time of hostility towards his kind? But Luigi was holding one of the child's tiny hands, and Alice's hand was on the other, and her left hand was around the little boy's shoulder. The child looked loved.

'The four girls, they look like strong characters.'

'Well, they had to be, I suppose, in those days. Life wasn't easy.' Gina peered at the photograph. 'Violetta and Edith both married railway men. The railway was everything then, my grandmother used to say. My mother, Alicia, married a mechanic. Harry Knowles, my father. But poor little Esther never married. She had a crippled leg. She died in an old ladies' home in Levin.'

His eyes dwelling on the man in the photograph, William said, 'Did anyone ever say why Luigi left Italy.'

'No.'

'He must have told Alice, though, surely.'

'Well if she did know, she told no one else, evidently.' Gina heaved a sigh. 'Why don't people take the trouble to find out about their family's past, while there's someone still alive to tell them?' Picking up the photograph, chuckling, she added, 'If Luigi was here, we'd have so much to ask him.'

'Indeed we would.' For months William had been thinking the same thing.

'They say the Maoris do – know all their genealogy, I mean – but, I'm not sure about that. There must be lots of their history that gets misplaced too.' She took off her glasses. 'Oh, there're a couple of other things here too, William.' Picking up the envelope, she gave it a little shake. A small coin and a sheet of folded blue notepaper fell onto the table. She picked up the coin and handed it to him. It was tarnished, with an uneven edge. There was the faint profile of a man's head on one side, an ancient trading ship on the other, and just-visible Roman numerals beneath the head.

'Where did it come from?'

'My mother was given it. By her mother. Luigi's wife. But I've no idea where it was from before that.'

Examining it, he said, 'It looks as if it might be Roman. If it is, presumably it came from Italy.'

'But the Romans were everywhere, weren't they? In Europe. So it might've come from England, where Alice's family were from originally.' Gina shrugged. 'Anyway, you can have it.'

William looked up. 'Really?'

'Yes. You've done all this work, trying to trace Luigi, you deserve something for your troubles.'

'Thank you. I'll take it to a coin expert, get it dated.'

Gina picked up the sheet of notepaper. 'And there's this letter. I don't know why my mother bothered to keep it. She didn't read Italian.'

'Italian?'

'Well I think it's Italian. Here, have a look.'

He unfolded it, a single sheet of heavy blue paper, covered in small, neat hand-writing, in ink, faded to pale brown. And it was in Italian. At the top was the word, Pesaro, a date, 23/11/1879, and the salutation, Caro Fratello. The letter was signed, Tua sorella, Violetta.

William stared at the letter, the date and place in particular. Luigi's home town, in the same year that he'd left it. From another Violetta. A relation, perhaps? Still clutching the unexpected find, he said to Gina, 'I'd like to borrow this, and get someone to translate it. Will that be okay?'

'Yes. It's no use to me.'

Peter Dellani taught Italian at the local college's night classes, a couple of kilometres from where William lived. Now in his eighties, but still spry and alert, Peter had been born to Italian parents in Island Bay, and had fought as an infantryman with the New Zealand Division during the Italian campaign of 1944. William visited Peter at his Johnsonville home, gave a photocopy of the letter to him, along with some money, to translate it.

Grizzled, with bushy sideburns, Peter squinted at the neat hand-writing and the date. 'Pesaro, eh? Eighteen seventy-nine, eh? From another age all right.'

Four days later, the old man posted the letter and a typed translation back. It read:

Pesaro, 23/11/1879

My Dear Brother,

I was overjoyed to learn from your letter that you are now safe and well in the new world. By now I hope you are with Leopoldo and helping him to work his land. But your letter shocked me too, Luigi, when I read of what Father Benassi tried to do to you the night you left. That our priest, of all people, could assault you indecently, could attempt such an abomination. He who had first given us the sacraments, who taught us history and language, who administered the last rites to our mother. No wonder you were forced to strike him. It became known quickly in the town that the priest (I can no longer bear to write or speak his name) was discovered the next morning by one of the sisters, bleeding from a serious head wound, and was admitted to the hospital. He told the doctor there he remembered nothing of what had happened to him. Then, another very strange thing happened. A month later he left the hospital, just before he was to be discharged, and did not return to the rectory. He has vanished from Pesaro and has not been seen anywhere since. Then, after the Bishop came from Urbino to investigate, it was discovered that our priest had been stealing money from the church funds, instead of taking it to the bank. Hundreds of thousands of lire were discovered in his rooms behind Sant'Agostino, money which should have gone to the poor and to help the nuns and the doctor at the hospital. And just as strange, fine clothing was found in his rooms, suits made of Torino cloth, silk shirts and ties, shoes of the finest leather. Because of the theft of the church funds, the poliziotto are searching for him throughout the Marche. The Bishop has appointed a new priest, Father Botterini, to Sant' Agostino, to replace the other. The new priest is elderly, and his health is poor, but he is undoubtedly devoted.

Here at home, Papa copes. He works as hard as ever on the boat and in the garden. Although he never says so, I know how much he misses you. Please write to him again when you can. I miss you so much. We both do.

Please give my fondest regards to Leopoldo.

Your loving sister,

Violetta

William put down the letter. So that was it. A priestly betrayal. Truly an old story. He read the letter again. 'An abomination', in Violetta's word. And yet, William reflected, had the abomination not been attempted, he – William – may not be here today. Nor would all the others who had come after Luigi. How randomly significant the events of the past could be, how wide the ripples spread, how insistently they lapped at lives. He picked up the original of the letter, studied once more the lines written by his great-great-aunty. Next year he would go to Pesaro, see for himself the town where Luigi and Violetta had been born, visit the church of Sant' Agostino.

He had deliberately left the last documents until the end. Now the time was right. Again he called the Births, Deaths and Marriages Central Registry, gave them the names, made the request over the phone. Copies of the two certificates came in the post a week later.

First names Luigi Giuseppe
Surname Galoni
Date of Death 29 February 1912
Place of Death Paraparaumu
Causes of Death Carcinoma of bowel – 12 months
Certifying Dr W H J Huthwaite
Date Last Seen 24 February 1912

Sex M
Birth Date Not recorded
Age at Death 57 Years
Birth Place Pesaro Italy
Number of years lived in New Zealand 33
Occupation Fisherman
Date of Disposal 2 March 1912
Place of Disposal Cemetery Waikanae
Marital Status Married
Marriage Place Wellington
Spouse's First Name Alice
Spouse's Surname Harris
Spouses's Age 40 Y

First Names Alice Maud Mary
Surname Galoni
Date of Death 6 August 1949
Place of Death Levin
Causes of Death Myocardial failure, fracture of thigh
Certifying Dr E T G Miller
Date Last Seen 1 August 1949
Sex F
Birth Date 15 October 1871
Unmarried Name Harris
Age at Death 77
Birth Place Westport
Place of Disposal Cemetery Levin
Marital Status Widow
Spouse's First Name Luigi
Spouse's Surname Galoni (Deceased 1912)

There was a fascination about cemeteries, William thought as he wandered about the paths of the one at Waikanae, searching the graves and headstones. They were necropolises, full of buried secrets. He had no idea where Luigi's grave might be, and the cemetery was large, spread over undulating land for several acres. He wandered around the graveyard, concentrating on the older headstones. Some were broken, their inscriptions indecipherable, but the oldest ones he could read dated back to the 1880s. After half an hour's searching he still hadn't found it. Even Luigi's last resting place, it seemed, was elusive. Passing an acmena hedge, he came to the last area, where there were only shiny black tablets. There must be a record, a plan, he thought, in the administration building. He would go back and enquire there. Then he looked over to his right, where there was a grassed knoll, topped by a few older-looking graves. He climbed the little hill, and there were the words he had been seeking, lichen-covered, but to him standing out as if they were in letters ten feet high.

The headstone was topped with a cross, standing on a small plinth; the grave a concrete trough. Sprouting from the grave were mauve agapanthas, bright now at the height of summer. The lichen encrusting the headstone was yellow, and growing in patches, obscuring some of the lettering. Carefully, William rubbed the dry growth away.

Loving Memory Of
Luigi Giuseppe Galoni
Who died 29 February 1912
Aged 57 Years
At Rest

Struck with the plainness, the simple dignity of the headstone, he sat alongside the grave, recalling the death certificates. Alice had outlived him by nearly forty years. She must have come to this place often, to tend the grave and remember her life with him. William decided that later he would come here again and clean the headstone properly.

He took from his shirt pocket the coin he had had cleaned and dated. It was Roman. 'Silver, from the first century BC,' the numismatist had pronounced. 'Quite valuable. The head's of the emperor who was known as Caesar Octavianus.'

Gripping the coin in his palm, eyes fixed on the headstone, William felt certain that the coin had been his. He stood up, and as he did so his eyes suddenly, unexpectedly moistened. Staring down at the concrete grave, he said quietly, 'Thank you, Luigi. Thank you from all of us.'

Before walking back down the hill, William looked over towards the sea. From the little hill and its grave there was a wide view. Right across the plain to the sea. To where the shadow of Kapiti Island loomed, dark across the horizon.

ACKNOWLEDGEMENTS

Several references provided valuable background material for the writing of *Alice & Luigi*. Associate Professor Hugh Laracy of the History Department of the University of Auckland first alerted me to the failed nineteenth century migrant settlement at Jackson Bay in his paper, The Italians in New Zealand (1973); Alan Poletti, Emeritus Professor of Physics at the University of Auckland, provided practical advice on tracing Italian ancestry in his paper Digging for our Italian Roots (2002), while the 2004 exhibition of Wellington's Italian fishing communities at the Museum of Wellington City & Sea helped considerably in stimulating my imagination. The book *Alla Fine Del Mondo - To the Ends of the Earth – the story of Italian migration to the Wellington region*, by Paul Elenio (published by the Petone Settlers Museum and the Club Garibaldi, Wellington, 1995) is a comprehensive account of the Italian migrant communties of Wellington, including the fishing village at Makara, while the book *The Far Downers The People and History of Haast and Jackson Bay* by Julia Bradshaw (University of Otago Press, 2001) is a mine of information on the the nature of pioneer life in south Westland. The book *Portrait of Frances Hodgkins* (Auckland, 1981) by the late art historian E.H.McCormick attests to the artistic significance of the Hodgkins painting, 'Babette', the model for which was my grandmother's sister, Alice Berretti. I must also express my deep gratitude to the Dowse Gallery, Lower Hutt, where the painting is held, for permission to reproduce 'Babette' on the cover of *Alice & Luigi*. I am grateful to the Alexander Turnbull Library for permission to reproduce the back cover photograph of Makara beach in the 1890s, and the *New Zealand Herald* for the author photograph. The book *The Celebration History of the Kapiti District* (compiled by Olive Baldwin, 1988) describes in detail the social and political history of the Paraparaumu district, and as such was a reference which I referred to frequently. Family records, anecdotes and photographs from Betty Box and Alan Lay, both of Auckland, were most helpful, and included the 1983 newspaper article, 'Babette remembers', a personal reminiscence of Alice Capewell (nee Berretti), of Otaki. I am indebted to Kevin Ireland for his advice on everything from explosives to cursing to gaming, to the skilled editorial assistance of David Ling and Christine Cole Catley, to Max Cryer for his musical and linguistic knowledge, to Sandra Fresia for her Italian language expertise and to the late Michael King for supplying the words of the prayer for the dead in Latin. The crude prejudice expressed by politicians of the period against assisted Italian immigrants to New Zealand can be read first-hand in the Appendices to the Journals of the House of Representatives of the late 1870s and early 1880s, in the sections pertaining to the failed settlement at Jackson Bay.